PENGUIN BOOKS
RAJ

Gita Mehta was born into a prominent Indian family and was educated in India and at Cambridge University. She has written, produced, and directed a number of documentaries for American, British, and European television companies and has published two books, *Karma Cola* and *A River Sutra*. She is married, with one son, and divides her time among India, England, and the United States.

by the same author

KARMA COLA: MARKETING THE MYSTIC EAST

RAJ

Gita Mehta

PENGUIN BOOKS

Penguin Books India (P) Ltd., 11 Community Centre, Panchsheel Park, New Delhi 110 017, India
Penguin Books Ltd., 80 Strand, London WC2R 0RL, UK
Penguin Group Inc., 375 Hudson Street, New York, NY 10014, USA
Penguin Books Australia Ltd., 250 Camberwell Road, Camberwell, Victoria 3124, Australia
Penguin Books Canada Ltd., 10 Alcorn Avenue, Suite 300, Toronto, Ontario M4V 3B2, Canada
Penguin Books (NZ) Ltd., Cnr Rosedale and Airborne Roads, Albany, Auckland, New Zealand
Penguin Books (South Africa) (Pty) Ltd., 24 Sturdee Avenue, Rosebank 2196, South Africa

First published by Jonathan Cape Ltd. 1989
Published by Penguin Books India 1993

Copyright © Gita Mehta 1989
Introduction copyright © 1990 by Gita Mehta

15 ·

Printed at Basu Mudran, Kolkata

for
A
S

Acknowledgments

MAHATMA GANDHI once advised a visitor wishing to learn about India to study India's villages and her women.

To the many women from the former princely families of India who were so generous with their memories, I am indebted.

I am equally indebted to the many former Indian kings who shared their views and pasts with me as they described their transition from ruling monarchs to ordinary citizens, as I am indebted to their sons and daughters for being my guides to their former kingdoms.

Because they were so generous with their time and recollections, and to avoid any inference that the fictitious characters in this novel might be derived from any one of them, I take this opportunity of thanking them collectively for their kindness rather than naming them individually.

In studying India during this period I am also indebted to two great British institutions: the India Office Library for its exhaustive archives, and the London Library for its wide and eccentric span of books on India.

To my parents, from whom I learned about the nationalist movement and the partition of India; to my uncle, who at the age of fourteen was sentenced by the British Empire to two decades of penal servitude in the Andaman Islands; to the many leaders of the nationalist movement and the many former rulers with whom I talked, I am grateful for teaching me the grace of that generation of Indians who speak of the past without bitterness and mention those responsible for their misfortunes only with rueful reluctance.

My special thanks to Lalit and Mapu and Anthony for providing me with places in which to work; to Rudi and Lee for their advice on the text; to my brothers for their erudition and encouragement; and to my editors for their patience.

Finally to the friends on three continents who so often saved me from the tyranny of the blank page – thank you, and God rest you merry, gentlemen.

Prologue

ON A COLD January morning when Jaya was five years old, her father insisted she accompany him into the jungle. The Maharani objected. The Maharajah overruled her.

'You coddle the children too much. Tikka's feet weren't allowed to touch the ground until he was old enough to ride a pony. Now you're doing the same with the girl.'

Under her veil the Maharani frowned in concern. The crown prince of Balmer, known to everyone as Tikka, was a sturdy nine-year-old with his mother's fair skin and the hard black eyes of his father. Tikka stood respectfully enough while his mother lectured him about the target practice that littered the ramparts of the Fort with dead pigeons. Minutes later the Maharani would hear shots and turn, half remorseful, half proud, to her attendants, 'What can I do with this boy and his love of guns? It's his Rajput blood.'

Tikka's younger sister, on the other hand, was a gentle child who had inherited the Maharani's green eyes and her father's dark skin. The Maharani frequently wondered if that dark skin would create problems when the time came to arrange Jaya's marriage. She worried about Jaya's temperament too. In the evenings when the Maharani untied bundles of brittle miniature paintings to show her children their ancestors, Tikka always demanded to see scenes of battle. He loved the ancient Rajput weapons, the great crossbows and the evil short spears which opened like shears in a man's belly. But Jaya stared silently at the strange, almost mystic paintings in which a horse was composed from trees and mountains and kings, and the Maharani did not know what went on behind her daughter's wide green eyes.

TWO HOURS before dawn Maharajah Jai Singh swung his excited daughter onto his saddle, cursing when her long skirt caught on the pommel of his saddle, as officers of the Household Cavalry, rifles slung across their shoulders, reined their skittish horses, casting strange shadows on the cobblestones outside the stables. Jaya settled back into her father's arms, the unfamiliar cartridge belt pressing against her spine. Someone wrapped a cotton quilt around her. In a clatter of hoofbeats through which Jaya could hear the sound of her anklets as her short legs hit the side of her father's mount, they rode down the ramparts of Balmer Fort.

The city below the Fort was silent. A few lamps in the lakeside temples showed that here and there a priest was waking. The metallic ring of horseshoes on the cobbled streets set dogs barking, and irate voices from lampless windows called the dogs to be still. Then they were in open country, fields on their left, the flat blackness of Jalsa Lake on their right.

The riders tunnelled through the dark by the light of the lanterns swaying on the riders' lances. The steady rhythm of her father's horse lulled Jaya to sleep. When she awoke, farmers were moving towards their fields behind black buffaloes dragging wooden ploughs, and smoke from cow-dung fires was rising above the mud walls of the villages.

A line of camels approached, cushioned feet making no sound on the road. Men covered in rough shawls swayed on their backs.

The dozing camel herders were startled awake by two shikaris, royal huntsmen, galloping towards the ruler.

'What news?' the Maharajah shouted.

'Panther, hukam! Six or seven miles into the jungle.'

'It's a big one, hukam. Better not take the princess.'

They wheeled their horses behind Jai Singh as the riders approached the elephants waiting at a village on the edge of the jungle. Maharajah Jai Singh dismounted, watched by a group of village women with veiled faces. 'Take care of the child, daughters. I will send for her later.'

Surrounded by cooing women who pinched her cheeks and marvelled at her green eyes, Jaya did not notice her father's entourage
climb onto the waiting elephants.

The women dispersed, and a ring of village children appraised
Jaya through kohl-lined eyes, waiting to see what would happen
to this Bai-sa, or royal sister, from Balmer Fort.

A boy of perhaps ten years asked, 'Bai-sa, have you ever
drunk cow's milk?'

'Of course I have. All children drink cow's milk.'

'But you must drink out of a big golden glass, Bai-sa.'

'No, I don't,' Jaya retorted. 'I have a glass from England
with a picture of a red soldier.'

'It's still a glass. Do you want to try it our way?'

A cow was chewing sugar cane beside a tree. The boy clambered
under the cow, pulling Jaya behind him. Jaya obediently squatted,
her head pushing against the cow's soft belly. The boy squeezed the
full udders, directing a stream of warm milk into her hair and eyes,
and the crowding children hooted in delight.

The village women broke through the cordon. Seeing Jaya covered
in mud and milk, the women held their earlobes in mortification.

'What will Maharaj say when he sees his daughter?' they
shrieked.

'It was only a game,' the boy wailed. 'She wanted to try it.'

Ivory bracelets clattered as the women beat the children.

'What will Durbar say?'

'Junglies! That's what you are!'

Tikka came striding through the crowd of bawling children. In
the sudden silence the women tried to clean Jaya with their veils.
Tikka winked at the ten-year-old before turning in disgust to his
sister. 'You'd better stop crying and get on the elephant. Bappa's
caught the panther.'

Lashed on the elephant's back was a shooting howdah, a canvas
box with sides high enough for a grown man to stand and take
aim. Jaya and Tikka clambered onto stools inside the howdah, their
waists held by shikaris as the elephant keeper, the mahout, sat on
the elephant's neck, stroking the back of the elephant's ear with a
steel prong.

'Gently, my beloved. Step as lightly as a dancer, my graceful
one,' the mahout chanted.

3

The elephant moved off the road, uprooting young plants and dusting them against its knees before looping the plants in a crackle of breaking stems into the soft maw of its mouth.

'Lightly, lightly, my beloved.' The elephant flapped its ears at the mahout's whisper, and the sound of those huge ears brushing against the leaves was like the sound of sails filling with air or the wings of some mighty bird about to alight.

The moisture of the night had not yet evaporated. Sunlight glinted off cobwebs stretching across the thorned bushes where a herd of blue bull deer was feeding. Jaya shouted in excitement. The herd turned for a second, then, in a rush of leaves and trampled branches, broke into flight. 'You're not supposed to talk in the jungle,' Tikka hissed. 'You'll frighten the animals away. And if a tiger hears, it will attack.'

In the distance an animal roared. The elephant trumpeted in fear. Wild boar squealed and wheeled out of the elephant's way, tusks shining white in black-tufted snouts. The roars got louder, and Jaya crouched on the floor of the howdah, gripping her brother's ankles.

Tikka pulled her plaits. 'Stand up, Jaya. It's the biggest panther you'll ever see!'

Under the insistent blows of the mahout's steel prong the elephant reached the Maharajah's position, but Jaya stubbornly clung to her brother's ankles, eyes shut in panic. Only when the shikari lifted her up did she open her eyes, terrified she might fall from the howdah rocking on top of the agitated elephant.

Through the undergrowth she saw her father and his men facing a large black panther chained to a sal tree. Blood dripped from the panther's neck as it leaped against the steel links of the chain, and roars of rage filled the jungle. Jaya clung to the shikari, eyes squeezed shut, even as she felt herself being lowered into someone's arms and carried closer and closer to that sound.

When she dared open her eyes she was standing less than a foot from the lunging animal. Spittle and drops of blood fell on her skirt. She tried to hide behind her father's legs. Maharajah Jai Singh prised her fingers loose and forced her to face the panther.

For what seemed like hours they stood in front of the sal tree, her father, her brother and herself, almost within reach of the enraged panther's claws. After a long while Jaya's terror subsided.

4

It was as though she had lost the capacity to fear and was watching the proceedings from some distant vantage point where she was not threatened. She even wondered if the sal tree was trying to comfort the panther as it dropped red blossoms like silk handkerchiefs on the captured animal's back.

The Maharajah took her hand as they walked back to the waiting shikaris. He put his other hand on Tikka's shoulder. 'Rulers are men and men are always frightened. A man cannot govern unless he confronts his own fear.'

Jaya was too young to understand that Maharajah Jai Singh was teaching his children Rajniti, the philosophy of monarchy, as it had been taught to prince after prince of the House of Balmer. Not until she became a ruler herself did she comprehend that the Maharajah taught his children the traditions of courage when he was himself a frightened man.

BOOK ONE

Balmer

I

1897

THE LAND of Jaya's birth lay beyond the desert known as the Abode of Death.

Even that year, three years before the start of a new century, the small tribe of bards making its way to the kingdom of Balmer saw many auguries of death. Water holes and village wells were dry. The artificial lakes which watered the great desert kingdoms of Jodhpur, Bikaner, Jaisalmer were covered with green slime, their levels sunk so low the foundations of water palaces stood revealed, ringed by brown-scaled crocodiles dozing in shallow water.

There was little food to spare for the storytellers as they converged on village squares at nightfall to tell their tales for a place to rest, and yet they became a caravan. Throughout Rajputana it was known the Maharajah of Balmer awaited the birth of his first child. Families in search of a season's work, other storytellers and tinkers and acrobats, called to the bards, 'Do you go to Balmer for the birth?' Learning it was so, they grabbed sleepy bullocks by their vermilion-painted horns and shouted 'Hut! Hut!' urging the animals onto the road.

Once a group of ash-covered sadhus lying naked in a broken pavilion built by a forgotten king waved their iron tridents and clambered into a crowded camel cart.

Sometimes the carts were pushed aside by the crested carriages of rajas who lived in the stone fortifications that outlined the treeless black hills. When the sun was at its height, the fortifications seemed to breathe, expanding and contracting in the haze as though the hills were massive, brooding lizards from the time of mythology and the motion of the stone battlements the sluggish shifting of their spines.

Sometimes the caravan attached itself to the procession of court ministers journeying to Balmer with secret messages from their maharajah to the ruler of Balmer, in defiance of the laws of Imperial Britain. Then an elephant led the way, flanked by cavalry units holding banners. When the processions moved on, a silver coin, embossed with a maharajah's symbol on one side and the profile of the English Empress on the other, was gifted to each member of the caravan, even the children.

Scrub jungle gave way to sand dunes. At sunset, the sudden darkness brought a feverish chill to the empty landscape. The travellers willed their emaciated animals to reach the shelter of villages spaced farther and farther apart before the demon women who had died in childbirth came howling through the night in search of children to replace the stillborn infants they had never suckled.

Now the caravan was so large no village could contain it, and the travellers pitched their own camps.

While their children slept in the cloth cradles tied between the brass spokes of camel carts, the bards, the gypsy genealogists of royal India, talked through the night, exchanging news of the Rajput kingdoms.

'Our rulers are preparing to travel to London for the Diamond Jubilee of the White Widow, the Empress Victoria.'

'The retinues and gifts they must take to impress the British Empire will dangerously impoverish their treasuries.'

'At least in London they can speak together. Here, Britain still fears conspiracy and will not allow the kings to meet except in the presence of Englishmen.'

'But court astrologers are reminding their maharajahs that famine has come every twenty years since the rise of British power.'

'And twenty years have passed since the last famine.'

The bards shook their heads, dismissing astrology for the reality they had witnessed on the road. They had seen the villagers praying for rain. The farmers knew already. Another famine had begun.

2

FEW EUROPEANS had travelled to Balmer in previous centuries, and those who had survived the dangerous journey had confused Balmer with the desert, calling it the Land of Death. In the half-century since Balmer had signed a treaty with the British Empire, Europeans had visited the kingdom more frequently. Only ten years ago the Tsarevitch of Russia, accompanied by two Grand Dukes of the Russian court, had passed a fortnight with the Maharajah of Balmer. Earlier, the son of the German Kaiser had stayed in the capital. These recent visitors had found Balmer to be a land not of death, but of prosperous farmers.

Even now it seemed as though the drought which threatened the outside world had stopped at Balmer's borders. Fields stretched in patchwork circles around villages shaded by towering silk-cotton trees, and the main avenue which led to the capital city, broad enough to accommodate a marching garrison, was lined with banyan trees spreading their branches over pergolas covered with nesting pigeons. The bards knew each pergola enshrined the ashes of some Balmer noble who had died in battle and the wives who had burned themselves on his funeral pyre.

Night had fallen when the bards finally saw the marble cenotaphs of the Balmer maharajahs glowing like a ghost city on the outskirts of the capital. The caravan hastened past the monuments of death through the elephant arches guarding the capital, and entered bazaars blazing in the light of kerosene lanterns.

From behind mountains of marigold garlands, hawkers called

to women on their way to the temples on the edge of Jalsa Lake. In the wide octagon of the central piazza, shopkeepers sat cross-legged inside wooden shops selling gold or quilts or medicines and fragrant sandalwood, dusty mirrors behind their heads reflecting their gesticulating customers.

Children came running to direct the caravan.

'Maharajah Jai Singh has built a tent city for you.'

'Where the elephants wrestle at the Dasra festival.'

Led by shouting children, the caravan moved past the ornate houses of the merchants and up the steep ramparts of Balmer Fort to the elephant grounds, where haphazard cloth tents clustered around a central cooking area, disguising the smell of camels, horses, and bullocks tethered in the adjoining field.

In front of the tents the eighty-foot-high wall of the inner fort rose with perpendicular austerity. Messengers were waiting to guide the bards into the inner fort. The Maharani was near her time. It was auspicious that her unborn child should enter the world hearing the stories of his ancestral line.

Through the carved zenana walls, the Maharani's attendants watched the bards unroll cloths painted with the histories of the Rajput kings so that moving pictures would illustrate their recitations.

The Maharani lay on a cushioned pallet, a woman with skin the colour of milk and the green eyes of the mountain kingdom of her birth. Her women cooled the soles of her feet with henna paste while in the courtyard outside, the bards declaimed:

'May you bear sons to increase the sons of the Sun.

'Two thousand years ago the great Queen Pushpavati was all that remained of the Sons of the Sun.

'Her father, her brothers, her husband, all her great line lay slaughtered in the City of the Hundred Temples.

'Her sisters and daughters had burned themselves, running past each other to enter the flames of the funeral pyre.'

The cloistered audience listened with familiar horror to descriptions of lost battles and burning women as the illustrations rolled on the painted screens.

'Why did Queen Pushpavati remain a living widow? She was the most valiant and honourable of Rajput women. It was her duty and her honour to mount the funeral pyre first.'

In a swell of drumbeats, the curtain moved upward. The Maharani's attendants peered at the cloth painting, admiring the overexplicit artwork.

'Because she was with child. An unborn infant waited in her womb to avenge the honour of his ancestors.

'For this reason only, Queen Pushpavati endured the taint of widowhood.'

Other people who lived in Balmer Fort, the elephant boys and the grooms, members of the household guard, even the administration clerks, came to sit in the courtyard and listen to the bards declaim the history of their clan.

'Queen Pushpavati

'The greatest queen in India

'Famed for her prowess with a sword

'Who could draw a bow almost as well as a man

'Who rode at the side of her husband in pursuit of the cheetah.

'This warrior queen was now a widow.'

Everyone knew the story. Still, they muttered at the indignity of the queen's fate as the tale unfolded: the child's birth, his martial feats as a boy, the growing suspicion that he was of royal blood.

When the painting of a white-turbaned king holding a rose rolled onto the cloth screens, the audience knew the narrative was ending even before the bards sang in unison:

'Thus did Queen Pushpavati give birth to the son of the Sun, and then ascend her funeral pyre

'Thus did the son of the Sun sire a hundred sons

'Thus, each son became a king

'And thus did our Empire come to be known as Rajputana, the Empire of the Sons of the King.'

The pleased Maharani sent her eunuchs out with a bag of gold coins for the bards. That night, while the bards feasted in the tent city, the earth began to shake. Sudden light pierced the darkness, catapulting flocks of frightened birds into the sky. Panicking animals fought against tethering ropes and small children hid in their mothers' laps, not understanding why their mothers laughed and tossed them in the air.

Thirty-nine times the deep roar of the cannons burst through the night, announcing the succession was secure. The Kingdom of Balmer had its thirty-ninth heir. Maharajah Jai Singh of Balmer was blessed with a son.

3

FOR ELEVEN centuries Balmer Fort had stood on the hill overlooking Jalsa Lake, a monument to proud isolation. Inside its massive yellow stone battlements there were silver fountains and pillars inlaid with lapis lazuli and gardens linking courtyards painted by master artists brought from the ateliers of Delhi. But these concessions to pleasure had the air of afterthought. It was the underground passages which led to Jalsa Lake so that water could be procured in time of siege, the narrow stone corridors with ceilings so low no traitor could raise his sword arm high enough to strike a death blow to an unsuspecting king, which gave the true profile of Balmer.

Now, inside the fort, Maharajah Jai Singh of Balmer gave audience in the great Durbar Hall, accepting gifts from the nobles who represented the kings of India. Every day he took his place on the gaddi, the wide cushion covered in crimson brocade that was the traditional throne of Rajput rulers. Behind him stood the chattri-bearer, holding the royal canopy over his sovereign's head as in time of war he would hold his sovereign's standard.

The Maharajah's head was covered by the red turban of festivity, tied with a simplicity that lent dignity but no decoration to the narrow face with the severe eyes. His stern mouth was partially hidden by a beard, divided in the centre and swept backwards into black wings across an austere white tunic broken only by a bandolier of emeralds.

Before him nobles sat in rows down the expanse of the Durbar Hall, their ceremonial swords laid across their knees, the jewelled hilts tied with gold gauze to signify they came in peace. Relays of dancing girls separated the Maharajah from his guests with their billowing skirts as certain nobles edged closer to the gaddi for a private word.

'You must go to London, Highness,' whispered a noble from Udaipur. 'We are bound by the vow we took four hundred years ago that we would not bow before alien emperors. But you are not restricted.'

His companion leaned closer to the King. 'Highness, your izzat, your honour, is unchallenged. Tell the Empress famine is upon us. Tell Victoria the speech of Britain is golden, but her taxes are more savage than the sword of the Moghuls.'

Another noble from another kingdom took their place, his lowered voice urgent in Jai Singh's ear. 'Maharaj, be cautious. Britain cripples us with her greed. Half of India's money goes to fatten England. The other half is spent on an army in which no Indian can be an officer. On more railways to move British goods, more police. The Angrez are weaving a spider's web of power from which we will never disentangle ourselves.'

For a week Maharajah Jai Singh listened to messages carried by the representatives of other Indian courts. In the end, it was the promptings of his wife which tipped the balance. The Maharani lifted her arms over breasts swollen with milk so her husband could bless the new heir to the sacrament which bound the kings of Balmer to the gods in whose name they ruled.

'Go to London, Durbar. You are the voice of the people's assembly. Victoria must listen to you. India's Empress cannot ignore India's suffering.'

4

LINES OF weary peasants stumbled beside the railway tracks leading to Bombay, where Jai Singh would board ship for England. Jai Singh stared at the devastation that had overtaken British India in the past year as frightened passengers told his ministers of the riots that had broken out when British officials had evacuated whole villages before setting every house on fire to prevent the spread of plague.

The railway stations were crowded with families fleeing the famine and disease in Bombay itself. They spoke of the sanitary cordon that had been created around the houses of the British residents and the rich Indian merchants who managed British interests.

'But everyone else is foraging for food, or dying of cholera.'

'Grain, robbed from cargo ships exporting Indian wheat to foreign markets, is being sold in the city's bazaars at exorbitant prices, and starving factory workers are deserting British factories in defiance of armed overseers.'

When he reached Bombay, Jai Singh could not decide whether he was waking from a nightmare or entering a dream. Inside imposing homes, Indians and Englishmen alike discussed how magnificent the Indian rulers would look when they paid public homage to Victoria in the Jubilee procession. Not once did they mention the famine.

At the docks, royal women were taking leave of their maharajahs inside screens held by armed eunuchs. From the upper deck, Jai Singh watched the temporary zenanas moving like giant silk balloons in the crush of horses and men as the young Lancers from the Indian kingdoms, who were to ride as the Empress's guard of honour, boarded

17

ship for London. As the ship cast anchor and Bombay harbour receded into the harsh glare, a premonition of doom enveloped Jai Singh.

He was unable to shake the mood during the voyage. Sitting at the Captain's table or promenading on the deck with the young Lancers, Jai Singh listened silently to the excited talk of the Jubilee celebrations and did not say he feared India's wealth was providing a carpet for Victoria's feet, leaving India no protection from the pitiless sun.

IN LONDON, unbalanced by the strangeness of his surroundings, Jai Singh briefly forgot the famine. In the unfamiliar rented house in Mayfair he crossed and uncrossed his legs, trying to accustom himself to sitting upright in chairs. At night, he tossed in the high four-poster bed into which a man's body sank like a corpse - so unlike the short, hard bed of the Rajputs, which ended at the ankles so a warrior would always sleep lightly.

During the day, the Balmer grooms negotiated his coach through streets crowded with hansom cabs and buses, and Jai Singh marvelled at the unending, alien wealth of England. Wherever he went he saw preparations for Victoria's parade. Wooden stands were being constructed along the route of the procession. Union Jacks festooned the facades of the buildings, portraits of the Empress stared from every window.

Only on a visit to the Stock Exchange did he feel briefly at home. The ordered confusion was so like an Indian bazaar. Men chalked figures onto blackboards, listened to names being called out across the smoke-filled chamber, erased the figures, chalked up larger sums. Then Jai Singh began to recognize the shouted names, and his throat tightened as he heard the calls for British companies that shipped Indian goods and Indian labour around the world. Returning home, he read the inscription engraved on the stone portals of the Royal Exchange: THE EARTH IS THE LORD'S AND THE FRUITS THEREOF, and remembered that each day of his stay in England he had seen how the fruits of the earth fed only the appetites of the British Empire.

At last, Jai Singh was summoned to the India Office, which governed the affairs of the Indian kingdoms. Accompanied by two young aides-de-camp and the corpulent figures of his court ministers of Trade and Foreign Affairs, Jai Singh mounted the marble staircase to a gallery dominated by a large oil painting depicting the conquest of an Indian king. The black frock coats of the three British officials who ushered him into the spacious office with moulded ceilings seemed to reprimand the brocade tunics of his own delegation.

Jai Singh took his place on a sofa, a young Indian lawyer in an English suit and wing collar perched nervously next to him, his ministers on chairs behind. 'Tell the Angrez there is famine in British India. Our trade routes pass through British India. We are landlocked kingdoms. Everything that enters or leaves our borders is taxed twice over by British India. Now the famine in British India is crippling us.'

As the lawyers translated his words, Jai Singh read indifference on the faces of the Englishmen, and the misgivings he had felt on the ship returned.

'Britain is conscious of the situation. Indeed, the Lord Mayor of London has begun a Famine Relief Fund.'

Jai Singh rested his hand on the lawyer's arm. 'Tell the Angrez the Lord Mayor's fund is of little use when the Empire's taxes inflame the famine. Explain to them when British India starves, royal India dies.'

A thin Englishman with sharp features consulted the Balmer file, the expression of contempt in his eyes at odds with the smiling mouth. 'Ask His Highness how much of his revenue goes towards the maintenance of his harem. Does he not feel that a railway would add to his country's wealth and create more revenue for his pleasures?'

'A railway will flood my country with cheap goods made in British factories. My revenues are already limited by Britain. How shall I pay for a railway?'

The Englishman flushed. In a soft voice, almost as though he were paying Jai Singh a compliment, he said, 'But surely His Highness has extensive funds. After all, Balmer no longer maintains an army. Britain must pay to defend Balmer, since Balmer is defenceless.'

The veiled threat hung like smoke in the air. Even now the British were preparing to hang the Maharajah of Manipur, who had challenged the British, as a common criminal. Jai Singh could feel the anger of the Balmer delegation pressing like a knife against his spine at his reply. 'Balmer is grateful for the protection of the British Empire. Observe our gratitude. We spend as much revenue paying homage to England as we once spent on our armies.'

Convinced he would not receive a sympathetic hearing from the men who governed India from the India Office, Jai Singh waited impatiently for the Jubilee celebrations to end so he could seek a private audience with Victoria.

He paced the overfurnished rooms of his Mayfair house, glaring at the expensive objects which crowded every table. He stared at the men in frock coats and the women in elaborate hats walking in Brook Street below him, and longed for the stone parapets of Balmer Fort above which desert eagles glided in an empty sky.

At night he attended the balls which preceded the Jubilee Parade and listened to stories of the Prince of Wales's partiality for actresses and other men's wives. He heard other scandals about one of Victoria's grandsons, who was said to frequent homosexual brothels, marvelling that the British were so unafraid of contamination when some disease in Victoria's blood had already poisoned the bloodlines of the crowned heads of Europe, even Tsar Nicholas II of Russia.

Two days before the Jubilee, Jai Singh received news that an old friend of his father's, the Maharajah of Dungra, had arrived in England and wished to see him.

Watched by a curious crowd, Dungra was waiting for Jai Singh on the pavement outside his house in Belgrave Square, his rotund form clothed in a deep blue tunic broken by a dozen rows of baroque pearls which fell from his neck to his ample waist. A man with a cap pulled low over his forehead nudged the woman standing next to him. 'Look at the old bugger,' he said scornfully. 'Wears more gew-gaws than a music-hall harlot.'

Jai Singh dismounted from his carriage. To the sound of a desultory cheer from the pavement spectators Dungra led Jai Singh inside the house, and London melted away in the hiss of starched turbans as the Dungra guards came to attention. The doors behind the guards opened to reveal a semicircle of barefoot and turbaned retainers.

Jai Singh followed his uncle into a room from which all foreign furniture had been removed. Low silver beds were placed around a dais which held the crimson gaddi of the ruler. In one corner of the room was a silver urn the height of a man, guarded by a bare-torsoed priest. The rulers held out their hands to be cleansed of the pollution of the foreigner with the purifying water of the holy river Ganges. Only then did Dungra motion Jai Singh to a silver divan.

'Tell me, Jai,' the old Maharajah settled his heavy frame into the cushions, 'what do you think of our imperial masters, now that you have seen them at such close quarters?'

'What does it matter what I think, hukam? I have no army to give weight to my views.'

Dungra raised a languid eyebrow. 'Be careful, Jai. That is a seditious remark. You are in England. For such sedition you could lose your throne.'

'I speak the truth, hukam. The proudest warriors in the world have become toy soldiers to decorate British parades. Armed with guns we cannot fire because the firing pins and the ammunition are kept in British India. We owe fealty to an empress whose guard are called Beefeaters. But we are Rajputs who hold the cow sacred because it nurtures life. Countless Rajput soldiers died of thirst in besieged forts rather than drink water from streams into which enemy armies had poured the blood of slaughtered cows.'

Dungra folded his hands over the pearls sliding across his stomach. 'I often think we Indian kings are like old courtesans, Jai. Decking ourselves in gems and stories of our glorious past because we fear the present. We speak of our warrior blood. But for three generations there has been no war in India. No trumpet of armoured elephants, no cavalry charges. Only the insolent silence of the Empire's Pax Britannica.'

Placing a paan made of betel leaf covered with beaten gold into his mouth, Dungra leaned forward. 'We all inherited treasuries to raise armies. Now that we have no armies, some of us squander our wealth on pleasure. Others like yourself hope one day to rise against the British Empire.' A plump finger wagged at Jai Singh. 'Yes, you do. You are young and all young men dream impossible dreams. As for myself, I have taken the money in my treasury and invested it in the wealth of the West. For twenty years my subjects have paid no tax. I have imitated the actions of the British Empire. Foreigners pay the costs of my government.'

Jai Singh interrupted the older ruler. 'Are you suggesting that the warriors of India should become moneylenders? It is against our dharma, the righteous action prescribed for us in the ancient scriptures.'

The mask of the merry clown slipped for a moment from Dungra's features. 'You speak like a child, Jai. The ancient scriptures enjoin us to spend only seven per cent of our wealth on ourselves and our governments. The rest we are to multiply for our people.' He spat a red streak of betel juice into a silver spittoon. 'Come, let us not be so serious. Tell me how you find London's social life.'

Jai Singh wondered if he should mention the India Office official sneering at the forbidden zenanas of India when his own princes risked disease from shared women and boys bought in homosexual brothels. 'I think, Highness, their idea of dignity must differ from ours.'

Dungra's thick lips, stained red with betel juice, opened in laughter. 'Dignity? Dharma? You live in the past, Jai. Such words have lost their currency. Now the world runs on money.' He clapped his hands and a servant entered, carrying a parcel tied in crimson muslin. 'You have been blessed with an heir. Regard this gift as a prophecy of the times we must live in, if we are to leave our sons kingdoms, not cremation grounds.'

ON THE EVE of the Jubilee Parade, the Indian rulers were summoned to a reception by the Empress at Buckingham Palace. Jai Singh followed the Beefeater guard through the halls which led to Victoria's Drawing Room, wondering if Victoria would be wearing the bracelet of flawless diamonds sent by the Maharajah of Jaipur to avoid losing caste by eating at the same table as the untouchable who was his Empress. The bracelet made Victoria the Maharajah's sister, and an Indian could take nothing from a sister's house, not even a sip of water. Learning of the custom, the Empress had excused the other Indian rulers from attending the state banquet which preceded her reception.

Jai Singh heard his name and titles being announced, and for a startled moment he felt himself an intruder who had wandered into the imperial toshikhana, the very treasury of the British Empire.

The human symbols of Britain's power - the British cabinet in their court dress of knee breeches and silk stockings, the foreign ambassadors wearing the insignia of their nations, the crowned heads of Europe connected by treaties and marriage to the Empire - stood in stiff circles under the chandeliers. On a dais, the focus of that power sat on a red velvet chair, an old woman in a black dress embroidered with gold suns and silver stars, her feet covered by the jewel-encrusted border of her long skirt.

Jai Singh saw that Victoria wore Jaipur's bracelet as he answered her queries about his stay in London. He moved on to exchange a few words with the Prince of Wales and the British princes and princesses standing on the dais beside their mother.

Others of Victoria's children were in the room. The Empress of Prussia with her two sons. The Princess of Naples. The Duchess of Teck. The Grand Dukes representing Tsar Nicholas II broke from their conversation with Archduke Ferdinand of Austria and Hungary to reminisce with Jai Singh about their visit to Balmer. Beside them the son of the Japanese Emperor, heir to the Chrysanthemum Throne, looked blankly at the Heir Apparent of Siam.

There was a sudden lull in the murmur of polite conversation. Jai Singh turned and saw a stocky little man striding down the room, dressed in an unadorned tunic coat and cotton pyjamas. Amusement rippled through the gathering as Sir Pratap Singh, the Regent King of Jodhpur, approached the Empress. His crumpled leggings were now being imitated by European riders who called them jodhpurs after this eccentric figure, reputed to be the finest rider in the world and famous as the man who had actually made the Prince of Wales dismount from his horse because he found the Prince's hands too hard.

Ignoring the stir, Sir Pratap reached the dais and raised his sword above Victoria's head. There were frightened gasps from the gathering. The Prince of Wales stepped forward to protect his mother, stopping in confusion when Sir Pratap placed the sword at Victoria's feet.

'Bloody native!' an outraged British official hissed behind Jai Singh. 'What on earth does he think he's doing?'

The whisper was silenced by shock when Sir Pratap took Victoria's small hands from her lap and placed them on his eyes.

Jai Singh knew Sir Pratap was obeying the Rajput code of honour. The sword Sir Pratap was forced to carry by British protocol, his honour demanded he place at Victoria's feet. Now, where other rulers had presented the Empress with superb gems, Sir Pratap was offering Victoria his eyes, the most precious possession of a warrior.

Moved by the simplicity of Sir Pratap's gesture, Jai Singh glanced around the crowded Drawing Room. The greatest names in India were in Buckingham Palace that night. The kings of the Maharatta Confederacy - Gwalior, whose armies had fought Wellington and caused Napoleon to dismiss Wellington as the 'Sepoy General'; Baroda, with the famous cannons cast from pure gold. The Sons of the Sun, the Rajput kings, all conscious that the senior Rajput king of Udaipur had declined to pay obeisance to this foreign Empress. The mighty rulers of Northern India, whose armies had come to Britain's aid at the time of the Mutiny. The Muslim rulers, led by the frigid Nizam of Hyderabad. The kings of the torrid Hindu South; the Maharajah of Mysore, the Elephant King of Travancore.

They lit up Victoria's Drawing Room with their tunics of gold brocade and aigrettes secured by gems that dwarfed the Koh-i-noor. Ropes of pearls and emeralds and rubies swept in waves under their beards and across their chests. Holding their jewelled swords in their left hands, they stood with the customary immobility of Eastern rulers among the circulating guests.

But Jai Singh knew all their shining splendour could not disguise the impotence of kings without armies who had been forced to travel thousands of miles to pay homage to an empress twice untouchable, a widow and a foreigner.

That night, propped up in the unfamiliar four-poster bed, Jai Singh unwrapped the muslin from Dungra's gift. Lines creased his forehead as he studied the documents which informed him that he, the ruler of Balmer, now owned shares in the Canadian Pacific Railway and a railway in Brazil, part of the American Fruit Company, smaller parts of Bell Telephone, an Australian gold mine, three banks and a dozen other foreign enterprises. Refusing to accept the defeat represented in the file, Jai Singh thrust the documents from him, vowing to guard Balmer until his son could mount the throne in full dharma as a warrior and protector of the people.

RAIN THREATENED on the morning of the Jubilee Parade. Looking through the windows while the servants wrapped the eighty-foot length of starched muslin turban around his head, Jai Singh felt sorry for the people milling behind the British troops who defied the grey sky with their scarlet coats and burnished silver helmets.

A huge cheer went up as the Maharajah of Balmer and the

Balmer Lancers, mounted on black chargers, made their way to Buckingham Palace. Jai Singh could feel the charged anticipation in the air, knew anything that broke the boredom of the two million people who waited for the Jubilee procession to begin would elicit applause.

Near Whitehall there was a confusion of colours as the colonial cavalries moved their horses into position. Behind the Australians. in their yellow coats, the New Zealanders in their cavalier hats with sweeping coloured plumes, the Sikhs in their bright red turbans, Jai Singh saw the colonial infantries, Chinese troops in triangular straw helmets, Trinidadians in spotless white puttees, Maoris with shields and spears.

The Balmer Lancers wheeled their horses through the gates of Buckingham Palace, to ride in Victoria's guard of honour. Jai Singh watched them, his heart aching for these proud young men who could never fulfil their dharma as warriors.

In the square outside the palace, rulers from a quarter of the world, their armies now absorbed into the great ocean of British power, waited on their horses, holding emblems heraldic of more glorious times to add their own bright pageantry to the triumphant display of conquest, and people hung from the branches of trees, waiting to witness the magnificence of imperial power on a scale such as the world had never seen.

The parade began, led by British heroes who had brought foreign governments to their knees. On the balcony of Buckingham Palace Jai Singh could see the small figure of the Empress taking the salute of the Englishmen riding by on prancing horses named after defeated kings, and he knew the paper treaty that called him Victoria's brother was meaningless in the face of such proud power.

Six naval guns on their gun carriages rolled below Victoria's balcony, separating the troops of the colonies from the troops of the Motherland. The cheers rose to a crescendo as Life Guards, Dragoons, battery after battery of Hussars and Lancers preceded by their mounted bands came down the Mall.

The sun burst through the clouds as the Indian Imperial Cavalry rode out in front of Victoria's carriage. A roar of applause went up from the crowds crushed against the troops. Never had the sun failed to shine for Victoria, and here it was again: Queen's weather for the Queen of Queens.

Forty Indian rulers, faces impassive, spurred their horses behind the carriage of their empress. Jai Singh saw that only Victoria's young godson, Maharajah Victor of Sirpur, waved with spirited enthusiasm at the cheering crowds.

IN THE DAYS that followed, unable to penetrate the euphoria that surrounded Victoria's court, Jai Singh failed to gain a private audience with the Empress. Britain was drunk on its own glory and wanted to hear no tales of death.

The long journey back from Bombay to Balmer was bleak evidence of the extent of the famine. Land taxes had not been lessened in British India. Dispossessed farmers, unable to scratch a living from soil that had become as unyielding as rock, were moving across India like clouds of dying birds. At every railway junction Jai Singh overheard accounts of the British revenue officers who had been beaten to death on the very day of Victoria's Jubilee Parade, and there was open talk of insurrection against the Empire.

On the borders of Balmer a delegation of anxious village elders surrounded their ruler.

'Destitute peasants have been streaming into Balmer, hukam.'

'Now moneylenders are coming in their wake, trying to buy land at derisory prices in the hope of capitalizing on the continentwide panic created by the famine.'

Then an old man, bent double with age, asked the question Jai Singh could not answer 'We still own our land, hukam. But if the rains fail again, what shall we do?'

5

IN THE EARLY years of the drought, the Maharani did not know that one day she would cling to her veil as a dying soldier clings to his standard, afraid to dishonour the memories of the Balmer maharanis who had preceded her.

Although her days were filled with the anguish of refugees, the Maharani rose before dawn and went to the Temple of the Balmer Maharanis to sit in solitary communion with the spirits of her predecessors. The knowledge of continuity in those dark hours, while the rest of the zenana slept, gave the Maharani a serenity which sustained her through the deprivation she witnessed daily.

When her pujas, her devotions, were completed, the Maharani watched through the carved zenana walls as her husband mounted his horse, surrounded by runners who came daily with news of those parts of the kingdom most severely affected by the drought.

Some days, the Maharajah rode beside the mile-long processions of bullock carts carrying water in kerosene drums which moved night and day down the dusty avenues of the country. Other days, he accompanied the elephants and camels which left Balmer Fort loaded with grain from the state granaries.

While her husband travelled the countryside, the Maharani supervised the relief camps for women inside the inner fort. Occasionally she held an assembly, a durbar, for the refugee women. Although the durbars were held after nightfall, the heat of the day's sun still seeped through the stones of the zenana courtyard. The lanterns, almost hidden by haloes of buzzing insects, had to be placed at a distance so their heat would not add to the intolerable closeness of the night.

Flying foxes wheeled so low their black wings touched black hair as the Maharani asked the refugee women why their children could neither read nor write. 'The boys of Balmer spend six years under the tutelage of the pandits. Even the girls receive three years of schooling. Why are children from British India, which is so far in advance of royal India, illiterate?'

The younger women covered their faces with their saris in shame, and in the silence the wild laughter of hyenas echoed from the darkness beyond Jalsa Lake.

An old woman finally answered. 'Our stars are bad, hukam. We once owned our lands, and the lives of our children were filled with studies. But the Angrez passed a law saying the tax collectors owned our lands. Overnight the Angrez made us into beggars.' With an expression of self-loathing, the old woman pulled down the sari covering her head and held the fabric by the edges to form a cloth container. She thrust her cloth begging bowl towards the Maharani in the gesture of the beggar. 'The moneylenders gave us no credit, and the landlords threw us off lands we once owned. Our arms ache from going through life like this.'

That night, lying beside her husband, the Maharani asked, 'Did the British really do such a thing? Did they take land from the poor and give it to the tax collectors?'

Jai Singh sighed. 'Yes. Cornwallis, a good moral man, passed that law and called it justice. He believed he knew what was best for India. You see, the British Empire can believe its fairy tales of justice because its soul is five thousand miles away in London, too far to learn the price of its justice.'

By the third year of the drought, the Maharani could no longer ignore signs that the balance of Balmer's government was being disturbed. The heat was like a wall imprisoning the flesh. The trickles of water from the reservoirs evaporated before they could moisten the mud canals, and village wells dried up completely.

The Maharajah came to her apartments after longer and longer absences, his severe face scored with deep lines, his parted beard

28

streaked with white. Slumped against the balcony, he railed against the nobles whose families had stood steadfast through centuries of battle and who now connived against him as he taxed them with increasing severity to combat the famine.

When the wives of the nobles who formed Jai Singh's Council of Ministers called on the Maharani, their conversations were full of veiled references to dwindling dowries for unmarried daughters and households run on impossible budgets, and the Maharani grew afraid for her husband.

Jai Singh's despair gave confirmation to her fears. 'Greed!' he said, hitting his clenched fist against the fretwork of the balcony walls. 'Dead cattle litter the countryside, yet my ministers want to lease land to British companies to build railways and factories. They say it is for Balmer's progress, but the ministers will become partners with the Englishmen, fattening on the misery of Balmer's starving farmers.'

Jai Singh rubbed eyes bloodshot with the irritation of dust. 'At the last British Durbar in Delhi, my own cousin, Raja Man Singh, told the British I do not want British factories in Balmer because I am hostile to the Empire. Now I must counter those rumours by sending my Lancers to Peking to fight Britain's war against the Dowager Empress of China.'

He ran his hand along the intricate carving of the balcony, unaware that a thick film of dust was covering his fingers. The Maharani reached for the hand, felt the calluses on the palm as she gently led him through her chambers. Jai Singh followed like a sleepwalker, his words heavy with dejection. 'Perhaps Dungra was right. Perhaps this new century will be devoted to the mysteries of money as sorcerers are devoted to the mysteries of the blood.'

In the little courtyard adjoining the Maharani's chambers, clay lamps lit a wall carved with erotic bas-reliefs from Indian temples. In the flickering light the marble figures seemed to writhe as the Maharani removed her husband's dusty clothes and pulled him onto the floor.

She could hear him grumbling that he had to study the plans for the new State Secretariat to be built on the eastern bank of Jalsa Lake, to provide jobs for dispossessed farmers, as she massaged him with sandalwood oil, her fingers searching out the knots of tension in the body between her knees.

29

Half-asleep, Jai Singh lowered himself into the bathing pool. The Maharani loosened her clothes. The silk garments slid to the floor. She reached for the long plait hanging like a thick black snake down the ivory nakedness of her back. Conscious that Jai Singh was watching, she slowly wound the long plait around her head, knowing her pale body with its heavy breasts and tapering legs, her rounded belly with the three lines like half-moons below the naval, still pleased her husband.

IN THE NEW YEAR the Balmer Lancers left for China. By the Christian calendar it was the beginning of a new century, and still it did not rain. Farmers trailed into the capital, to the brackish drinking water provided by Jalsa Lake, leaving their dying cattle licking salt from the cracked surfaces of fields baked hard as clay in the kiln of the fierce sun.

The Maharajah reluctantly closed Balmer's borders to refugees but continued his implacable resistance to a British presence within the country. Sometimes he carried copies of London newspapers, a month old by the time they reached his kingdom, to the Maharani's balcony. Unfolding the brittle pages, he read aloud news of the China war. Once he brought a thick envelope from the Viceroy. The black-banded letter informed them that the British Empire had lost its soul. Victoria, Queen of Queens, was dead.

As summer approached, the wives of the nobles became openly rebellious. Led by the wife of the Prime Minister, an austere woman emaciated from the three full days she fasted in the week, they came in a delegation to the Maharani.

The Prime Minister's wife spoke for the noblewomen, her delivery dry and bloodless like her husband's. 'The Maharajah is unreasonable, hukam. He has not allowed us to take a paisa from the farmers in the last four years, but we have had to pay our taxes just the same. We have not been allowed to charge for irrigation and seeds. We have been forced to open our granaries to feed starving refugees.' She coughed delicately behind her hand, as the other wives nodded in assent. 'How does the Maharajah expect us to live, hukam? Even the best cow runs out of milk when it is not fed.'

The Maharani tried to speak of duty. 'Surely if you fast for three days each week, you cannot have forgotten the principle of sacrifice for a common good?'

The wife of Jai Singh's cousin, Raja Man Singh, cleared her throat. The Maharani smiled encouragingly at the young woman whose pregnancy was visible under the folds of her garments, certain of her support.

'But, hukam,' the young rani said shyly, 'my husband says the British have not lifted the taxes on the farmers. Britain even taxes the cloth the farmers weave to cover their bodies. He says the British Empire will be twice as strong after the drought but Balmer will be bankrupt.'

The Prime Minister's wife patted the young rani's lap approvingly, and the Maharani realized that the pyramid of Balmer's government was crumbling.

THE DAY the Maharani was sure another child stirred inside her womb she sat on her balcony and waited for her husband's return, thinking how year after parched year she had seen the ordered world which gave purpose to her existence turned upside down, seen the sun suck all the moisture from once-fertile fields, witnessed the depth of her husband's despair as his country became a wasteland ready to be exploited by the machines of a new age without customs or humanity.

The curtains of the inner chamber were swept aside and Jai Singh strode onto the balcony. Taking her pale face between hands blackened from days on horseback, he said, 'You must break purdah.'

He said other things, but the Maharani heard nothing more. A paralysis held her motionless as she waited for the moment to pass and her husband to withdraw those few words which would destroy a thousand years of tradition.

When Jai Singh did not reverse his command, she pulled the veil from her head, holding the two edges in her outstretched hands to make a begging bowl. 'Hukam, ask anything from me but this.'

Jai Singh tore the veil from her hands. 'Savage times require savage measures! Your sacrifice will not be unique. The Tiger Queen of Baroda has come out of purdah and is travelling in her country to assist in famine relief. The Regent of Jodhpur's wife has moved out of Jodhpur Fort. Now she lives in a mud hut and cooks food for

31

the drought kitchens with her own hands. I require your presence in the camps. Ask yourself this, woman. What is more important, your veil or your people's despair?'

The Maharani scooped up the thin fabric from the floor. She could not explain why a piece of cloth woven to such fineness that she could see through it as clearly as she saw through a pane of dusty glass and which in a breeze clung to the delicate contours of her face seeming to reveal more than it hid, was the membrane which separated a life of honour from the ways of alien chaos. But she was convinced the new child she carried in her body would have a troubled life, robbed of the protection of those time-honoured ways as immutable as the laws of nature.

Struggling to regain some semblance of control, the Maharani sent for the Baran, the senior maid who performed all her pujas when she was menstruating or otherwise indisposed.

The heavy chunking of golden anklets that proclaimed the Baran the Maharani's surrogate in the zenana sounded in the corridor, and a tall woman with almost masculine features entered the painted chamber.

'The Maharajah wishes me to break purdah. During my absence from the Fort, you will ensure that there is no neglect of the refugee women. . . .'

The Baran gasped. 'You cannot do this, hukam. You must not. The zenana will lose the reason for its existence.'

'The Maharajah wishes it, Baran. Tell Kuki-bai I wish to call on her.'

Tears welled in the Baran's eyes, but she folded her hands. 'Your command, hukam.'

There was no slump in the Maharani's carriage as she walked to the rooms of Jai Singh's grandfather's favourite concubine, no hesitation in her voice as she dealt with the palace women waiting outside their chambers with complaints against the eunuchs.

Only when she saw Kuki-bai's plump form struggling to rise from the silver bed suspended on four silver chains did she reveal her anguish. The old concubine had guided her as a lonely bride, only thirteen years old, through the intricacies of a strange zenana and the politics of an alien court. The Maharani had often wept in Kuki-bai's lap, and the familiar smell of cloves and cinnamon comforted her as again her tears soaked into Kuki-bai's garments.

Kuki-bai stroked the Maharani's long hair with small, still shapely hands. 'Oh, child, you are too rigid. You must learn to bend with the times, or you will snap in two like an old neem twig.'

'He wants me to break purdah. If I obey, I will become like the zenana eunuchs - neither a woman within the protection of women, nor a man in the world of men.'

'Your husband may be forced to leave for London, to attend the coronation of the new Emperor. He no longer trusts Raja Man Singh or the Council of Ministers. While he is away he expects you to keep an eye on what is happening in the state. You cannot do this from the zenana.'

'My predecessors would have killed themselves rather than endure such dishonour.'

Kuki-bai clucked impatiently. 'Your husband's grandfather, the Lion of Balmer, prohibited the women of Balmer from ever burning themselves again on their husbands' funeral pyres. But you young women are still blinded by the heroic tales of the sati queens of Balmer. Now compose yourself so that you do not shame the ruler before his subjects.'

That evening, during the half-hour when the cruelty of the day's heat was forgotten in the magnificence of the sunset, Jai Singh came for the Maharani. In an unusual gesture of public affection, he held her arm as she walked beside him down the corridors that connected the zenana to the public courtyard.

Through her veil, the Maharani could see blurred figures in the courtyard – the eager face of her husband's cousin, Raja Man Singh, and the pinched face of the Prime Minister. Beside them stood the other ministers of the council, prurience and boredom fighting for dominance on their features. At the back of the courtyard, hundreds of Balmer men shuffled from foot to foot in embarrassment.

The Maharani shrank back into the doorway, knowing that the act of unveiling her face would be as final an act of immodesty as unclothing her body; and she could not force her limbs to cross the marble lintel, or bare her face before men who were not father, brother, husband or son to her.

Jai Singh was speaking. Locked in her private nightmare, the Maharani did not hear him. 'Woman, do they not call me Bappa? Father?' he repeated. 'Unveil your face and bless the brothers of your son.'

The Maharani willed her fingers to lift the veil. For a moment, the flimsy fabric shielded Jai Singh and herself from the gaze of the spectators. In that instant, she recognized his shame that her pale face should be naked before other men. Giving him a small smile of reassurance, she turned her bared head to the courtyard. The people of Balmer lowered their eyes in respect. Only the Council of Ministers stared with barely disguised curiosity at her naked face.

The next day, the Maharani moved out of Balmer Fort and took up residence in a cluster of mud huts on the east side of Jalsa Lake, where a temporary city of huts and sorry tents stretched out to a distance almost as great as the capital itself.

Attended by the daughters of village elders, she accommodated herself to her new life with characteristic energy. But in the shifting pattern of her days, which encompassed everything from celebrating the birth of a child to ensuring the cremation of dead bodies, she still made time before sunrise for three hours of prayer at a small altar in the corner of her hut, swearing to the spirits of her predecessors that when the rains came at last, she would re-enter purdah.

Sometimes the Maharani hurried from some conclave of complaint to find her husband mounted on his dusty charger, Tikka sunburned and asleep on the pommel of his saddle. Conscious of the crush of people outside the mud walls of her hut, the Maharani never found occasion to tell her husband she had conceived.

ON THE DAY of the Spring Festival, when in better times the farmers would have put on garments of yellow cloth to celebrate the end of the spring harvest, but which, that fifth year of the drought, was only another cruel reminder of how nature had disinherited them, the Maharajah recalled the Maharani to Balmer Fort.

Swaying in the double-swing cradle strapped on the back of a camel, the Maharani tried to re-create in her mind the image of the Temple of the Balmer Maharanis. The camel sank onto its front knees, taking the Maharani unawares. As she fell forward she saw eyes watching her from behind the zenana walls and felt a flash of fear. Jai Singh's arms lifted her from the camel cradle. 'Go see to your women. Tonight you will dine with me in the King's View.'

The Maharani entered the harem. Grateful for the shade of the high zenana ceilings and the cool marble floor under her feet, the

Maharani was too exhausted to notice that the maids were bowing from a distance, their backs pressed against the stone walls of the corridors.

Outside her apartments, four eunuchs stood guard beside the Baran, flanked by priests. The Maharani stared at the strange reception committee, wondering if fatigue had rendered her brain too slow to remember some essential ceremony of return. As she moved forward, the eunuchs shrank from her shadow falling in a diagonal slash on the marble floor. Then the Maharani saw the massive iron padlock lying against the silver-and-gold inlay of her doors.

The Baran folded her hands in supplication. 'You have sat with potters and sweepers and other untouchables. The priests say you are polluted.'

The Maharani stared in disbelief at the Baran. 'You know the rulers have always been above caste. We are mother and father to everyone in Balmer; we enter every home and eat at every table.'

'The Maharajah is the anointed of the gods, hukam. He cannot be polluted. But you are only his wife. The priests say you carry pollution on your person.'

'The priests are aware that the principle of matrimonial unity makes me my husband's equal half. I am not bound by the superstitions of pollution.'

The senior priest inclined his fat torso, naked but for the sacred thread disappearing into the folds of the silk dhoti, his deferential attitude a subtle blend of conciliation and clerical reticence. 'It is a problem of precedence, hukam. In our eleven-hundred-year history, no Maharani has ever broken purdah. It is only a matter of the prescribed baths and ritual fasts of purification. We wish to make sure that you do not – by our neglect and poor ignorance – pollute the zenana.'

The Maharani recoiled from the unctuous insult as the Baran pleaded, 'I beg you, hukam. If you enter the chambers without purification, the priests say we will all be polluted.'

A clash of heavy jewellery echoed down the stone corridors. Kuki-bai was hurrying down the sunlit halls, shooing pigeons away with claps of her painted hands, a stream of courtly insults issuing from her mouth at the maidservants huddled against the stone walls. She advanced on the horrified priests and the eunuchs smiled

35

slyly at each other in anticipation of a full-scale confrontation which would break the tedium of the zenana. 'There is famine in the land. If these priests were not so plump, we could say their excess of zeal comes from fasting for the people of Balmer. But they have sold their office to the council, and in the boredom of their newfound wealth they have come to the zenana to turn the minds of simple creatures with tales of pollution.'

The old concubine grabbed the keys from the Baran and unlocked the doors. The eunuchs giggled behind their hands, their overrefined sensibilities immediately registering the shift in the balance of power. Kuki-bai turned on them. 'As for you hermaphrodites who fatten on the frustrations of your wards! Tell me, you grotesque creatures, does an emerald necklace still buy a tola of cocaine? How much jewellery have you taken from the women in these last months for opium, for liquor? And what new aphrodisiacs have you concocted for the zenana this season?'

Quailing at Kuki-bai's accuracy, the frightened eunuchs waited outside the Maharani's apartments until she had bathed, to lead her through the passageways of the zenana to the King's View.

ORIGINALLY CONSTRUCTED to give the ruler a clear view of the surrounding countryside and deny an enemy army the advantage of surprise, the King's View was a terraced tower approached through a high doorway curving three times under gold banners embroidered with the crest of the Balmer rulers.

The Household Guard presented arms as the Maharani entered the terrace for the first time in her life. Jai Singh was sitting on a marble bench inlaid with precious stones. Behind him, the lights of the city merged with the stars in the black sky.

Alone after months of separation, the Maharani at last told her husband she was expecting another child.

Jai Singh's arm tightened around her. 'I may not be here for the birth. The Viceroy has finally given me permission to travel to England for the coronation of the new emperor.'

'Why do you ask the Viceroy's permission to travel?'

'It is a fresh incursion on our treaties. The new Viceroy, Curzon, looks like a bamboo pole but he is not a bad man. He has already frozen taxes in British India and asked the British Parliament to lift

36

the Empire's tax on salt – to give some relief, as is always done at the coronation of a new emperor. Of course Britain's Parliament refused.'

'If he is such a good man, why is he breaking our treaties?'

The Maharani felt her husband's chest fill with air, heard the long sigh. 'Because Curzon thinks he has been sent to India to be our father. First the British thought the maharajahs were too primitive, so they encouraged us to travel abroad. Now Curzon thinks we spend too much time imitating the Europeans and he wants us to stay at home.'

'Must you really go to England for the coronation?'

'The coronation is only an excuse so I can raise funds from the Tsar without arousing the suspicions of the British Empire. The treasury is nearly bankrupt. I have to raise funds from somewhere. The Tsar is my only friend in Europe.'

Fear opened like a trapdoor beneath the Maharani. 'You cannot do this! If the British ever discover you have broken the terms of your treaty with the Empire and dealt independently with a foreign power, especially Russia . . .' Jai Singh's hand covered her mouth, but the Maharani's muffled words continued to describe the consequences of his act. 'The British will exile you from Balmer! They will take your throne! They will refuse to recognize Tikka as your heir, or invest him with his rightful ruling powers! You know they can invoke their terrible Doctrine of Lapse.' She found it hard even to speak those words, by which the British forced an Indian ruler's abdication, disinherited his heirs and simply absorbed an Indian kingdom into the red ocean of the British Empire.

The Maharajah took his wife's face in his hands and tried to explain the political realities which cornered him like a trapped animal. 'If the rains fail again, I shall have to construct a railway and allow foreign factories to be built in Balmer. I must arrange loans so the farmers don't have to sell their land to the Angrez companies at unreasonable prices. All this costs money. When the Tsar stayed with me as Tsarevitch, he admired the Balmer Navratan. I plan to sell it to him. He will not reveal the sale to England.'

'The Balmer Navratan is priceless. Why don't you ask the British Empire to negotiate the sale? At least the British will be able to ensure the necklace is kept safe.'

'Already the Raj believes I am anti-British. What redress do I have if I entrust the sale of the necklace to the British Raj and it gets lost?'

The Maharani stared at her husband. 'That's impossible.'

Jai Singh laughed cynically. 'Wasn't the Koh-i-noor stolen from a child under the protection of Britain? And publicly presented to Victoria? Why are the necks of the wives of so many English officers encircled with gems extorted from the courts of India? Empress Victoria herself has condemned the practice.'

IN GREAT SECRECY the Maharani helped Jai Singh make his preparations for London. Although the treasury was under the Maharajah's jurisdiction, all contents were described in the treasury files in minute detail. The file that recorded the presence of the Balmer Navratan had to be removed and altered. Night after night the Maharani sat with her husband in the King's View and rewrote the file in her own hand, eliminating any mention of the Balmer Navratan.

The day before Jai Singh's departure, he placed the heavy necklace made up of the nine gems of Indian good fortune on a table in her chamber. Sapphire, ruby, diamond, emerald described huge coloured arcs on the polished walls, their facets catching the light of the afternoon sun. The Maharani gazed in awe at the jewels, assembled over hundreds of years for their perfection and their auspiciousness, each stone heavy with priceless carats.

Wrapping the gems in silken flax so they would not be damaged, the Maharani reluctantly folded the flax into a cummerband for her husband to wear around his waist on the long journey to Paris and his rendezvous with the emissaries of Tsarist Russia.

TOWARD THE END of the fifth year of drought, when the rains should have come but still did not, and a desolate people had ceased to ask why the gods were so harsh in their anger, the Maharani gave birth. This time there were no bards at the gates of the inner fort, no feasts of celebration. But the birth provided a topic other than death to villagers exhausted by the endless contemplation of devastation.

It was as well, the villagers said, that the new child was a daughter. The state could ill afford the celebrations due a son. Otherwise, were not the times similar to those prevailing at the birth of Tikka? See, the Maharajah was again in England to attend the coronation of the British Emperor. But now there was a man, not a widow, sitting on the throne of England. Who knew? Perhaps India's luck would change at last.

On his return from Europe the Maharajah looked more spirited. The villagers remarked on his relaxed manners as he rode the streets of the capital, stopping to accept their withered garlands and their congratulations on the new child.

Even the Maharani, lying ill with the after-effects of a difficult birth, noticed the change in her husband's demeanour when he entered her chambers.

Tikka was tickling the feet of the new baby with a long peacock feather. The baby let out a yell of protest. Jai Singh laughed and bent over his daughter's cradle. 'That is not the sound of a crying baby. That is a battle cry. If the name is auspicious, let's call her Jaya, Victory.'

The Maharani smiled at the lightheartedness in her husband's voice and knew his negotiations with Russia had gone well.

6

JAYA WAS THREE years old before she saw rain, although she heard the maidservants speak of it often, the way people speak of the dead.

Seven long years the unrelenting sky had stretched out into the horizon like a vast copper thali, throwing the heat of the baked earth back on itself as farmers without hope searched for clouds behind the vultures circling their fields. Twice the Maharajah had gone to Delhi with his elephants and cavalry to attend the elaborate durbars staged by British viceroys to remind India of the power of the British Empire. Each time he had raged at the drain on his dwindling treasury, while the Maharani silently counted the cost in lost honour.

The night the rains came was a night the people of Balmer talked about long after they had again become accustomed to the routine cycle of seasons. The inner fortress of Balmer Fort was opened for the music festival that night. Lightning crackled in the dry air, its bright geometry lighting the black clouds moving in from the jungles beyond Jalsa Lake, as crowds flooded into the wide courtyard where previous maharajahs had assembled their cavalries before riding out to battle, and where maharanis had burned themselves on funeral pyres when their men had not returned.

On either side of the ramparts a marble pergola perched like a jewelled box. In the open pergola, Maharajah Jai Singh leaned against a bolster cushion, his sword nudging the thigh of his excited seven-year-old son.

The other pergola was so highly carved it seemed as though

delicate lace curtains hung from its dome; concealing the zenana women sequestered inside. Jaya and the Maharani took their places on the stairs leading to the purdah pergola, their heads bare, their faces uncovered.

The Ustad, the music guru of Balmer, sat on a raised platform abutting the ramparts, his long white beard partly hidden by the five-stringed tanpura resting on his left shoulder.

The fragile figure of the Ustad bent forward, and the buzz of conversation in the courtyard ceased abruptly. In the silence the old man's voice swelled across the night in the Raga Agni, the raga of fire and heat so brutal in its power it was said that when the immortal Tansen sang it to the Emperor Akbar, the flames of a thousand clay lamps had leapt into the air and the dry leaves on the trees had burned to ash. It was said the raga had set Tansen's throat ablaze and he would have been consumed in the conflagration created by his own voice if his daughter had not sung the raga of rain and moved heaven to tears.

Now the force of the raga pouring from the old Ustad's throat immobilized the silent audience, reminding them of the seven years of drought they had endured, of their dead animals lying in parched fields, of the walls of their houses too hot to touch under the incinerating sun.

Jaya scratched her cheeks. The hot wind blowing across the stone parapets made her skin prickle, drying the drops of perspiration on her forehead almost before they had formed. She barely noticed that the Maharani had also begun to sing until the opening notes of the Maharani's raga reminded her of the empty cry of the koyal, that desolate sound which had echoed throughout the drought, the cry of the rainbird thirsting for water.

As the music gained momentum Jaya thought she could hear what she had never heard: breaking monsoons, peacocks dancing, trees bending under torrential rain. The harsh rage of the raga of fire, the melodic pleading of the raga of rain rose through the night. The ragas ended and although the crowded courtyard was not drenched with rain, there seemed to be a coolness in the wind blowing over the stone battlements.

The Maharani covered her head, pulling the gold fringe of her veil towards her waist. A drop of rain fell on Jaya's head. Jaya ignored it, unable to understand why her mother's familiar face was now obscured.

The Maharani took her hand and led her up the steps to the purdah pergola. Black eyes moved like small bats behind the carved screen. Jaya pulled back in fear. Her mother urged her forward. Jaya did not understand that the drought had broken and the Maharani of Balmer was re-entering purdah.

FROM THE MOMENT Jaya was born, the Maharani had vowed her daughter would be raised in the ways of her predecessors, which alone could protect the child from the harsh, changing world beyond the zenana walls.

Before dawn, maidservants awakened Jaya, joking the irritable child through a bath of purification before taking her to the Temple of the Balmer Maharanis, in the central courtyard of the zenana.

One maidservant preceded Jaya with a lantern to light the ornamental canals leading to the temple; another held Jaya's hand. On the grass verge beyond the courtyard, disturbed frogs filled the night with deep-throated belches.

While the Maharani sang to awaken the gods, Jaya sat on the temple floor in front of the idols, watching the sky turn crimson as though the sun were clawing the sky as a tiger claws its kill. As the sky lightened, the Maharani's voice was drowned by clouds of birds flying in from Jalsa Lake to their ritual feeding at the temple.

Taking her daughter's chin in her pale hand, the Maharani made the child recite the ancestral litany of the Balmer Maharanis.

'Like the great sati, Queen Pushpavati, may I bring honour to the Rajput blood that runs in my veins and bear sons to increase the sons of the Sun.'

'Like the great sati, Queen Sita Devi of Balmer, I shall wear no cloth of gold, but collect its value every year to buy food for the poor in time of famine.'

Morning after morning Jaya recited the names of the sati queens of Balmer who had put on their bridal clothes, dipped their hands in red powder and placed their small palmprints on the outer walls of Balmer Fort before walking behind their husbands' corpses to immolate themselves on their husbands' funeral pyres.

Every day Jaya was reminded of their last and binding command to the kingdom before they fell unconscious into the flames.

'Like the great sati, Queen Asha Devi of Balmer, I shall fast two days in every seven, to recollect my respect for my people.'

Jaya squirmed and wondered why there were so many satis and so many vows: no fish to be eaten by the women of the royal house until their desert lands had an abundance of water; no meat to be eaten during the breeding season of animals; no songbirds to be kept in cages until the foreign usurper had left India.

She was on her feet before she finished the prohibition on songbirds. It was the last vow. Now she could race outside to scatter grain and watch the birds pick their way around the temple courtyard, sunlight glancing off their coloured feathers.

AFTER THE SATI VOWS, Jaya wolfed down the morning meal and changed into her riding clothes to join her father for the precious daily excursion outside the walls of the Fort.

Tikka was already a fine rider, always impatient for a gallop. Jai Singh restrained him, forcing him to slow his horse to the pace of his sister's pony. Accompanied by officers of the Household Cavalry and the Maharajah's military aide-de-camp, Major Vir Singh, they took long morning rides in the dense jungle beyond Jalsa Lake.

On their way to some overgrown temple or broken cenotaph the children were tested on different plants and species of bird, told which herbs had medicinal qualities or how to apply clay from an anthill as a poultice against snakebite. Sometimes they listened spellbound as their father and his officers spoke of experiences in the jungle when they had tracked a rogue elephant or a wounded tiger.

On their return, Tikka accompanied his father to the new Secretariat on the east bank of Jalsa Lake, where he studied administration. Once a month, Tikka and the Maharajah left on a tour of the countryside to attend the court of appeal, where, under the shade of silk-cotton trees, the Maharajah held monthly durbars to rule on those cases which had not been settled in the village and district courts.

But Jaya was only a girl and had no such respite from the routines of the Fort.

43

7

THE MAHARAJAH had decreed that his daughter was not to be raised in purdah. In every other particular, the Maharani insisted that Jaya be educated in the traditional manner of the princesses of Balmer.

First there were the music lessons with the old Ustad, whose temper and ear seemed to sharpen with his increasing age. Jaya looked longingly at the kites floating over the stables as the nearly blind Ustad shouted at her inattention, making her repeat the scales over and over again.

From the music room the Baran collected her for the rangoli classes. Jaya sat on the floor in the cool verandah outside her rooms, circled by lacquer baskets filled with coloured powders, while above her head the Baran recited the aesthetics of colour and design.

'The mango design for the Spring Festival,' the Baran instructed, and Jaya traced an elaborate pattern with coloured powder onto the marbled floor.

'The clay lamps for the Divali pujas.' Jaya wiped the floor clean with a damp cloth and carefully sprinkled the powders so that arches of lamps and garlands of flowers appeared on the floor.

Once a week, accompanied by a group of little girls, she followed the Maharani to the chambers below the zenana, for the dispensing of the Fort stores. Jaya clapped her hands furiously to frighten the monkeys grimacing on the stone balustrades, while her friends with less restraint screamed and giggled, their voices echoing in the stone stairwell.

At the bottom of the stairs, catacombs of storerooms occupied an area the entire length of the zenana. Light from distant skylights fell on clay floors polished to look like crimson marble under the dark, high-ceilinged galleries.

The Controller of the Household opened the iron padlocks and the air in the galleries took on the rich smells of a bazaar as one door after another in the long row of storerooms was flung open, and the Maharani read out the week's requirements from the list held under her veil.

The little girls sat on the floor next to massive iron scales, watching palace servants hoist dusty gunny-bags dripping grain onto the scales, weighting them down with iron weights almost the size of the children. Grunting with effort, the servants hauled creaking cane baskets filled with onions and potatoes from the storerooms while the eunuchs gossiped in the corner.

As the morning wore on, the crimson floor was covered with a thin film of rice dust. The young girls disguised their boredom by drawing patterns in the white dust, and the Maharani engaged the palace servants in seemingly desultory conversations about crops or prices so that, without knowing it, her daughter would absorb information about her country.

BUT THERE WERE two moments in her day which Jaya would not have traded for the world outside the zenana – the afternoons in Kuki-bai's chambers and the evenings with Major Vir Singh on the polo ground.

It was not that Jaya enjoyed the massages, or the sharp remonstrations when she missed a shot, but she considered such discomforts worth enduring for the stories.

In fact, Jaya had fought so often with Tikka as to who was a better storyteller, Kuki-bai or Major Vir Singh, that Tikka suggested they let a jury of children decide the matter once and for all.

Kuki-bai laughed and laughed when Jaya warned her about the competition, the silver bells on the chains which held her bed jingling noisily with her delight. 'And what does your mother say about all this?'

45

Jaya's eyes rounded with fear. 'Oh, you mustn't tell her, she would never approve. We might have to cancel the whole competition.' There was an implacable composure about the Maharani which rather inhibited Jaya. The Maharani never looked over her shoulder, no matter what the provocation. She always stood still, eyes directed forward, while the maidservants hovering at her side explained the nature of the disturbance, and Jaya doubted that she could ever attain that cocoon of remote and motionless dignity by which the Maharani imposed order on the crowd of palace women who surrounded her like buzzing flies wherever she went in the zenana.

Kuki-bai pulled at Jaya's lower jaw and popped a sweetmeat into the child's open mouth. 'How are we going to keep it from Maharani-sahib? She knows everything that goes on in the Fort.'

Jaya stared at Kuki-bai in consternation. 'What shall we do? If you don't take part, Tikka will think you were frightened of matching yourself against the Major.'

'Frightened? Your father's grandfather, the man the world knew as the Lion of Balmer, said he loved me because I was the only human being apart from himself who did not know the meaning of fear.'

A maidservant entered the room with a silver thali, a wide platter, filled with pastes and wheat grain. Jaya fidgeted as the maidservant stripped off her clothes and pushed her naked body onto the cane mat. Afraid that Kuki-bai might back out of the competition, Jaya grudgingly allowed the maidservant to rub her limbs with the wheat mixture so that every hair would be pulled out by the roots.

By the time Jaya had bathed and raced to the rifle range, the panel of judges, three boys and two girls, were already sitting on the stone ramparts.

Major Vir Singh strode towards a box of cartridges, a tall figure in khaki jodhpurs and high boots, his starched green turban rising above his head in a wide fan, the handlebars of his moustache bristling from the sides of his face.

'Pull!' the Major shouted. Jaya fired at the clay disc spinning through the air. The disc shattered. 'Pull!' Two more discs shot into the air, visible only for a second before Tikka, firing both barrels in quick succession, sent shards of clay exploding over the field.

The judges applauded as the children cooled the barrels of their guns in a copper bucket filled with water, grabbed fresh cartridges and exchanged positions.

At the end of the session Major Vir Singh professed to be astonished by their accuracy. Tikka winked conspiratorially at Jaya as they walked to the unsaddled horses waiting at the polo grounds. The other children crowded into a carriage.

Jaya grabbed her mount's bridle, sure she would do badly on the jumps and the Major would get into a bad mood. She cantered to the water troughs that marked her course. The Major handed her two coins. She bent over the bare back of her pony to slide the coins between her knees and the warm skin of the horse. As she urged the pony toward the fence, she prayed that the coins would not fall, although Tikka had given her two more coins to put into the pockets of her tunic in case she lost the originals.

The Goddess was with her that day. She did not lose her coins or miss a single jump. Major Vir Singh rode up to retrieve the coins, followed by the carriage filled with cheering children. Jaya's pony took fright at the sudden noise. It reared, and Jaya somersaulted backward.

When she regained consciousness she was propped in the Major's arms. Peering through the Major's impressive moustache, she whispered, 'I never dropped the coins, Tikka.'

Tikka was proud of his sister for not crying. He did not know that whenever Jaya threw herself into her mother's lap with a cut hand or bruised knee, the Maharani tended her with efficient but unsentimental sympathy, explaining that a Rajput princess had to learn endurance. Now Jaya opened her eyes wide and asked with transparent guile, 'Please, Major-sahib, my head still hurts. May I rest here for a little while?'

The Major patted Jaya's cheek. 'Of course, of course. You're a very brave little girl. Would you like to hear a story?'

'Tell about the China campaign, Major-sahib,' Tikka demanded as the judges pulled grubby pieces of paper from their pockets. 'How you freed the European Legation.'

Major Vir Singh cleared his throat theatrically. 'As you know, the British have not allowed us to keep armies since the Mutiny. They are terrified that we might rise against them again. But Britain needed soldiers for China, and the warriors of royal India are

47

the linest fighting forces on the continent. So the Viceroy asked Sir Pratap Singh, the Regent King of Jodhpur, to form a special cavalry corps of Rajputs.'

He did not notice the children's eyes glaze over with the historical background or brighten when he spoke of the voyage to Shanghai, the typhoons and the panicking horses.

'The old Empress of China was an opium addict. They say she took a shoeful of opium every day and trusted only her eunuchs. But it was the Angrez who forced opium on China. Although the Empress was an addict, she was fighting to throw the Angrez out of China.'

'So then what happened, Major-sahib?' the children chorused.

'How can I describe it?' He pulled at his moustache, and the waxed hair snapped back against his cheek. 'What a gathering of riders there was outside the walls of the Forbidden City of Peking! The Cossacks of your father's old friend the Tsar of Russia. The Prussian Junkers sent by the Kaiser of Germany. The Americans. The cream of the British Indian Cavalries – Hodson's Horse, Skinner's Horse, the Central India Horse. But most impressive by far, ourselves. The Imperial Cavalry Corps, the warriors from the kingdoms of India.'

Jaya could see the hero worship on boys' faces and hoped the two girls would be more objective.

'Every night Sir Pratap visited our tents to remind us that our ancient enemy, the Maharatta cavalry led by the Maharajah of Gwalior, would be watching to see who were better horsemen, the Maharattas or the Rajputs.'

Then Major Singh launched into the story of the attack. Although Jaya had heard it often, she still swelled with pride when he described how the Balmer Lancers, mounted on their surefooted Marwar horses bred for speed, had galloped behind Sir Pratap, outflanking the Cossacks and the Prussians, riding neck to neck with the Maharajah of Gwalior's Maharatta horsemen toward the waiting guns of the Boxer troops.

'You should have seen the dust as we made our cavalry charge through the thunder of Chinese cannons, the bright sparks when the hooves of our galloping horses hit the paving stones. At full gallop we rode into the midst of the waiting enemy. Lances reversed. Each man holding steady in the face of death. We could see the faces of the Boxer troops, and still not a Rajput or a Maharatta righted his lance until he heard the shout of the commanders, "Has the Anointed killed? Has the Maharajah drawn first blood?"'

Major Vir Singh straightened the starched sash of his turban. 'And when Sir Pratap raised his bloodied lance, you should have heard the roar. A thousand Rajputs shouting our battle cry, "Jai Mata ki! Victory to the Goddess!"'

There was an expression of such intensity on Tikka's face that Jaya was almost frightened. 'And those Maharatta horsemen must have remembered how their battle cry terrorized India for two hundred years, because even in the heat of fighting, when Maharajah Gwalior raised his bloodstained lance to show his cavalry that battle had been joined, my blood ran cold to hear his Maharattas roar, "Har! Har! Mahadeva!"'

Tikka could contain himself no longer. He raced up the stone steps shouting, 'Jai Mata ki!' The other boys raced behind him with bloodthirsty yells of 'Har! Har! Mahadeva!' Jaya was relieved to see the girls looking primly disapproving of the high spirits of their fellow judges.

'After the Dowager Empress had sued for peace there was a big banquet. All the troops attended, except the Cossacks. You see, Sir Pratap had nearly killed some Cossack officers who were assaulting a group of Chinese women.'

The children nodded knowingly. It was the dharma of a warrior to protect the defenceless.

'At the banquet the British officers accused us of being stupid, riding into battle with our lances reversed. They said if the enemy were good shots, half the attacking force would be dead before we reached the enemy lines. Foreigners don't understand that war is our dharma. Our kings ride first into battle, protecting the thousand sons of their kingdoms who ride behind them, because only an anointed king can authorize a just war with the blood on his lance.'

Major Vir Singh looked at his watch. 'My king will be playing polo in half an hour and I haven't yet seen to the polo ponies.' He patted Jaya's head and ran towards his horse.

The judges filled in their points, refusing to let Jaya or Tikka see the scores as they approached the elephant stables. The sky was already beginning to streak with colour. It was time for the elephants' evening baths. Broken rainbows splintered above the stone corrals as the elephants sprayed high fountains of water into the air, drenching their mahouts and the row of high silver-and-gold howdahs glistening in the evening light.

Kuki-bai sat on the edge of a howdah watching the oldest tusker, a huge beast nearly ninety years old with four-foot-long tusks, having iron fetters removed from its hind leg.

'Come, beloved of the gods. Come, protector of the weak,' she chanted. The tusker lumbered towards her and wrapped her plump body in the wrinkled coils of its grey trunk. Holding the ivory tusks with her small painted hands, Kuki-bai spoke the elephant's name as she might have addressed a lover: 'Ah, Moti, you make me feel like a young woman again. Come, show these children of a new generation what we did in our youth to amuse the Lion of Balmer.'

The tusker raised Kuki-bai gently over his left tusk and swung her onto his neck. In a cloud of billowing silk she settled behind his massive head. Jaya was pleased to see Tikka looking worriedly at the judges staring up at the painted soles of Kuki-bai's feet, bright crimson against the blue-grey skin of the elephant.

'How he loved us, eh, Moti? The Lion of Balmer?' Kuki-bai chanted. 'Do you remember the meeting of the five kings in the deserted Fortress of Chittore? The great clans of the Rajputs, gathered together for the puja of the horse? Hundreds of thousands of people were there that day. We could not recognize the turbans they wore. We did not know where they came from or what battles they had fought. And do you remember the horses that covered the whole plain below the Fortress, crowded next to the camel camps and the fairs?'

The elephants were still spraying each other with water, but the mahouts had left their charges to crowd around the children. 'Do you remember the nobles from each kingdom performing feats of horsemanship such as we will never see again? And the polo games at night, the metal balls flashing across the field, as though the black mud were the sky and the lighted balls streaks of lightning? And then, Moti, when the trumpets sounded for the end of the polo game – do you remember how we stole past the guards with some silly story of a sage and a prophecy and moved into the centre of that dark field? Weren't we frightened, Moti, when we saw the five Presences sitting on their howdahs with their chattri-beaters standing behind them, jewels shining in the night?

'We sat on the string bed lashed to your back, shivering in fear, my two small brothers and myself, one with his drums, one with his flute. I whispered, "Now! Start now, quickly before we are taken away!" and Munna said, "I can't sister. My mouth is dry. There is no spit to wet the end of my flute." And Latu began to play the drums so loudly you thought the show had begun.' She patted the tusker's broad back. 'Hut! Moti, hut!'

The elephant wound its trunk around Kuki-bai's waist and lifted the small figure into the air, holding her suspended until her vermilion-painted soles found balance on the ivory tusks.

Kuki-bai closed her eyes. Jaya held her breath, sure the old concubine would fall. Kuki-bai began raising one eyebrow, then the other as though a ripple of black water were washing over her forehead. The closed eyelids lifted over the kohl-lined eyes. The painted fingers opened, like a lotus opens in the sun. The elephant gently uncoiled its trunk until Kuki-bai was balancing unsupported on its tusks, her fine features framed in the bright henna of her open hands.

The children applauded wildly as Kuki-bai leaned back on Moti's broad forehead.

'That night I danced on Moti's tusks for an hour. I did. the warrior's moves, raising my hand like the flat blade of a sword, and the kings threw coins at me. When I did the mudra of the petitioner, kneeling on Moti's tusks with real tears falling from my eyes, I could see the gold coins shining in the mud.'

Kuki-bai laughed. 'Eh, children, you think these are an old woman's fantasies, don't you? But four kings diced for me that night. Your great-grandfather won, and asked what I desired. We were so poor, we three children, since our father died. Our only inheritance was the elephant. I asked for some land for my brothers and a home for Moti. But the Lion asked what I desired for myself. He was famous for his kindness to women. In those days when poor people could not afford to marry off their daughters, rather than kill the babies they left them outside the zenanas of the maharajahs. The Lion had built a special home for them so that when the girls came of age they could choose between the zenana and life outside.'

Kuki-bai looked down at her painted hands. 'But even if he had been the cruellest ruler in the world, I knew when I looked into his eyes that I was lost. He gave me a house on the edge of

Jalsa Lake. The Chand Mahal, the Palace of the Moon. There was a marble pavilion by the side of the lake and we . . .'

Shaking her head as though clearing her mind of memories, she waved her painted palms at the children. 'To mourn the Lion would insult the years of happiness we shared in the Chand Mahal. That's why you see me in jewels with henna on my hands. But in the old days, during the great puja processions, the Lion sat in his golden howdah here, and I danced there.' She pointed to the ivory tusks curving against the yellow stones of the courtyard. 'And the people of Balmer thought we were like gods as we made our way to the Temple – the Lion of Balmer, Moti and myself. Hut, Moti, hut!'

The children watched in silence as the small round figure of the old concubine, swaying with the motion of the tusker, turned towards the zenana.

To Jaya's disbelief, Kuki-bai did not win the competition. The three boys voted for Major Vir Singh. But listening to the judges arguing furiously over their scores, Jaya could see that some of the magic of the Fort had taken hold of their imaginations and she felt better about her own isolation.

8

EVERY YEAR after the monsoon rains, fresco painters came to repaint the walls of the inner Fort. Followed by a horde of other children, Jaya and Tikka raced through the courtyards outside the zenana, splashing vegetable dyes from the clay vats on to each other.

High on their bamboo ladders, the fresco painters shouted at them to stop.

'What's the good of all this paint to you?' the children taunted. 'You don't even know how to draw a bullock cart. The wheels are much bigger than that.'

The exasperated artists shouted back, 'God knows what era you live in. Can't you tell the difference between a bullock cart and a rail-train?'

Humiliated by their ignorance, the children stopped throwing paint on each other and sat down to watch the symbols of a new world being projected like images in a stereopticon onto the stone walls of the ancient fort.

In the bright colours of folk art Jaya learned about the changes in her father's kingdom. Long before she ever saw an Englishman she had been aware that a group of English people had come to live in a new colony on the west bank of Jalsa Lake, factory owners and engineers. But in her imagination the Angrez were pictures frozen on the painted walls of the zenana, driving orange Rolls-Royces or sitting in trains spouting blue smoke, or forever going for stiff-backed rides in hackney carriages.

Soon Jaya found that she alone of all the children racing under the bamboo ladders was unable to offer advice on the strange machines appearing on the walls outside the zenana. She could not go to watch the railway lines being laid outside the city or see the organ pipes being fitted into the church her father had built for the Angrez, and she felt that she might as well be living in purdah.

On the rare occasions Jaya was allowed out of the Fort, she sometimes found reality better than the bright images in her fantasy world.

There was the day the Balmer State Train steamed into the brand-new railway station on the outskirts of the capital. Jaya could not stop staring at the English men and women sitting under an embroidered canopy to the left of her father. She thought they must feel hot in their long dresses and heavy coats, but otherwise they looked quite kindly, not at all like the British Political Officer, present for the official opening of the Balmer Railway, who didn't smile once during the entire morning and stood as straight as a ramrod when the cannons on the Fort fired a thirteen-gun salute for him. After the lengthy ceremonies the children were allowed to enter the train. Tikka rushed to see the engine. Jaya bounced on the sofas and switched on the electric chandeliers in the carriages, convinced she was in a dream machine fashioned on some other, superior planet.

Then the first motorcars arrived in Balmer Fort. Jaya clambered up the elephant gates to watch the Duisberg and the Hispano Suiza being attached by ropes to the Palace elephants, and the straining elephants haul the glittering machines up the steep ramparts. But when the cars reached the courtyard she thought they looked too practical, not at all like the chariots fit for divinity which decorated the outer walls of the zenana.

She sulked and would not be persuaded to go for a ride. Only when her cousin and enemy, Raja Man Singh's daughter, clambered onto the running board did Jaya knot her veil around her waist and climb in next to the aide sitting at the steering wheel.

Jaya hated her cousin's father, Raja Man Singh. He was a dedicated Anglophile who had already engaged English tutors for his daughter and his small son, John, next in line after Tikka to the Balmer throne. Now his children were known by English names and ate with knives and forks and called their parents Mummy and Daddy.

Jaya thought her cousin's affectations silly most of the time, but she still felt inferior that her cousin should belong to the energetic and changing world outside the Fort walls, until the day Maharajah Jai Singh entered his wife's chambers and sent Jaya out to the balcony.

Alarmed by the expression on her father's face, Jaya hovered behind the curtain.

'Is there no alternative?' the Maharani's low voice asked.

Jaya lifted the edge of the curtain and saw her parents standing in the middle of the room.

'None. The British have signed a treaty with the Russians. It is only a matter of time before my dealings with the Tsar become open knowledge.'

'If the British and the Russians have overcome their differences, why should your actions matter now?'

'The British do not like rulers with independent minds. We are dangerous. They prefer us to be drunk in our zenanas, too busy to care how the Empire encroaches upon our rights.'

'And an English tutor for Tikka will change that?'

'No, but it might convince the British that I am training my son to be loyal to the ideals of the Empire.' Jaya did not understand the conversation, but she was shocked to see her formal mother rest her head on Jai Singh's shoulder.

That afternoon, Jaya squashed into the curtained Duisberg, between her veiled mother and the four maidservants crouching on the floor. The car drove out of the Fort, past the city and the Angrez colony, to Kuki-bai's old home, the Chand Mahal.

Jaya ran towards the swing suspended from a mango tree while the Maharani and the maids inspected the marble pergola at the side of the lake before making their way over the green lawns towards the arched balconies of the Chand Mahal, now being altered to accommodate the Englishman who had been hired to teach Tikka.

Jaya followed, curious to see how the Angrez would live. Inside the high brown doors, a feeling of strangeness overwhelmed her. Sofas with overstuffed cushions, a leather-topped desk, numerous stiff chairs were all lifted off the ground by strange clawed feet that seemed to grip the white and black marble squares of the floor with evil talons.

She held her mother's hand tightly as the veiled women moved through bedrooms with high four-poster beds, into bathrooms where white porcelain tubs were raised on more clawed feet.

Jaya pointed at the bathtub. 'Is that for washing clothes?'

The Maharani laughed. 'No, for washing their bodies.'

'But how do they change the water?' Jaya persisted.

The Maharani steered her out of the bathroom. 'The container is filled and then the Angrez wash themselves.'

'They can't wash their feet and their faces in the same water. Where do they wash their feet? In those other things? Those white chairs without handles?'

'That is enough curiosity, Jaya,' the Maharani said, sweeping her out of the house.

As they made their way back to the car, a maidservant giggled in her ear.

'They sit in chairs to do their business?' Jaya asked in astonishment. 'Why? Have they got stiff legs or something?'

Then she told the maid that she doubted that Tikka could be taught anything by people who bathed in dirty water and had stiff legs.

9

THE ANGREZ TUTOR turned out to be a fine polo player and an excellent shot, carrying his six-foot frame with a military austerity which belied the laughter in his grey eyes when he was inventing stories about the wild tribesmen in the Khyber Pass.

Captain Osborne was the third generation of his family to have had a distinguished career with the British Indian Army. On formal occasions he wore the many decorations which excited Tikka's admiration – the India Medal, won for campaigns on the North-West Frontier, the Tibet Medal and, most impressive of all, the Distinguished Service Order, awarded for his valour against the Afghans.

Tikka was fascinated by Captain Osborne. The amused tolerance with which the Captain attended state functions suggested a man who saw himself as a spectator at a colourful but irrelevant pageant staged by children. His air of faint boredom exuded the confidence of someone who knew he was a member of a superior civilization.

Kuki-bai's old palace became the centre of Tikka's world. As soon as he finished his administration lessons at the State Secretariat, Tikka collected his friends and raced to the Chand Mahal to demand a game of cricket with Captain-sahib. At the end of the game, Mrs. Osborne sent the servants out with pitchers of cold limewater. The boys sat on cane chairs, the grass under their feet growing damp with evening dew as they listened to the Captain speak of the underground railway that ran beneath the city of London, the factories that had

57

already begun to manufacture aeroplanes and cars, the explorers who were racing each other to the two poles of the earth.

Tikka did not know how it had happened, but the Captain's presence diminished Balmer. With a deepening sense of disloyalty, he regarded his father as a ruler blind to the advances of the real world outside the orders of his kingdom. He avoided his mother, embarrassed that he now saw her as a woman steeped in the superstitions of the harem. He despised himself for despising his parents and desperately wanted the Angrez tutor to acknowledge that he was not like them.

In his anxiety to impress the Englishman, Tikka applied himself to his lessons with an ardour that surprised his sister. Jaya was afraid that her brother was becoming an Angrez himself as his rooms filled up with British newspapers and magazines. The servants had strict instructions not to touch the catalogues piled next to his bed marking the goods he had ordered from the Army and Navy Store in London.

Often Tikka returned from the Chand Mahal with his arms full of books to add to the books already crowding his desk: Kipling, Burke, Baden-Powell, Macaulay. When Jaya flipped idly through a volume, a fresh smell came off the pages and she thought it must be the smell of England. England stared from Tikka's walls too. The ivory paintings of the gods had been replaced by black-and-white photographs of English sportsmen. An entire wall was covered with pictures of a young Indian maharajah holding a cricket bat in his hands. The brass plates under the pictures read RANJI – SUSSEX, RANJI – LORDS, RANJI – SURREY.

At Captain Osborne's suggestion, a cricket pavilion was constructed under the brooding shadow of the Round Tower which had once imprisoned captive nobles, its clean wooden lines contrasting with the rough stone slabs of the tower. Now Tikka spent all his spare time practising in the nets near the pavilion. When Jaya called with some message from the Maharani, he lectured her on cricket all the way back to the zenana until Jaya thought she would scream if she heard another word about Maharajah Ranji's famous leg-glance stroke.

'You are becoming a half-caste like John! I spent hours dipping the strings of your kite in diamond chips, and then you didn't even care when your kite was killed!' she said accusingly. 'All you can talk about is England or your beloved Ranji.'

58

Tikka gripped her arm. 'The British said no native – that's what they call us, you know, natives – could ever play cricket properly. But an Indian has become the greatest player in the world. Ranji was invited to play for England itself!' He stared fiercely at his sister. 'And still the sahibs in Bombay will not let Ranji, a close friend of their own King, join the Cricket Club of India because of the colour of his skin. We have to change such things.'

Jaya rubbed her arm, suddenly conscious of the difference between her brother and her cousins. Tikka did not want to imitate the Angrez; he wanted to be better than them and force their admiration.

Even her father seemed obsessed by the Angrez. After dinner the Englishman and Maharajah Jai Singh had fallen into the habit of disappearing together to the King's View. On her way to the zenana, Jaya would peer past the upright figures of the Household Guard and see the tutor leaning back in an armchair, sparks from his Havana cigar lighting the darkness while her father drew on the hookah at the side of his marble bench.

'Excellent thing that Lord Curzon forced the Maharajah of Rewa's abdication as one of his last acts as Viceroy,' the Angrez would remark in his clipped voice. 'Imagine tying human beings to a carriage.'

'Those men were moneylenders who had exploited peasants during the great famine,' Jai Singh explained. 'Maharajah Rewa tied them to his carriage as warning.'

'Rewa should have tried the moneylenders in a court of law, not punished them in that barbaric way. Lord Curzon nearly killed himself trying to teach justice to the Indians.'

'It is true that Lord Curzon loved justice and hated barbarity,' the Maharajah agreed. 'Yet during the Imperial Durbar, Curzon could not stop his fellow Englishmen from saluting the British officers of the Ninth Lancers, when all India knew those officers had killed their defenceless Indian servants for sport, making them crawl on all fours and piercing them with lances until they died of their wounds. If I had not heard it with my own ears, I would not have believed the British people would save their loudest cheers for murderers.'

'You are being unfair, Your Highness. Despotic Indian rulers do worse things every day.'

'Many Indians think Curzon was a despot, Captain-sahib. He closed Indian newspapers. He prevented Indians from sitting for competitive examinations. He partitioned Bengal with one stroke of his viceregal pen and annexed half of Hyderabad with another, without a care for the Nizam of Hyderabad's treaty with the British Crown.'

'But surely you don't deny that Lord Curzon was a great viceroy?' the Angrez asked incredulously. 'He worked tirelessly to shape this huge continent into a country. He improved the roads, the railways, the telegraphs, the irrigation systems. Maybe he broke a few eggs in the process, but it was done for India's good and India should be grateful.'

Once, when she was running past the King's View, Jaya heard her brother's name. 'Why not send Tikka to school in England, Your Highness? He is a bright boy, eager to improve himself. The Maharajah of Cooch Behar and the two Sirpur princes, Maharajah Victor and Prince Pratap, were all educated at Eton. The broadening of Tikka's outlook will make him a more effective ruler.'

Jaya was surprised at the harshness of her father's reply. 'An effective ruler, Captain, is a man who knows the needs of his own people. I find it difficult to believe this information is available in an English school, however large its playing fields.'

Walking with her brother past the Fort zoo, Jaya repeated the conversation. 'I might as well be a prisoner in the Round Tower,' Tikka said bitterly. 'If Bappa has his way, I'll never leave this old fort beyond the desert. Raja Man Singh is sending John to the British school in Ajmere. Why can't Bappa be modern like Raja Man Singh and send me to the British school too? Or even England?'

Jaya looked at the wooded acres of the zoo, not knowing how to comfort her brother. Deer were feeding near the bamboo thickets, and the cry of peacocks filled the afternoon. A striped hind leg pressing against a boulder indicated the tigers were asleep in the broken caves of an abandoned watchtower.

'I don't want to be buried in Balmer! The British will think John is much better equipped to rule than I am. After all, what will I have seen except this country stuck in the past?'

Jaya's skin burned with shame. Only a few days before the English tutor's arrival, Tikka had completed the elaborate course that tested a Balmer heir's horsemanship. Jaya had carried the gold thali filled

60

with cane sugar to feed his horse. She could still remember standing there, the sweet smell of cane sugar overpowered by the odour of the sweating horse, so proud of her brother that she had not wanted to giggle even when she saw him winking at her. She could not believe this angry youth, his lean figure taut with fury, was the same brother who had sat high above her on his saddle, his shadow cutting a black line across the courtyard while the Lancers cheered.

'Bappa is right not to send you away,' she blurted. 'You hate India and it's all the Englishman's fault.'

'That's not true!' Tikka shouted. 'Captain-sahib loves India. You've heard him talk about the Indian soldiers he commanded. Has he ever done anything but praise them?'

'So what? Indians still can't be officers in the Indian Army.'

'Oh, you're just a girl. How can you understand these things? Come on, I'll race you to the polo grounds.'

Relieved at the truce, Jaya ran behind her brother. After all, Captain Osborne did tell dramatic stories of his experiences with the Indian Army. She had often edged towards the circle of young cricketers to listen to the Captain's account of survival marches, his face expressionless as he described how he had eaten the eyeballs of dead Afridi tribesmen when the food ran out.

'What do eyeballs taste like, Captain-sahib?'

'A bit slimy. Rather like eating grapes, once you get used to the way they stare at you as you pop them into your mouth.' There would be a chorus of groans as the boys realized the Captain was teasing them. Then the Captain's face would soften, and he would speak about Indian soldiers.

'Marvellous fighting men,' he would say, rubbing the cricket ball against his white trousers, leaving red streaks on the cotton. 'The snobs in the British Army look down on us because we command native troops. In England they don't understand there is nothing an Indian soldier will not do for a few kind words from his officers. My own batman was killed giving us covering fire in the Waziristan campaign. The man may have cleaned my shoes, but I thought of him as a brother.'

One day Jaya found Major Vir Singh standing next to her, a frown cutting deep lines across his forehead. She looked from the strong features bracketed between his upswept moustache and starched turban to Captain Osborne's ginger hair and grey eyes which changed colour like glass marbles, and she wondered if the Major was jealous that Tikka's loyalty had shifted.

Major Vir Singh waited until the Captain left before warning Tikka, almost hesitantly, not to believe everything the Englishman said. 'I am not calling the Angrez a liar. I am only saying men see things in a way that justifies their own actions.'

Jaya did not understand the meaning of Major Vir Singh's words, just as she did not understand why she no longer felt comfortable with her brother. In only a year, the Englishman had changed the atmosphere in the Fort as he had changed Kuki-bai's old home. She did not know that the confusion in the Fort reflected the changes throughout India. Indian newspapers, freed at last of Viceroy Curzon's censorship, were filled with passionate editorials demanding Home Rule for British India. Indians were boycotting British goods to show their resentment of the Empire's exploitation of India's resources. Nationalist leaders were being sent into exile. From America, Europe, Africa, Japan, the exiled leaders continued to demand representation in the government that ruled their country. Realizing that the momentum of nationalist feeling had become irreversible, the new Viceroy had invited Indians to sit on the Imperial Council which governed British India, and called the first conference ever held between the kings of India and the representative of the British Crown.

But Jaya did not know these things. She only knew that when she had entered the rooms of the Chand Mahal, described by Kuki-bai so often through the long afternoons of her childhood, and found them whitewashed of their frescoes, when she had peered into courtyards where musicians had once sung through the night and seen them filled with heavy furniture, she had known something precious had been violated. Now she could feel the same thing happening inside the Fort itself.

Sometimes she felt safe only inside the carved walls of the zenana, fearful that if she stepped outside the world of women, she would be swept away by the restlessness blowing through the ancient Fort like the hot winds that warned of desert sandstorms.

IO

DURING THE nine-day fast which preceded the Dasra procession, Jaya pretended she was in a time machine from one of Tikka's story-books.

In the morning she tried to stay awake through the singsong monotony of the priests' voices reciting the epic battle between the God Rama and Ravanna, many-headed god of darkness, while sputtering clay lamps threw shadows on the wall. Half-asleep, she followed her mother into the glaring sunlight where the symbols of the day's puja were piled high in the temple forecourt.

Each day's puja had its specific task of commemoration – food, learning, music. For the puja of weapons, lances and unsheathed swords glittered like shards of broken glass on the stone pathways. By the end of the morning, they had disappeared under offerings of coconuts and marigold garlands.

Enormous cooking pots, their insides newly silvered, were hauled from the Fort kitchens for the puja of vessels. Jaya poured holy Ganges water into the vessels, and seeing her reflection swimming in the polished curves, she was again aware of the relationship between herself and the artifacts of her life.

The sense of permanence evaporated the moment she saw the fresco painters on their bamboo ladders. This year, the enthusiastic artists had covered an entire wall of the zenana with a flamboyant pink zeppelin. On the adjoining wall, above the precisely curved waves of the English Channel, a goggled Blériot waved from his biplane at the circle of inattentive maidservants gossiping in the sun. Jaya wanted to laugh when she saw the turban balancing on top of Blériot's helmet, but for the first time she felt insignificant in the presence of the painted foreigners. Their brilliantly coloured machines made the implements of the daily pujas seem primitive, as though the price of the future promised by the frescoes was exile from all that she held familiar.

Not until she left the last fresco did she feel free of the zenana walls with their weight of tradition on one side, their threat of change on the other.

At the King's View, her father was waiting to bless her before he departed for the Viceroy's conference. Jaya hesitated behind the Guard. The Maharajah was not alone. A thin woman was leaning against the parapet. For some reason, Jaya felt self-conscious that her long skirt was embroidered with gold thread, and she rubbed her nose, hoping to hide the diamond winking in her left nostril from the cool appraisal of the stranger.

Maharajah Jai Singh beckoned Jaya to his side. 'This is my daughter, Mrs Roy.' The stranger raised her joined hands, but did not bow. 'Mrs Roy's husband is going to redesign Balmer's irrigation system and increase our electricity supply. While he creates miracles in Balmer, Mrs Roy is going to create one in the zenana by making you fluent in the English language.'

Jaya had never met an Indian woman like Mrs Roy. She dressed in austere homespun saris, the rough white cotton broken only by a coloured band at the border to indicate she was not widowed, and she was fiercely anticlerical, refusing to attend the Maharani's religious functions if priests were present.

Jaya had never heard an Indian woman talk like Mrs Roy either, her gentle voice in such contrast to the virulence of her views on the British Raj.

Jaya no longer resented the fact that Tikka was too busy with his Angrez books to join her and the maidservants in midnight games of hide-and-seek in the zenana. Mrs Roy's lessons were much more interesting than Tikka's books, full of bloodcurdling accounts of the injustices of the Empire. Once she even mentioned a cousin who had been shot by the British police.

From the cloth satchel hanging from her shoulder, its weight unbalancing her slender frame, Mrs Roy produced a seemingly endless supply of nationalist Indian newspapers, until Jaya became quite adept at reading aloud from the coarse sheets of newsprint with the black ink that came off all over her fingers.

As her lessons progressed, Jaya began to understand Major Vir Singh's warning to her brother. There was no similarity between the Captain's account of British India and Mrs Roy's version.

In the evening, Jaya joined the boys lounging on the slatted wooden benches in the cricket pavilion and listened to the Captain speak of an India which three generations of his family had helped to mould.

'Men like my batman are the real Indians. Brave, honourable, loyal men. Their oath is "Sahib, we have eaten your salt. Our lives are yours." But these city lawyers from Bombay and Calcutta, who call themselves the voice of India and burn British cotton on the streets, these ungrateful scum forget what England has given India.'

The next afternoon, Mrs Roy waved her sari in the child's face. 'Shall I tell you why I wear this? Because it is woven in my own country, not shipped as raw cotton to the millowners of Manchester and Lancaster. Each time I buy a garment like this I put food into the mouths of Indians.'

At the cricket pavilion, Tikka and his friends nodded agreement with the Captain. 'The Viceroy should ban the native press again. These babu editors only encourage sedition against the British Raj.'

The following day, Jaya looked into Mrs Roy's eyes, bright with passion behind rimless glasses. 'The British Raj has jailed another great patriot, Tilak, but his words have already become a slogan throughout India, spread by our own newspapers. "Freedom is my birthright and I shall have it!" A hundred thousand people chanted that slogan when they heard Tilak sentenced to six years in a British jail.'

A few days later, Captain Osborne waved a copy of the London Times at the boys sitting in the pavilion. His face was flushed with rage. 'Didn't I say it was dangerous to allow these damned city lawyers to publish their scurrilous rags and incite violence? The Assistant to the Secretary of State for India has been shot in London. At point-blank range, in front of his wife, while attending an At Home for friends of India. The assassin is an Indian student who says he will go to the gallows proud of his filthy act of murder. He calls it a blow for India's freedom.'

Jaya hugged her knees as Captain Osborne's rage broke in

65

waves over his shocked audience. Earlier in the day, Mrs Roy had said, 'Our leaders counsel moderation. But how long can you gag the anger of the young when they see signs all over their own country saying "Dogs and Indians are not allowed"? In three months, a British judge assassinated in Calcutta, British millowners bombed in Bombay and now a British cabinet minister shot dead in London, the very heart of Empire. The British Raj is reaping the harvest of its own injustice.'

Jaya listened to the contradictory views of the two tutors as she might have listened to the bards, weaving passionate mythologies about another world, the world of British India where white men ruled like anointed kings and Indians challenged the might of their masters with smudged articles in badly set newspapers.

When she visited Mrs Roy's house, Jaya was surprised to find in the high-ceilinged rooms no evidence of the violence that coloured Mrs Roy's lessons, as though her tutor's strident nationalism were an armour donned for the outside world.

The sparse austerity of the cotton mattresses placed on the floor was broken by terra-cotta bowls filled with marigolds, the silence seldom interrupted by anything more urgent than the clicking of yellow lizards. Black-and-white photographs hung in disarray on the whitewashed walls.

'Who are they, Mrs Roy? Your brothers?'

'My husband's cousins. One was shot by the Angrez. That is why my husband and I left British India.' She pointed to a photograph of two young men laughing at something beyond the camera. 'Poor boy. He had only been married a year; his wife was expecting a baby. When Curzon partitioned Bengal, there was a riot. The police fired at the crowd, and he was killed. Now, less than ten years later, the British have reversed Curzon's partition. What a pity the British Raj cannot reverse their bullets as well as their laws.'

'And the other one?'

'The surviving brother, Arun Roy. A lawyer, and a very active nationalist in Calcutta.'

Jaya studied the square face with the thin moustache stretching above the laughing mouth. There was something conspiratorial in the lawyer's bright eyes, as if he were sharing an intimate secret with her. 'Is he married too?'

'Not yet. But he should be. A wife would control his wildness.'

A tenderness entered Mrs Roy's voice as she spoke of the family left behind in Calcutta, and she fetched a clothbound photograph album filled with pictures of Arun Roy.

'See this?' Mrs Roy pointed to a picture of the lawyer dressed in a kimono, sitting between two ladies with long needles in their hair. 'We had to send Arun to Japan after the British shot his brother. We were afraid he might do something rash if he stayed in India. Many Indians were travelling to Japan in those days to pay homage to the Japanese people for winning their war against Russia. You see, it was the first time in modern history that an Asian country had defeated a European empire.'

Jaya looked through the album, fascinated by the lawyer's ability to assume a different role in every photograph, though the lips were always parted in a smile beneath the thin moustache and the eyes always seemed to be looking past the camera, into her own.

Mrs Roy opened a lacquer basket cracked with heat and usage, and rummaged through old letters before extracting a creased paper. 'He wrote this from Japan: "Sitting in Japan, it is hard to believe that only ten years ago Europe brought China to its knees. If the Chinese had been ruled by someone like the Japanese Emperor Meiji, they could never have been defeated. If we had an Emperor Meiji in India, what couldn't we achieve as a people? Perhaps we need a war. Look what war has made of the Japanese! From farmers they have become manufacturers of poison gas!" '

She looked at Jaya above her spectacles. 'I'm afraid Arun wants vengeance, not justice. I wish he were like that lawyer in South Africa who wants change without bloodshed. Gandhi is probably a crackpot, but at least he doesn't think poison gas is a sign of progress. Still, Arun is young, and I suppose young men always think of war as a game.'

Noticing Jaya's inattention, Mrs Roy straightened the ruched sleeve of her blouse in irritation. 'You must interest yourself in the outside world, Bai-sa. Did you know that your father and his fellow rulers have asked the Viceroy to stop British officers from meddling in the affairs of their kingdoms? More important, they have said they want their children brought up as Indians, not bullied into becoming sahibs by the British Raj.'

Jaya thought of Captain Osborne's influence over Tikka as Mrs Roy declared, 'The maharajahs have asked for a Chamber of Princes to protect themselves from the treaty violations of the British Raj. Everywhere in India the people are linking arms. One day the Empire will wake up and find itself strangled in our embrace.'

11

When the Maharajah returned from the Viceroy's conference, no one was permitted to enter the King's View. Standing behind the Household Guard, Jaya and Tikka watched engineers drill through the stone walls to extend electrical wiring onto the terrace and the Fort carpenters tightening the ropes on the purdah tent, but the Guards refused to explain the sudden activity.

At sunset the doors to the terrace were finally opened. Hidden by silk screens, the Maharani and purdah ladies filed into the purdah tent, while children and courtiers, their voices shrill with anticipation, crowded onto the carpets spread on the stone floor. When Jai Singh had seated himself on the marble bench, the lights were extinguished.

A solitary lamp illuminated a young man standing behind a black box. Jaya shrank against Tikka's shoulder. The single light shining on the stranger's chin made an ominous mask of the high cheekbones and hooked nose, as though he were a gypsy from the troupes who told tales of black magic.

'Your Highness, ladies and gentlemen,' the stranger began. 'We have seen with our own eyes wonders we once read of in our holy books and dismissed as the dreams of sages. The horse has been replaced by the car, the elephant by the train, the bird by the flying machine. Magic becomes reality every day, and the magicians are not gods but men.'

The stranger's long teeth snapped down like boar's tusks at the end of each incantation. 'Two such magicians, the Lumiere brothers, came to Bombay and taught their magic to a genius from our own land. Tonight it is my privilege to show you the fruit of that encounter – Dadasaheb Phalke's masterpiece.'

With a dramatic gesture he slid a steel cover over the lamp. Whirring filled the darkness like the insistent beat of insects' wings. There was a clicking sound as celluloid strips caught ratchets. Then flickering images appeared on the white sheets.

Jaya sat on the carpet unable to comprehend what was happening. This was not like the rolling cloth paintings used by the bards. Trees and animals were expanding and contracting like sequences in a dream. Real people filled the night, faces large as houses swelling across the screen.

'The Lord Krishna.' The Maharani's clear voice pierced the muslin curtains of the purdah tent. 'See, it is the Lord Krishna as a child.'

Whispers of recognition filled the terrace. Jaya felt the blood rush to her head when she saw the mighty cobra rising from the parted river to open its hood like a canopy over the laughing baby. She shouted with relief when the river crashed down like a tidal wave separating the Lord Krishna from the furious soldiers, but she could not hear her own voice in the loud chanting from the purdah tent. The Maharani and the purdah ladies were reciting the Krishna Hymns. Their voices reached a crescendo as the film ended with the child Krishna flying above the humans he had astonished, into the pantheon of waiting gods.

Long after the screen went blank, the audience sat transfixed in front of the white sheets glowing dimly in the night, unable to tear themselves away, as though they had been present at an oracle.

Had the Maharajah not brought the magic of cinema to the Fort, other things would have claimed Jaya's attention. Captain Osborne and Mrs Roy got very agitated in different ways about the bomb that had nearly killed the Viceroy in Ahmedabad. Raja Man Singh went to Ajmere to leave John in the British school. The King Emperor, Edward VII, died, and the flags at the Fort flew at half-mast during a full week of official mourning.

A new viceroy, Lord Hardinge, came to India, bringing the astonishing news that the new King of England, George V, wished to be crowned Emperor of India in the imperial city of Delhi. Jai Singh went to Delhi to discuss arrangements for this momentous event. The Osbornes travelled with him, because their son, James, had finally arrived in Delhi from England.

But Jaya was so busy trailing behind the projectionist, asking him how people could fly, and where he stored the pictures in his black projector, that she didn't even see the Angrez tutor's son until days after his arrival in Balmer, when Kuki-bai pulled her by the hand to the carved wall of the zenana.

A car bounced over the yellow flagstones of the outside courtyard. The fan of the chauffeur's turban quivered with the impact of the brakes, and he leaped out to open the door.

Behind her brother Jaya saw a young man, taller than Captain Osborne, with a thin neck made longer by the close crop of his black hair, descending from the car.

Kuki-bai sighed. 'No wonder the girls in the zenana are excited.'

Jaya peered through the carving. 'He looks like a crane. Why should that excite the zenana ladies?'

Kuki-bai laughed at the disappointment in Jaya's voice. 'Wait. You'll change your mind when he comes to the zenana.'

Jaya was shocked. 'A man coming to the zenana? That's impossible!'

'No, it's not, if your mother and father invite him. They have done so because the new Viceroy wants your father to send Tikka to school in England, and if Tikka goes . . .'

'You're teasing, Kuki-bai. Bappa told the Angrez tutor that Tikka would never be allowed to study in England.'

Kuki-bai lowered her eyes, and Jaya saw the network of veins on her wrinkled eyelids. 'Sometimes your father has no choice. Many years ago, Balmer needed money during a terrible famine and your father went to the Tsar of Russia for help. Now he is no longer trusted by the British Raj. The new Viceroy says that if Tikka is to remain heir to the Balmer throne he must go to England. Maharani-sahib is anxious to meet the Angrez boy because Tikka may have to travel to England with him.'

In the corridor behind her Jaya heard the zenana eunuchs teasing the purdah women. The women shrieked with laughter, pushing the eunuchs out of their way as they hastened down the stone corridors to the Baran's chambers to select their jewellery.

'The Angrez is a man in his prime – sixteen years old!' the eunuchs shouted after the purdah ladies. 'At last you hot-blooded

71

creatures will have something to fill your empty dreams.'

Infected by the excitement, Jaya found herself submitting meekly when the maidservants flattened her long hair with scented oil, and applied kohl in sweeping lines to accentuate her green eyes.

'What a beauty you are turning out to be, child!' Kuki-bai cracked her knuckles against her temple to remove the evil eye. 'Your husband will have to keep you in purdah or you will break hearts just by crossing a room.'

Jaya examined herself in Kuki-bai's mirror and felt the thrill of vanity. Large eyes stared at her above a nose straight as the turned blade of her father's sword. The diamond in her left nostril gleamed against the dark skin that so worried her mother. She swung the long hair which fell to her knees, laughing as the thick black curtain swirled above the orange silk skirt, and for the first time she thought of herself as a woman and not a child.

As a special mark of favour, the Maharani received the tutor's family on the balcony outside her private chambers. The gentle light of late afternoon softened the bright paintings on the wooden windows opened to admit the breeze from the lake. Sparrows swung on bougainvillea vines covering the courtyard below with fallen flowers.

With an exaggerated flourish the zenana eunuchs ushered the Angrez onto the balcony. The veiled purdah ladies commented on the Angrez woman's wide-brimmed hat, and the white silk dress that hung like a shift from her shoulders to her ankles, showing only an inch of white stocking above high-heeled shoes. They whispered to each other that Mrs Osborne's feet were really quite small for a mem-sahib.

A young man followed nervously behind. Gauze veils clung to moist lips as the purdah ladies turned their attention to him.

'Look at his eyes. The Goddess must have created a special colour for this boy's eyes.'

'No, no. That is the colour of the monsoon sea. See how it changes from blue to green. I swear no mortal was given such eyes before. And look at the lashes.'

'Hai, as thick as elephant grass. And so black, like his hair. Do you think our blood runs in his veins?'

'Chee! Chee! Why do you call this young god a half-breed? But if he were one of us, what a husband he would make for Bai-sa.'

'Truly. Put a turban on his head, a sword in his hand and with all the other parts the Goddess must have given him, he could tame our little panther.'

They laughed behind their hands, joined by the sniggering maid-servants.

Jaya could not think of a tart reply to the teasing. In her new self-consciousness the jokes of the women became a fearful possibility.

'Mind your desperate tongues, ladies,' Kuki-bai rebuked the laughing women. 'At least our Bai-sa will be taken by a man. She will not need to break her hymen with smuggled vegetables.'

Jaya looked up, afraid the Angrez might understand, and saw James Osborne giving Kuki-bai surreptitious glances from under the long eyelashes that had charmed the purdah ladies. Jaya realized the old concubine might look odd to a stranger in her bright silk garments, tracings of henna on her small palms, the rich decorations in such contrast to the wrinkled skin and the sparse hair.

'Did you know you are living in Kuki-bai's old house?' Jaya asked, forgetting that she was speaking directly to an Angrez for the first time in her life. The boy shook his head. 'Well, you are. My great-grandfather built the Chand Mahal for her, because she was his favourite concubine. Kuki-bai is a great dancer. She used to dance on Moti the elephant's tusks.'

The Maharani and Mrs Osborne, deep in inconsequential conversation about the beauty of Jalsa Lake, did not notice the colour rising above James Osborne's white collar at the word concubine. Not knowing why she had the advantage of the Angrez, but pleased that Tikka was attending a court of appeal and could not stop her, Jaya pressed on.

'Yes. There were wonderful paintings of love on the walls of the Chand Mahal. They had to cover them all up with whitewash because the Angrez don't like looking at such things.'

James Osborne flushed bright red. The purdah ladies stopped chattering among themselves and turned their veiled heads to stare at him.

The Maharani leaned forward. 'What are you discussing with Tikka's friend, child?'

'I was only asking if it is true the Angrez don't like paintings in their houses.'

The Maharani frowned, but Mrs Osborne said, 'Please, Your Highness, let the child ask. Yes, Princess, we have many paintings in our lovely new home. My favourite is a magnificent oil painting of Clive's defeat of Tippu Sultan.'

'Dying men? Would you not have preferred the old paintings of beautiful women and kings in love, like those we have in the zenana?'

Mrs Osborne stopped laughing. 'You must visit the Chand Mahal and judge for yourself,' she said in a distant voice. 'Perhaps next week, Your Highness, during the cricket match?'

TIKKA ISSUED furious instructions to the maid accompanying Jaya to the Chand Mahal that his sister was not to speak at all to the Angrez except to answer yes or no in response to direct questions.

'Why is Tikka so angry with me, Devi?' Jaya asked as they were driven to the Chand Mahal.

The maidservant sniffed. 'Because you lack the modesty of a normal girl.'

Jaya dug her elbow into the maid's shoulder, uncertainty audible in her defiance. 'That is not true.'

Hearing the unsureness, the maidservant patted her young charge's knee. 'You are not a bad child, Bai-sa. But young girls do not ask total strangers why they don't like to look at naked women sporting with men. The pictures on the zenana walls are about pleasure, Bai-sa. Foreigners do not discuss such things. It is said the Angrez do not even enjoy pleasure. They only like power.'

The car turned into the drive of the Chand Mahal, past the marble pavilion on the lake. The green lawn in front of the swing was now a cricket pitch, looking just like the pictures in Tikka's Angrez magazines. Cane matting stretched between wooden wickets, where James Osborne was preparing to bowl. Jaya stepped out of the car. Behind Mrs Osborne's outstretched hand she saw her brother attempt Ranji's leg-glance stroke and be clean-bowled by the Angrez. There was a cheer from the fielders. Captain Osborne declared Tikka out as Jaya put her hand in Mrs Osborne's cool palm.

The Angrez ladies were sitting on the verandah. Servants passed trays of sandwiches. Jaya nibbled on the sandwiches, nodding mutely to any questions. Obedient to Tikka's instructions, she did not speak to the ladies, only to the servants.

At last the cricketers joined the ladies and helped themselves to sandwiches and thick slices of cake.

The maid poked Jaya through the slats of the chair. 'Don't talk to the servants, Bai-sa.'

'Why shouldn't I? What would they think if I didn't return their greetings?'

'Don't you see the Angrez pretend the servants don't exist? Follow the custom of the house, Bai-sa. You are a guest.'

Captain Osborne tapped a silver spoon against his cup to attract attention. 'His Highness has very kindly lent us the film which he brought from Bombay.'

There were exclamations of 'Marvellous!' and 'What fun!' as the gathering trailed through the drawing rooms. Oil paintings tilted from the walls, brown backgrounds broken by blood running down bright uniforms. Jaya remembered to smile and answer 'Yes, mem-sahib' when Mrs Osborne asked if she liked the paintings.

In an enclosed coutyard Mrs Osborne's piano had been pushed aside to make room for rows of chairs. Jaya settled between Tikka and the Angrez boy, curious to see how the Angrez would respond to the film.

For the first ten minutes the Angrez audience reacted like the viewers in the King's View, such was the power of cinema to astonish. But they did not know the story of God Krishna as the Balmer boys in their white cricketing clothes knew it. They had not heard the legend of the god recited by maidservants, or accompanied their mothers to the temples of Jalsa Lake to offer fruit to the deity. The very sequences that had moved the Maharani and the purdah ladies to prayer led the Angrez to try to suppress their laughter behind their hands. As the miracles became more flamboyant, the audience's hilarity increased.

The projectionist stood behind the revolving wheels of the projector, his mouth tight with anger. But Tikka was laughing with the Angrez. James Osborne twisted in his chair. 'Don't mind them, Princess. They don't understand what they are seeing.'

Jaya was ashamed for her brother, even as she asked in surprise, 'Do you know about Lord Krishna?'

'I was born in India, Princess. Of course I know.'

'Your mother told you?'

'My ayah, my Indian nurse, told me. She used to scold and say I was even naughtier than Krishna when I was a child.'

THAT SUMMER James Osborne became a regular member of the Maharajah's morning riding party, and Jaya fell into the habit of riding next to him. Unlike Tikka, the Angrez boy did not gallop off suddenly, causing her pony to shy and pull at the reins.

He seemed interested in everything about Balmer. Soon she was acting as his guide to the Fort. They visited the elephant corral, where she told him how Kuki-bai and Moti had come to Balmer. At the stables, she pointed out the battle honours engraved on the stone arches and repeated Major Vir Singh's account of the Balmer Lancers in Peking. While James Osborne ran his fingers along the stone hands carved into the Fort gateway, Jaya explained how the sati queens had placed their dyed palms on the stones to bless the Fort as they made their way to their husbands' funeral pyres. Seeing the disapproval on the Angrez boy's face, she told him the sati queens were considered saints for their sacrifice. The expression of disapproval grew stronger. Jaya looked into his blue-green eyes, remembering the comments of the purdah ladies when they had seen that deep changing colour, and for some reason she felt weak, almost as though she were going to fall.

That afternoon when she was having her massage in Kuki-bai's courtyard, she could not understand why she was so angry when the old concubine asked, 'Do you still think Tikka's friend looks like a crane?' Or why she felt so desolate when Kuki-bai studied her face saying, 'Ten years old. You are half-woman already, child. It is time that you were married.'

Bumping into the Angrez boy on her way to the polo ground, Jaya kept her eyes firmly on the ground and mumbled some indistinct greeting. His gentleness confused her. When he asked if he had offended her in some way, she opened her mouth but could not answer because her tongue felt heavy and the words seemed to stick in her throat.

Overcome with shame, she raced into the zenana. The maidservants caught her as she ran into the stone corridors and took her, arguing and pulling, to the Maharani's balcony.

The Maharani's regal posture contradicted the excitement in her eyes. She placed a parcel in Jaya's hands. 'You have received a gift, child. A portrait of the man you may one day marry.'

Jaya's humiliation at her encounter with James Osborne dissolved in waves of apprehension as she took the ivory miniature between two fingers, as though it were a live coal.

'The Dowager Maharani of Sirpur has sent a portrait of Prince Pratap, the younger brother of the Maharajah of Sirpur. She wishes to know if your father is agreeable to the alliance.'

Nausea clenched Jaya's stomach and she could feel her childhood slipping away like wet sand though the fingers holding the ivory miniature.

'Don't be frightened, child. Prince Pratap is one of the most handsome men in India. And his brother, Maharajah Victor, rules a powerful kingdom. If you marry into Sirpur, you will be kept like a nightingale in a golden cage.'

Jaya forced her eyes to the ivory disk and found herself looking into the oval face of a grown man. Long eyes sloped over high cheekbones. Heavy eyelids drooped as through in boredom above lips lifted in an unconvincing smile. Jaya thought he looked just like an animal stalking its prey.

The purdah ladies ran out in confusion as Jai Singh strode onto the balcony: 'Why is the child being shown that picture? An alliance between Sirpur and Balmer is unthinkable. The Sirpurs are the lapdogs of the British Empire. The ruler is Victoria's godson. He even flaunts her name. Maharajah Victor he calls himself.' Jai Singh's eyes blazed with anger. 'Isn't it enough that the British Raj threatens me with the consequences if I do not send Tikka to England? Must I lose my daughter to an Angrez lackey also?'

There the matter ended, except that Jaya realized with an aching sense of loss that she had ceased to be a child. In only a handful of years she would be sent away in a palanquin to live with some stranger whose features she had only seen painted on a piece of ivory. Overwhelmed by the enormity of the realization, she did not find James Osborne threatening any more.

12

IN THE DAYS of preparations for the Dasra puja, which celebrated the triumph of good over evil, the Keeper of the Elephants paced the stone elephant stables, issuing instructions to the artists tracing patterns on to the elephants' wrinkled hides.

Moti's grey skin slowly disappeared under the rich tones of vegetable dyes. Cobras wound around his legs and under his great chest. Tigers plunged down Moti's flapping ears, deer raced across his haunches. Other artists painted a jungle onto Tikka's elephant. Garlands of flowers covered the elephant that would draw the two-storeyed wooden purdah carriage for the Maharani and the ladies of the zenana.

On the morning of the puja Jaya clambered into the purdah carriage. She had a clear view of Major Vir Singh sitting astride his charger at the head of the Balmer Lancers. Tikka, in the silver howdah of the Heir Apparent, led the line of elephants carrying the Ministers of the Council. At the rear of the procession she could see the spears and shields of the Household Guard.

The chattri-bearer appeared, holding the state umbrella. The mahout struck Moti's forehead with a steel prong, and Moti lumbered to his feet. Two soldiers hurried forward to place a wooden staircase on the right of the tusker as Maharajah Jai Singh walked to the waiting procession, his erect carriage defying the weight of jewels cascading down the front of his brocade tunic.

Major Vir Singh unsheathed his sword. The ruler placed his foot on a step. Major Vir Singh's arm swept down and the Fort cannons fired a salute. Jai Singh mounted the next step. The cannons fired again. Seven times the sound of cannon fire shook the Fort as Maharajah Jai Singh climbed to the golden howdah.

In the silence that followed the crash of cannon, Major Vir Singh spurred his horse. The Balmer Lancers, pennants lifting in the breeze, trotted behind him. The sigh of moving elephants was drowned in the deep thud of two nagara drums, each drum the size of an elephant, which straddled the outer gates of the Fort, announcing as they had announced for eleven centuries, the departure of the Maharajah and his forces from the fastness of the Fort. Now the deep pounding of the nagaras bounced off stone battlements and echoed down the narrow streets of the capital, louder than the noise of the purdah carriage bumping on its wooden wheels over the stones.

The procession reached the city and the sound of the nagaras was lost in the shouts of people flinging marigolds and roses at the Maharajah from carved balconies. Cheering crowds jostled each other on the streets. Through the latticework of the purdah carriage Jaya saw streaks of colour where Moti's feet, encircled in gold anklets, had trampled the showers of blossoms.

The procession halted. Concealed by the vermilion silk screens held by the eunuchs, Jaya followed her mother into the temple. Through the thin fabric of the purdah tent she could see the sacrificial ram tethered at the altar, its white hide carrying no blemish that might render it unfit for the Goddess. Oblivious of the crowds, the ram was nibbling at the fruit resting on pyramids of rice grains.

Maharajah Jai Singh stood before the altar as the priests recited his lineage and titles. Then he drew the Balmer sword, lifting his arm so that the flashing blade was visible throughout the temple. People pressed their palms together, and the relentless thud of the nagaras filled the silent temple like a heartbeat. Suddenly Jai Singh's arm swept down. Naked steel disappeared into flesh. Blood spurted onto the fruit and plantain leaves. A cheer rose from the crowd. It was quickly stifled when Jai Singh did not raise the sword. In that endless moment, Jaya felt her heart pounding in rhythm with the nagaras. At last the Maharajah's arm lifted, and the severed head of the ram bounced down the rice, black tongue protruding, eyes still rolling in fear.

The priests rushed forward to press their silver bowls to the open arteries of the ram. Cries of 'Victory to the Goddess! Victory to the Maharajah!' filled the air.

A priest appeared behind the muslin curtains holding a bowl of blood. The Maharani smeared her own forehead, then Jaya's, with the warm liquid. Jaya felt the blood congealing on her skin like a scab as she stared at the priests being mobbed in the temple courtyard. Red splashed everywhere. People were fighting to dip their hands into the blood of the sacrifice.

'It's all right, Maharani-sahib. The Maharajah did not lift the sword twice,' Kuki-bai whispered.

'The sacrifice was not performed with a single stroke,' the Maharani repeated like an incantation. 'Therefore the sacrifice is unholy.'

Jai Singh walked back to the temple, the sword in his right hand dripping blood onto the stones. Jaya was frightened by the expression of weariness on her father's face. Her fear doubled at the certainty in her mother's next words. 'The Maharajah knows the sacrifice was unholy. There will be bad luck on the house.'

As soon as the procession returned to the Fort, Jaya raced to tell Tikka about the Maharani's prediction.

'Superstitious nonsense,' Tikka said irritably. 'I don't understand why Bappa continues to perform the sacrifice. Doesn't he realize we are living in the twentieth century?'

SOON AFTER the Dasra puja the Fort began to empty. The court was moving to Delhi to take part in the greatest spectacle ever mounted by the British Empire in India, the Coronation Durbar for George V. At last Indians would see the figure in whose name the Angrez ruled their country. For the first time a British monarch was to be crowned Emperor in India.

The Viceroy had spent lavishly to create a magical city of tents to house the guests and participants. Forty thousand tents, with elaborate apartments consisting of drawing rooms and dining rooms and bedchambers and studies, had been erected in Delhi. Rose gardens and polo grounds had been laid out and thirty-six railway junctions built to accommodate the influx of visitors.

Raja Man Singh and the Prime Minister left Balmer first, taking the cars and the state carriages. Then Major Vir Singh and the Balmer

Lancers went away, their horses neighing and kicking against the horse boxes mounted on the train.

'Why aren't you in Delhi, Mrs Roy?' Jaya asked, resentful that the Maharani had not allowed her to accompany the Maharajah and Tikka to Delhi. 'The Coronation Durbar is the most magnificent sight India will ever see.'

Mrs Roy banged her teacup down on the tray. 'Every five years the British Raj bankrupts India with such shows of magnificence. First Victoria's Diamond Jubilee. Then Curzon's Imperial Durbar. Now this totally unnecessary Coronation Durbar.'

'But Mrs Roy, imagine a whole city made of tents!'

'When will you learn that life is not a fairy tale, Bai-sa? Even now, there is a famine throughout western India. Indians are dying like flies, but the indifferent British Raj has spent a million pounds of India's money on tents, and another half-million pounds on an imperial crown.'

'But the King is going to be crowned Emperor. You have to have a crown for that.'

The tutor sighed, and her thin body shuddered under the coarse cotton sari. 'Power crowns kings, Bai-sa, nothing else. George the Fifth does not need a crown. Who can deny the power of the British Raj? The Angrez have decided to shift their capital from Calcutta to Delhi and build a new imperial city that will cost millions of pounds. But no Indian can tell the British not to squander the wealth of an impoverished country. And you ask why I am not in Delhi to admire their mad spectacle of vanity!'

Silenced by Mrs Roy's anger Jaya sipped her tea, no longer so envious that Tikka was in Delhi and she was not.

While the Court was away Jaya found she had the rifle range to herself, and she organized the stableboys into relays of throwers. Afternoon after afternoon she fired at the bursts of clay pigeons, bottles, tin cans appearing with unexpected suddenness in the sky, determined that when the tiger season began the day after the Court returned to Balmer, she would be a good enough shot to bag at least one tiger and put an end to Tikka's complacency because three tiger skins hung on the walls of his study.

But when the Court arrived, Jaya forgot Mrs Roy's objections in her wonder at Tikka's excited descriptions of the Coronation Durbar.

81

'Ranji drove in a solid-silver coach! And Maharajah Patiala is nearly seven feet tall in his turban. But the King of England, unfortunately, is very short. When he made his state entry into Delhi, we couldn't even see him. Everyone said he should have come on an elephant, but the King said if a horse was good enough for the King of England it was more than good enough for the Emperor of India.'

'And the Durbar?'

'Their Imperial Majesties sat on two thrones with their trains falling for miles and miles down the steps. The Maharajah of Baroda didn't wear any jewels and then made the insult worse by turning his back on the King Emperor in front of the whole of Delhi.'

'Will he lose his throne for that?'

'That's what everyone says.'

'And then?'

'There were parties every night. Each ruler had his own quarters, just like a palace, with Lancers mounting guard in front of the tents. There was a long line of camels in front of Maharajah Bikaner's apartments. He brought the Bikaner Camel Corps as his personal guard. Oh, and one night there was a big fire and all the fireworks for the Coronation burned up. Anyway, the best parties were in the Sirpur quarters. The Sirpur brothers had a ballroom tent with a huge chandelier and a twenty-five-piece dance band. Maharajah Victor and Prince Pratap are great sportsmen. All the foreign women are in love with them – Russian countesses, French marquises and even film stars all the way from America.'

Tikka smiled mischievously at his sister. 'If you were only older, Jaya. You could marry one of the Sirpurs and I could come and visit you and we could play polo and cricket and dance with beautiful firengis.'

Jaya's hands grew cold as her brother chattered on, remembering the ivory miniature of the bored man with a face like a predator.

That afternoon Jaya sat with the Maharani on the purdah balcony that overlooked the Durbar Hall, filled with people waiting to pay obeisance to the Maharajah on his return to Balmer. The British Political Officer was the guest of honour. In his severe black suit, he sat stiff with dignity next to the Maharajah.

The morning wore relentlessly on and the Angrez grew restless in their chairs, seeing the lines of visitors still waiting to offer gifts to the ruler. Dancing girls swirled in the centre of the Durbar Hall, opening their ranks to admit another subject hurrying forward to make his bows to the Maharajah, then closing, like the slow opening and closing of the jaws of a crocodile sunning itself on a sandbank. Jai Singh's mouth lifted as he acknowledged his bowing subjects but the smile did not reach his eyes.

Sleepy with the long ceremony, Jaya tried to remember the rifle her father had brought her from Delhi, its engraved barrel and its wooden stock inlaid with a hunting scene of a Rajput princess driving her lance into the neck of a tiger.

The Maharani pointed to Raja Man Singh and the Prime Minister whispering to each other. 'See their pleasure. This morning your father finally agreed to let Tikka study in England. How hard the Angrez are, to steal a son from his father. And that, too, in a time of peace. If we had been at war with England, if they had taken your brother to England as hostage, then. . . .' The Maharani's voice petered out in unhappiness. Jaya craned forward and saw Tikka laughing as he talked to James Osborne. She didn't think her brother looked at all upset.

THE NEXT DAY the tiger season began at last, and an hour before sunrise, Jaya climbed into the car, to sit between her father and Captain Osborne on their way to the jungle.

Half-asleep, Jaya heard Jai Singh ask, 'How long can the Angrez remain in India, Captain-sahib? Would it not be better to leave India in the hands of her own rulers?'

The Englishman tapped his cigar ash out the window, and sparks disappeared into the dark. 'Would the people of India return to their rulers if we left, Your Highness? Most of those rulers care only for the vulgarities of splendour.'

'And what of the splendour of the British Raj which we witnessed in Delhi?'

'That was a symbolic event, sir. Besides, King George is only a figurehead. He does not have absolute power like India's rulers. A saint would have difficulty governing with such absolute power, and there are few saints among the five hundred maharajahs who rule royal India.'

'But there are saints among the ten thousand Englishmen who have absolute power in governing British India?'

'Our laws remove the need for saints. That is why Tikka will profit from his stay in England.'

A group of villagers stood at the side of the road. Jai Singh dismounted. Jaya waited impatiently for her father to end his conversation, afraid that Tikka and James Osborne would already be sitting on an elephant making their way to the tiger.

Jai Singh got back into the car. 'At least, Mr Roy's canals have helped this year's crop. Do you know the worst thing the British Raj has done, Captain-sahib? We, the kings of India, no longer need to fear our subjects. They cannot punish us. Only foreigners have that power now.' He patted Jaya's knee. 'Well, child, you might shoot a tiger today. So tell me, what is the most dangerous animal in the jungle?'

Jaya gripped her gun, thrilled that the conversation had at last turned to the shikar. 'Everyone knows that, Bappa. A wounded tiger.'

'Why?'

'A wounded tiger cannot hunt its natural prey, so it becomes a man-eater, hukam.'

Captain Osborne laughed, and Jai Singh turned to him. 'I can see that you have been called out into the jungle with your rifle to protect the villagers, Captain. And known that fierce excitement when a shikari begins to stalk the wounded animal that is stalking him.'

Captain Osborne lit a new cigar, cupping his hand over the flame. 'And I have known pity, too, Your Highness, when I saw the mangled bodies of the villagers attacked by a man-eater.'

'What about the people who create a man-eater by wounding a tiger without killing it?'

A stern expression darkened the Captain's features. 'Such men are either criminals or amateurs, Your Highness. In all justice they should be banned from the jungle.'

Jai Singh hit his fist on his knee. 'Justice! How the Angrez love that word. We had a system of justice once, Captain. We had laws. But your Empire absorbed our armies, castrated our nobles, confused our scholars, diminished our priests. You deposed the guardians of our laws and left only – what is it you Angrez

84

say? – the Oriental despot. Any vice was smiled on by the British Raj except the vice of independence. You wander so confidently in the jungles of India. But what are you, Captain-sahib? Amateurs or criminals? Why do you not kill us instead of only wounding us?'

Even though the windows were open, Jaya could feel her father's rage fill the car like the heat from a bonfire, and when the car stopped she fell over Captain Osborne's knees in her haste to get away from the grown-ups.

To JAYA'S RELIEF, she was not positioned with the adults. The Maharajah and Major Vir Singh climbed into the howdah on the lead elephant, followed by Tikka and Captain Osborne on the second elephant. Jaya stood next to James Osborne in the canvas shooting box lashed onto the back of the third elephant.

Birds lifted in noisy clouds as the elephants cut like grey arrow-heads through the scrub jungle. Monkeys swung from vine to vine, away from the clattering sound of sticks beaten against copper trays. The beaters moved in a wide circle from the far end of the jungle, shouting to prevent the tiger from slipping through their lines to the waters of Jalsa Lake. Jaya caressed the ornate steel barrel of her rifle, praying to the Goddess that today it would be her name the shikaris praised when they measured the shot tiger.

The sharp report of a pistol signalled the tiger had been sighted. James Osborne released the safety catch on his gun. Jaya's finger tightened on the trigger of her rifle. There was a sudden blur of black and yellow stripes in the undergrowth in front of Tikka's elephant, but Tikka fired into the air. Jaya realized that her brother was directing the running tiger toward her. She stared at the bushes, her gun held high above the mahout's turban.

The sharp crackle of breaking sticks sounded behind her. Jaya swung around. The tiger had moved downwind to the elephant. Only a hundred feet away, it was crouched on its powerful hind legs to spring. Without conscious instruction from her brain, Jaya squeezed the trigger. The tiger spun backward from the impact of the bullet and Jaya shut her eyes for a split second. When she opened them, the tiger was preparing to spring again.

The elephant panicked and bolted. The tiger bounded behind the elephant, its speed unhindered by its wound. Branches whipped into Jaya's face and shame and fear flooded through her, hearing the mahout shout to the beaters walking defenceless through the brush, that a wounded tiger was at large in the jungle.

James Osborne was trying to keep his balance against the canvas walls of the shooting box. Jaya dropped her gun and seized his waist to steady him. With a mighty roar, the tiger made its death charge, springing into the air, claws caked with mud, massive jaws stretched in pain and rage. James Osborne fired. For a moment the tiger seemed to hang suspended in the air as the bullet tore a gaping hole in its throat; then it fell to the ground, inches from the elephant's tail, dull red soaking into its striped chest.

The mahout steered the trumpeting elephant around. From the small cloth bag tied to his waist he took out a handful of pebbles and threw them at the fallen tiger. One by one the pebbles bounced off and the animal did not twitch. Only then did the mahout stand on the elephant's head to shout that the tiger was dead.

Jaya felt her body shaking with fear. James Osborne put his arms around her, and she could smell the acrid gunpowder on his skin. He held her for a long moment until her shivering stopped. When she looked up, once again she felt she was swimming in the blue-green eyes as he said gently, 'Your first tiger, Princess. Congratulations.'

13

THE OSBORNES remained in Balmer after Tikka and James Osborne left for England. The Maharajah had asked Captain Osborne to assist him in expanding Balmer University.

A new science college became the focus of the evening gatherings in the King's View. Mr Roy and Captain Osborne often joined the Maharajah to study architectural plans, or draw up lists of names for possible professors. Only occasionally did Jai Singh refer to his son.

Tikka's letters from England bravely disguised his homesickness, but in the scribbled pages no friends were mentioned. Even the excited letter informing the Maharajah that Tikka had scored the highest number of runs in the school cricket game was followed by a terse note stating that he had not been selected to play in the school team.

Overhearing her brother's name, Jaya lingered at the doorway of King's View. 'You told my son cricket illustrated the British ideal of fair play, Captain-sahib. Why is my son not in the school team when he is a better cricketer than his fellow students?'

'If only we could rid the world of the cruelty of children, Your Highness . . .'

'Unfortunately, my son's exclusion was not brought about by the cruelty of children but by school rules which prohibit a native from equal participation in school activities. Rules that are similar to the practices of the Empire itself, wouldn't you say?'

Captain Osborne's face reddened, and Jaya did not think it

was from the glow of his cigar. 'Perhaps Tikka will profit from the experience and learn to stand on his own feet.'

Jai Singh moved to the parapet to look down at the lights of the city. 'It is curious how events repeat themselves, Captain-sahib. I did not understand that we must stand on our own feet, as you put it so admirably, until I visited your country. If England teaches my son, as it taught me, to hate injustice in those who are all-powerful, then I shall be content.'

But Jaya knew her father was not content. For no reason that she could fathom, the Maharajah instructed her to learn the texts on Rajniti, the classical art of government, which Tikka would have studied had he not been in England. Her music classes with the old Ustad, even the lessons with Mrs Roy, were curtailed, and now most of her time was spent in the Fort Library, a long chamber, running above the length of the old government offices, deserted since the construction of the State Secretariat.

Paintings of hundreds of figures deep in study or contemplation extended below the ceiling of the Fort Library. Jaya often climbed the library ladders for a closer look at the portraits of the great astronomer Maharajah Jai Singh of Jaipur or the famous scholar Maharajah Verma of Cochin. She enjoyed peering at the other paintings and guessing which figures represented Manu the Law Giver and Brighu the Prophet and Shankarcharya the Philosopher. Sometimes the armies of scholars – mathematicians, grammarians, poets, philosophers, scientists merged into a giant atlas of human thought, making her head swim as she balanced on the top rungs of the ladders.

When Jaya pulled out a volume from the bookshelves she had to hold the covers tight so that the palm-leaf pages with their illuminated borders and spidery Sanskrit script did not slip loose. Standing in the middle of the empty chamber, she would read aloud at random, marvelling how monumental each syllable sounded in the cadence of the line, as though written to be chanted by a hundred scholars at a time.

A dry cough would interrupt the echoes of her voice and Jaya would turn nervously, knowing the Raj Guru, the High Priest, of Balmer was in the room.

Jaya was a little afraid of the Raj Guru. He rose at three o'clock in the morning to perform his yogic disciplines before presiding over the daily state pujas at the Fort Temple. Then he worked for several hours on his own commentary on the *Arthasastra*, yet there was never a crease in his spotless silk dhoti and shawl, and Jaya had never seen him take so much as a sip of water, no matter how hot the afternoon.

Still, it was not the old High Priest's austerity or erudition that frightened Jaya but the knowledge that this fastidious scholar was the man who consecrated the rulers of Balmer.

So when the dry voice, like the sound of grass crackling in a summer dust storm, whispered, 'Name the four arms of kingship, Bai-sa,' Jaya stuttered in her anxiety to please him.

'*Saam*, a king must serve his people's needs. *Daan*, he must provide for their welfare. *Dand*, he must be implacable in the punishment of injustice. *Bhed*, he must intrigue on behalf of the kingdom, with treaties and alliances.'

'Name the duties of a king, Bai-sa.'

Jaya recited the many duties of a king

'And if a king fulfils all these duties, Bai-sa, what are his rewards?'

'Men bow their heads to him in recognition of his merit.'

'And if a king has no merit?'

'He forfeits the right to govern.'

'The Angrez have written of the divine right of kings. Do we hold this belief?'

'No, hukam; merit, not birth, is the attribute of kingship.'

'And how does a ruler gain knowledge of merit?'

'First he must study the *Arthasastra*'s texts on government and Rajniti.'

'Very good, Bai-sa. Now we will examine the teachings in the *Arthasastra*.'

Over the months, Jaya studied the *Arthasastra*'s tenets on civil and criminal jurisprudence. She learned that the revenue system of British India was still modelled on the revenue system of Chanakya. She was taught the different punishments to be meted out for crime and was surprised to learn that the harshest sentence was exile, and could not help thinking of Tikka's exile in the cold country of the Angrez.

The lessons in the Fort Library added to the contradictions that increasingly confused her. When the Raj Guru discoursed on monarchy in his dry whisper, Jaya believed the old priest was speaking of a world that was inviolable. Then, at her English lessons, Mrs Roy made the position of kings sound as precarious as that of men drowning in quicksand.

'Make a note of what has happened these last years, Bai-sa. The King of Portugal assassinated and Portugal declared a republic. The end of the Manchu Dynasty in China. The King of Greece assassinated by republicans. The Sultan of the Ottoman Empire practically deposed by revolutionaries who call themselves the Young Turks. The Prime Minister of the Russian Empire assassinated, with the Tsar unable to do anything while his wife allows a mad priest to rule Russia.

'And as for the mighty British Empire – in Ireland there is open rebellion against the Angrez. And here, a bomb was thrown at the Viceroy when he tried to make his triumphal entry into Delhi.' Mrs Roy gave a grim laugh. 'Mark my words, Bai-sa, the British Empire will bleed to death from the wounds inflicted by these two lances – Home Rule for Ireland, Home Rule for India.'

Sometimes Jaya felt that the evenings with Major Vir Singh were the only constant moments in her life. If he was pleased with her shooting, he took her to buy falcons from the falconers waiting outside the stables, the hooded birds clawing at their gloved hands. If she won his special approval, the Major permitted Jaya to ride with him to the cheetah cages, where the dangerous coursing cats, kept for the Maharajah's deer hunts, lapped warm blood from wooden gourds, tails twitching in warning, yellow eyes fixed on the riders.

WITHIN THE YEAR, construction began on the new college, and Mr Roy and Captain Osborne were often delayed at the building site. While the Maharajah waited for them, he sometimes asked Jaya to join him in the billiard room.

Flattered that the Maharajah was able to spare an hour of his time, Jaya climbed onto a high stool at one end of the billiard table. Long lights focused on the clay armies – soldiers, armoured elephants, cavalry units – covering the green baize that separated her from the bar of shadow falling across her father's face.

Grasping a silver cue with a carved hook, Jaya manoeuvred her forces around the billiard table, crowing with delight when her clay cavalry achieved a surprise approach from behind a papier-mâché mountain to capture her father's miniature cannons.

Once when Jaya was arranging the troops of the British Indian Army, the Maharajah asked, 'Has the Raj Guru taught you the four arms of kingship yet, Bai-sa?'

'Oh, Bappa, we finished that long ago.'

'Then you should be able to recite them to me.'

Jaya straightened in her chair. In a passable imitation of the Raj Guru she whispered, 'These are the four arms of kingship. A king must tend his people. He must provide for their welfare. He must be implacable in dispensing justice. A king must intrigue with other powers for the welfare of his state.'

She waited for her father to express approval. When he spoke, it was as though he had forgotten she was in the room.

'*Saam*, I tended my people, putting their survival above the vanities of an empire, and I was called seditious. *Daan*, I provided for the state, and my only son was taken hostage by the Angrez. *Dand*, how can I be just when I cannot give sanctuary to those who fight injustice in the British Raj or try a man who has the ear of the Angrez? What then remains of monarchy but *bhed*? Intrigue, flattery, imitation – the weakest arm of monarchy. This is what it means to be an Indian king in the British Empire.'

The Maharajah seized his cue. From the expression in his eyes Jaya knew this was no longer a game. There was a sudden desperation in his concentration, as if he were seeking a significant battle, some precise moment of inattention that had led rulers like himself to their present impotence.

An armoured elephant lay on its side. Above the howdah fluttered a simple red pennant emblazoned with the full sun, marking the Maharana of Udaipur's proud title 'Sun of the Hindus'. Jaya gently hooked her cue over the howdah. Her father's cue descended on top of hers.

'Forget Udaipur! His days are numbered. This morning the British took his mint. Now they are trying to gain possession of his mines. Udaipur's treaty has not protected him from Britain's greed.'

He shook his open palm at his frightened daughter. 'And the Maharajah of Baroda has been told by the British that if he continues to order books written by the republican writer Mazzini he will jeopardize his throne. Are we schoolchildren that our English masters dare tell us, the kings of India, what we may read?'

91

He swept the toy soldiers of the Manipur army to one side, and Jaya winced at the sound of breaking clay. 'Why waste time playing games of war? We have treaties with the British Raj. Let's see what their Pax Britannica has brought us. In the northeast, Manipur hanged. In the centre, Rewa gone. Indore threatened. In the Deccan, half of Hyderabad's kingdom removed on a viceroy's whim.'

The peculiar darkness lent a sinister edge to Jai Singh's anger as his hand swept down again and again on the map of India. 'To the west, Baroda threatened because he turned his back on the Angrez Emperor's coronation and reads books by Italian writers. Our proudest Rajput king, Udaipur, hanging by a thread to the honour that the Moghul Empire could not wrest by war but the British take by peace. In the south, thrones trembling because their kings dare to be more progressive than the Angrez themselves. All over India, rulers exiled or forced to abdicate while Britain replaces their ancient lines with lackeys.'

He turned from the room. 'Will our people ever forgive us for these ignoble treaties?'

Jaya looked around the table in horror. Broken elephants and horses were strewn against the cushioned sides, metal pins exposed, limbs sticking at strange angles into the green cloth.

Jaya wondered if she should write to Tikka about the Maharajah, then dismissed the thought, reluctant to add to the burden of unexpressed unhappiness in her brother's letters.

IN THE TWO years that Tikka had been in England, his letters reflected his natural high spirits only when he spent time with the Sirpur princes.

When the Sirpur Polo Team was competing for the Hurlingham Cup, Maharajah Victor invited Tikka to stay in his country house in Surrey.

'Maharajah Victor has a weakness for American film actresses and Prince Pratap likes French ladies,' Tikka wrote. 'I asked Prince Pratap why they don't ever spend time with Indian women. He said, "Because they are just a lot of overfed buffaloes." '

Another letter said, 'Prince Pratap has hired a Spaniard to teach me a new ballroom dance called the tango. It is all the rage this season. Prince Pratap calls anyone who cannot do it a peasant.

When I learn the tango he has promised to invite a film star for me and take us dancing at the Ritz.'

One evening she returned from the polo grounds to find a letter from Tikka lying on her bed. She tore open the envelope. A photograph fell to the ground. On the back Tikka had scribbled, '*At the Savoy to celebrate my birthday.*' Jaya turned the photograph over, and her heart lurched. James Osborne towered over her brother. The Angrez boy's long neck was no longer vulnerable, filling the stiff collar of his dress shirt like a marble column; and the youthful features had strengthened into a man's. But his mouth still turned in that half-shy, half-knowing smile.

Jaya tried not to resent Tikka's affection for the Sirpurs, and wished he would say more about James Osborne. Since leaving Balmer, the Angrez boy had written to Jaya twice a year – a card on her birthday and a letter at Christmas. His casual expressions of goodwill made her stomach somersault, and she was ashamed at the violence of her response.

14

ALARMED BY the changes in Jaya's education, the Maharani complained to Kuki-bai and the purdah ladies, 'Who will marry such an overeducated girl? Her in-laws will resent her. Her husband will be insulted when she flaunts her learning in front of him. She is twelve years old. At that age I was already engaged to be married. At the very time she should become a woman, her father is trying to make her into a son.'

With these words the Maharani announced her decision to undertake Jaya's training herself, and repair the damage done by the Raj Guru and the Maharajah.

Jaya was no longer able to spend the hot summer afternoons in Kuki-bai's chamber, listening to the old concubine's tales while the water-soaked vetiver screens cooled the painted room and the little bells tinkled on the chains of the swaying bed. Instead, she was surrounded by eager purdah ladies vying to teach her the sola shringar, the sixteen arts of being a woman.

Some of these arts Jaya knew already. Her body had always been massaged with turmeric paste to lighten its complexion. Her skin had always been rubbed with wheat and cream so that even the lightest down was removed. Now the purdah ladies brought ivory jars and glass caskets filled with unguents. Jaya sat on her mother's balcony, twisting her long plaits around her fingers as the purdah ladies droned on in the heat about the oils that restored life to dull hair after childbirth, the scents that heightened a body's natural odours to act as an aphrodisiac on the senses of a lover.

Some afternoons she was taken to the Baran's chambers. The purdah ladies unfolded stacks of garments, and the rita leaves that preserved the clothes dropped onto the floor like dun-coloured confetti as they taught her to match ornaments to clothes. They squatted around her, explaining which gemstones were auspicious for which occasions, and tried heavy earrings on her small earlobes, arguing over which nose ring would soften her sharp profile. They fastened anklets on her slender feet and made her pick her way between the clothes, shouting at her when she walked too quickly.

Jaya found their attentions oppressive and could not wait to escape to the cavalry grounds, where her humiliations were at least of her own making and not because her nose was too sharp or her skin too dark.

Major Vir Singh's indifference to the fact that she was a girl was most apparent at the tent-pegging session. Sometimes, she missed her peg as often as seven or eight times in an afternoon. The Major made her repeat the manoeuvre in front of all the officers. Embarrassed at having to ride down the field witnessed by men who had performed cavalry charges in China and who spent at least one day a week spearing wild boar in the nullahs beyond Jalsa Lake, she begged Major Vir Singh to allow her to practise on her own. He refused brusquely, and Jaya wondered if there was any truth in the Maharani's observation that the Maharajah was trying to make her into another son.

But the afternoons with the purdah ladies did not make her feel like a woman either.

'Look at all those old prunes who are teaching me the arts of the female,' she complained to her favourite maidservant, Chandni. 'They would frighten any man away.'

The maidservant, married for almost six months, replied loftily, 'What do they know, Bai-sa, locked away in the zenana? I can teach you to be a woman. A woman is a mood. My name is Chandni, moonlight, so I must always have some element of mystery about me, as there is in the moonlight.'

Jaya snorted in derision. 'Marriage has curdled your brains, Chandni. You never used to talk such nonsense before.'

'And too much riding and studying have turned yours, Bai-sa. You forget that you come from a great family and will have to make an important marriage. If you marry a ruling maharajah he will probably have other wives. He will certainly have a harem. How will you survive in such a crowd unless you understand the art of being a woman?'

'Hush, Chandni. You are telling me to be like a concubine. If my mother ever heard, she would dismiss you from the zenana.'

'The concubines know more about the art of being a woman than the purdah ladies. You could learn something from meeting them.'

Jaya clapped her hands over her mouth, and the maidservant laughed at her shocked expression.

'How could it be arranged, Chandni?' In Balmer's history only one concubine, Kuki-bai, had been elevated to the royal apartments out of respect for the Lion of Balmer's memory, and Jaya was intrigued at the thought of meeting those other women whose presence sat like a weight over the zenana, presenting the constant threat of an infatuated ruler raising a favoured concubine above his own wives, or even above his heir.

'I'll take you.'

'What if the eunuchs see me and tell my mother?'

'Those corrupt creatures? They spend their afternoons lying on their beds, gloating over the jewellery they have extorted from the concubines and planning new forms of blackmail. Don't worry. No one will know.'

Terrified by her clashing anklets, Jaya followed Chandni down the steep stairway to the dark corridors below the zenana. The passageways behind the storerooms twisted and turned, ending abruptly in front of a huge wooden door.

It swung noiselessly open. Jaya barely had time to smile at a dark-skinned concubine before Chandni took her hand and pulled her inside. Grey-haired women stood in the halls, whispering behind their hands.

An old woman stretched out her arms as the noise of anklets signalled Jaya's approach. Bony fingers clawed at Jaya's clothes. 'Is it true? Has a woman of the royal family come to visit us at last?'

Jaya gently pried the fingers loose, surprised at how fragile and weightless they were in her palm. Then she saw the cataracts over the woman's eyes and realized with horror that she was blind. The woman's quavering blessing followed Jaya down the corridor: 'Go with God, Bai-sa. Go with God.'

They entered a maze of courtyards, deserted except for monkeys bounding up the carved balconies. 'Where is everybody, Chandni? Why are there only old women in the harem?'

The dark-skinned concubine was urging them into a stone tunnel. Jaya stumbled, blinded by the unexpected darkness. Chandni grabbed her arms, supporting her towards the glimmer of illumination at the far end of the passage.

Suddenly the tunnel opened into an octagonal chamber, half the size of the Durbar Hall itself. The afternoon sun blazed through carved windows, fracturing in geometric shadows onto green malachite terraces where maidservants were tending wicker baskets filled with smoking incense.

A marble pool in the shape of a lotus dominated the chamber. Fresh rose petals had been sprinkled on the water. Under the petals Jaya saw another lotus, in palest pink marble, inlaid in the floor. Silver peacocks spouted jets of perfume into the pool, and half-clothed girls dangled their feet in the scented water, rose petals clinging to their skins.

The concubines surrounded Jaya.

'It is a hot afternoon, Bai-sa. Take off your clothes.'

'Come and swim with us, Bai-sa.'

Afraid of giving offence, Jaya reluctantly stepped out of her garments, and the concubines stared with frank interest at her naked body. Jaya grabbed at Chandni's veil to cover herself. The concubines laughed.

'We are all women here, Bai-sa.'

One of them patted the silk scarf that barely covered her ample breasts. 'But you are as slender and supple as a lotus stalk compared to me, Bai-sa.'

Another concubine stepped out of her thin muslin shift. 'Look at me, Bai-sa. I am like you. I have small breasts also. The purdah ladies are teaching you the sola shringar, but have they taught you this?' She took a wisp of silk, dipped it into a jar of red powder and spread a red shadow under her breasts to make them seem fuller.

A green chameleon with a tiny gold chain around its neck was placed on a concubine's lap, and it slowly faded, as though it were haemorrhaging colour onto her pale skin. The concubine turned to Jaya, swatches of coloured silks dangling from her fingers. 'You are a beautiful girl, Bai-sa. But suppose your husband thinks your breasts are too small? It is one thing to put shadows under them, but a man's hands learn a truth of their own.' She passed a piece of scarlet silk over the chameleon and its scales slowly took on a red glow. 'Suppose your husband does not approve of your dark skin. Or does not think green eyes are becoming in a woman. How will you keep his interest then?'

At the periphery of Jaya's vision, rose petals swirled slowly in the water. Hypnotized by the motion of the concubine's fingers, dazed by the unreality of the setting, Jaya was hardly able to concentrate on the concubine's words. 'No one understands how the attraction between a man and a woman is born, Bai-sa. Even worse, no one understands why it suddenly dies. We poor creatures must use every aid to keep a man's affections constant. Take the gold chain from your husband's neck and put it on a chameleon. Then you will always be able to control your husband.'

Jealous that the princess was being monopolized, the other concubines pulled at Jaya's hand, and Jaya felt herself sliding over the edge of the pool. The concubines splashed energetically around her, diving to grab her limbs. Water sprayed high into the air. Laughing mouths spouted perfumed water under eyelashes stuck together with petals. Long hair streamed down smooth brown limbs, plastered to breasts and slender waists. Aware of her own body for the first time, seeing it reflected in the women around her, Jaya felt her self-consciousness vanish.

She climbed out of the pool, and once again the concubines crowded around her, naked bodies dripping water onto the terrace. As Chandni dried her hair, the concubines spoke to Jaya of their families, of the poverty and ambition that had led parents to leave them outside the walls of the zenana. They told her about the malicious power of the eunuchs and the daily bribes the eunuchs forced them to pay. Haunted by their denied humanity, Jaya was relieved when Chandni pulled at her arm to leave.

At the door, she looked back and saw the concubines lying on the malachite terraces, drying their hair around the baskets filled with incense. Their long black hair had vanished into clouds of smoke, but their naked bodies shone like bronze stars against the green stone.

15

THROUGH THE MONTHS that Jaya's metamorphosis from girl to woman was being guided by the purdah ladies, she was barely conscious of events in the outside world. She knew that something sinister was happening in Europe because she often saw Mr Roy and Captain Osborne sitting knee to knee with her father around the large telegraph receiver in the King's View, reading out the news from London, and sometimes she overheard their worried voices discussing Kaiser Wilhelm.

'Europe is hardening into alliances which will almost certainly result in war,' the Maharajah observed worriedly. 'I don't like the idea of Tikka remaining in Europe at this time, but the Viceroy will not let the boy return to India.'

'Nothing can happen to Tikka in England, Your Highness,' Captain Osborne assured him. 'King George is not one of these excitable European fellows like the Tsar who let their wives run riot. He won't allow England to get into a mess, whatever happens in the rest of Europe.'

At the English lesson, Mrs Roy thrust a newspaper into Jaya's hands. 'The British nearly lost India in 1857 because they made Muslim soldiers grease their bullets with pork fat. Think how much worse it will be when war is declared and India's Muslims are asked to fight against the head of their faith, the Sultan of Turkey.'

Jaya stared inattentively at Mrs Roy, the newspaper stretched between her hands. The tutor sighed in exasperation. 'Bai-sa, do pay attention. Even with all your daydreaming you must have heard of the man the Angrez are hoping to make into the new leader of Indian

Muslims in case Britain goes to war against the Sultan of Turkey. Haven't you noticed how this Aga Khan person is suddenly to be seen with the Viceroy at every important function?'

'Mrs Roy, is it true that if you lie with your husband on the night before a big puja you will give birth to a demon?'

Mrs Roy swept the newspaper out of Jaya's hands, then paused when she saw the anxiety in the green eyes. 'Where on earth did you hear such nonsense, Bai-sa?'

'From the purdah ladies. They said if I conceive at the time of the full moon I will bear a blind son, and the concubines told me to keep a chameleon with a gold chain around its neck if I want my husband to stay faithful, and—'

Mrs Roy tightened the cotton sari around her thin waist. 'What do concubines know about childbirth? They are kept as slaves for one man's pleasure. They make up these tales to console themselves for the children they will never be permitted to bear.'

'No, Mrs Roy. You don't understand. This is the wisdom of the harem passed down through generations of concubines.'

'It is the foul stench of ignorance,' Mrs Roy said severely. And if you do not attend to your lessons, Bai-sa, you will become as superstitious as the concubines. Repeat what I have just told you about the Aga Khan.'

A maidservant interrupted the lesson with a summons from the Maharani. Relieved to escape Mrs Roy's disapproval, Jaya followed the maid from the room.

On the zenana balcony, the Maharani and Kuki-bai were examining the papers lying on a table between them. A group of purdah ladies settled themselves on the carpets, giggling as the Maharani took Jaya's chin in her long fingers and tilted it toward the open window. 'What do they call this light, child?'

The evening breeze from Jalsa Lake felt cool on Jaya's face. 'The cow-dust hour, hukam. The hour when the farmers herd their grazing cattle home.'

The Maharani smiled. 'In eastern India, this light is thought to make a woman appear at her most beautiful. They call this the hour of the bride.'

The purdah ladies chorused their assent.

'How true, Maharani-sahib.'

'See how Bai-sa's skin glows in this light.'

The Maharani released her daughter's chin. 'Your father has finally agreed that you must be betrothed. After all, you are a woman now, nearly thirteen years old. You will be attending the manwar ceremony for the first time this year.' She waved towards the photographs on the table. 'These are from the families whose sons have been suggested for you.'

Jaya glanced at the scattered images. Turbaned strangers sat on heavy Victorian chairs, elbows resting on tables crowded with signed portraits of European monarchs. Other strangers leaned on bolster cushions and pulled at hookahs. A few photographs had been tinted, and bright green plants and unnaturally red lips broke the monotony of those portraits.

The Maharani picked up a tinted photograph. 'Look, Kuki-bai. Wouldn't he make a good husband for Bai-sa?'

The old concubine held the portrait close to her watering eyes. 'He is no prince. With those small eyes, he must be a moneylender.'

'Well, this one is definitely a maharajah. A thirteen-gunner.'

'No amount of thirteen-gun salutes is going to change this family's preferences. The whole of India knows they are pederasts.'

At a third portrait Kuki-bai sneered, 'Are those legs or what? His feet don't even touch the ground.'

The purdah ladies snatched at the portraits, snickering at the old concubine's caustic observations. Jaya wanted to laugh too, but alarm knotted her stomach when she saw the Maharani's expression of disapproval.

With studied indifference the Maharani examined each compartment of her betel-nut casket. Finally she extracted a wet betel leaf and began smearing lime paste onto it. Even the purdah ladies were silenced by the Maharani's demeanour. They watched nervously as she dusted the paan leaf with a pinch of pure tobacco, secured the ends with a clove and pushed the paan into the side of her mouth.

The Maharani chewed slowly on the paan, spitting red betel juice at intervals into a nearby spittoon. At last she said, 'As you are so critical, Kuki-bai, perhaps you would care to suggest a bridegroom for Bai-sa?'

The concubine accepted the challenge. 'If only the Angrez boy, Jam-iss, were one of us, he would be my first choice. . . .'

The blood rushed to Jaya's face, and the purdah ladies stared at her in concern.

'As he is not, we must be practical about Bai-sa's future. First, she will live in a world where the Angrez have undisputed power, so she should marry into a kingdom friendly to the British Raj, like the kingdom of Gwalior. Second, she has been taught all this business with guns and tent-pegging, so she must definitely marry a good sportsman, like Maharajah Ranji or the Maharajah of Cooch Behar. Third, she is highly educated, so her husband must be an erudite man like the present rulers of Mysore and Baroda.'

Kuki-bai dropped her hands. 'Since these rulers are already married, I can see only one proposal that satisfies Bai-sa's requirements. Prince Pratap of Sirpur.' Jaya shook her head furiously, but the old concubine ignored her. 'There are other things I like about the Sirpur boy also. . . .'

Jaya could not contain herself. 'He is not a boy, Kuki-bai. He is a man.'

The purdah ladies laughed uproariously at Jaya's outburst. 'And what good would a boy be on your wedding night, Bai-sa?'

'You will need a man to turn you into a woman, Bai-sa.'

'An excellent suggestion, Kuki-bai.' The Maharani nodded her approval. 'Prince Pratap is a modern prince. His grandmother, the Dowager Maharani of Sirpur, has already expressed delight with Jaya's education.'

Jaya stared at her mother as though she were a cobra. The Maharajah had expressly forbidden any marriage alliance with Sirpur.

The Maharani said gently, 'Your father's antagonism to the Empire is so widely known you can be married only where there is no fear of the Angrez, Bai-sa. The Sirpurs are close to the British. A marriage with Balmer could not endanger them.' Jaya lowered her eyes, and the Maharani took her hand. 'Still, if you prefer one of the other men, we will consider the proposal.'

That night, the Baran came to Jaya's room with a box containing the photographs and miniatures. Jaya held the pictures to the light of the lamp, and the maidservants pressed her feet in silent sympathy, knowing the intensity of speculation that centred on each portrait as Jaya searched the features of strangers for some map of her own future.

When the maids left, Jaya took out the photograph of James Osborne. She studied it in anguish. There was something so clean about the Angrez, so untouched by the rigid traditions which tainted the faces of the men whose portraits she had examined while the rest of the zenana slept.

Hoping to reverse her mother's decision, Jaya decided to petition her father against the marriage. But when she reached the billiard room, the velvet covers were still on the table. The clay armies and silver cues had not been set out. Jaya sat on the edge of a bench, staring at the table standing like an empty altar under the triangular lights.

The Maharajah entered the room waving a buff-coloured envelope. From long experience Jaya knew it was a communication from the British.

The Maharajah's eyes were alight in a way Jaya had not seen in a long time. 'Tikka is coming home!'

Jaya cleared the distance between her father and herself in one leap. Laughing, Jai Singh caught her in his arms. 'He boards ship next month and he will be in Balmer by the end of July.'

'Oh, Bappa, we must have a big fireworks display. You know how Tikka loves fireworks. And then—'

The Maharajah shook her shoulders. 'Tikka is returning to Balmer because there is fear of war in Europe.'

'The Europeans are always fighting somewhere! Now, let's see. We will have to get records from Bombay and a phonograph of course. Tikka can do ballroom dancing, even the tango, and he will have to teach me!'

The Maharajah's stern voice cut into her incoherent plans. 'Baisa! If there is a war, Balmer will have to send troops. We cannot celebrate one son's return when five hundred others are going to war. Captain Osborne's son, James, has already joined his father's regiment. Things are moving so quickly that the boy is remaining in England to be close to the front if England enters the war.'

Unaware of the shock in his daughter's eyes, he added, 'It is a pity Tikka cannot reach Balmer in time for the manwar ceremony.'

16

The MANWAR ceremony was an exuberant celebration of the warrior caste. In the outer Fort the nagara drums were beaten for the men, and all through the night the bards sang the glories of past battles. But the manwar ceremony of the zenana was shrouded in secrecy.

From early that morning the eunuchs sat in the zenana courtyard choosing opium pellets as hard as areca nuts, discarding any pellet from which the resin still leaked.

The eunuchs knew other caches of opium were hidden in the concubines' chambers, under ivory beds or behind painted windows. They even knew that enterprising maidservants sometimes visited the houses of pleasure in Balmer City to obtain the precious white-lightning powder from South America for their sequestered charges. But these drugs might not be of the best quality, capable of rendering the most powerful women in the kingdom indiscreet.

The Chief Eunuch grunted with effort as he struck a particularly hard opium pellet with his pestle. 'This is for the wife of the Prime Minister, that dried old bamboo!'

Shrill laughter echoed in the courtyard as the eunuchs ground the opium pellets into paste, regaling one another with tales of the past misbehaviour of the ladies. The laughter died abruptly as the Household Controller approached. Now the eunuchs became obsequious, trailing behind the Controller into the stone corridor leading to the lower Fort.

The Controller slid aside the heavy bolt on the palace cellar and turned up the flame of his kerosene lantern. Suddenly the room was ablaze with reflections from rows of bottled asha, the spirit drunk by Rajput warriors.

There were ashas made from sapphires. Other bottles took their colours from amethysts, turquoises, emeralds. One shelf held the rich red asha, a century old, into which palace brewers had crushed rubies from Burma; another shelf, the asha made from black pearls.

In Jaya's apartments, her maidservants had laid out long skirts with matching chemises on the bed. At thirteen years of age, Jaya was more than a little self-conscious about her appearance, and she changed fretfully from the orange skirt to the yellow one, trying to forget Mrs Roy's remarks at her lessons the day before.

'So at last you are being allowed to celebrate your warrior blood, Bai-sa,' Mrs Roy had said. 'You Rajputs are so vain about your courage. But I am told the manwar ceremony consists of women drinking themselves into insensibility so they can speak the names of men whose children they have borne.'

'The ladies never take their husband's names, Mrs Roy. It would be disrespectful. My mother has never spoken my father's name, no matter how intoxicated she becomes.' Mrs Roy had waited for Jaya to add something to her lame explanation, but Jaya had known she could never make Mrs Roy understand why the Balmer ladies had to become intoxicated before they dared speak those names, which dismantled whole lifetimes of custom. When she remained silent, Mrs Roy had said, 'Suppose your husband is cruel. How will you resist him when you dare not speak his name? Remember, Bai-sa, even small children are taught to call things by their right names. It prevents confusion later.'

The maidservants peered through the windows at the terrace filling up with women, urging Jaya to hurry. A distance from the visiting wives, the zenana concubines sat on carpets, watching the eunuchs fill the glasses of the guests with asha. The laughter of the visiting ladies rose above the voices of concubines humming scales to each other. Later, as the visitors got drunk or began hallucinating under the influence of opium, the gentle voices of the concubines would cease embroidering classical airs.

Still dissatisfied with her appearance, Jaya took her place next to the Maharani and tipped a glass of ruby asha to her lips. The Maharani pointed to the Prime Minister's wife: 'They say you are the bravest woman in all Balmer. You shall have the honour of commencing the ceremony.'

'Well, hukam, I call my husband . . . that is to say, I call the father of my children . . . that is, the person who is the Maharajah's Prime Minister . . . well, I call him . . . uh . . . Andatta.' The Prime Minister's wife smiled with relief as she ended her speech.

'This is not a name!' shouted a young woman with plump cheeks. 'Andatta means provider of seed. That is a *function*.' She prodded the Prime Minister's wife's angular hip. 'But we all know how he provides *you* with seed.'

The visiting ladies giggled hysterically as the Maharani motioned to another woman, who pulled her veil down until it almost covered her face, muffling her words.

The eunuchs placed honey and liquid opium in front of the ladies. Jaya's head was already swimming, and she held her glass carefully, afraid her fingers would inadvertently crush the glass like an eggshell.

The visitors tossed back the opium, removing the bitter aftertaste with honey. Thalis heaped with spiced meats and saffron rice were brought onto the terrace. The rich smell of food, mixed with the musky scents of the ladies' attars, hung over the hot afternoon like incense.

On an ordinary day, the ladies would now retire to their siestas, and gossip with the women of the household. This afternoon, they curled like sleepy cats on the bolster cushions, the absence of men suggesting desire more acutely than if men had been lying between them. Perceiving their lethargy, a bright-eyed concubine sang mischievously:

> See, her body is as hot
> As a tava heated on the coals.
> Poor man, he is only cold dough,
> But he will rise like fresh bread
> Between her thighs.

The visiting ladies screamed in mock horror and fell laughing into each other's arms. Two concubines grabbed an oblong drum and placed it between their knees. The eunuchs crowded around them, clapping to the accelerating beat. One eunuch began singing in a high-pitched voice:

106

> *Oh, there is a lovely woman*
> *Who lives in a magic garden*
> *Filled with honey and fruit.*
> *But the gate to her magic garden*
> *Lies, alas, between her thighs . . .*

He raised his eyebrows archly, and another eunuch took up the song:

> *Oh, there is a great warrior.*
> *Between his thighs*
> *He has a thick knobbed stick*
> *As round as my arm . . .*
> *As long as my leg . . .*

The concubines groaned with simulated desire. Coquettishly covering their faces, both eunuchs sang together:

> *For so long the great warrior*
> *Has tried to enter the magic garden*
> *To speak of love to the lovely woman,*
> *But she will only let him*
> *Knock*
> *Knock*
> *Knock*
> *At her gate!*

Now the concubines and eunuchs began competing with each other in the lewdness of their song. The visiting ladies, immobilized by opium, ceased pretending outrage. There were songs of eager breasts and restless thighs, of organs the size of a peanut and organs the size of a crocodile. Dusk fell and still the songs continued, while the insistent drumbeat filled the terrace, plunging like a phallus through the high voices.

Clay lamps and bronze candelabra were brought onto the terrace. Bats dipped over the courtyard like great black kites swooping in a monsoon breeze. As night descended on the courtyard the music turned melancholic. Songs of unfulfilled desire hung heavy in the air.

A pretty young concubine was smiling at another concubine holding a sitar to her shoulders. The musician's sweet voice lifted in the night:

She takes no pleasure in the palace courtyards,
She avoids the parks,
She turns her back on her painted playmates,
Her gossamer veil burns her fingers
With the heat of her desire . . .

Jaya recognized the song. It was the prayer of a devotee which the Maharani often sang in the temple. Now the concubine's voice caressed the darkness, imbuing each word of the hymn with erotic suggestion.

Murmurs of appreciation rose from the somnolent shapes lying on the mattresses, and sexual longing seeped into the marble courtyard like moisture. The visiting ladies moved on the mattresses, whispering their husband's names into the nearest ear. The Maharani motioned the eunuchs to offer trays of sweets to the visitors, and grotesque shadows slid across the walls as the eunuchs passed between the candelabra with their offerings.

Jaya's head felt as though it were floating several feet above her neck. She couldn't move her eyes from the twin turrets at the end of the zenana, stone prisons built by a jealous ruler to incarcerate two concubines who had become lovers. Jaya knew that the imprisoned concubines had died of old age in their separate towers, never again looking upon another human face, and she had heard the purdah ladies whisper to one another that the towers were haunted, that on nights of the full moon the stone walls grew damp with the tears of the separated lovers.

The singer turned her head, long eyes closed as though absorbed in a trance:

Absent, He sets my limbs on fire;
When near, He makes me jealous . . .

Jaya stared at the singer, wondering what it was like to spend a lifetime waiting on the pleasure of a king, adorning oneself for seduction, listening night after night for the sound of a maharajah's footstep outside the chamber, knowing it might never come. The smiling concubine still had not moved her gaze from the singer. A gentle sadness shaded the singer's features. Then the long eyes opened, and the singer reached across her instrument to touch the pretty concubine's forehead.

108

Seen, He steals my heart away;
When near, I am in his power ...

With sudden ferocity Jaya remembered strong arms around her own body, the smell of salt and gunpowder on skin, deep blue eyes smiling down at her, pulling her into them like the undertow on Jalsa Lake when it was swollen with monsoon rain.

17

THE TEDIOUS weeks till Tikka's return were made longer by the savage heat of summer, but the purdah ladies could hardly contain their anticipation.

'Sixteen years old! Your parents won't worry about you any more, Bai-sa.'

'The Maharani will be looking for a bride for your brother.'

'And he is England-returned! Only the best states will be considered now!'

For Jaya, the preoccupations of the zenana were little distraction from the thought of James Osborne on his way to war.

Every evening, she stood anxiously in a corner of the King's View while electric fans whirred behind blocks of ice to cool the terrace and insects spun through the air like black dust. Names which Jaya half remembered from Mrs Roy's lessons gained a chilling significance as the clerks read aloud news of the latest developments in Europe.

The war receded briefly into the background with Tikka's arrival. Cannons were fired from the Fort, and the Maharajah held a welcome durbar for his son. The fireworks display was brought to an abrupt halt as the first storm of the monsoons deluged the courtyards with water. Wringing their turbans dry, the villagers told each other that Tikka's return was auspicious for the kingdom.

As soon as the ceremonies of return ended, Tikka stopped visiting the zenana. On her way to the Fort Library, Jaya would find him running behind Mr Roy. 'Is it true the Japanese used poison gas against the Russians? Do you think the Germans will use gas in Europe?'

Through the library windows she could hear his urgent questions, followed by the patient tones of Major Vir Singh or the Commander-in-Chief, explaining the firing capacity of the Hotchkiss gun, trench mortars, the Maxim gun.

Each evening, Tikka was the first person in the small drawing room adjoining the King's View where the telegraph had been moved at the onset of the monsoons, waiting eagerly for news that England had mobilized.

When Jaya told Tikka of the Maharani's decision that she must marry Prince Pratap of Sirpur, Tikka brushed her aside. 'You needn't worry about all that. Prince Pratap is not thinking of marriage. He is taking the Sirpur Lancers to Europe.'

And when she asked shyly about James Osborne, Tikka's features creased with envy. 'He has already joined Captain Osborne's regiment. I bet he sees active service before I do.'

On a stormy August night, Jaya ran through the puddles from the zenana to the King's View to find everyone in the drawing room crowded around the telegraph machine. The sound of clacking keys was drowned by the heavy downpour beating against the stone walls as they waited for the long transmission to end. At last, the clerk handed the message to the ruler, and the Maharajah read the message aloud: 'Yesterday the Prime Minister, Mr Asquith, informed Parliament that Germany had been given an ultimatum expiring at midnight. The Speaker of the House and Members rose to their feet as the Prime Minister read out a Mobilization Proclamation from His Majesty, George V, King of England and Emperor of India. At midnight Great Britain declared war on Germany and Austria. Also yesterday, Japan declared war on Russia and the —'

Captain Osborne was on his feet before the Maharajah had finished. 'Your Highness, I must leave immediately to rejoin my regiment.'

The Maharajah motioned to the aides standing behind his chair. They followed Captain Osborne from the room. The Maharajah turned to Mr Roy. 'You and your wife will teach our troops the rudiments of the English language. The men must be able to read simple road signs and maps in case they are cut off from their regiments.'

He beckoned to Major Vir Singh. 'Inform the Senapathy that all troops are to be put on battle alert from tomorrow morning. Full combat training is to commence immediately.'

Major Vir Singh raised his arm. 'Bal-hukam!' Jaya huddled in her chair. It was the first time she had heard the battle cry of Balmer spoken in time of war.

IN THE DRIVING monsoon rain, Jaya and Tikka rode to the cavalry grounds to watch the Balmer Lancers being drilled. The Senapathy, the Commander-in-Chief, sat astride his horse at the edge of the field as the two companies of Lancers, three hundred cavalrymen in all, practised their manoeuvres under the command of Major Vir Singh.

The precision of their formations when they wheeled at the trot on the waterlogged field, the magnificence of the full charge as all three hundred Lancers thundered down the field, regimental pennants whipping in the rain, made war appear a brilliant spectacle of glory, and Tikka became increasingly desperate to join them.

The whole of India seemed drunk on the war. In the King's View the telegraph keys clacked out the numbers of men who had volunteered for army service that day, and at Jaya's lessons, Mrs Roy threw her nationalist journals in front of Jaya. 'Look at these newspapers! Hundreds of thousands of Indians have already volunteered for the army. Do they think the British Empire will be grateful for such sacrifice?'

Ignoring Mrs Roy's anger, every morning Jaya joined Tikka to watch the mounted manoeuvres and the rifle practice. In the afternoons they followed Major Vir Singh around the stables, oblivious of the rain soaking through their garments as the Major inspected bits and harnesses, berating the sowars, the grooms, who would accompany the troops to Europe if he found even a smudge of rust on the metal. In the evenings they sat in the archive rooms, helping the exhausted soldiers to master the English alphabet, staying on when the Senapathy entered with his maps of Europe marked with thick black arrows and listening to him describe the movements of the armies of Russia, France, Great Britain, Germany and Austria.

The Maharajah was in constant communication with Sir Pratap Singh, the Regent King of Jodhpur, who had led the Balmer Lancers in China. At the age of seventy years, Sir Pratap had once again been appointed Commander-in-Chief of the Imperial State Forces, the cavalry regiments from the kingdoms of India.

At last the Maharajah received news that Sir Pratap was taking the first contingent of Imperial Service Troops to Europe. 'They leave tomorrow. Our troops are to travel with the second contingent.'

Jai Singh looked down at the telegram with a grim smile, and the gathering in the King's View watched him in silence. 'Sir Pratap has sent me the details of the troops raised by the Indian kingdoms. Fifteen cavalry regiments. Thirteen infantry battalions. Three Camel Corps, to be used as infantry on the western front or for desert warfare in defence of the Suez Canal. Two mountain batteries. Supporting services of medics and transport units. I need hardly say these contributions are far in excess of the requirements of our treaties.'

Ignoring the anger in his father's voice, Tikka leaped from his chair. 'If our Lancers are travelling with the second contingent, there is still time for me to join.'

'Don't talk like a fool, Tikka! You are only sixteen years old.'

'Sir Pratap is taking the Maharajah of Jodhpur. He is only sixteen. And he is also taking his own son, Hanut Singh, who is even younger than I am – he's not even fifteen yet.'

'That is Sir Pratap's affair. I will not allow my son to come to the aid of the British Raj.'

'But the Balmer Lancers are going. It is a matter of honour that one of us lead them!'

'What honour is there in strengthening those who have made us a subject people, forced to plead for what is ours? I am accepting an intolerable blackmail to consolidate your rightful position as heir to the Balmer gaddi.'

In bitter arguments between father and son October crawled by. Tikka received a letter from Prince Pratap of Sirpur when the Sirpur Lancers arrived in France. '*Six Rajput Kings are fighting in this war. Your men will never forgive you if you do not take part in what people here are already calling the Great War.*'

Crumpling the letter into a ball, Tikka flung it at the wall. 'Six Rajput kings! Why must Bappa cut off our noses with dishonour? Sending our troops to the battlefield without a member of the royal house to lead them!'

'But, Tikka, no member of the family led our troops in China.'

'I was not old enough then. Now I am.'

Sir Pratap sent a telegram from London issuing instructions that all ranks of the Imperial Service Troops were to familiarize themselves with the bayonet in case they were asked to fight as infantry. When they found straw dummies waiting on the cavalry ground the bayonets fixed to their rifles, the Balmer Lancers refused to dismount from their horses. They demanded the Senapathy call the Maharajah.

Jai Singh rode onto the cavalry ground and patiently explained why the bayonet exercises were necessary, but the Lancers remained rebellious.

'We are cavalry, hukam. We ride into battle. We do not crawl on the ground with knives fixed to our guns waiting to disembowel the unsuspecting.'

'Have you heard the cries used by the Indian Army soldiers when they make a bayonet charge? Only the godless Angrez officers could have made abuse of mothers and daughters into a battle cry, hukam.'

'If we died with those words on our lips, raping the honour of women, we would not die as warriors. The pandits would refuse to cremate us according to our caste.'

The Maharajah counselled them to use their own battle cry. When that did not placate them, Jai Singh said harshly, 'You speak of honour but forget your oath of obedience to the Balmer Durbar. As your Durbar, and the voice of your assemblies, I demand this obedience.'

Tikka jerked angrily at his horse's reins. 'This is only the first of many strange and distasteful things the Lancers will see abroad. Bappa is foolish not to send me with them to calm their fears.'

Jaya dug her heels into her horse and galloped after him.

At the far end of the Fort, a small temple broke the line of jagged battlements. Tikka dismounted and flung himself against the temple wall. 'Why can't Bappa see reason? If I go to France, all of Bappa's sins will be wiped away with one stroke. The British don't understand the pride we have in our dharma as warriors. Both our pride and our honour are heathen to them. I tell you, the only way to make them respect us is to impress them by their own standards.'

Jaya remembered her brother's fury when Raja Man Singh had sent John to the British school and Bappa had refused to let Tikka go too. Now Tikka was a man. In less than a month he would be seventeen years old. There was a determination in his voice that had been lacking in the frustrations of the boy.

Tikka pulled at her hand and dragged her to a stone image of the Goddess tilting against a broken pillar. Vermilion marked the idol's forehead and a few fresh flowers curled on its teet, showing that someone in the Fort still came to worship here. 'Before the Goddess I take this oath. I will take the Balmer Lancers to France. With or without Bappa's blessing. Even if I have to join hands with Raja Man Singh against him.'

A WEEK BEFORE the Lancers departed to board ship for Europe, there was a full-dress parade of the troops. Tikka sat astride his horse next to Jaya, sullenly watching the Senapathy issue orders to the Lancers. The first hint of winter chilled the wind blowing through the battlements, and the pennants of the Lancers, embroidered with the icons of past battles, floated like colourful bunting above the sowars standing to attention, their hobnailed boots and white puttees contrasting with their orange turbans.

Major Vir Singh rode to the front of the parade carrying the Balmer flag. For a moment the heavy crimson banner was lifted by the wind, revealing a great bird with a gout of flesh gripped in its left claw: the Balmer crest, a bird of prey feeding on the carrion of fallen enemies.

Jai Singh's white horse trotted slowly past the targets rising at the end of the field. The Maharajah was dressed in the garments of war. On his head was the red turban that signified shakti, power. The sun struck shafts of light from the two enormous diamonds enclosing a ruby on the armlet worn high on his right biceps. The diamonds represented the eyes of a warrior, the ruby the energy of the sun, and the armlet itself signified the strength of a warrior's sword arm. A thick red cummerbund encircled his waist, and the Balmer sword slapped against his right leg as he reined his horse in front of the Lancers, motionless on their horses.

Major Vir Singh dipped the banner, shouting the war cry of the Rajputs: 'Jai Mata ki! Victory to the Goddess!'

Five hundred men responded with the battle cry of the kingdom: 'Bal-hukam! By the command of Balmer!'

Jai Singh raised his voice to address his troops. 'Lancers of Balmer! Fourteen years ago you went to the aid of the Angrez in Peking. Today you go to their aid in France. England has not honoured its treaties with us, and none can say that we have eaten England's salt. But the British Empire is at war and our treaty demands that we send troops to aid them. Once again you are the proof of Balmer's honour, and this time the world will bear witness.'

'Bal-hukam!' the ancient oath of acquiescence echoed around the cavalry ground.

'You all know that the premier Rajput ruler, the Maharana of Udaipur, the Sun of the Hindus, has refused to fight, saying the war of a foreign usurper cannot be an honourable war for Rajputs. He has insulted the British Empire by paying the Empire money to hire other soldiers. For this insult the Maharana of Udaipur and the Rajput warriors of his kingdom have been called cowards in the messes of the Indian Army – that army of mercenaries where no Indian, not even a warrior, is allowed to hold the rank of officer.'

The atmosphere changed on the cavalry ground as the ruler's voice, strong with controlled rage, shouted, 'I say to these Angrez officers who draw their wages from war, by what right do they call Udaipur a coward? Let them call up the ghosts of a thousand kings who have died in battle, ten thousand queens who have burned themselves for honour, before they dare speak the word coward to the scion of Chittore and the line of Rana Pratap.'

A roar of agreement swept across the open field.

'It will never be said the Balmer Lancers fought for payment. We are kshatriyas, the warrior caste. We fight for dharma. On the battlefield you are the standard-bearers of Rajput honour, vindicating the valour of the Maharana of Udaipur and every other Rajput warrior who does not have the good fortune to ride at your side.'

He drew a paper from his tunic. 'I have today received a communication from Sir Pratap Singh of Jodhpur. The British Empire wanted us to police its Suez Canal. Sir Pratap ignored orders and took our troops to France and to war, cabling this explanation to the Viceroy: "TO US KSHATRIYAS THE CHANCES OF UPHOLDING OUR DHARMA ARE RARE."'

Jai Singh looked at the end of the field where Jaya and Tikka were sitting on their horses. 'My son has asked long and bitterly to be allowed to fulfil his dharma. After reading Sir Pratap's message to the Viceroy I can no longer find it in my heart to refuse. Let it be known that my son, who will one day be your king, takes my place beside you on the battlefield.'

Tikka's bellow of triumph was almost drowned by the battle cries bursting from five hundred throats. 'Jai Mata ki! Victory to the Goddess!' The litany of blood echoed off the ramparts. Visualizing the stone idol in the Fort temple with the garland of skulls around her neck, Jaya suddenly understood why, from the whole pantheon of divinity, it was the Goddess whose name was invoked in time of war.

THE ZENANA was thrown into chaos at the news of Tikka's departure. The purdah ladies insisted on making Tikka's uniforms with their own hands, cutting the thick cloth with their heavy steel scissors as the Maharani recited mantras of protection for her son.

Tikka's menservants soaked yards of orange muslin in starch. Jaya stood forlornly in a corner of her brother's room watching the servants wind the wet cloth around her brother's head, before placing the turbans on the window ledge where the sun would dry them into shape.

Tikka's guns were dismantled and laid in pieces on the bed. Jaya polished the barrel of his rifle with a chamois cloth while Tikka oiled his shotgun.

'I can hardly wait to see James's face when we meet in France. By the way, I hope you are sending something for him.'

'I've already packed a shawl and written a letter. How should I address him? Is "Esteemed James-sahib" all right?'

Tikka almost dropped the steel rod. 'Don't be so silly, Jaya. You should write "My dear James".'

'That is too intimate. What would he think?'

'He would think you had learned something better than babu English from Mrs Roy.'

'If we show respect, it is considered uneducated? No wonder people call the Angrez junglies.'

'All right, all right. What have you said in your letter?'

Jaya pulled a paper from the waistband of her skirt and shyly read it out. 'Dearest friend of my brother, esteemed James-sahib. You have been on the battlefield three months. Every day of that time we have done a puja for you in my mother's temple. I see the Goddess very well by the light of the lamps. Be assured you have her protection. Now we are sending my brother and his Lancers to your assistance. With the aid of Tikka Raja of Balmer and the Balmer Lancers you must surely win this war. With deepest respect from your friend's sister, Rajkumari Jaya of Balmer.'

Tikka saw tears swimming in the green eyes and put his arms around her shoulders. 'Now, Bai-sa,' he scolded gently. 'You know Rajput princesses are not allowed to cry. Especially on the eve of a warrior's departure.'

'First you were sent away to England. Now you are going to France. And if anything should happen to you. . . .'

Tikka hugged her and went back to assembling his weapons. 'Nothing is going to happen to me. I shall defeat the Huns with some splendid cavalry charges and return to entertain your bride-groom with bloodcurdling war stories.' Jaya winced, and he shook his finger mockingly at her. 'Remember what the Raj Guru says, Jaya. Duty is honour. These are our duties. War for me, Bai-sa. A bridegroom for you.'

On the night before Tikka's departure the women of the harem queued to mark his forehead with vermilion and sprinkle his turban with petals that had been offered to the Goddess in the Temple of the Balmer Maharanis.

The Maharani lifted a goblet of asha, offering it as a mother's libation of courage to a son departing to the battlefield. Tikka emptied the goblet and bent to touch her feet. For a long moment the Maharani's pale hands rested on her son's black hair; then Tikka left the balcony.

'Stand up, Jaya. The Baran is going to dress you for tomorrow's puja. There must be no mistakes. Any error made by a sister doing the puja when a brother goes to war would be most inauspicious.'

Jaya was awed by her mother's control, giving no indication of the anguish she must feel that the son of whom she had been deprived for more than three years was leaving her again, this time for war.

The Baran took out a jewelled ornament in the shape of a large berry and twisted it into the hair above the centre of Jaya's forehead.

'A thousand years ago, we came as warriors to this desert. Our only food was the fruit of the bher tree. Out of respect, we wear an ornament in the shape of that fruit at the highest point of our body.'

The purdah ladies helped to fasten heavy jewelled collars around Jaya's throat.

'Our treasuries were converted into gems, easy to carry as we moved from battlefield to battlefield. While our men were at war, our women guarded the nation's wealth. Your jewellery symbolizes that guardianship.'

The Baran unwrapped a large bundle.

'The clothing you will wear at the time of the puja recalls the colour of the Goddess.' Jaya put on the long skirt and chemise, dyed to deep crimson, and could not help thinking it was also the colour of blood.

From the last parcel the Baran unfolded a veil, which she draped over Jaya's head.

'In time of war, the royal women were charged with securing the Fort. Tomorrow your body will be veiled with the battlements of our citadel. Remember, the sanctity of Balmer Fort passes into your care when you put the tilak of blood on your brother's forehead. . . .' The Maharani's voice broke for the first time. Jaya could feel the tears pricking her own eyes, and she stared at the ramparts of Balmer Fort embroidered onto her veil, trying not to cry in front of the purdah ladies.

EARLY THE NEXT morning Jaya dressed in the puja garments and took her place in the forecourt of the Fort Temple next to the Raj Guru and Maharajah Jai Singh. In front of them, a ram pawed and butted at the stake which tethered it to a stone ditch.

The Lancers' horses were lined up on one side of the temple, nuzzling against the sowars holding their reins. The other side of the temple was blocked by the tusker, Moti. The nagara drums from the gateway of the Fort, each immense drum itself the size of an elephant, were strapped on the tusker's back, and Moti's mahout was crouched forwards on the elephant's neck to make room for the drummers.

Three hundred Lancers in dress uniforms, headed by Tikka

and Major Vir Singh, sat on the ground outside the temple, their brightly polished weapons – lances, rifles, bayonets, swords – lying in neat rows on the red carpet before them. A line of priests chanted the mantras auspicious to the warrior caste, deep voices rolling in waves across the open ground, drowning the sighing of the tusker and the whinnying of the horses.

The Raj Guru unsheathed Tikka's sword. Jaya grasped the rough hilt, knowing all eyes were on her, as Tikka marched forward.

The weapon felt heavy in her hand when she lifted the naked blade between herself and her brother. She fought back the urge to take Tikka's proud figure in her arms and lock it into a steel embrace from which he could not escape to some distant and desolate battlefield, but Tikka's eyes bored into hers, commanding her to complete the puja.

She swiftly sliced the soft cushion of her thumb. Blood ran in a thin stream into the fork of her elbow. Conscious of the glass bangles clinking on her wrist, she helplessly smeared a long streak of blood onto his forehead.

Tikka took the sword. As he walked to the ram, Jaya saw he had only one finger balanced against the blade and realized he was going to perform the sacrifice with the most difficult stroke. She tried to remember a mantra to give Tikka's sword arm strength when suddenly Tikka shouted, 'Jai Mata ki!' The sword slashed down. The ram's cleanly severed head bounced into the stone ditch, blood gushing like a vermilion geyser from its throat.

The priests rushed to hold goblets to the gaping wound as the nagara drums began to pound. The Lancers stepped up to let the priests anoint their foreheads with the blood of the sacrifice. Shouts of 'Jai Mata ki!' tore through the steady chanting of the priests and the thudding of the nagaras. The Raj Guru sprinkled blood onto the weapons, then moved on to smear the tossing heads of the horses. Jaya could see blood caking Moti's tusks as the Lancers performed the last ritual of the puja, the manwar, draining asha from their clay cups and smashing the empty cups into the ditch until the ram's head disappeared under shards of broken clay.

Moti moved away from the temple, the nagara drums vibrating at his sides. The Lancers queued to touch the Maharajah's feet. Shouting 'Bal-hukam!' they turned on their heels and marched to their mounts. When Major Vir Singh bent down, the Maharajah clasped him in an embrace. 'May the Goddess make your arm strong in battle, my friend,' he whispered, and Jaya felt tears collecting in her throat.

Then Tikka was at his father's feet. For a long time Tikka bent before him and the Maharajah did not place his hand on Tikka's shoulder. Jaya stared at him, refusing to believe his rage with the Empire would let him withhold his blessing from a son departing for war.

Jai Singh slowly eased the armlet from his right arm and tied it high on Tikka's biceps. The gesture was visible to the Lancers on their horses. In the noise of their cheering, only Jaya heard her father's voice break. 'Today the Empire takes the dearest part of myself. This is the armlet of sovereignty – symbol of my eyes and my protection. May its strength guard you from harm until you wear it as your country's king.'

Tikka's collar bulged as he raised his arm to salute the Maharajah. 'Bal-hukam!' he said fiercely, then wheeled towards his horse.

The Lancers were grouping in lines of four behind Moti. A convoy of cars drove up, and the grooms squeezed into the seats. Jai Singh mounted his horse to lead the procession to the first gateway of the Fort. Jaya flung herself onto her horse and galloped to the ramparts in time to see the Maharajah rein his horse underneath the high stone arch.

Major Vir Singh unsheathed his sword as the Fort cannons began to fire. The deep fusillade crashed through the thud of the nagaras, and the Lancers trotted in formation past the Maharajah, down the ramparts. Before them swayed the tusker carrying the drums announcing war. People crowded on the stone battlements to throw marigold garlands in front of the horses. The crash of cannon, the pounding of the nagaras, the harsh ring of iron hooves on stone shook the ancient fortifications as Jaya craned to watch the fanned plumes of Tikka's turban disappear under the arches of the outer Fort.

Long after the shriek of the train whistle announced the departure of the troops, the nagara war drums still pounded from the elephant gates of the Balmer Fort, warning the kingdom that the Balmer Lancers had gone to war.

18

By March 1915, India had raised an army of a million men to defend the British Empire, and in the House of Lords, Lord Curzon, that unbending Viceroy who had once treated India's kings as recalcitrant children, acknowledged Britain's debt of honour to her proudest colony.

Tikka's letters had already given a human dimension to Curzon's tribute.

'*November 25, 1914. Yesterday we docked at Liverpool. The streets were packed with Angrez cheering the arrival of the Indian troops. Women rushed to put flowers in the turbans of the Sikhs, and the horses pranced about, showing off for the crowds.*'

'*December 10, London. We visited the hospital for wounded Indian soldiers in Victoria Street. The Baluch regiment lost 500 men out of 560; the Brahmin regiment lost even more! The British are finally thinking of awarding the Victoria Cross to Indian soldiers. What a pity so many men have had to die before the Angrez recognize our valour.*'

'*December 30. France at last! But this is no war for cavalry charges. The soldiers live in trenches dug into hard winter mud, sheltering like rats against enemy guns. The artillery is so close you can see the enemy gunners priming their cannons. And our beautiful horses are being used to pull supply wagons!*'

The war slowly gained a life of its own in the archive rooms below the Palace Library. The walls of one chamber were covered with maps of the main theatres of the European war. In another room, the Senapathy marked on large charts the escalating contributions made by the Indian kingdoms, while clerks transcribed telegraph messages from Delhi into reports for Jai Singh to read on his return from the State Secretariat.

In the largest chamber the Maharajah and the Senapathy held their nightly discussions, before dictating a condensed version of the day's events for Jaya to read aloud to the zenana.

The Maharani responded to the war by spending entire days in the Temple of the Balmer Maharanis doing pujas for the welfare of the Balmer Lancers. As the situation in Europe worsened, the Maharani's devotions became lengthier and increasingly secretive.

Often Jaya had to wait in her mother's apartments, surrounded by purdah ladies eager to interrupt the tedium of their lives with the savagery of the European campaign, a barely concealed excitement visible on their features when they heard the horrifying casualties exacted by the war.

'February, 1915. Poor horses – like ourselves, they hate this mud and snow. Yesterday there was a dress parade of the Indian Imperial troops. The men were thrilled when Field Marshal Sir John French spoke a few words of Hindustani to them. They are very proud that the Commander-in-Chief of the British forces once commanded the Indian Army.'

'March, 1915. Off to the Front at last! Cannot write any more – must get the men ready to leave for Ypres.'

After that letter there was silence from Tikka, made worse by the telegraph messages reporting a new and terrifying dimension to the war. Aircraft were being used to bomb the troops from the air. The Germans had tanks and trench mortars, and their new guns – the Big Berthas – far outdistanced anything possessed by the British.

As the weapons became more incomprehensible, the Maharani searched for solace in the dark regions of tantric worship. A pallet was moved into the Temple of the Balmer Maharanis so she could spend her nights in solitary worship. Jaya knew that behind the locked temple doors her mother was performing sacrifices to the Goddess with open coconuts, the symbol of human sacrifice, to give Tikka the powers which confounded death.

As news of the Maharani's obsession with the supernatural spread, mendicants and holy men began appearing outside the walls of the zenana. Jaya watched the purdah ladies shrinking from the emaciated figure of her veiled mother hurrying down the corridors to consult with naked, ash-covered ascetics through the stone lattices of the harem walls.

By May, there was still no word from Tikka, and the haze of summer lay like the heat from a funeral pyre over the Fort. The Baran entered Jaya's rooms. 'Get ready to accompany your mother, Bai-sa. She wishes to consult a woman who lives in a cave at the edge of the desert.'

'Why doesn't my mother send for her?'

'Your mother has sent for her many times, but she has refused to come. She is called Sati Mata. They say she is of royal blood and became an ascetic when she was prevented from burning herself on her husband's funeral pyre.' The Baran looked nervously around to make sure no one was listening. 'She lived in Benares for twenty years, next to the burning ghats and the corpses. They say she has eaten the flesh of dead children.'

'Why must we see her?'

'Because she has great powers, Bai-sa, and Maharani-sahib . . .' The Baran's voice petered out uncertainly.

'Go on, Baran!'

'I should not say this, Bai-sa, but your mother is too much involved with prophecies and unnatural powers. And her fasts are too severe. I worry for her mind. . . .'

But when Jaya joined her mother in the curtained Rolls-Royce, she saw no lunacy in the Maharani's serene eyes. The pale face was a little drawn, but the long fingers turned the beads of her mala as they had always done, and the low voice still held its gentle note of command. Beyond the glass partition the Chief Eunuch sat next to the chauffeur, holding the rolled screens to protect the Maharani from watching eyes when she dismounted.

The car twisted through the narrow streets of the capital and slid past the marble cenotaphs of the rulers into the monotonous landscape. The reservoirs were dry, baked into vast ditches of cracked mud, and the branches of dying trees angled like lightning against the glassy blue sky. Occasionally Jaya saw a slab covered with stone hands, marking the spot where women had committed sati. Other stone slabs commemorated the place where a warrior and his steed had fallen in battle, and Jaya thought of Tikka sheltering in a trench while his horse was used to pull supply wagons.

On the southern boundary of the kingdom, stone fortifications stretched across the spine of the Arravalli Hills, enclosing abandoned forts and temples. As the chauffeur manoeuvred the heavy Rolls-Royce up a hillside, the car scraped a Flame of the Forest tree and violent red blossoms burst through the dust, hurting the eyes with their brilliance.

Halfway up the slope, the Maharani tapped on the glass partition. The Chief Eunuch leaped out, holding his screen wide so the Maharani, followed by Jaya, could descend without being seen by the chauffeur. He stumbled up a steep path behind them, struggling not to drop the basket filled with fruit and flowers that hung from his elbow.

At a clump of black rocks, the Maharani motioned to the eunuch to wait and took the heavy basket, in which the flowers had already wilted in the heat. She climbed up the steep incline, carelessly brushing aside the locusts whirring above her head. Jaya stopped to free her veil from the thornbushes, but the Maharani did not seem to notice the thorns or the dizzying sun. By the time they reached the top of the hill, Jaya's head was swimming from the heat, and looking down she saw the parched fields undulating in the haze like a mendicant's shawl.

The Maharani clambered up to a broken cenotaph with hands carved in its yellowing marble, the sign of the sati. Green pigeons flew in and out of the crumbling cupolas, and monkeys chattered noisily on the wide platform as the Maharani removed her sandals and mounted the broken steps, slabs of loose marble shaking under her bare feet.

Jaya followed the Maharani into the tomb, grateful for the darkness after the glittering sunlight, until her eyes adjusted to the heavy shadows and she saw bats hanging like rotting fruit from the broken dome. The Maharani pulled aside a dusty antelope skin that covered a small doorway. The skin swung back, leaving Jaya alone in the dark tomb with the bats and the monkeys. Something wet slithered over her feet. With a scream, Jaya tore the skin aside and ran out into a courtyard, practically falling into the lap of a woman sitting on a tiger skin at the base of a mango tree.

The woman laughed – a deep, throaty sound that seemed to well up from her belly. Her body was partly covered by a coarse cloth the colour of dried blood, and light shone off bare shins crossed in the lotus position. An iron trident was thrust into the ground at her side. Her black hair fell onto the tiger skin, where a coconut shell was seeping white liquid onto the stripes.

A cobra slithered onto the tiger skin and lapped at the liquid spilling from the coconut shell. Jaya suppressed a scream behind her fist, crouching against the woman's bare brown shoulder.

The woman stroked Jaya's cheek with dry, hot fingertips. 'Ah, child, if terror of a harmless serpent is the sum of fear you will know in your life. . . .' She took Jaya's hand and placed it near the snake. The cobra slithered up Jaya's forearm to coil itself around her wrist. The forked tongue darted out, striking at the glass bangles sliding down her arm.

'Go towards your fear, child. Only then can you find the courage to endure the life that stretches before you, exiled from your sex.' Black eyes glowed in the ascetic's smooth face, compelling Jaya to meet their gaze.

'I warned her father!' The Maharani said bitterly. 'I told him he is educating his daughter to be a man!'

The ascetic ignored the Maharani's outburst. 'Few will understand the high cost of your valour, child, the impoverishment of your spirit. But you must find the courage to live with your own barrenness.'

'Barren?' the Maharani almost shouted. 'Is my daughter barren?'

'Do not alarm yourself, Maharani-sahib. Your daughter will be married, and she will bear a son.'

'I did not think the Goddess could be so cruel. Whom will the girl marry?'

'A great sword.'

'A ruling king?'

'A great and ancient sword.'

The Maharani was worried again. 'Is the girl to be third or fourth wife to an ageing maharajah? Her father would never permit such a union.'

The Sati Mata shook her head indulgently at the urgent questions. 'Your ambitions are so young, woman. Marriage, youth, power – all these are dreams that drift away like dust before the inevitability of death. Twenty years I sat on the banks of the holy river at Benares. I watched sons break open their fathers' skulls. I saw women fighting to throw themselves into their husbands' funeral flames. I heard

126

priests haggle over the price of grief and watched holy men pluck flesh from half-charred corpses and consume it in the belief they would gain powers.'

'But your name. Are you not called Sati Mata because you tried to die on your husband's funeral pyre?'

The ascetic flung her head back in laughter, and the coarse cloth almost slipped below her breasts. Jaya looked at the pink tongue protruding from between the full lips, and wondered if the woman was a dancing girl who had come to Balmer hoping to make a fortune from her mother's frailty.

The Sati Mata tightened the garment over her breasts. 'The title sati should not be given to a woman who burns herself, but to a woman of virtue. And the greatest virtue is endurance. I am called the Sati Mata because my gurus are the Five Satis, those five virtuous women who refused to burn themselves on their husbands' pyres. The true sati has the will to continue when the familiar world fragments around her.' The ascetic paused. 'You will also be known as a Sati Mata, Maharani-sahib. When the nagaras of Balmer Fort are smashed before your eyes.'

'The Balmer nagaras can be broken only when Balmer Fort is conquered. You speak in riddles that I do not understand. But if there are evil influences which we have released by foolish actions, show me a way to make reparation.'

The Maharani prostrated herself on the tiger skin, ignoring the cobra turning towards her. 'Our motives were always governed by the country's welfare. Surely the Goddess will forgive us. Give me a mantra to placate the anger of the Goddess.'

Jaya was shocked at her mother's loss of dignity; but the coiled cobra, the broken monument of death shimmering in the heat, gave an urgency to the moment, as though they were in another world where the present was a mirage and only the future concrete.

The ascetic pried the Maharani's pale fingers loose from their grip on the tiger skin. 'Are you a child, Maharani-sahib, to believe in goddesses and mantras?'

The Maharani sat back on her heels and lowered her head. 'Only one who has achieved detachment could speak such words without profanity. But I am an ordinary mortal. My son fights another nation's wars. My husband is under siege from his governing council in his own citadel. You say the nagaras will be smashed before our eyes. Your words are full of death.' Tears fell on the tiger skin, and the cobra fanned its hood. 'We have need of help, Sati Mata. I beg of you, give me a mantra to protect our house against the threat of destruction.'

The Sati Mata sighed, raising her hand in benediction. Jaya thought she was hallucinating when she saw the red glow enveloping the ascetic's palm. 'You have insisted on a mantra and I must give you one. This will be your talisman against fear, Maharani-sahib. Ram Nam Sat Hai. The Name of God is Truth.'

'The mantra of death!' the Maharani gasped. She stood up to confront the ascetic. 'If the foundations of our house tremble, so be it. But I will not speak a mantra that should fall only from the lips of a widow following her husband's funeral pyre! I am the wife of Jai Singh-ji. I shall never live on as Jai Singh's widow!' Jaya could not believe that she had heard her mother speak her father's name. 'I am a Maharani of Balmer. Like my great predecessors, I shall burn myself, before I speak your mantra.'

The ascetic's stern voice sliced through the Maharani's anger. 'You have asked for a mantra against death as a child asks for a toy. Repeat your mantra until you have understood its meaning.'

She closed her eyes and appeared to enter a trance. The cobra curled at one naked knee, staring at the ascetic with glittering eyes. For a long time there was silence. Then a voice that seemed to swell up from the earth resonated in the stillness: 'Ram Nam Sat Hai. The Name of God is Truth. Shanti! Shanti! Shanti!'

The audience was over, but the ascetic's voice echoed in the cenotaph as Jaya followed the Maharani into the darkness. 'The Name of God is Truth. Let there be peace and peace and peace.

19

Ten years after the war King George V made his first radio broadcast to the British Empire. The King Emperor's speech was written by Rudyard Kipling, that dreamer who had once believed the loyal native soldiers and dashing British officers of his beloved Indian Army would police the civilized world for a civilized Empire.

Kipling's text made no reference to the slaughter that had reduced his civilized world to a charnel house, leaving half the British army dead in the mud of Flanders within the first three months of the war.

No mention of the quarter-million Turks of Enver Pasha's army who had died in their attempt to capture Russia's oilfields before sweeping through Afghanistan to conquer India; or the Australian and New Zealand troops who had proudly landed at Anzac Cove only to be mown down by machine-gun fire, the first casualties of the half-million men who died at Gallipoli. No mention of the million German soldiers who had died at Verdun; or the millions dead on Russia's eastern front; or the British soldiers shot in a single morning at the Somme; or Kut-al-Amara, when an army that had moved too far and too fast was besieged and fifteen thousand Indian troops starved to death.

Perhaps Kipling could not find adequate words for a world that had moulted an entire generation, shedding human corpses like old skin before it came of age.

Even Lord Kitchener, the great soldier who had fought Lord Curzon for control of Kipling's beloved Indian Army, could not decipher a meaning in the massacres. Like Maharajah Jai Singh and all the other men who believed in the cavalry charge, Lord Kitchener had despaired when he saw the soldiers frozen in their trenches. He had heard the awful silence that punctuated the crash of trench mortars and said, 'I don't know what is to be done. This isn't war.'

But when Jaya listened to the Emperor of India addressing 'the men and women cut off by the snows, the desert, or the sea, that only voices out of the air can reach them,' she remembered how the telegraph had once seemed a voice out of the air. She recalled the clacking telegraph keys that pounded out the campaigns of Ypres, Aisne, Gallipoli, Kut-al-Amara, Cambrai, like the thudding of global nagaras, and the long-delayed letters that gave immediacy to killings already six months old.

'*The Germans are using poison gas against us,*' Tikka wrote from Ypres. '*But we have no gas masks and have to cover our faces with handkerchiefs soaked in urine. The men complain that when the wind is carrying the gas in our direction and they are trying to get covers over the heads of frightened horses, their bladders dry. They want to fight as cavalry. They say it is always easy to piss before a cavalry charge.*'

'*Do you remember how furious you were when the British refused to allow the Balmer Lancers to train with real arms, for fear they would train their weapons on Delhi?*' Tikka reminded the Maharajah in another letter. '*Now there is such a severe shortage of arms that we are making hand grenades out of jam jars and firing petrol cans into enemy trenches with catapults. We stuff bits of steel pipe with dynamite to blow up the barbed wire – the British soldiers call it the Bangalore torpedo. Sometimes we pack tree trunks with explosives, hoping the Germans will be deceived into thinking we have cannon.*'

The Maharajah's hands tightened on the flimsy paper. 'Why don't the British take these?' He waved angrily at the iron barrels of cannon piercing the stone ramparts, ready to destroy the city stretching beneath if threatened by siege. 'We are no longer permitted to use them except when we appear like actors in a village drama to the sound of firing guns!'

As though unwilling to accept his own powerlessness, Jai Singh spent hours in the Palace Library studying the military campaigns of the European powers. At the other end of the long chamber, Jaya tried to concentrate on the Raj Guru's instructions, but her eyes kept wandering to her father hunched over a table, pulling at his white beard until it fell onto the pages of his book like a bird with a broken wing.

Tikka's letters made it clear that neither cannon nor study would end the war. *'James Osborne's regiment has joined us in Neuville. What a reunion! Men are dying in such numbers that it is a shock to find people still alive. We are all old hands at trench warfare now, even the horses. If there is a mist we know the Germans are going to gas us or bomb us, and we promptly dive into the nearest ditch.'*

In October he wrote: *'Captain Osborne, James and I were riding out to see our aeroplanes when a sortie of thirty German Fokkers attacked. Captain Osborne's horse bolted, dragging Captain-sahib behind him. German aircraft were dropping 120-lb bombs all around us and we couldn't see anything through the smoke. By the time we caught the horse, Captain-sahib was bleeding badly. A piece of shrapnel had torn a hole in his throat. The doctors at the field hospital could do nothing. '*

The Maharajah decreed a day of official mourning for Captain Osborne, and Jaya wrote a stiff and inadequate letter of condolence to his son.

That winter, the war was eighteen months old. In the archive rooms below the Fort Library the clerks had invented their own pictorial codes for the changes sweeping the world. Russia was a bleeding egg held in the hand of a black-robed priest. Africa was a naked warrior pierced by two spears flying the flags of Britain and Germany. Turkey was a torn book, its pages falling into the water. On one page was drawn the figure of a Bedouin Arab with a single eye, the new king of the new country allied to the British Empire, King Ibn Saud of Arabia. Behind the symbols of a disintegrating world the court artists had laboriously reproduced serene jungles filled with grazing deer and dancing peacocks, as though denying the horrors of the present.

Jai Singh often interrupted Jaya's lessons to read Major Vir Singh's reports to the old Raj Guru.

'The trees have all been cut down to heat men freezing to death in waterlogged trenches. We are fortunate. We have only lost four

men. But for the first time the Lancers are afraid of dying. There is no wood to burn for their funeral pyres.'

The old high priest remained silent for a long while, then whispered, 'Only action frees us from the wheel of action. Those are the words of the Gita. Let each man do his duty.'

'But we no longer know our duties!' Jai Singh shouted in frustration. 'When death falls from the skies, what is the duty of a warrior? When bombs and mines destroy fields, what is the role of the farmer? When factories manufacture death, what is the role of the merchant?'

He picked up a heavy volume, waving it at the Raj Guru. 'A Polish nobleman wrote this book – *Is Another War Impossible?* – seventeen years ago. Listen to his words: "There will be increased slaughter on so terrible a scale it will be impossible to get the troops to push the war to a decisive issue ... the soldier has so perfected the mechanism of slaughter he has practically secured his own extinction." That is what Major Vir Singh means! This is no war for men. It is a war between the mechanisms of slaughter! Perhaps there will never again be a war for the kshatriya or the Rajput.'

Jaya pressed her hands together, trying to re-create in her mind the pastoral backgrounds with which the court artists had reassured themselves the war would pass, and envied her mother's oblivion, lost in clouds of burning camphor and a constant parade of ascetics.

IN THE SUMMER of 1917, it was as if the Goddess had decided to answer the Maharani's fasts and prayers. Tikka was wounded at Cambrai.

From his hospital in Paris, Tikka wrote: '*At Bullecourt when we entered No Man's Land the snow and slush were so bad we had to dismount and lead the horses. The shell craters are so deep a horse can easily drown. Suddenly machine-gun fire opened up from a group of destroyed tanks. We realized too late that the Germans were using the tanks as pillboxes. We were completely pinned down by crossfire, and we would all have been killed but for a heavy snowstorm. We have taken an oath never to curse the snow again! An officer from Jacob's Horse was awarded the Military Cross for our action. I think Prince Pratap should have got one too. He crawled under enemy wire to rescue me and carry me back to our lines. Every time I regained consciousness I could hear him cursing the Sirpur retainers for lying drunk in their villages on the one occasion when he really needed their help. Of course, our Balmer Lancers now treat Prince Pratap like a god!'*

As soon as she read Tikka's letter, the Maharani moved on her advantage. 'We owe the Sirpurs a debt which can never be repaid. Prince Pratap has saved Tikka's life! You cannot delay this marriage any more!'

'Must your son's life be bought with your daughter's?' the ruler argued.

'But Jaya will be happy in Sirpur! The Dowager Maharani wants an alliance. She will educate and protect the girl!'

'Who can protect a wife from her husband?'

'You speak as though Prince Pratap is a monster! Have you forgotten already that he has saved your son's life?'

'For men like Prince Pratap, danger is a drug. He is courageous only because he is adventurous.'

'Meaningless theories! He and his brother, Maharajah Victor, have always been kind to Tikka. Now Tikka owes them his life. What further proof do you need that they will be kind to Jaya?'

'Then why is Sirpur demanding a huge dowry for Jaya?'

'That is the price of your own folly in antagonizing the British Empire. Tikka has already paid with years of his life. We are lucky that for Jaya, the price is only wealth.'

The Maharajah shrugged, his head bent down on his chest as though trying to see into his own soul. Sitting in a corner, Jaya recognized her father's helplessness, but when he said, 'I never wished the children to pay for my beliefs. Do as you think best,' the blood pounded in her ears like the warning thud of the nagaras.

THE DECISION about Jaya's marriage seemed to free the Maharajah and Maharani from their separate isolations.

The Maharajah immediately departed to attend a secret meeting of Indian kings and Indian nationalist leaders, the first such clandestine gathering ever held in India, taking place in the Sikh kingdom of Patiala.

Inside the zenana, the Maharani's interest shifted from solitary pujas for her son's welfare to exchanging family horoscopes with the Dowager Maharani of Sirpur. She even sent the Dowager copies of her son's letters from Paris.

Prince Pratap had joined the convalescing Tikka in a city filling up with refugees from the dismantled Austrian Empire or fleeing the chaos in Russia since the Germans had sent the Bolshevik leader Lenin by secret train to Moscow. Tikka's letters indicated why Prince Pratap was such a heavy financial burden on the Sirpur treasury. Every night Prince Pratap gave dinners for fifty people at a time, as though presiding over a frenzied masque. Tikka revelled in the elegant eccentricities of the White Russians, the bohemian writers and artists of Montparnasse, the spoiled French courtesans who seemed to form Prince Pratap's intimate circle, and his accounts of Paris were filled with the dazed pleasure of a young man who had escaped from death into a maelstrom of pleasure.

In Prince Pratap's company Tikka became familiar with the opulent Paris brothels. *'The French are especially proud of the Hôtel Chabannais. Can you imagine, they even bring visiting heads of state to see it. Edward VII honoured Queen Victoria by calling one suite the Hindu Room, though the old Empress of India would have been quite shocked if she had seen some of the contraptions in it! Naturally, Prince Pratap always insists on booking the Hindu Room.'*

Jaya felt her brother was living in a fantasy world, holding the horror of the present at bay with his pen, and from the Dowager's letters Jaya realized that Sirpur was banking on her dowry to take the pressure of Prince Pratap's extravagance off the state.

On the day that Jaya's nuptial arrangements were concluded, the Sati Mata sent a garland of marigolds in blessing and repeated her prediction that Jaya would marry a great sword. The Maharani was more excited by the garland than depressed by Tikka's letter saying he was rejoining his regiment at Cambrai.

Soon engagement gifts began arriving from Sirpur. Heavy steel trunks, painted an auspicious crimson, were unloaded at the outer walls of the zenana. The eunuchs groaned under the weight as they carried the trunks inside, shouting at the purdah ladies standing in their way, speculating on the contents.

Jaya sat dispiritedly on her mother's balcony while the purdah ladies examined the weight of gold in the sari borders. Holding delicate filigree necklaces studded with precious stones to the light, the ladies checked for flaws in the gems, and asked the Maharani when the miserly old Dowager would send the famous Sirpur emeralds instead of these silly trinkets.

Despite the engagement presents, Jaya's lessons with the Raj Guru continued. When the Maharajah had been gone three weeks from the Fort, Jaya heard a car drive into the courtyard below the Library. Then the Maharajah and Mr Roy, dusty from their journey, entered the room.

There was a febrile brightness in the Maharajah's eyes as he poured himself water from the clay ewer. 'Guru-ji, I have thought hard about what will happen to small powers like ourselves when the European empires disintegrate.'

At the edge of her vision Jaya saw Mr Roy circling the Library, his head tilted back to examine the frescoes on the ceiling.

'Many years ago in London, His Highness Dungra tried to warn me the world we knew was already finished, and to prepare for a new age. I would not listen to him. I fought against allowing the British to bring their factories and railways to Balmer. Like the Maharana of Udaipur, I argued that once we adopted the machines and institutions of the Angrez, we would adopt their ways, and in the process lose our souls.

'During this secret conference in Patiala, I met the representatives of many Indian rulers who have experimented with parliamentary representation – Bikaner, Baroda, Travancore, Mysore. I also met many nationalist leaders. It is now clear to me our very survival as independent countries depends on imitating Angrez institutions and including the people in the running of the state's affairs.'

He sighed as though exhausted from solving a difficult mathematical equation. 'For so long I refused to acknowledge the fact that our dharma as warriors is over. How could it be otherwise for me? Is it not said in the Laws of Manu that a man without dharma may not presume to govern?'

The Raj Guru had been listening with distant interest to the Maharajah. Now he spoke as if instructing a child. 'Why do you hold the Angrez responsible for change, hukam? Read the scriptures. In our long histories there is no form of social organization we have not tried. Great republics; countries governed by scholars; kingdoms

135

ruled by holy orders. Our governments have always been run by the counsel of the people. How else could decisions taken by the elders of five villages overturn the laws decreed by a king?'

'No longer, Guru-ji. The British Empire has changed such traditions forever. The Empire can ignore the decisions of the village elders. England believes only in what is written.'

'Dharma, Maharajah-sahib, is righteous action.' Mr Roy stopped looking through the books, compelled by the authority of the Raj Guru's dry whisper. 'If you can use these months when the Empire is preoccupied with its own survival to ensure that the people of Balmer exact a just price for their sacrifices, then you have not forfeited your dharma.'

Jai Singh gave him a grateful smile. 'Maharajah Dungra became a constitutional monarch years ago. He has agreed to visit Balmer and advise me. And Mr Roy's cousin, the lawyer Arun Roy, is also coming to Balmer. I hope he will be able to devise a constitution which the British Empire cannot alter to its advantage.'

THE FOLLOWING MONTH, the Maharajah reluctantly tore himself away from his plans for changing the system of Balmer's government only once, to attend the short ceremony finalizing Jaya's engagement to Prince Pratap of Sirpur.

Three Sirpur priests had endured the inconvenience of the long journey across India to bring the gold thalis filled with sweetmeats cooked in the Sirpur Palace kitchens.

Dressed in red and gold, her head covered with a veil, Jaya was led by the purdah ladies to the courtyard outside the zenana and placed on a low ivory throne. Through her veil, Jaya watched the hazy figures of the Ministers of the Council laying coins in front of the visitors.

The Sirpur head priest, acting for the Dowager Maharani of Sirpur, broke a coconut sweetmeat and offered it to Jaya. For a long time Jaya did not move, her hands clammy with fear. Once a sweetmeat from the Sirpur House touched her mouth, there would be no turning back. Then the Maharani lifted the edge of Jaya's veil, and the strong smell of coconut assailed her nostrils as she obediently opened her lips.

But when the Sirpur priests unveiled a large portrait of Prince

136

Pratap and Jaya saw again the heavy-lidded eyes and bored smile, her stomach contracted, regurgitating the sweetmeat, bitter with bile, back into her mouth.

The portrait of Prince Pratap was given pride of place in Jaya's rooms. It seemed to chill the chamber, as if the thick stone walls that kept out the desert frost could not warm the frigid features. Every morning the Baran brought a garland of fresh flowers for the portrait and stood next to Jaya as she woodenly recited prayers for the well-being of her future husband.

When she was alone, Jaya tried not to look at the portrait. But as the weeks passed and the chill of December turned into the cold of January, her eyes seemed drawn to the stranger's face, and at night she shivered as though she had a fever, and sent for more covers for her bed.

20

The Maharani's jubilation at Jaya's engagement was matched by Jai Singh's delight when he received the news that the lawyer, Arun Roy, and the old Maharajah of Dungra were on their way to Balmer to assist in the drafting of a new constitution.

Both were pleased with Tikka's next letter.

'We all knew Field Marshal Haig would make the first cavalry attack of the war at Cambrai. The Germans have demolished every town and village, making the ground perfect for cavalry. In fact, the entire region is now known as the Devastated Area.

'Early on the morning of November 20 the Cambrai offensive was launched. Under the command of Sir Pratap Singh of Jodhpur, we were with the Fifth Indian Cavalry Division. I must say, old Pratap doesn't seem at all conscious of the fact that he is seventy-two years of age. He was chafing away as our tanks cut through the formidable German defences.

'I almost felt ashamed of our horses when I saw the sun striking against the tanks and their gun turrets swivelling from side to side. But their magnificent attack was halted by one canal. The tanks were too heavy to cross the rickety old wooden bridge that separated them from the enemy. We laughed so much we nearly fell off our saddles watching the tank commanders pound their useless machines with their fists.

'With our mobility, we could easily have got behind the German lines. But the cavalry was ordered back to billets. We were disgusted. Instead of a cavalry campaign, Cambrai had become a tank battle!

'For the next ten days we sat in trenches, although the situation was desperate. On the morning of November 30 the Germans launched a surprise offensive, and we were finally ordered to carry out a mounted attack on Gauche Wood, to divert German fire.

'Although the area was strongly held, one of our squadrons found a gap in the German wire and galloped through. Our next squadron was decimated. Then the rest of the brigade – the Eighth Hussars, Hodson's Horse and ourselves – attacked.

'We charged in perfect diamond formation with drawn swords in spite of the exploding shells, the ground erupting in front of us and the clods of mud practically blinding our horses. The Lancers followed at a steady trot, pennants and lances held upright like battlements. Enemy troops as well as our own cheered our advance. In the middle of this ugly war, with corpses and burnt-out tanks strewn all over the field, it was as though our charge were a reminder of what a noble calling war had once been.

'As we were regrouping we saw a terrible sight. The Mhow and Sialkot brigades were sitting on their horses in full range of the German guns. Some idiot of a British commander must have told them to hold their positions, even though their closely packed formations presented a perfect target for enemy artillery. They were being mown down by shells. Torn limbs and horse-flesh were flying everywhere. But the two brigades remained motionless throughout the massacre.

'Without firepower, we couldn't advance. Apart from the German artillery, our own aircraft machine-gunned us three times. In desperation at the slaughter, the Second Lancers of the Indian Cavalry charged the German guns. We cheered wildly when a group of Lancers jumped a fence at the gallop and went after the Germans with lances.

'We held the front line as the Germans attacked in waves against our positions. After three days of continuous attack we were finally relieved by the British Cavalry. But the Indian Cavalry had acquitted itself well. We stopped the German advance, our own Lancers made a cavalry charge and what's more, we took part in the first tank battle in history!

'Oh, by the way, we are leaving Europe to join General Allenby's army in Palestine.'

SOON THE WHOLE kingdom knew that Tikka and his Lancers would be a thousand miles closer to India, and with the arrival of the Maharajah's visitors, Balmer Fort suddenly came alive again as it had been in the days before the Lancers left for Europe.

Jaya and the purdah ladies went early to the enclosed purdah balcony of the Durbar Hall on the day Jai Singh was receiving the Maharajah of Dungra in formal durbar.

Below them, small iron braziers heated the Durbar Hall against the dry cold of a late-January morning, and the scent of burning sandalwood filled the air. Thin tendrils of smoke were reflected in the mirrored pillars that lined the outer perimeter of the audience chamber, where rows of villagers wrapped in heavy blankets were already crowding the public entrances.

Venetian mirrors, ordered a century ago, hung on the walls of the ladies' balcony, ornate frames peeling, glass smoky with age. One mirror reflected the domed roofs where the craftsmen worked, and Jaya could visualize the weavers throwing their shuttles across their looms as they wove garments for her trousseau, the jewellers crouched over wax tablets, designing her bridal ornaments.

'A handsome man, for an Easterner,' a purdah lady whispered. Jaya looked down. Mr Roy and his cousin, the lawyer from Calcutta, were entering the audience hall. Arun Roy's tall frame was draped in a long silk shirt and a white dhoti which fell to the floor in elegant folds. A brown shawl lay across his broad shoulders.

'He certainly has a noble manner,' the Maharani observed. Hearing her approval, the other purdah ladies pressed against the stone screens until every aperture was filled with eyes. The lawyer seated himself next to a brazier. He pulled a hookah closer and placed the mouthpiece between his teeth. There was a sudden flash of white teeth under the thin moustache, and Jaya heard the woman next to her gulp loudly.

Mr Roy handed the lawyer a sheet of paper. The lawyer reached under his shawl for a pair of spectacles. When he placed them on his nose, there was a groan from the purdah ladies.

'The gods are too cruel!'

'To make such a handsome man blind!'

Steel lances crashed against marble floors as Raja Man Singh entered the Durbar Hall carrying the symbol of sovereign sway, a white horse tail falling from a golden cone. The Senapathy followed with the symbol of war, a sheaf of peacock feathers. Behind him came the Ministers of the Council bearing silver staves crowned with the insignia of abundance - the head of the tiger, the head of the elephant, the head of the crocodile. The Prime Minister of Balmer held in front of him the sign of administration, a red hand.

The crash of lances striking marble floors echoed again in the corridor.

'Take heed! Take heed!' the heralds shouted.

'There approaches
'The Provider of Grain
'The Protector of the People
'The Source of Bounty
'Maharajdhiraj
'Jai Singh Ji
'Defender of the Goddess
'Ruler of Balmer.'

Jai Singh sat down on his gaddi, the fanned plumes of his turban brushing against the crimson canopy of state, the symbols of monarchy circling his erect form.

The purdah ladies pointed to an archway where the Maharajah of Dungra was being ushered into the audience chamber.

'He looks like a fat black duck.'

'Why does he wear so many pearls?'

The Maharajah of Dungra's son entered behind his father. Poking her finger through the lattice, a purdah lady choked into her veil. 'They may be dripping with pearls, but look at the size of their backsides. Just like a pair of buffaloes!'

'At least the son's parentage will never be questioned.'

'And he is called Tiny! Can you believe it?'

As if on cue, the son's head rolled back onto the rolls of flesh squeezed above the tight collar of his tunic and the rows of pearls.

'Now see what you have done. Our guest has heard you,' the Maharani whispered.

'But, hukam, how can such a fat man be called Tiny?' Jaya could barely get the words out, and the purdah ladies tried to stifle their screams of laughter.

'Be silent, Jaya, or you will have to leave,' the Maharani com-

141

manded. 'His Highness Dungra will say the women of Balmer make their presence known at durbars, like dancing girls.'

Embarrassed, Jaya tried to control herself as the lines of nobles came up to offer gold coins in nazaar to her father. Dancing girls whirled in the centre of the Durbar Hall. Presents were placed before the Maharajah of Dungra and his son, Tiny. The lawyer, Arun Roy, seemed amused by the ceremony and occasionally made notes on his paper.

Then the Raj Guru was standing before Jai Singh for the Aashirvad, the blessing which ended a formal durbar. The crowds peering through the open arches rose to their feet, and there was silence as the old priest's cracked voice dominated the vast chamber with the ancient Sanskrit phrases.

THAT EVENING there was an entertainment for the visitors. The stilt dancers performed on the cobbled stones outside the King's View, and a group of boys executed the Balmer sword dance. The Maharajah of Dungra presented them with a bag of gold coins before following the other guests to the small drawing room next to the King's View.

Hookahs had been placed near the divans and a log fire burned in the blackened fireplace. The Maharajah of Dungra insisted that Jaya sit next to him. She sank into the springs forced down by his heavy frame, inhaling the strong smell of rose water from his clothes, trying not to stare at the thick lips, stained red with betel juice, as he spoke.

'The Secretary of State for India was in Dungra last month. I think this resolution in the British Parliament indicates the Angrez are drawing closer to the idea of Home Rule for India. After the war Britain is almost certain to give the rulers a Chamber of Princes and Assemblies to British India.'

Arun Roy smiled at the old ruler. 'For years Britain has promised to make India a Dominion, like Canada and Australia. Let us see if she fulfils her promises at last. After all, one and a quarter million Indians joined up to defend Britain's territories in 1915, and £100 million was sent from India's exchequer as an outright gift to Britain. Since then India has paid Britain a further £30 million every year.'

Mr Roy broke in. 'And at the very time that the Irish rebellion was at its height in 1915, we Indians stopped all agitation against the Angrez – no more bombs, no more assassination attempts. If the Angrez do not give us representation after the war, they will not be able to control the situation. We are not next door to England like Ireland. Our frustrations can't be quelled by British troops.'

'There is a sinister aspect to any concessions we may receive after the war.' Mrs Roy peered at the gathering through her rimless spectacles. 'Britain is setting Hindu, Sikh, Moslem against each other. Royal India against British India. We must not allow this to continue.'

Tiny Dungra shook his head in objection. 'The Moslems are already in communication with the Sikhs, and both groups are joining hands with Gandhi, who heads the Indian National Congress.'

'Tell me about this Gandhi,' Jai Singh said.

Without bending his plump torso, Maharajah Dungra spat into the spittoon at the foot of the divan. 'He lived in South Africa for a number of years, where he agitated against the pass laws. He wants to use his techniques from South Africa – the system of nonviolent resistance – to demand Home Rule for India.' Dungra crossed his hands over his belly, and Jaya's attention was momentarily diverted by his splendid rings. 'But Gandhi is a little too austere for my taste.'

'Gandhi's austerity will move the Indian masses to throw off the yoke of the British Raj.' Arun Roy was suddenly serious. 'He speaks to their strength – numbers and passive resistance. He dresses like them. He lives like them. Mark my words, he will turn their fear into courage.'

The divan shook with the Maharajah of Dungra's laughter. 'First, we, the kings of India, must show courage. Tell us about your secret meetings in Patiala with the Indian nationalist leaders, Jai.'

'We have agreed to work together to curtail the Empire's authority over our affairs.'

The lawyer looked at Jai Singh with renewed interest. 'But surely the rulers support Britain?'

'We must appear to support Britain or lose our thrones, Mr Roy,' Jai Singh replied coldly. 'But if we get a Chamber of Princes, perhaps our true views will be known at last.'

Dungra patted Jaya's knee. 'We must have confused you, child.

143

What will you dream of tonight after all our talk of Gandhis and Chambers of Princes?'

Jaya gave him a shy smile. 'I shall probably dream of ships, hukam. At this very moment my brother and the Balmer Lancers are sailing to Palestine.'

THE NEXT DAY, a convoy of cars left the Fort taking Maharajah Jai Singh and his guests on an extended tour of Balmer. In the weeks that they were gone, the Raj Guru was occasionally called to explain matters to a village council, or the shikaris loaded the coursing cheetahs into the shooting brake because the Maharajah's party was taking a day off to hunt deer. Once Jaya saw four Household Guards riding down the ramparts, hooded birds clinging to the heavy leather gauntlets that covered their hands, and she knew her father had reached the southern border of the country and was falconing in the desert.

Whenever someone trusted left to join the Maharajah, the Maharani sent her husband reports of the Council meetings and Raja Man Singh's movements. Jaya carried the heavily sealed envelopes to the messenger, sometimes adding a note of her own.

She was in the process of enclosing Field Marshal Haig's tribute to the Indian Cavalry when she received a summons to join her father herself.

In the harsh light of the afternoon, the Senapathy drove Jaya through the bazaars of Balmer city, past the tea sellers heating iron kettles on stoves and the butchers hauling haunches of goat meat from their carts. He turned the car onto a twisting dirt track leading into the jungle, and braked near an abandoned fort.

Stone blocks had come loose from the fortifications, and a banyan tree spread like a pillared pavilion at the gateway to the fort, shading the waiting horses. The Senapathy handed Jaya a lance. 'There is no question of your trying to stick a pig yourself, Bai-sa, but your father wants you to gain some experience riding with a spear. In case you get thrown, use this pistol to frighten away any animals.' Jaya detected a note of disapproval in the Senapathy's terse instructions as he swung himself into his saddle.

An hour's hard riding brought them to the rocky nullah, the gorge, where the other spears were waiting. Arun Roy was slipping the leather thong of his lance over his wrist. Tiny Dungra stood next

144

to him. Jaya was surprised to see the Dungra heir and wondered if he even knew how to ride.

Tiny Dungra swung onto the saddle with surprising grace and followed Arun Roy down the nullah toward the cane fields. The shouting of the beaters sounded faintly in the distance as the two riders galloped through the undergrowth, sending flights of bright blue kingfishers and scarlet minivets flashing into the glazed sky.

Jaya walked her own horse closer to a lake covered with oval lotus leaves. Crocodiles sunned themselves in the mud. On the bank a clutch of peahens picked at red flowers the size of melons; then a peacock strutted into view, its brilliant tail feathers sweeping the ground. Once a harsh cough echoed from the opposite bank, the sound of a tiger warning its mate. She clutched her lance, searching for signs of wild boar, but there was no sound from the bushes. All that could be heard was the popping of lotus buds opening on their swaying stalks.

Suddenly a streak of dull black flashed through the grass, evil-looking tusks curving above a long snout. Jai Singh's horse shot past Jaya. The Maharajah's hand was lowered, holding a dagger parallel to his horse's head as he accelerated towards the boar. Jaya felt a rush of pride, knowing that only three men in the world dared hunt wild pig with daggers and not spears – the Maharajah of Alwar, Sir Pratap and her father. A herd of Nilgai antelope were running in the opposite direction. The boar disappeared into the herd, pursued by the Maharajah. Unable to keep pace with the antelope, the pig dropped back, and the Maharajah closed, his dagger only inches from the boar's head.

The pig jinked, racing towards the rocky nullah as Arun Roy galloped down the slope, displacing rocks and stones in a small landslide. The pig jinked again and vanished into the cane fields. Tiny Dungra materialized through the waving sugar cane, his lance raised like a javelin. The wild boar stopped dead in its tracks. Jaya searched for her revolver and found it gone as the boar spun around at full speed only to find Arun Roy's lance raised for the strike. Jaya distinctly heard the blade hitting bone before the lance snapped from the momentum of the animal's leap.

The wounded boar turned toward the lake, the broken lance sticking out from one shoulder. Blood darkened the boar's dusty hide as it moved in a straight line toward Jaya's horse, its small eyes fixed on her. She knew if the pig slipped between the horse's legs it would disembowel her mount with its tusks. Major Vir Singh's instructions at tent pegging echoing in her head, Jaya dug her heels into her horse, trying to gain momentum so that speed would add strength to her blow. The boar's ugly snout was pulled back in pain and rage as she steadied the lance in her grip, hardly aware of the other riders shouting to distract the wounded pig.

The wild boar was nearly under the horse when she brought her arm down. The tip of the lance disappeared into the boar's neck. The blade sliced through gristle and flesh as she put all her weight behind it. An earsplitting squeal shattered the silence of the jungle, and the boar fell to the ground, the wooden lance snapping under the weight of its body.

A group of beaters appeared over the ridge. The Maharajah waved at Jaya, letting the shikaris know it was Jaya's kill. Loud cheers rolled down the rocky nullah, and the disturbed crocodiles lashed their huge tails against the mud, as Arun Roy galloped toward her. 'Nicely done, Bai-sa! That was a perfect stroke. You've shamed me!'

The rest of the day passed uneventfully. Occasionally Arun Roy would rein in his horse next to Jaya's. Although he said nothing of importance, Jaya found herself blushing at his approach, confused by his playful manner and his careless compliments. By the time the day's sport had ended, the total bag was nine wild boar, and the sky was red with the setting sun, throwing the brilliant plumage of the roosting jungle birds into black silhouette.

As they rode back to the tents, Arun Roy and Tiny Dungra discussed recipes for cooking wild boar, their enthusiasm echoing in the silent cane fields barely visible in the thin light of a new moon.

Jaya quickly bathed and changed her clothes while the shikaris waited in the cold night air with kerosene lanterns to light the mud pathway.

At the far end of the tents, a log fire blazed in a large pit. Arun Roy and Tiny Dungra leaned back in canvas chairs, drinks in their hands, their legs stretched to the warmth of the fire. Near them, the carcass of a wild boar swung from a long iron bar, steam rising from the pans of boiling water being poured over it.

Jaya joined them, but they barely acknowledged her, their attention taken by an old man with a magnificent white moustache. The villager pointed a crooked finger at the boar half-skinned on its iron rod. 'The pig-pearl hukam. Your men have forgotten to look for the pig-pearl.'

Tiny Dungra bent forward eagerly, almost tipping his chair into the mud. 'What is a pig-pearl?'

'The Bai-sa's boar was old enough to have a pearl in its head, hukam. As is sometimes found in the head of an old elephant. No pearls from the sea can compare with the pig-pearl, hukam.'

'What does it look like?'

'It shines like moonlight, hukam. It has magical properties. Bai-sa's boar must have one in its head.'

'You mean if we find the pig-pearl it belongs to Bai-sa?' The disappointment was clear in Tiny's voice. Jaya giggled, remembering the remarks of the purdah ladies when they had seen the pearls around Tiny Dungra's neck. Arun Roy threw his arm across the back of Jaya's canvas chair, laughing with her, and Jaya suddenly felt she had known the lawyer all her life.

IN THE MAHARAJAH'S durbar tent, rows of villagers sat cross-legged on the carpets, and village headmen in brilliant turbans, their high-waisted jackets almost hidden by their shawls, waited for Jai Singh to speak.

The Maharajah leaned forward on his gaddi. 'The elders of every village in this area are here tonight. According to our ancient ways a decision made by the elders of five villages can overturn the laws made by a king, but tonight I have called you from your homes to tell you that I fear your counsels will no longer carry weight. Our ministers now give preference to ways of governing that are alien to us.'

The villagers were silent, taking in the meaning of the Maharajah's words. An imposing man with an upswept beard asked, 'How can we prevent this, hukam?'

'If you wish your words to be heard then you must learn the new language of government.'

'We till our fields and tend our herds. We have no time to learn the language of the Angrez.' The other villagers noisily echoed his sentiments.

'I am not talking of the language of the British. I speak of a new language of power. Each village must choose someone to represent its interests who can attend the Secretariat and learn this new method of government. When the clash between your interests and those of the nobles comes, as it surely must, you will be able to voice your concerns effectively, even making them heard by the British Empire itself. As soon as the war is over, we shall start a school of administration for your sons. The governing council of Balmer will be chosen by vote, and you will share equal power with the nobles.'

The villagers turned to each other, anxiety visible on their faces as they discussed the Maharajah's suggestions. An elder raised his joined hands. 'The nobles will resent this, hukam. They will not wish to share their hereditary powers with us.'

'No one has hereditary powers, only hereditary duties. It is my responsibility to protect the people against the anger of the nobles. Remember this. This war has changed the balance of our world. We can never return to what we once were. If we are not prepared to change, we will perish.'

RETURNING TO the Fort, the Maharajah's guests set to work on the new constitution, anxious to complete the document before they journeyed back to their homes in time for the Divali celebrations which signalled the Hindu New Year.

In that time Jaya seldom saw the visitors, except for one occasion when she was summoned by her father and the old Maharajah of Dungra to Jai Singh's office.

The table in front of the two rulers was covered with green files. 'These are stock certificates, Bai-sa,' Jai Singh said. 'I am making them over into your name. You are to tell no one about them – not your mother or even your husband.'

Jaya stared at the engraved lettering on the papers, chilled by the note of conspiracy in her father's voice.

'Every good housewife keeps a secret cache of money for hard times, Bai-sa,' Maharajah Dungra reassured her. 'You are taking a huge dowry to Sirpur, but there may come a time when you need something for yourself. Until then, Tiny and I will keep this wealth safe for you in Dungra.'

'Are these papers wealth, hukam?'

Dungra laughed. 'A new kind of wealth, Bai-sa. I bought these for your father in London in 1898. In twenty years, their value has already multiplied many times over.'

The reminder of her impending wedding dispersed the carefree mood created by the visitors, and Jaya felt burdened by her future, hardly able to smile when Arun Roy came to say goodbye and handed her a small package.

Under the moustache, Arun Roy's lips stretched in a smile. 'I believe this belongs to you, Bai-sa.'

Jaya opened the wrapping. A large pearl nestled in the velvet like a misshapen egg. Jaya gasped. 'The pig-pearl!'

'Next time, we'll find an elephant pearl together,' the lawyer teased, and Jaya flushed as she watched him walk away, his dhoti sweeping against the stone floor, wondering why she felt his conspirator in a plot he had not yet revealed.

21

THE FRESCO PAINTERS came and went and it was time to prepare for Divali night, when every house in the kingdom would be lit with clay lamps to attract the Goddess of Wealth.

While you are getting ready for Divali we have been guarding the Jordan Valley and watching the men go down with malaria and dysentery,' Tikka wrote from Palestine.

'Sir Pratap has already become a legend here. He insisted on sleeping in the stables with his horses to make sure they were over their seasickness. Although the temperature is 115 degrees in the shade - quite a difference from the snowstorms of France — he kept the Imperial troops fit by making them walk down the polo field, four hundred men at a time, to remove every stone so we could play polo without endangering our horses. Lord Allenby tried to make Sir Pratap remain in a hotel in Jerusalem. But the old man would have none of it, worse luck for his son, Hanut Singh, who has to get up at five in the morning and jump his father's pony over a five-foot bar for two hours, while his father inspects the troops.

'Poor old Sir Pratap fell ill with fever on the night of July 13 and missed all the fun when the Turks attacked. One squadron of the Jodhpur Lancers carried on too far and were all killed. Sir Pratap is now claiming to be a blood relative of every man who died. He is bursting with pride because one of his officers, Major Dalpat Singh, got the Military Cross for galloping on an enemy machine gun, killing the gunners, taking the gun and then capturing the Turkish commanding officer with his bare hands.

'Sir Pratap has broken his legs so often in the past, he now finds it painful to mount or dismount. Despite the pain and the fact that he is seventy-four years old, he stays in the saddle for thirty hours at a time. We honour him as the very image of a Rajput warrior, and we are performing a special puja for him on Divali.'

Jaya watched the shouting potters whip their donkeys up the ramparts of the Fort, stacks of clay lamps shaking on their over-loaded carts, and wondered when Tikka would be in Balmer for Divali again.

Inside the zenana the maidservants took out silver cups, so that when Divali night ended they could collect the streaks of lampblack from the silver and make kohl for the purdah ladies to line their eyes. And the eunuchs unrolled the tent where the ladies would usher in the new year by dancing for the ruler. On their balconies the purdah ladies played cards, laughing when they saw the eunuchs struggling to raise the tent on its poles.

Then it was Divali night. Above the city, the illuminated Fort loomed in the darkness, thousands of clay lamps flickering on its battlements. Crackers burst like gunfire in the narrow streets of the capital, and fireworks shot into the night from roof terraces and bazaar corners.

In the zenana tent, Jai Singh sat on a cushion facing the ladies. Warm breezes carried the sound of laughter from the city as the Maharani rose to dance for her husband. For a long moment the Maharani danced alone, glass bangles shining on her narrow wrists. One by one the purdah women joined her, turning in skirts so heavily encrusted with gems that the next morning the maidservants would bandage their bleeding waists. But now the women dipped in the dance of the peacock, the jewelled ornaments which held their veils to their foreheads throwing coloured patterns onto the gold canopy of the tent. Turning round and round, her skirt ballooning against the others, Jaya saw fireworks appear for a bright moment in the sky, then fragment into coloured ash, and she imagined that Balmer was like a great Catherine wheel, spinning through the night for the pleasure of the God-dess.

TWO DAYS LATER, it was as if Divali had come again. Maharajah Jai

Singh strode into his wife's apartments, and placed a sweet between her lips, saying, 'You gave birth to a lion.'

Behind him, the Chief Eunuch carried a sheaf of telegrams. Jai Singh picked out one. 'This is from your son's commander-in-chief, General Allenby: "CONGRATULATE YOU ON THE BRILLIANT EXPLOIT OF YOUR MEN WHO TOOK THE TOWN OF HAIFA AT A GALLOP, KILLING MANY TURKS WITH THE LANCE IN THE STREETS OF THE TOWN, AND CAPTURING 700 PRISONERS." '

He rifled through the telegrams. 'And this is from the Viceroy: "A BRILLIANT FEAT OF ARMS." '

Jai Singh turned to the report from Major Vir Singh: 'ACTION OF IMPERIAL LANCERS AGAINST HEAVILY FORTIFIED TURKISH POSITION RESULTED IN CAPTURE OF 2 GERMAN OFFICERS, 23 TURKISH OFFICERS, 700 OTHER RANKS, 2 NAVAL GUNS, 10 FIELD GUNS, 10 MACHINE GUNS AND A LARGE AMOUNT OF AMMUNITION, PROVING BEYOND DOUBT ROLE OF CAVALRY STILL VITAL IN WAR. ALLENBY CALLING HAIFA CHARGE "A BRILLIANT LITTLE SCRAP BY ALMOST OVEREAGER INDIANS"!'

There was little time to dwell on Tikka's glory. Although it was November, long past the monsoon season, it was still raining heavily in Balmer, increasing fears that the influenza epidemic sweeping through India would at any moment reach Balmer. Numerous cases had been reported in the town, although as yet there were no deaths to add to the horrifying toll of three million dead in the rest of India.

Kuki-bai developed a high fever which did not respond to the herbal potions sent by the ayurvedic doctors or the medicines prescribed by the Western-style doctors. Jaya sat by the old concubine's silver bed, listening to her incoherent ramblings about the Chand Mahal as a solitary lamp, rocked by gusts of heavy wind, threw strange shadows on the painted walls and maidservants entered with burning camphor to disinfect the air.

On the evening that Kuki-bai's fever broke, Jaya was called to the Maharani's balcony. She scrubbed herself with disinfectant before joining her parents, who were worriedly discussing the influenza epidemic.

The agitation was clear in the Maharani's voice. 'The monsoons have failed in the rest of India, but here it is as if the Goddess were trying to drown the kingdom. And with each storm the influenza cases increase.'

The Maharajah shook his head wearily. 'The situation is critical everywhere, even in Damascus. Of Tikka's whole division there remain only twelve hundred men. Already four hundred soldiers have died of influenza.' He unfolded thin sheets of paper and read out his son's latest letter.

'I suppose it is no surprise that the men are going down like ninepins to the influenza. In the past two weeks we have covered nearly three hundred miles on horseback, and in all that time the men have lived on tea, biscuits and jam. We will not touch the tinned food for fear it has beef.

'We have been charging Turkish columns and taking prisoners all the way. On the Homs–Damascus road one of our squadrons saw a party of Arabs and charged. The Arabs bolted, leaving a solitary Arab in a car. Risaldar Major Hamir Singh immediately accused him of being a Turkish spy. When the prisoner finally convinced the British officers of our unit that he was none other than the legendary Lawrence of Arabia, I thought Prince Pratap of Sirpur was going to die laughing. But I fear Colonel Lawrence will never forgive the Indian Army!

'We entered Damascus on October 1, and were given a tumultuous welcome. Allenby wants all troops who are fit enough to advance on Aleppo at once. Everyone hopes it will be the last serious battle fought on this front. The men are very tired and anxious to go home. So am I.'

Beyond the painted wooden windows, lights moved in the Temple of the Balmer Maharanis where the purdah ladies were performing their evening puja.

The Maharajah put his arms around his wife. 'It will soon be over. Think, your son may be here to celebrate Divali with you next year.'

The Maharani wept in her husband's embrace. 'After all these years that he has been in school and then at war!'

Jaya left the balcony, embarrassed at her mother's display of emotion. The Baran blocked her path, thrusting a paper into her hands. 'The telegraph clerks say the Durbar must read this urgently.'

Jaya reluctantly returned to the balcony. His arm still around his weeping wife, Jai Singh took the message. The paper slipped from his fingers and Jaya stepped forward to retrieve it as Jai Singh flung the Maharani from him.

'No!' he shouted, drawing the dagger from his cummerbund and smashing the hilt against the painted windows. 'Anything but this!' Women appeared in the courtyard below, staring in consternation at the ruler as they shielded their faces from the falling splinters. 'Not this!' the Maharajah bellowed like a wounded animal, smashing the dagger again and again on the windows.

Jaya read the message: 'YOUR GALLANT SON FELL GLORIOUSLY AT THE HEAD OF HIS BALMER LANCERS WHILE CHARGING THE ENEMY TROOPS AT ALEPPO. HE WAS CREMATED WITH FULL MILITARY HONOURS. ALLENBY.'

'The lamps, Bai-sa.' Seeing her mother's bloodless face, Jaya knew she had guessed the contents of the paper. 'Tell the women to stop the puja and extinguish the lights in the zenana immediately.' The Maharani's low voice was steady as she gave her instructions, and Jaya wondered why she was not crying now, when her son was dead, as she had cried at the thought of his return. 'Tell the zenana ladies they must cease speaking.'

Jaya turned and fled down the stairs. The Baran ran after her. 'Is it Tikka-maharaj, Bai-sa? Has something happened to Tikka-sahib?'

'We must put out the lamps, Baran.'

The Baran tore the veil from her head, wailing to the women crowding the corridors. 'The Tikka-raja is gone! The Angrez have killed the Tikka-raja!'

At the Baran's words the women bared their heads. Jaya ran past them, her feet sliding on the veils which now covered the marble floors. Hardly able to see through the hair falling over their faces, the women reached out to steady her.

In the Temple of the Balmer Maharanis, the purdah ladies were sitting in prayer in front of the stone image of the Goddess. Jaya lit a lamp from the flame burning before the Goddess and placed it on the arch of the temple. As she did so, an eerie silence fell on the zenana and the whole harem was plunged into darkness.

Jaya heard the crash of breaking clay as she stumbled back to her mother's balcony. The eunuchs were smashing the cooking vessels in the zenana kitchens to ensure no food was cooked in the palace for the thirteen days of mourning. In the darkness a flame leapt high above the main gates of the Fort, and Jaya was almost sick on the steps. The flame, taken from the Fort Temple, signalled to the whole country that the heir to the Balmer throne was dead.

For the next thirteen days the Maharajah sat in open durbar, a white turban of mourning on his head. The carpets in the Durbar Hall were shrouded in white sheets, and the Fort priests, led by the Raj Guru, chanted the scriptures in an unbroken relay through the long days and nights of mourning as the people of the kingdom came to sit with their ruler.

On the fifth day of mourning, Maharajah Jai Singh informed the Durbar Hall that the war in the Middle East had ended and the Ottoman Emperor had accepted an unconditional surrender. His voice was so weak few heard him, and people whispered to one another that the ruler looked very ill.

22

THE SLOW THUD of the nagara drums sounded above the elephant gates. Jai Singh leaned on the old Raj Guru for support as the Balmer Lancers advanced towards him.

Jaya stood at the zenana walls watching the bareheaded Lancers, their lances reversed, ride up the stone ramparts. In front of them trotted Tikka's riderless horse, a piece of homespun cotton covering its black muscles. At the rear of the procession, Major Vir Singh carried the urn containing Tikka's ashes.

Seeing her son's ashes, the Maharani's grief finally broke through her control. 'Your father and his senseless, hopeless rebellions against the Angrez!' she screamed, beating Jaya's shoulders with her fists. 'He has killed my son! Your father has killed my son!'

Kuki-bai pulled the Maharani into an embrace, muffling the shrill voice. 'Send for the Sati Mata, Bai-sa. Your mother is not in possession of her senses. She might say anything now.'

While they waited for the Sati Mata, Kuki-bai sequestered the Maharani in her own chambers. The Baran informed the avid purdah ladies that the Maharani was performing a special puja for her son, and Jaya was sent to inform her father of the Maharani's condition.

The Senapathy and the Raj Guru were conferring worriedly outside the Maharajah's bedroom. 'The doctors are with your father, Bai-sa,' the Raj Guru said. 'He cannot see you now.'

Jaya returned to Kuki-bai's chambers. The Maharani was clutching the armlet Jai Singh had given his son on his departure for the war.

Shafts of light from the two diamonds fell on the Sati Mata, sitting impassively on the floor, her snake coiled in her lap.

'This was meant to protect his son,' the Maharani said bitterly. 'How can he protect anyone? He paid homage to a widowed empress, an unholy creature! He forced his own wife to break purdah! His Dasra sacrifices to the Goddess were unclean! He has cursed our house with his profanity!'

The Sati Mata raised her hand. The Maharani fell silent and sat down heavily on Kuki-bai's bed, setting the silver bells clashing.

'Have you told your father, Bai-sa? What are his instructions?' Kuki-bai whispered.

'They won't let me see him. He is ill.'

'Is it influenza?' Kuki-bai asked in an urgent voice. When Jaya shook her head, Kuki-bai slumped as though she could no longer carry the burden of her own suspicions. 'Run, child. Tell your father he must not eat food from Raja Man Singh's house!'

Jaya raced through the corridors of the zenana to convey Kuki-bai's message, but the Household Guard barred the doors of her father's apartments with crossed lances. Behind the lances Jaya saw the Balmer crest, the vulture with carrion clutched in its claws. 'Durbar is in session with his Council, Bai-sa. They are not to be disturbed.'

She sat down to wait, staring dully at the rows of the Ministers' slippers lying outside the doors. After a long time the doors opened. Raja Man Singh came out, fury contorting his face. At the sight of Jaya, his expression changed to one of sorrow. 'These are terrible, terrible times, Bai-sa. We must pray that everything will be all right soon.'

The Raj Guru was beckoning from the doorway. Jaya ran past Raja Man Singh into her father's darkened bedroom. The Maharajah's left foot, exposed at the end of the short bed, was not encircled with the heavy gold anklet of sovereignty. Jaya's eyes adjusted to the dark and she saw that her father was holding the anklet in his hands.

Jai Singh painfully raised his head. 'I have informed the Council that you are to become ruler of Balmer, Bai-sa.' He handed her the anklet. 'Raja Man Singh must rule as Regent until you come of age, but after that . . .' He sank back onto his pillow with a sigh of exhaustion. 'Guard the honour of the people, Bai-sa. Complete the reforms I have begun.'

Jaya bent forward. "Hukam, you must not eat food from Raja Man Singh's house.' She could see her tears falling on the pillow stained with her father's sweat. But his eyes were closed, and he hadn't heard. 'Bappa, listen to me. Don't touch any food from Raja Man Singh's house.'

The Raj Guru tapped Jaya's shoulder. She turned, weeping, to him. 'Bappa must not eat food that has been prepared in Raja Man Singh's house!'

The Household Guards looked on in surprise as the old high priest drew her into his arms. 'Don't look for conspiracy where there is none, Bai-sa. You know how many deaths there have been these last weeks.' He looked sternly into her eyes. 'Your father is dying because his time has come. Call your mother.'

Jaya did not know where her mother found the reserve of will to compose herself into a figure of serenity as she sat by the Maharajah's deathbed. It was as though the Sati Mata had instilled into the Maharani her own strength, and when the doctors pronounced Maharajah Jai Singh dead the Maharani only said, 'Hai Ram!' as though she had been preparing for widowhood a long time.

She knelt and removed her diamond anklets, throwing them on the floor under the bed. She loosed her long hair from its thick plait and unfastened the jewelled collar of matrimony that had enclosed her neck since she had become a bride at the age of thirteen. Jaya saw white marks around her mother's throat where the collar had protected the skin from the sun as her mother reached up and with slow deliberation rubbed the red tilak of marriage off her forehead.

Denuded of any sign of matrimony, the Maharani sat on the floor next to her husband's bed while the priests prepared the Maharajah's body for cremation. Once, she motioned for a pair of scissors. When Jaya brought the scissors, the Maharani lifted handfuls of heavy hair and cut it off close to her scalp, until the floor around her was carpeted with her hair.

The priests dressed the Maharajah's body in ceremonial clothes and placed it on a flower-strewn stretcher. In the courtyard outside, an elephant waited to carry Jai Singh's body through the streets of the capital to the cremation ground.

The Maharani followed the stretcher to the doorway of the Maharajah's apartments. Crowds of men thronged the corridors.

Seeing the Maharani's bared head, shorn of its hair, they crushed together, away from the pollution cast by a widow.

Inside the zenana, it was as though every old woman in the kingdom had crowded into the marble halls to scream at the Maharani.

'Unfortunate woman, your life has ended!'

'Widow! You are unclean! Widow!'

A slab of rough stone was pushed into the Maharani's path. Colour streaked its crevices, showing where spices had been ground for cooking. The Maharani dropped to her knees. Jaya pushed her way through the shrieking women and saw her mother raise both wrists and smash them against the stone until broken glass bangles splintered into the rough surface. The old women fought each other to grasp the stone rolling pin and grind the Maharani's bangles into glass dust.

Jaya hit out blindly at the old women. For a moment her flailing fists silenced the obscene litany. Then the shrieking accusations doubled in volume:

'Widow!'

'Unclean!'

'Unholy!'

Without a change in her regal carriage the Maharani passed through the lines of cursing women and under the high wall that separated the concubines from the rest of the zenana. Broken glass fell on her head; the concubines were throwing their broken bangles over the wall, their shrill voices sending up a steady wordless wail. Jaya wondered if their long plaits lay sheared on the floor, and whether the eunuchs were sweeping up the hair to sell in the bazaars.

At the zenana temple, the Maharani said gently, 'Your father's last rites will take place at any moment. I wish to be alone when the cannons announce the end.'

She entered the Temple of the Balmer Maharanis, barring the wooden doors behind her. Jaya stood forlornly on the pathway, watching the fish swimming in the ornamental canals. The sudden crash of cannon fire made the wooden doors of the temple rattle, announcing to the city that the Maharajah's funeral pyre had been lit. Jaya knew that her cousin John, acting in Tikka's place, was breaking her father's skull to release his soul. She looked at the elephant gates and saw the flame that signalled Tikka's death still burning next to the nagaras.

Remembering her father's rage that the British had not taken his cannon for their war, Jaya cursed herself aloud for being born a girl, banned from the last rites.

Kuki-bai and the Sati Mata came running down the pathway between the canals. 'Why are you shouting, child? Where is your mother?'

Jaya wondered what the ascetic had done with her snake, and she giggled through her sobs, visualizing the cobra sliding on the zenana floor among the old women.

Kuki-bai hammered on the locked temple doors, screaming the Maharani's name, and the Sati Mata tightened the red cloth around her breasts as though preparing for battle. The doors of the temple were flung open. The Maharani stood in the entrance, smoke enveloping her slim form, her hands hidden behind her back. Tears of smoke streamed from her green eyes.

'What have you done, woman?' Kuki-bai's voice was almost inaudible with rage. The Maharani looked at her placidly. For a long moment the two women confronted each other through the crash of firing cannon. Then the Maharani thrust her hands in front of the old concubine's face. Jaya vomited into the canal near her feet. The pale hands were wrapped in rags that had been set on fire.

'I am sati now!' the Maharani said with fierce pride. She pressed her burning hands against her long skirt. The skirt immediately caught fire. The Maharani began chanting 'Ram, Ram,' as though she were sitting on the funeral pyre cradling her dead husband's head in her lap.

The Sati Mata pushed Kuki-bai to one side. Lifting the Maharani's burning body in her arms, she flung it unceremoniously into the nearest canal. Jaya saw her mother's shorn head go down into the water once, then again, but she was paralyzed, unable to force her limbs to her mother's rescue.

The Sati Mata gripped the Maharani's arms and dragged her onto the pathway. Kuki-bai crouched next to the Maharani and gently examined the burned hands. 'Why did you do it?' she asked in a sickened voice. 'The Lion of Balmer banned this practice forever.'

The ascetic turned to Jaya. 'Get some balm for your mother's burns. The Raj Guru will be sending for her soon. Tell the Baran to fetch clean clothes.' Jaya stood rooted to the pathway, staring at her mother. 'Your father wanted you to govern a whole kingdom. You cannot stand about looking shocked.' The cold, unsentimental voice shook Jaya out of her paralysis, and she hurried into the zenana to fetch the Baran.

Urged on by the ascetic, the Baran changed the Maharani into clean white garments and bandaged her blistering hands. A frightened purdah lady brought an urgent summons from the High Priest of Balmer, and Jaya wondered if the Sati Mata really could see into the future.

The Raj Guru was pacing up and down the zenana courtyard. When he saw the Maharani's bandaged hands, tears glistened in the severe eyes. 'The Maharajah's soul has been released, hukam. I require your presence at a final ceremony.'

Like a sleepwalker the Maharani let Kuki-bai and the Sati Mata lead her out of the zenana. An assembly of mourners filled the outer courtyards. Before them stood the Ministers of the Council and the senior nobles, their heads covered with the white turbans of mourning.

The Raj Guru's harsh whisper broke through the sound of muffled weeping. 'It is the sacred task of the Raj Guru to guide the ruler so that his reign is marked by tolerance, wisdom, humility. As guardian of the honour of the Balmer throne, I can say that Maharajah Jai Singh, in his every act, fulfilled our teachings.'

Shouts of 'Maharajah Jai Singh amar rahe! Maharajah Jai Singh's soul is immortal!' rose above the ramparts, and anger flashed across Raja Man Singh's features.

'Our greatest blessing has been the continuity of our kings. For thirty-nine generations the anointed son has taken the throne of the anointed father, and we have never endured the cruel wars of disputed succession. But any priest unfortunate enough to be Raj Guru of Balmer when the line of direct succession is broken is enjoined to mark the solemnity of the event by breaking the nagara drums of Balmer Fort.'

Moti lumbered through the crowds, the drums tied to his sides knocking white turbans off heads, and a current of fear passed through the packed courtyards. Raja Man Singh shouted angrily, 'The nagaras can be broken only when we lose our citadel. I am Regent of Balmer. I will not permit this madness.'

161

The Raj Guru ignored the outburst. The elephant sank to its knees. Watched in apprehensive silence by the crowd, the drummers unstrapped the nagaras and dragged them to the priest. Holding the hilt of the Balmer sword with both hands, the Raj Guru brought the steel blade down again and again on the skin stretched tight across the drums, and at each blow the assembly winced.

The Maharani turned abruptly towards the zenana. Jaya barely heard her mother's low voice chanting, 'Ram Nam Sat Hai. The Name of God is Truth. Ram Nam Sat Hai. Let there be peace and peace and peace.'

IN THE FOLLOWING days of mourning, Jaya sat in the Temple of the Balmer Maharanis with her mother, praying for the Maharajah's soul, unaware of the upheavals in the Fort except on the infrequent occasions when she went to her chambers and the Baran repeated the rumours circulating in the kingdom.

'Everyone is saying your father was poisoned by Raja Man Singh, Bai-sa. And now Raja Man Singh has gone to Delhi to petition the Viceroy to overturn your father's decree and let his son, John, succeed to the Balmer gaddi.'

On his return from Delhi, Raja Man Singh summoned the Maharani to the public courtyard outside the King's View.

The Maharani had last stood in the courtyard to break purdah at Maharajah Jai Singh's command, but she was no longer attired as a queen. Now she wore garments made of coarse white cotton, and around her shoulders hung a white cloth printed with the prayer she would repeat for her dead husband until her own death.

'This woman's association with the House of Balmer has ended,' Raja Man Singh shouted. 'She has neither husband nor son to keep her in her old age. What shall we give the widow?'

The question echoed in the courtyard. Jaya stared at the crowds, unwilling to believe they would permit such humiliation on their maharani.

'What shall we give the widow?' Raja Man Singh shouted again, revelling in his triumph. 'It is written in our ancient scriptures that we owe the widow nothing – not the food from our cooking vessels nor the water from our wells. What shall we give the widow?' Turbaned heads were lowered, and people shuffled their feet in embarrassment, but no one challenged the noble. Jaya could see the marks around her mother's throat where the collar of matrimony had sat, the shorn hair sticking out in grey tufts above the pale face drawn with grief, and she clenched her teeth in revulsion at customs which could so strip her regal mother of dignity that pity and disgust marked the features of everyone in the courtyard.

The Raj Guru advanced on the crowds, his spare frame shaking with rage. 'Cruel and heartless race, you have called this woman Mother. It is your duty to succour her.' He raised his hands above his head, and gold glittered between his fingers. 'Fortunately, the Maharani of Balmer does not need the charity of those she has treated as her sons. The Maharajah of Dungra sends these as the sign of the brother.'

He tilted his hands so that everyone could see the gold bangles in his palms. 'A stranger opens his house to your maharani. A stranger places at her feet a brother's wealth. Tomorrow I anoint Raja Man Singh's son Maharajah of Balmer. In the ancient texts which chart the destiny of our country it was written that this be so. But I will break the silence of the Raj Guru to tell you this. It is also written that the man who so eagerly mounts the Balmer throne after the nagara drums are broken will be your last king.'

23

ROYAL PROCLAMATION OF 1919

'George V, by the grace of God, of the United Kingdom of Great Britain and Ireland and of the British Dominions beyond the seas, King, Defender of the Faith, Emperor of India.

'To my Viceroy and Governor General, to the Princes of Indian States, and to all my subjects in India, of whatsoever race or creed, Greeting.

'Ever since the welfare of India was confided to us, it has been held as a sacred trust by Our Royal House and Line. We have endeavoured to give to India's people the many blessings which Providence has bestowed upon ourselves. But there is one gift which yet remains and without which the progress of a country cannot be consummated – the right of her people to direct her affairs.

'The Act which has now become law entrusts the elected representatives of the people with a definite share in the Government. The burden is too heavy to be borne in full until time and experience have brought the necessary strength, but opportunity will now be given for experience to grow.

'Simultaneously I have gladly given my assent to the establishment of a Chamber of Princes. I trust that its counsel may be fruitful of lasting good to the Princes and States themselves, and may be to the advantage of the Empire as a whole.

'I take this occasion again to assure the Princes of India of *my determination ever to maintain unimpaired their privileges, rights and dignities.'*

IN 1919, JAYA was married by proxy to Prince Pratap of Sirpur, and King George issued a royal proclamation promising limited self-government to India.

But the events of that year had drastically altered the relationship between Indians and their British rulers. Publication of the details of the reforms promised in the King Emperor's proclamation had horrified the British community in India, and their newspapers waged a sustained campaign against the idea of natives being competent to govern themselves.

The situation was further exacerbated by international pressures. India's sixty million Muslims believed that British troops had profaned the holy cities of Mecca and Medina during the war, and were now humiliating the defeated Ottoman Emperor, Commander of the Islamic Faith. From the northern borders of India, the Afghans called upon Indian Muslims to join them in overthrowing an infidel empire.

The economic situation was equally perilous. The influenza epidemic, which had taken a toll of five million lives, was followed by a disastrous monsoon. Despite the severe shortage of food, the Empire continued to export Indian grain, refusing point-blank to reduce land tariffs on a starving peasantry, and Gandhi led movements among Indian peasants to withhold taxes until the Empire recognized the seriousness of their plight.

In reaction to the perceived heartlessness of the British Empire, many Indians embraced the doctrines of Marx and Lenin, actively encouraged by the one-year-old Bolshevik government of Russia. Other Indians took their inspiration from President Wilson of the United States, that passionate advocate of self-determination, regarded by many Indians as the most powerful figure in the world.

The spark that ignited the multitude of inflammatory situations was the imposition of a new law. Instead of instituting its promised reforms – at the very time when Indians believed their sacrifices in the war had earned them such reforms – the Imperial Government proceeded to pass the Rowlatt Acts, under which Indians could be tried in special British courts with no right of appeal. Anyone believed to constitute a threat to the peace was to be detained in jail or in the dreaded penal colony in the Andaman Islands, where prisoners were kept in chains, often for the duration of their ten- and fifteen-year sentences. Those Indians who published or circulated documents which the British believed to be seditious could be imprisoned indefinitely.

Muslim leaders called upon all believers to stop working for the British Empire, and Gandhi launched a nationwide noncooperation movement to show Indian displeasure with what was being called the Black Act of the British Raj. The Empire responded by making it illegal for more than five persons to congregate in British India. Indians immediately convened mass protest meetings. Thousands were jailed.

Violent speeches were made, and violent tempers flared. Two prominent nationalist leaders were forcibly deported from the city of Amritsar. Their enraged followers burned down banks and public buildings, killing five Englishmen and severely beating a woman missionary. Although many Indians protected Englishmen from the mob, the martial-law administrator of the Punjab, General R.E.H. Dyer, declared it illegal for any Indian to walk upright through the Amritsar streets where the crimes had been committed. Drums beaten at dawn and dusk warned all Indians to crawl on their hands and knees through these streets.

A mass meeting was held in Amritsar to protest General Dyer's ordinance. Armed troops surrounded the walled park where the meeting was taking place, and blocked the park's only exit. No warning was given to the crowd to disperse. On General Dyer's orders, the troops fired directly at unarmed men, women and children. Every bullet, of each round fired, killed or wounded a demonstrator. Subsequently, no assistance was rendered to the wounded.

A total news blackout sealed off the Punjab from the rest of India, and other Indians could only speculate as to what was happening, but as rumours of General Dyer's massacre spread, Indian disaffection with the British Empire grew critical. The Indian poet and Nobel Prize laureate Raja Rabindranath Tagore returned his knighthood to the British. Thirty other Indians followed suit, refusing to wear the decorations given them by an unjust Empire.

General Dyer applied martial law in the Punjab even more

harshly, now decreeing public floggings and more crawling orders. A new ordinance required all Indians to salaam any person with a white skin.

Village after Punjab village – which had provided many of the troops used by the Empire in the war – rose against the British. In retaliation, the British bombed the villages from the air.

After six months of public agitation, the Empire finally instituted an inquiry into the Amritsar massacre, to defuse a dangerously explosive situation. General Dyer, who had ordered the shooting, defended his actions with these words: 'It was a merciful act but at the same time it was a horrible act, and it took a lot of doing . . . or they would come back and laugh at me. . . .'

Indian political leaders and seven Indian maharajahs were brought to London to explain to an anxious England that vengeful Indians were not on the verge of murdering every Englishman in his bed. The Maharajah of Alwar observed that it was the first time the British Prime Minister had deigned to receive a delegation of Indian rulers, despite the numerous occasions when Indian princes had sought to meet the Prime Minister to explain the exigencies of imperial policy as they affected Indians.

To most Indians, the incidents of 1919 had rendered King George's proclamation irrelevant. Indeed, on the very day of Jaya's marriage, in the city of Amritsar, where General Dyer had fired on an unarmed crowd, the leaders of the Indian National Congress responded to the King Emperor's proclamation with a new resolution.

'*This Conference is of the opinion that the Reforms are inadequate, unsatisfactory, and disappointing.*

'*This Conference reiterates its declaration that India is fit for full responsible government and repudiates all assumptions and assertions to the contrary.*'

ONLY HOURS after the Indian National Congress passed its resolution, Jaya stepped into her bathing pool and was almost suffocated by the heavy scent of attar of roses.

For seven days her body had been caked in clay, until she had left a trail of white powder wherever she went in the zenana. All morning the maidservants had been removing the white clay from her body with almond oil, their comments on the smoothness of her

167

skin almost drowned by the reed marriage instruments wailing from the walls of the outer Fort. Now, on the afternoon of her wedding, she gratefully submerged her body in the cloying scent that lay in an oily film on the surface of the clear water, thinking about the events that had led to her marriage.

In the last year she had been kept a virtual prisoner in the zenana, while rumours circulated in the kingdom about the sinister suddenness of her father's death. During that year, Raja Man Singh's son, John, had been crowned the Maharajah of Balmer, with the support of the British Empire.

The new ruling family had ruthlessly consolidated their position in the kingdom, heaping humiliation on the Maharani until the widow had fled Balmer to seek sanctuary with the Maharajah of Dungra.

Then the Roys were dismissed from Balmer, their nationalist sentiments publicly denounced as seditious, and Rani Man Singh had incarcerated the vociferously critical Kuki-bai in the concubines' quarters, abandoning the old woman to the capricious malice of the eunuchs and the jealousy of the other concubines.

In his eagerness to remove the only remaining threat to his son's throne, Raja Man Singh tried to hasten Jaya's marriage; but during 1919, Prince Pratap of Sirpur had remained in Palestine with his Lancers, assisting in the dismantling of the defeated Ottoman Empire. After protracted negotiations, and after agreeing to pay a large annual sum to Prince Pratap as well as Jaya's dowry, Raja Man Singh had finally prevailed on the Sirpur Council to permit Jaya to be married by proxy – to Prince Pratap's sword.

Jaya pulled her body out of the bath and went to her altar room to perform her final puja as an unmarried girl. As the Baran recited prayers, Jaya bitterly circled the elephant-headed god of protection and good fortune with sticks of incense. For a year the Baran had scrupulously followed Rani Man Singh's instructions to isolate Jaya within the zenana. The other purdah ladies, conscious of Rani Man Singh's power over their lives, had imitated the Baran. Jaya remembered how she had endured the sneers of the eunuchs in the lonely months when she had spoken to no one but Chandni. Tonight, Rani Man Singh would act as her mother in the wedding rituals. Raja Man Singh would perform the rites of her father. John, who had usurped the throne of Balmer, would act as her brother.

Cheering from below the Fort signalled the approach of the bridegroom's party. Already the bridal gifts had arrived: the famous Sirpur emeralds, and a tusker elephant. Now the wealth of Sirpur was on public display – painted elephants, trotting horses with gems plaited in their manes, cattle with gilded horns and gold cloths thrown over their creamy shoulders, horse carriages, fashionable Rolls-Royces, the elephant carrying the Sirpur nagaras.

Jaya garlanded the portrait of Prince Pratap of Sirpur. In the past year, she had stared so often at the features of the man who would release her from captivity that she had almost forgotten what other men looked like. Even when Chandni brought news from the bazaars that the Afghan War in which James Osborne was fighting with his regiment was not going well for the British Empire, she had felt only a remote regret, as if hearing the misfortunes of a stranger.

The Sirpur nagaras pounded through the shouts of street urchins, and Jaya's breath caught in her throat as she visualized the last elephant in the Sirpur procession, and Prince Pratap's sword swaying under the golden howdah flying the pennants of the House of Sirpur.

The Fort cannons fired as the Sirpur cortege approached the battlements of the Fort. Jaya could see the flash of gunpowder in the darkness as the zenana women delicately outlined the contours of her face with dots of sandalwood and helped her into the heavy crimson skirt encrusted with diamonds and tied the tassels of her silk chemise across her naked back.

Making no effort to be gentle, Rani Man Singh squeezed dozens of ivory bangles over Jaya's hands until both arms were circled from wrist to armpit in clashing bracelets. Jaya kept her face averted, for fear the Rani would see the hatred in her eyes. But when the purdah ladies fastened the veil of golden gauze on her hair, they also turned their faces away, embarrassed at the unseemly manner in which Jaya was being married off to a sword.

The Baran ran into the chamber. 'The Sirpur party is moving up the ramparts, hukam. You must hurry.' Thrusting the bag of jewellery into the Baran's hands, Rani Man Singh hurried down the corridor to light a clay lamp from the flame that burned in front of Jaya's altar, before placing the lamp on a thali filled with the symbols of fertility: milk, water, honey, rice, a coconut.

Infected by the excitement of the approaching procession, the purdah ladies fumbled as they fastened Jaya's jewellery. A golden nose ring obscured the lower half of Jaya's face, interfering with their attempts to get the collar of auspicious gems around her slender throat. Below the collar they fastened a ruby necklace in its European setting which had once belonged to a Queen of France. Jaya felt suffocated as the women scratched at her body with jewelled gauntlets and heavy anklets. One woman tied a blinker embroidered with pearl parakeets, the birds of passion, onto her veil. The other women crowded to the lattice screens to watch the arrival of the bridegroom's party.

Bursts of fireworks illuminated the zenana walls. Seeing the familiar chambers filled with hurrying women, Jaya forgot the oppressions of the past year and was conscious only of an immense and paralyzing reluctance to leave all that she had ever known for an uncharted life in a new world.

Lifting her head with difficulty under the heavy blinker, Jaya moved slowly to the screen. Scores of Sirpur dancing girls were whirling into the marriage courtyard, tossing showers of coins onto the yellow flagstones as they danced. The approaching elephants, lit by the bronze torches that lined the ramparts, threw huge shadows against the battlements of the Fort.

The Balmer dancing girls waited in the marriage courtyard with long-necked rosewater sprinklers in the shapes of peacocks and swaying lotus blossoms and opium poppies. Thousands of clay lamps flickered in the courtyard lighting the falling coins and silver sprinklers, so that the moving crowds looked like bursts of fireworks as they milled towards the marriage pavilion, shrouded in its three curtains of scented flowers.

The Prime Minister of Sirpur entered the courtyard. The Balmer dancing girls crowded around him, splashing his gold brocade tunic and the massive diamond in his aigrette with rose water.

'Look, Bai-sa! The Sirpur animals are forming a reception line on either side of the ramparts. The sword must be approaching.'

An elephant caparisoned in gold brocade moved to the front of the Sirpur procession, lamplight shining on the heavy gold anklets circling its legs. In the howdah sat the Sirpur Elder who would act for Prince Pratap and the Raj Guru of Sirpur, who would perform the marriage rituals jointly with the Raj Guru of Balmer. In front of the two men, shaded by the royal canopy of Sirpur, Prince Pratap's sword lay on a golden stand.

The elephant moved under the arch where a clay globe filled with puffed rice was suspended by streamers. The Sirpur Elder lifted Prince Pratap's sword and smashed the gourd. Puffed rice fell over the howdah, and the elephant raised its trunk, feeling blindly for the grains as Rani Man Singh spoke the ritual words.

'Why have you come to Balmer?'

'I have come to marry your daughter.'

'Our daughter is more than gold to us. She is the Goddess of Bounty, the Goddess Laxmi.'

'I will respect her as a goddess. I greet her in the name of the gods.'

The Sirpur Elder dismounted onto the chalk circle consecrated for the bridegroom, holding Prince Pratap's sword in both hands before him. A hundred conch shells blown from the stone ramparts sounded eerily through the Fort as Rani Man Singh circled Prince Pratap's sword seven times with the thali bearing the flame from Jaya's altar.

Raja Man Singh moved forward with a handful of gold coins, letting them fall in a glittering shower onto the sword to deflect the evil eye from the bridegroom.

Jaya looked down at the courtyard. Curtains of flowers enclosed the marriage pavilion, swaying gently in the breeze created by the crowds. Smoke from the holy fire wafted around the canopy of red cloth above the pavilion. She could see the seven steps leading from the marriage platform to the ground, the seven steps which would allow her to change her mind even after the rituals of marriage were over, and the thought that she could deny the wedding gave her a surge of hope. The feeling died as Raja Man Singh led the Sirpur Elder towards the marriage pavilion, where the old Raj Guru of Balmer was waiting.

Supported by the Baran, Jaya moved painfully through the stone corridors of the zenana for the last time. She could hear the voices of the two Raj Gurus intoning the lineages of their respective kings. Even from that distance Jaya heard the contempt in the voice of the Sirpur high priest. Balmer was an ancient kingdom - twelve hundred years old. But the kingdom of Sirpur was so old its origins were lost in myth, and that consciousness of superiority was conveyed to the entire assembly by the bored voice of the Sirpur priest chanting the three-thousand-year-old lineage of his rulers.

As she neared the marriage pavilion, the voices of the priests were invoking the blessing of India's most powerful river, the only river named as a man: the Brahmaputra – Son of the Creator. Jaya's eyes welled with tears at the thought of leaving Balmer's empty desert landscape for that ancient alien kingdom sprawled across the delta of the Brahmaputra River.

The two priests seated Jaya next to the sword. Tying a red cloth around its hilt they knotted the edge of the cloth to Jaya's veil. The Elder of Sirpur stood impassively behind the sword while they chanted the ancient Sanskrit prayers of marriage and duty. Jaya tried to keep her head upright as rice and flowers cascaded onto her veil, sliding to the clay floor. Hot tears fell onto the jewelled gauntlets that encased her hands, and she willed herself not to scratch her cheeks where tears had moistened the sandalwood patterns on her face.

Seven married Balmer women stepped up to the platform to perform the separate ceremonies that gave her away to the House of Sirpur with symbols of fertility and wealth. One smeared oil on her head. Another put a long line of collyrium under her eyes. Jaya saw their solemn faces and remembered them sprawled on mattresses at the manwar ceremony, laughing at the bawdy lyrics of the eunuchs. The last married woman gently pulled at Jaya's jaw to spoon curds and sugar into her mouth. As Jaya's tears flooded over her hands, the woman pulled Jaya's veil over her own head. Shrouded under the heavy fabric, she held Jaya's heaving shoulders as though her hands could exorcise Jaya's desolation; but the Sirpur Raj Guru was pulling at the veil, and she backed away.

The Elder placed Prince Pratap's sword in Jaya's hands. Jaya rose to her feet, invoking the sacred Fire, Destroyer and Creator of the Universe, to bear witness to her marriage. Carrying the sword in front of her, she began to circle the fire as the Elder, speaking for the bridegroom, said, 'I will guide you to the four directions of the universe.'

'I will guide you through the three worlds,' she whispered in response. 'The Gross. The Subtle. The Sublime.'

Holding the heavy sword in front of her, she stood before the seven steps that led from the marriage pavilion down to the ground where the bridal palanquin waited under the elephant arch, covered with mirrors to deflect the evil eye from her person when she followed her bridegroom's procession from Balmer Fort.

The sun was already rising as she descended the first step and whispered, 'If I am doing wrong, I call upon the morning star never to shine again.'

She paused on the next step. 'If I am doing wrong, I call upon the rising sun never to light the sky again.'

On the third step, she was surprised at the rage in her own voice as she demanded loudly, 'If I am doing wrong, I call upon the moon never to reflect the light of the sun again.'

She could see the morning star to the left of the fading new moon and the rose glow of the sunrise. 'If I am doing wrong, I call upon the planets to cease their revolution around the sun.'

The desolate moan of conch shells echoed in the half-light, and it was no longer anger but fear that made her raise her voice as she descended the next step. 'If the seven mothers of the world have any knowledge why I should not take this step, I call upon them to stop me.'

She halted before the last step and wept.

'The ascetics!' the Balmer Raj Guru whispered. Jaya started to speak, but her voice broke under her sobs.

'Say it, Bai-sa!' the old high priest urged. 'If you do not speak now, the Sirpurs will say you are bringing bad luck to their house!'

Drawing a deep breath, Jaya managed to gasp, 'If the seven great ascetics have any knowledge why I should not make this union, I call upon them to stop me.'

Now she was on the ground. Until this moment, her marriage was not final. She clutched Prince Pratap's sword, trying to muffle her sobs. But her grief seemed to have a force of its own, and her voice was unfamiliar to her when she spoke. 'Earth, you are the mother of us all. You know the future and the past. Swallow me up if you have any knowledge why I should not take this awesome step.'

For a long time Jaya waited, hoping that some supernatural event would save her from the palanquin, its mirrors winking fiercely in the sunlight, but the Sirpur courtiers were murmuring impatiently, and she bent to place the sword on the implacable earth. Weighed down by her garments, she pressed her forehead to the hilt of Prince Pratap's sword, as she would have pressed her head to Prince Pratap's feet, had he been there.

BOOK TWO

Sirpur

24

THE PEOPLE of Sirpur did not need the reassurance of history. Of all the great dynasties that had followed the God Krishna's chariot into battle, only two remained, Tripura and the House of Sirpur, and there was little need for a people to consult their records when the names of their ancestors were intoned throughout India by the devout.

Sometimes, in the tea shops on the banks of the Brahmaputra River, old men interrupted their chess games to slap their knees with bony hands and laugh at that moment of panic, three thousand years ago, when the kingdom's scribes, fearful of Sirpur's mortality, had commenced the written records which now gathered dust in tottering piles in the stone cells of the Kamini Temple. Their brief passions spent, the old men gazed with quiet satisfaction at the silver waters of the river, certain that, in Sirpur, history was younger than mythology, and mythology itself only an ambitious branch of geography.

The centre of Sirpur's geography, from which the country spun in sweeping emerald rice fields towards the Himalayas and China, was the ancient capital sprawled on the left bank of the Son of the Creator, the mighty Brahmaputra River. The people of Sirpur had reason to fear the Son of the Creator when its swollen waters burst over the foothills of Sirpur's northern boundary, drowning the bamboo villages of the tribals before surging across paddy fields to inundate the capital with human bodies tangled in fishing nets.

Every decade the river flooded its banks, forcing the capital to rebuild itself from its own ruins. It was a common sight in Sirpur City to find the stone lintel of a two-thousand-year-old temple adorning the doorway of a tea shop only just constructed from timber washed up on the riverbank after last year's monsoons, or the roofing from an upcountry lac factory now shading a rickshaw mechanic's shop. As one century faded into another and the written histories in the Kamini Temple lay unopened in their crimson covers, the buildings squeezed together in the narrow streets provided a haphazard record of the past to the kingdom's indifferent citizens.

As if the endless cycles of destruction and reconstruction had given them a special tolerance, the people of Sirpur viewed the half-naked tribals who lived in Sirpur's foothills with the same equanimity with which they regarded the practices in the Dowager Maharani's Purdah Palace, where it was said that many women had never even seen the front of the sprawling three-mile-square City Palace compound. And those harem women, insistent on maintaining their incarceration despite Maharajah Victor's frequent attempts to liberate them, speculated on the wild behaviour of the European guests living in the apartments of the City Palace when on warm spring nights they heard shrill cries for more champagne from mem-sahibs riding bicycles in midnight treasure hunts.

In the years between the floods, the Brahmaputra River fed the rice fields with rich silts until farmers, their pockets filled with coins, emptied the shops in Sirpur's busy bazaars, and barges poled towards Calcutta with the wealth from Sirpur's tea gardens and emerald mines. In those years the Sirpur population made sure of their kingdom's survival by paying homage to the Kamini Temple.

Every morning they recited the origin of the Kamini Temple, when the God Shiva, holding the Goddess in his embrace, had thundered across constellations in the Dance of Cosmic Destruction. In singsong voices they described how the fragile body of the Goddess, unable to contain the momentum of the dancing God, had fragmented into a thousand pieces, and the thousand temples that had been built where the disintegrating Goddess had fallen.

The womb of the Goddess had fallen here in Sirpur. No one knew when the first arches of the Kamini Temple had risen around the black stone vulva, or why for seven days in every year the clear water streaming through the stone lips turned red and sticky. But when the Goddess menstruated, pilgrims descended on the Kamini Temple from all over India, trampling one another in the stone corridors to anoint themselves and pray for the many miracles which it was said the Goddess sometimes granted in the kingdom of Sirpur.

FROM HER bridal conveyance, her husband's sword across her knees, Jaya looked through the garlanded windows, marvelling that the strictures which separated race from race, religion from religion in the British Empire had no meaning in this ancient land. In the narrow streets of the old city she could see Chinese watchmakers sitting under their ideogrammed banners, next to British Residency lawyers in shiny black suits and bare-breasted tribal women with cheroots as large as cigars stuck into their matted hair. On the broad avenues of the new city, European mem-sahibs in open-topped palace cars chatted animatedly with the aides mounted on horseback by their sides.

Passing the Sirpur Law Courts and Sirpur University, the garlanded car approached the City Palace, residence of the Maharajah and administrative centre of the Kingdom of Sirpur. Distant figures sunned themselves against the whitewashed walls, pointing lazily at the fishing boats with dirty muslin sails moving slowly down the river to catch the river fish and crabs for which Sirpur was famous in the East. On the other riverbank, the garden houses of wealthy merchants provided a pleasant interlude, opening onto terraced gardens and long verandahs where families could sit gazing at their great river in any season.

The car rolled through gateways lined with bowing guards and entered the bamboo thickets which separated the Purdah Palace from the many palaces inside the City Palace.

Outside the iron railings of the Purdah Palace, Abyssinian eunuchs were waiting to usher Jaya into the presence of the Dowager Maharani. Jaya followed them through high-ceilinged rooms with teak beds resting in water containers against the constant threat of snakes, into the Dowager Maharani's durbar room.

An old woman, crippled with arthritis, rose painfully from her gaddi. Hard knuckles cracked against Jaya's temples to remove the evil eye, then she pressed heavy iron keys into Jaya's hands, saying, 'These are the keys to your husband's storerooms, and these are the keys to mine.'

Jaya sat at the Dowager Maharani's side while she spoke of

her grandsons. 'Poor Victor. He was only seven years old when he became Maharajah. In spite of his youth, Sir Henry Conroy, the British Resident, forced him and Pratap to leave immediately for school in England.' The old woman gave Jaya a grim smile. 'But each time the boys returned to Sirpur, I told the younger concubines to remind them of their own customs.'

Jaya stared in shocked silence at the purdah garden as the Dowager Maharani's rasping voice described how she had sent girl after smooth-limbed girl from the harem to seduce the awkward schoolboys during their holidays, hoping to recapture her grandsons' souls from Britain through their loins.

AT LAST maidservants supported Jaya up the wide marble stairs to her new home, the Wales Palace. Originally built to house King Edward VII when he had visited Sirpur as Prince of Wales, the Wales Palace had been constructed in the Indo-Saracenic style, a blend of Victorian railway architecture and Indian grandeur favoured by Indian rulers for its supposed popularity with their British masters.

As though trying to impose Sirpur's suppleness on the unforgiving solidity of the British Empire, Prince Pratap had hung mirrors etched with elongated female bodies on the heavy walls. But when the bowing servants opened doors to chandeliered rooms with elaborate Indian marble floors and white dust covers shrouding European furniture, Jaya felt intimidated, and she stood on the balcony of her chambers looking lovingly at the familiar domes and tridents of the Kamini Temple rising behind the City Palace.

That evening, Jaya was officially received by the ruler in the opulent Durbar Hall of the City Palace. Through her veil, Jaya stared in wonder at the famous walls covered with the gilded frescoes which had attracted scholars from all over the world. While ministers presented her with gifts, Maharajah Victor smiled sympathetically from his gaddi, as if in recognition of her loneliness, and she noticed the weary gentleness in his eyes.

After the ceremonies he offered to take a photograph of her, as a souvenir of the day. She followed him to a private study with comfortable leather armchairs and photographs of winning racehorses on the walls.

'I'm mad about films,' Maharajah Victor announced, his voice muffled under his photographer's canopy. 'Do you like the cinema, Princess?'

'Oh, yes, hukam. My father brought a film to Balmer. About the God Krishna. We watched it many times.'

The handsome head appeared above the brown cloth, and the sloping eyes stared at her in astonishment. 'I meant proper films, with film stars like Mary Pickford and Douglas Fairbanks. Or Cora Hart.' The head disappeared under the cloth. There was a flash. Acrid smoke filled the air.

He pulled the plate from the camera in satisfaction. 'You must be so lonely without Pratap. Leave your veil here. Come and watch a film in my private cinema.'

He preceded Jaya into a screening room crowded with Europeans. Feeling absurd and clumsy in her bridal garments, she sat in one corner, not daring to move her hands in case her ivory marriage bangles clacked too loudly, while the Europeans exchanged easy banter with the Maharajah about polo matches and parties they had attended in Europe.

A mem-sahib, the thin straps of her evening dress cutting into her white flesh, attempted to engage Jaya in conversation. She held up a jewelled horse. 'Isn't this pretty, Princess? Of course, you must be so familiar with this sort of work. So amusing about the Nizam of Hyderabad asking the Fabergé craftsman to design a palace and then deciding Fabergé was too vulgar for Hyderabad.'

The tight curls shook with laughter. Jaya smiled warily, reluctant to admit she didn't know what the mem-sahib was talking about, grateful when the room was plunged into darkness.

Images flickered onto the screen, and the Europeans groaned.

'You're such a romantic, Victor. Nobody looks at these films any more.'

'It's Cora Hart again! We might have known.'

'She really is the worst actress in the world.'

The Maharajah ignored them, leaning forward each time the actress's pretty features were enlarged on the screen. In the darkness Jaya studied his gentle, weak face. The Maharajah's longing was the desire she had seen on the faces of the Balmer concubines, forbidden to touch each other, fearful of the power of the eunuchs. Noticing her scrutiny, the Maharajah smiled, as if they shared a common sorrow.

25

TO KEEP HERSELF sane in the strange limbo of being a bride but not a wife, Jaya recorded the events of her life in an album, treasuring inside its black pages the rare photographs sent by Prince Pratap.

Her husband's infrequent notes from France, where he had acted as aide-de-campe to the Maharajah of Bikaner at the signing of the Versailles Treaty which ended the Great War, or from Switzerland, where, again as Bikaner's aide, he was attending the opening ceremonies of the League of Nations, seemed to have been written to a younger sister. In between the breezy anecdotes Jaya searched for some acknowledgement of their marriage, and found none.

Her own days were filled with marriage functions. There was the day she was weighed in silver in the presence of the kingdom's Prime Minister and the British Resident. She sat cross-legged on a massive iron scale while the palace clerks emptied gunnysacks filled with silver coins onto the other scale to distribute to the poor, observing the two men who had been knighted for their services to the rulers of Sirpur.

The Prime Minister, Sir Akbar, leaned on a gold-knobbed cane, his patrician features crowned by a simple fez, his thin frame covered in a perfectly tailored tunic coat. Sir Akbar's restraint and suavity conveyed the sophistication of his noble origins in Hyderabad, the kingdom that had inherited the learning and world-weariness of the decaying Moghul Empire. Next to him, Sir Henry Conroy's shining bald head and round body suggested a jollity instantly belied by the lead-grey eyes coldly watching the proceedings. Jaya could visualize the British Resident sending two small boys halfway across the world, never doubting the rectitude of his decision, impervious to their tears.

A few days later, she received the aristocratic Sirpur ladies in the White Drawing Room of the Wales Palace and almost wept at their conversation.

'After all, hukam, the Kamini Temple is named after Kama, the god of love.'

'And your husband is a prince of the House of Sirpur, hukam. He is a guardian of the sanctity of the temple.'

Staring miserably at the pale carpet, Jaya was ashamed to be so unworldly among the voluptuous women of her husband's kingdom, with their fashionably bobbed hair and the sequins glittering suggestively through their sheer chiffon saris.

'It is your husband's puja to make love.'

'Many other husbands have reason to deplore Prince Pratap's prowess under the mosquito net when their lovesick wives turn away from their marital beds.'

Unaware how their teasing inflamed her mind with unformed desire, the ladies waved ivory cigarette holders in the air above their glasses of wine and assured Jaya that her unencountered husband was no ordinary man.

In the days that followed, Jaya heard the legend of the Kamini Temple so often it no longer startled her with its explicitness. She stared so often at the temple's iron trident, spearing the sky on the hill behind the City Palace, that in the secret shadows of her mind she even longed to be initiated by her husband into Sirpur's thoughtless pleasures. But in the evenings, when she stood at her balcony, watching the changing colours of the Brahmaputra, she sometimes felt the great river eroding her mind as a stone is eroded by the constant caress of water, and she became fearful that the desert certainties bred by her native Balmer would not withstand the corruption of Sirpur's fertility or the supple conjunctions of its ways.

As the weeks passed into months and still Prince Pratap did not return, Maharajah Victor often invited her to join him at the polo grounds. In the early mornings, as they cantered down the empty fields he sometimes spoke of the pain caused by the absence of loved ones. His distant tenderness to her, his gentleness with his horses, his unvarying courtesy to the grooms and the children

183

watching from the edge of the field made Jaya idealize the ruler, and each time she learned of his too-rapid compliance with some instruction from the Dowager Maharajah or Sir Henry Conroy, she converted the evidence of the ruler's weakness into further proof of his compassion.

ALMOST A YEAR after Jaya's arrival in Sirpur, the season of floods was over and the citizens had rebuilt those parts of the city damaged by a monsoon of only moderate severity.

The Goddess was again undergoing her mysterious transformation, and the bazaars were almost impassable with the crush of pilgrims buying clay lamps and flowers to offer in the many smaller stone temples that sprawled up the steep hillside to the main Kamini Temple.

The deep blast of a rubber-bulb horn cut imperiously through the clamour of rickshaws and black bicycles trying to move through the mass of men and women in the street, as the Rolls-Royce specially commissioned for the Dowager Maharani forced the crowds out of the way.

Behind the flag hanging limply on the hood of the Rolls-Royce, an open glass partition revealed the blue-black, hairless chests of the Dowager's Abyssinian eunuchs, who sat impassively beside the chauffeur, scimitars across their knees. Inside the six-wheeled car – narrow under the engine, then expanding into a metal balloon raised above four white-walled tyres – the old Dowager Maharani lay on her chaise-longue, cursing fretfully as the car bumped its way up the hillside to the Kamini Temple.

Eunuchs helped the Dowager from the Rolls-Royce into a curtained sedan chair. Shaven-headed women lifted the chair's long poles, and Jaya followed them up stone steps worn almost flat by generations of pilgrims.

Carved stone pillars lined the temple's sombre corridors. Jaya averted her eyes from the writhing figures, unable to find the link between this celebration of fertility and the insouciance of her husband's notes from Switzerland.

Bare feet slapping against the stone, the women descended the narrow steps that led to the inner sanctum of the temple, a cave with clay lamps flickering in its rock crevices.

Moisture seeped from the black rocks, reminding Jaya of the thin film of sweat shining on the naked torsos of the Dowager's Abyssinians. In the centre of the cave was a large black stone worn smooth by water flowing from some uncharted spring beneath the cave. The Dowager stepped painfully out of her chair and limped toward the stone.

Standing above it, Jaya saw the stone was shaped like a gigantic vulva, its thick lips glistening like black glass from daily anointing with coconut oil. The Dowager Maharani thrust her hand between the lips. Red liquid seeped through her stiff fingers as she smeared Jaya's cheeks and forehead, chanting, 'May your homage to the Goddess bring fruit to your womb and may you enrich our house with sons.'

Jaya bent down reluctantly to touch her forehead to the thick lips. The transparent liquid welling up from the smooth slit between the stone lips was turning red, and she felt soiled, remembering how her mother had not even entered the puja rooms in Balmer during her time of month. She tried to evoke the memory of the Maharani, but the image slid away and she imagined her familiar childhood self sliding away with it.

The temple votaries handed the Dowager a large photograph in a silver frame. The Dowager's rasping voice rose in a fresh supplication to the Goddess. Hearing the viciousness in the old woman's incantations, Jaya peered curiously over her shoulder, and saw a rosebud mouth pouting beneath tinted blue eyes staring out in innocent greed at the old woman. Large looped letters obscured the bare shoulders below the pretty face: *To my darling Victor from your adoring Cora.*

With a savage incantation, the Dowager smashed the photograph against the black stone lips. The sound of breaking glass echoed in the cave as thick liquid gushed over the stone lips and dripped onto the photograph, staining the blue eyes crimson.

The shrill voices of the votaries rose in an obscene litany. Jaya remembered the longing in the Maharajah's weary eyes each time Cora Hart's face had swelled onto the screen, and knew it was not the lust being exorcised so crudely in this rock cave. She turned away from the stone vulva, wondering if she would go mad in this strange country with its incomprehensible ways, and never set eyes on the man to whom she had been married.

26

WHEN NEWS CAME that Prince Pratap was finally on his way to Sirpur, almost two years had passed since Jaya's wedding, and the Sirpur newspapers were full of the reforms the King Emperor had promised India the year she was married.

For weeks there had been speculation as to whether the dashing young Prince of Wales would come to India to inaugurate the King Emperor's promised Assemblies. Then the British Raj decided it could not control the demonstrations by Indians angered that the King Emperor's heralded reforms granted India only the cosmetics of power, not power itself, limiting British Indians to partial representation in assemblies whose legislation was subject to overrule by the Viceroy; and confining Indian kings to a Chamber of Princes in which British officials would control the content of their speeches. The *Sirpur Herald* also expressed outrage that the Empire's Press Act, which had prohibited newspapers in British India from reporting on India's kingdoms, had been repealed, permitting salacious stories about the private lives of Indian kings to fill the British Indian newspapers.

India now awaited the arrival of the Emperor's uncle, the Duke of Connaught, to inaugurate the Assemblies and the Chamber of Princes, from which the people and kings of India would petition their imperial rulers.

WHILE HER husband's train was rolling towards Sirpur, Jaya dressed again in her wedding finery to greet her bridegroom. When the maid-servants announced a visitor in the White Drawing Room, Jaya almost ran down the wide marble stairs – only to find herself confronted by an embarrassed Prime Minister. 'Prince Pratap has been detained at the City Palace, hukam. He will lunch with you tomorrow.'

Jaya tore the flowers from her hair, crushing them underfoot as she fled to her chambers.

She scrubbed at the sandalwood decorations on her face, her enraged image multiplied a thousand times in the pastel mirrors that covered the bathroom.

Lying on the four-poster bed, she leafed through the album in which she had tried to understand her absent husband. She stopped at a photograph of Prince Pratap waving from the cockpit of an air-craft. A helmet was pushed back on his head; heavy goggles hung at one side of his laughing face. There was an excitement in his long eyes that had been absent from the other photographs, and Jaya was suddenly fearful he might resent their marriage.

All day she stayed secluded in her bedchamber, weeping that Prince Pratap had preferred to spend his first night in the City Palace with Maharajah Victor and his guests rather than with his new wife. Maidservants knocked at the door. When they entered with the food she had not eaten all day, she waved them away.

Moving onto her balcony, she watched the dusk turn into darkness. Night fell quickly in Sirpur. The far bank of the wide river was invisible at this hour, and lanterns were strung along the dim bulks of the river barges moving downriver, their gaiety belied by the mournful flutes of the river pilots guiding their vessels through the night.

Carriage lamps lit the gateways of the City Palace. The Prime Minister had told her that a handsome Sikh, the only Indian to have flown with the Royal Air Force in the Great War, had accompanied the Prince to Sirpur, as well as two Europeans belonging to that new breed of adventurers called aviators. He had not mentioned the beautiful women who must have joined the party, but Jaya knew they were there.

The City Palace was always filled with foreign visitors. She had seen the glamorous women who angled for invitations to Sirpur before the season began in Calcutta, hopeful, in the enforced intimacies of the City Palace, of gaining a protector from among the big-spending playboys who formed Maharajah Victor's inner circle.

She had met the wealthy, idle men who had arrived for a season's shooting and stayed on for a year, cocooned by the famous Sirpur hospitality from the disintegration of postwar Europe or the Prohibition laws of America.

The melancholy melody of the river flutes echoed Jaya's desolation as she wondered whether the succession of foreign women, who sometimes crossed the lawns of the Purdah Palace in tennis skirts to have awkward teas with the old Dowager Maharani, had already exchanged their handsome Sirpur aides-de-camp for Maharajah Victor's younger brother.

A car honked in the portico of the Maharajah's apartments. Loud laughter echoed across the lotus lake. Jaya angrily freed her tangled hair from a bougainvillea vine, certain her husband was escorting some white woman with bare shoulders and a half-exposed bosom into the Palace, joking about the wife he had never seen.

Under the canopied mosquito net, unable to sleep, she half-dreamed, half-imagined the meeting with her husband. She could no longer remember the alchemy by which the face she had hated in her youth had become the focus of her most complicated desires; but as her fatigued mind abandoned itself to its untutored longings, she dreamed she slept within her husband's arms and that his hands caressed her naked flesh.

The next morning, the maidservants came to dress her once again as a bride. Dipping their silver sticks into freshly prepared henna, they reddened her palms and feet, before throwing the veil over her head. Then Chandni handed Jaya the small square of red silk which had sat accusingly in front of Prince Pratap's image for two years. Inside was the gold coin that Jaya would lay at her husband's feet at last.

The maidservants guided Jaya past the oil paintings of Sirpur rulers into the White Drawing Room, where only yesterday she had fled the kingdom's Prime Minister. The mirror above the fireplace reflected her rich Indian garments framed against the white silk curtains. She turned nervously as the doors were flung open.

Through her veil she saw a tall figure in tight-fitting jodhpurs and a polo shirt standing in the doorway issuing instructions to a servant. Pale brown skin stretched smoothly over high, almost Mongol cheekbones. The long eyes were half-closed to the smoke rising from a cigarette. Highly polished riding boots reflected the tin of cigarettes held in one hand. An Alsatian growled behind his legs. The cigarette tin came down sharply in front of the dog's head, and the Alsatian sank to the floor.

The door slammed shut. Jaya could feel the blood roaring in her ears as he walked towards her. But he stopped in the centre of the room, nonchalantly ashing his cigarette onto the pale green carpet. Jaya stared at the ash drifting down onto the shining boots. When he did not move, she willed herself to cross the long expanse between them.

Her ivory bangles and heavy anklets echoed in the serene drawing room. Removing the gold coin from the crumpled silk, now soaked with perspiration, she bent awkwardly to place the coin before the polished boots.

Bare forearms came into view at the corners of her veil. Jaya stopped breathing, unable to take her eyes off the moving hands, wondering if the marriage was to be consummated here on the pale green weave of the Chinese carpet, with the breeze from the river blowing over their locked limbs. Long fingers, almost too elegant to belong to his powerful polo player's hands, moved towards her waist and gripped the edge of her veil. A faint smell of perspiration and cologne hit her nostrils as the muscled arms threw the veil back over her shoulders, sweeping it to the ground.

Jaya lifted her head so that he could see the long neck Kuki-bai had so often said was beautiful. As if in acquiescence to her silent display, Prince Pratap walked slowly around her. She swallowed, acutely aware of his eyes on her breasts.

A sleepy voice broke the silence. 'I'm afraid you won't do, Princess. You really won't do at all.'

'Hukam?'

'Wash all that nonsense off your hands and feet. And change out of these Christmas decorations.'

He tapped a cigarette on the back of the tin before placing it between his lips. 'By lunch I hope to find an improvement.' At the open door the waiting Alsatian sprang up, rubbing at Prince Pratap's legs as he sauntered from the room.

Delayed by the anxious scrubbing of her hands with lime juice, Jaya was late for her first lunch with her husband. When she reached the dining room, unused during Prince Pratap's absence, she saw the dust covers removed from the mirrored Lalique dining table and a silver centrepiece flanked by peacock feathers and flowers reflected in its surface. Prince Pratap lounged in his chair. Behind him stood a plump European in a tailcoat. Jaya hastily pulled her veil down over her unpainted face.

'Remove your veil, Princess. Michel is my personal attendant. Please treat him exactly as you would one of my grandmother's eunuchs.'

Reluctantly, Jaya slid the veil back, noticing the pained expression on the Frenchman's shiny features.

'Your clothes are a great improvement. But in Sirpur our women wear the sari. Kindly do the same. Do you know how to eat with a knife and fork?'

Jaya nodded, and he smiled in satisfaction, waving his hand at the array of wineglasses and gold-plated cutlery circling the plates. Seeing the graceful fingers with their manicured nails, Jaya hid her own hands in the folds of her long skirt, of the palest shade she could find in her trousseau.

Gloved servants entered with soup bowls. Jaya stared dubiously at the bits of meat floating in the clear brown liquid.

'We are the oldest Hindu kingdom in India, Princess. Three thousand and eleven years, to be exact. Is it likely we would be serving you beef?'

He waited until the servants left the room, then leaned over the mirrored surface of the table. 'On the other hand, the first time I tried beef, at university in England, I was sick.' He laughed at her shocked expression. 'I can see I have offended your caste sensibilities, Princess. If I came to your chambers tonight and demanded my conjugal rights, you would be polluted. What a dilemma.'

Jaya could not stop the deep flush reddening her face. Prince Pratap raised a mocking eyebrow. 'Rest assured that I shall never approach you without undergoing the necessary purifications in the Kamini Temple, Princess. In the unlikely event, that is, of my ever approaching you.'

Startled, Jaya dared to look at him for the first time. He looked back at her expressionless. 'Ours is strictly a marriage of convenience, Jaya Devi. Should the necessity for children ever arise, I am sure we can both rise to our duty, but until then . . .'

A servant entered carrying quail on a gold platter. Cold with shock, Jaya struggled not to drop the tiny birds onto the carpet.

With the precision of a surgeon Prince Pratap slit the small frame with the tip of his knife, as though the fragile bird were glued to his plate. But when she tried to cut the quail, her cutlery scratched loudly against the crested plate.

'By the way, what languages do you speak?' he asked, indifferent to her discomfiture.

The servants replaced the porcelain plates with thalis filled with Indian dishes.

'French?' the bored voice prompted. 'Italian? Spanish?'

Jaya's hunger evaporated. Mrs Roy had said her English was excellent. She could read and write four Indian languages, including the classical Sanskrit. Hoping to surprise her husband, she had also studied the Sirpur language and could now speak it almost as fluently as the local citizens. But this stranger was not interested in her achievements. She lowered her head as tears of anger and shame fell onto her raw, scrubbed hands.

Prince Pratap sighed. 'It is not a simple matter of cosmopolitan manners, Princess. But of politics. Despite my brother's almost suicidal devotion to the British Empire, its officials are convinced that Victor is flighty and squanders the kingdom's revenues on film actresses.'

He dipped long fingers into one of the many containers on his thali and extricated a small river fish. Putting the entire fish into his mouth, he added, 'Unfortunately, when the British Empire disapproves of the loyal Maharajah of Sirpur, it disapproves even more of the Maharajah's younger brother, whom the newpapers of British India are characterizing so unkindly as an irresponsible playboy. The Empire has instructed me to stay in India. If I am permitted to travel abroad again, I shall have to be accompanied by a wife. That's why I agreed to our marriage. So here we are, Jaya Devi. You cannot eat quail or wear a sari. You know no languages. Yet through you I must outmanoeuvre the Empire which forced me into this marriage.'

He pushed his chair back, and Jaya followed him onto the east verandah. Beyond the balustrades, a path lined with oleander bushes led down to the riverbank. As the Frenchman poured his master a large brandy, Jaya opened the enamelled paan casket, sure that her husband could not fault her at least in this traditional ceremony. Prince Pratap watched her preparations over the rim of his brandy glass. As she was about to place the paan in her mouth, he said, 'When the Prince of Wales comes to Sirpur at the end of this year, you will be our official hostess. I hardly think His Royal Highness will enjoy dining next to a woman with betel-stained teeth.'

Jaya obediently replaced the paan in the casket, her submission belying her rage.

'Victor and I are leaving for Delhi for the inauguration of the Chamber of Princes, but you can't possibly travel with us. You are still a rough diamond, Princess. Still, if you work very hard, you might be passably presentable in another year, by the time the Prince of Wales gets here.'

Jaya could not keep the note of rebellion from her voice. 'We received the last Prince of Wales in Balmer, hukam. And the Kaiser of Germany's son. And the Tsarevitch of Russia.'

Prince Pratap half-smiled at her first hint of spirit. 'That was before you were born, Princess. But, don't worry. I know a highly respectable Indian lady from Bombay who is just the person to teach you the intricacies of Western society. I shall invite her to Sirpur to keep you company, while Maharajah Victor and I are attending the inauguration of the Chamber of Princes.'

27

A BLACK PEKINGESE with silk bows in its long hair and a Borzoi wearing a wide diamond choker, which Lady Modi's French maid later declared had been fashioned after Queen Alexandra's jewelled collars, preceded Lady Modi into Jaya's life. The dogs bounded out of the crimson Rolls-Royce, clearing the white running board with single leaps, and dashed up the marble steps, barking at the row of maidservants who stood behind Jaya on the porch of the Wales Palace.

'Chantal, get hold of those damned animals!' a husky voice commanded irritably from the car.

A dwarf of a girl with long pigtails dangling incongruously over her ears leaped out as the Borzoi grabbed the end of a maidservant's veil and sped off into the flower beds at the edge of the lawn, followed by the yapping Pekingese. The French girl ran after them, shouting, 'Ali! Viens ici! Scott-Ward! Ali, Scott-Ward, attention!'

A foot in a high-heeled shoe appeared on the running board of the car, followed by a shapely leg in a white silk stocking. Above it, held like a horizontal spear, was the longest cigarette holder Jaya had ever seen. Almost three seconds elapsed before a body attached itself to the cigarette holder. A round stockinged knee, a short beige silk skirt and a cascade of swinging pearls came slowly into view. Then Lady Modi, all of her, stepped onto the ground.

Jaya stared at the elfin creature squinting at the bright sunlight. The creamy white skin and the shining chestnut hair lying flat against the delicately contoured face like a burnished helmet seemed proof that this doll-like woman could not possibly be the Indian friend invited by her husband to Sirpur. A lace parasol snapped open, and the husky voice issued a stream of gutter Hindustani curses to the animals destroying the flower beds.

Holding the parasol in a gloved hand, Lady Modi daintily mounted the marble steps. 'Darling child, do forgive my beastly hounds. They always go mad when they have been cooped up too long.' She placed one smooth white cheek against Jaya's face in the simulation of a kiss. 'Is the bar set up in the east verandah as usual?'

Without waiting for an answer, Lady Modi passed the bowing maidservants and entered the corridors which led past the aide-de-camp's office, the White Drawing Room, the billiard room, the study. Reaching the wide verandah, she sank into the deep cushions of a wicker sofa.

Transparent eyelids closed over the brown eyes. 'Your first lesson in international deportment, Princess. How to fix a martini.' She pointed to the drinks tray resting on a lacquer table. From beyond the verandah, the waving oleander blossoms threw shadows onto her white gloves. 'Pour some vermouth into a glass and swill it around.' She wilted into the sofa. 'Now throw it into the roses.' Jaya obediently flung the vermouth over the marble balcony into the flower bed below. 'Fill the glass from that green bottle, the one that says Gordon's Gin. Put in a few ice cubes, and bring it straight to me.'

Lady Modi sipped at the drink approvingly. 'No question, darling. You have a definite flair.'

The muscles in Lady Modi's delicate throat moved up and down as she swallowed. Without stopping for breath, she finished the martini. 'Another, darling.' Jaya returned to the drinks tray and was sharply corrected when she forgot to throw the vermouth into the flower bed.

'Green eyes, darling. Wherever did you get them? No secrets under your family's mosquito net, I hope.'

'Her Highness, my mother, was a Himalayan princess,' Jaya replied frigidly, appalled at her guest's bad taste.

'Don't waste your anger on me, darling. I am going to be the friend you so desperately need if you intend staying with that scoundrel Pratap.'

She pointed her glass at a cane stool. Jaya sat on the stool looking down at her hands while Lady Modi studied her face. 'Forgive my bluntness, darling, but you are rather hairy. Pratap hates that. I've often heard him say Indian women remind him of wild boars, bristling with coarse black hair.'

Jaya ran her fingers over her smooth arms, and laughter bubbled over Lady Modi's glass. 'Darling, if you had hair on your body, you would have been banished to the Dowager Maharani's palace immediately. No, it's your eyebrows. They're too Indian – all that black-bow-of-love business. I'll have Chantal pluck them for you. And of course she'll have to bob your hair.'

'Cut my hair?' Jaya was horrified.

'But darling, Pratap wants you to be fashionable. You must have short hair.'

Jaya shook her head stubbornly. 'Long hair is one of the emblems of a married woman. I will not cut it off. It would be inauspicious for my husband.'

Further discussion was ended by the appearance of the diminutive French maid holding the panting dogs. At the sight of their mistress, the dogs leaped forward, pulling the leather leashes free of the French girl's hands. They bounded around Lady Modi, licking her legs. A small foot kicked out ineffectually. 'Get away! Chantal, control these damned dogs!'

The French maid refused to move. 'Je suis femme de chambre. Je peux rien faire!'

The Borzoi rubbed its diamond choker against the slender legs, and the silk stockings began to run. Galvanized into activity, Lady Modi grabbed the thin leads. The dogs whined as their heads were pulled forward sharply and the husky voice repeatedly ordered them to sit.

Fatigued by her exertions, Lady Modi leaned back on the sofa. After a long moment, she opened her eyes and said with exquisite formality, 'Princess, may I present my dogs? This is Scott-Ward.' The Borzoi rose on thin hind legs and began to whine piteously. 'Named after my first husband, Rupert Scott-Ward – a bore, a miser, but also a British baronet. The dog shares one characteristic with Sir Rupert. Neither of them has ever exhibited a shred of pride.' She pulled the other dog forward. The Pekingese resisted and was rewarded with a sharp kick. 'This absurd thing is called Ali, in honour of my second husband, the Nawab Muammar Ali of Lucknow. A man of impossible beauty, but too degenerate, darling, even for me.' She kicked the Pekingese again. The dog yelped at the unprovoked attack. 'I didn't have the stamina to be Ali's stamp of respectability in front of those endless British officials. If I had stayed with him, I'm sure I would have taken to morphine and boys as well.'

She sighed and released the Pekingese. 'So now I am married to an elderly lawyer of great renown and wealth who spoils me hopelessly and hates politics. I'm more fortunate than my dear friend Ruttie Jinnah, whose asthma only gets worse and worse as Jinnah, her devoted elderly lawyer husband, gets deeper into politics.'

Unwinding herself from the sofa, she smoothed down her skirt. 'Darling, would you mind terribly if we lunched in my rooms? I can't bear the thought of seeing my crumpled old face reflected in Pratap's dining table.'

She tapped out of the room, followed by her maid and the two dogs straining at their leads.

When Jaya reached Lady Modi's sitting room, she stood at the doorway inhaling the unfamiliar smell of French perfume, unable to see her visitor. Every surface was covered with garments. The deep armchairs were invisible under silk, feathers, velvets, chiffons. Capes and Kashmir shawls hung from padded hangers on the wooden door leading to the bedroom. Saris spilled over the ornate bed to the carpet. Chantal edged into the room with a heavy cut-glass scent bottle, pressing its rubber bulb frenetically as though trying to remove some unpleasant odour from the clouds of clothes.

'Stop that at once, Chantal! The Princess will think she is in a bordello.' Lady Modi's head rose from a chaise-longue. Her delicate body was clothed in a pink peignoir. Across her shoulders was a pink silk wrap edged with dyed ostrich feathers. The feathers ruffled as she spoke, obscuring the features of the Pekingese nestling on her lap.

'Foreigners spray scent over everything to disguise the fact that they never bathe.' Lady Modi leaned over the back of the chaise-longue, where an open champagne bottle stood in a silver ice bucket, and filled her glass, cursing when the liquid bubbled over her hand. 'While we are on the subject, may I suggest a little less attar of roses for you, darling. I was quite overpowered when we kissed. I know you traditional girls are taught it's an aphrodisiac, but it has exactly the opposite effect on a sophisticated man like your husband.'

She waved her small hand to dismiss the maid. 'Now, darling, I shall need to take a closer look at you. Undress completely. Here, the champagne will help you overcome your shyness.'

Jaya felt powerless, as though the round brown eyes had cast a spell over her. She took the glass by its thin stem, gulping at the fizzing contents. A little light-headed, as though she had been drinking ruby asha at the manwar ceremony in Balmer, she stepped reluctantly out of her clothes.

'But, darling, you're beautiful! What on earth is Pratap moaning about?'

'Does my husband think I am very disgusting, Lady Modi?' Jaya was unable to keep the fear from her voice.

Lady Modi emptied the champagne bottle into her glass. 'Since you are traipsing about naked in front of me, darling, I think you should call me Bapsy. The truth is, he thinks all Indian women are disgusting.'

'Is it the colour of our skin? Our hair? Are white women so much more beautiful than we are?'

'Of course not, darling. It's just that you represent everything the British Empire has taught Pratap to despise. Haven't you read that Englishwoman's book, *Mother India*? The author is clearly mad, but the British believe every word she writes. Now, loosen your plait. Perhaps we can make a virtue of your long hair.'

Jaya unplaited the heavy hair and shook her head. Black waves dipped over her full breasts to fall in a thick curtain below her hips.

'I don't want to shock you, darling, but that lurid book says a lot of Indian women spend all day in the temples performing human sacrifices, or copulating with priests.'

Jaya trembled, thinking of the sati prayers she had recited every morning in her mother's temple. 'The sahibs believe that of us, who are taught to die rather than endure dishonour?'

'Darling, it is precisely because you are raised in purdah that such tales are credible to the British. Even Rudyard Kipling wrote that royal women from the Himalayan kingdoms are sold into prostitution. You see, the British never meet you. The Empire has no access to you or power over your lives.'

'But the Empire forced this marriage on my husband.'

'It's not that simple, darling. Since censorship on news from royal India was lifted, everybody in British India is glued to the newspapers, and Victor's and Pratap's reputations have been badly damaged. Some newspapers have even suggested that Victor is contemplating marrying Cora Hart. Naturally, the Viceroy would forcefully oppose the marriage and suggest Victor abdicate in favour of Pratap. Pratap needs you to improve his own reputation.'

'I'm married to him, Lady Modi. What more can I do?'

'Become chic, or course, darling. Elegant. Worldly. At the moment you threaten Pratap's vanity with your lack of sophistication. If you want to attract your husband, Princess, you must make the British envy Pratap, not patronize him. You must make yourself into a woman who is desirable to white men.'

The wooden blades of the ceiling fans sent currents of warm air through the room. Jaya pulled the crimson robe around her body, suddenly cold, as she contemplated the significance of Lady Modi's words. 'Must I flaunt myself before the sahibs like a concubine to win my husband's approval?'

Lady Modi clapped her small hands over her mouth, lacquered nails crimson against her white skin. 'Anything but that, darling. Pratap hates concubines. I can't imagine what the Dowager Maharani thought she was doing sending concubines to those boys when their British tutors were trying to make them into muscular Christians. But what can one expect from the Dowager, with her endless mumbo jumbo about the power of the Goddess?'

Jaya thought of the girls swimming in the scented pool in the Balmer zenana and knew her husband would have turned away in disgust from their hennaed hands and the incense smoking through their long hair.

'Does my husband want me to become a mem-sahib?' she asked, remembering the hot afternoons when she had learned the sixteen arts of being a woman, almost asleep as the voices of the purdah ladies droned in the heat.

'Not at all, darling. More like Indira, the Maharani of Cooch Behar. The whole of Europe is at her feet and she's as Indian as can be.' Lady Modi fitted another cigarette into her cigarette holder, and the Pekingese yelped as the ivory mouthpiece dug into its fur.

'Even if her father, the Maharajah of Baroda, hasn't spoken

to her since she got married in a frock at a registry office in London.'

Jaya's nerve failed. 'Shall I have to wear frocks?'

'Don't be foolish, darling. Indira wore one because she eloped with Maharajah Cooch Behar's younger brother a week before she was supposed to marry Maharajah Gwalior. You can imagine the scandal. Maharajah Gwalior is thick as thieves with the King Emperor, and ruler of India's senior kingdom.'

Lady Modi's huge eyes widened in emphasis. 'Think of the huge expenditure on a wedding between Baroda and Gwalior, two of the largest kingdoms in India. Every ruler and important official in British India had been invited to attend. The marriage arches were up. Some of the guests had already arrived. Then Indira bolted, saying she couldn't bear the thought of Gwalior's body between her linen sheets. The whole of India talked of nothing else for weeks.'

Jaya recalled how Maharajah Baroda had turned his back on the Emperor of India in Delhi and thought the Maharajah of Baroda's daughter must have inherited her father's spirit.

'Now she's the Maharani of Cooch Behar?'

'Another romantic story. The late Maharajah of Cooch Behar was in love with an American film actress. When the British forbade the marriage, he drank himself to death on champagne at the Ritz Hotel in Paris. Chic, don't you think? After his death, Indira's husband became the new Maharajah of Cooch Behar.'

Lady Modi pointed a long nail in the direction of the bedroom. 'Now, darling, let's get back to work.'

Jaya obediently followed the trailing peignoir and sat down at Lady Modi's dressing table, letting her hands run over the bottles crowded against the mirror.

Pushing aside the chiffons and silks, Lady Modi sank onto the bed. 'On Pratap's instructions, I brought hundreds of saris for you. Choose something.'

Jaya shyly rummaged through the heaped fabrics. Holding up a magenta sari for approval, she disappeared into the bathroom. When she reappeared, Lady Modi clapped in delight. 'Absolutely perfect, Princess!' Jaya looked at herself in the mirror. The shape of her slender body could be seen under the folds of silk clinging to her heavy breasts and her small waist. 'Maharani Cooch Behar has set a style with her pastel French chiffons, but I think strong colours make a virtue of your dark skin. And wear as much green as you can, darling, to draw attention to your eyes. Now for the gloves and the handbag.'

'Gloves?'

'Absolutely, darling. It's court etiquette, de rigueur when you are presented to the Prince of Wales.'

'But what use is a handbag?'

Lady Modi was bent over a chair on which beaded and jewelled handbags lay in disarray. She straightened at Jaya's question. 'You can't be serious, darling. To carry your handkerchief, your personal effects, of course.'

'The attendants carry anything I need.'

Lady Modi shook her small head in exasperation, and the helmet of chestnut hair glinted in the sunlight. 'Darling, your maidservants will not be present at the Calcutta races or when you are presented in London.'

'Will my husband's aides take their place?' Jaya asked, not knowing why her mentor was irritated.

'No one will take their place, Princess,' Lady Modi answered emphatically. 'Royalty is hemmed in with officials who represent tradition and power. But society concerns itself solely with fashion.' The long cigarette holder waved in the air like a schoolmaster's pointer. 'After all, darling, society is about fun. Even the Prince of Wales knows that.'

28

UNDER LADY MODI'S tutelage Jaya slowly lost her self-consciousness, but when Lady Modi grasped her waist and dipped her stiff body in the motions of a tango Jaya envied the laughing maidservants swinging on the rope swing that hung from the huge banyan tree outside, as she had once stared longingly at the kites flying above the stables of Balmer Fort.

She arranged flowers in long-necked crystal vases as impatiently as she had once sprinkled coloured powder on the cool marble floors of the Balmer harem, and the nationalist events that Mrs Roy had once read aloud from the newspapers in her cloth satchel had now been replaced by Lady Modi's articles describing the scandals of India's kings.

'It's not nearly so delicious reading this rubbish in British India,' Lady Modi would say, unfolding her latest clippings. 'But one can't help wallowing in things that are banned. Don't you think so, darling?'

She passed the articles to Jaya with screams of delight. 'If those fat old rulers had really had quite so many dancing girls or pretty boys or drugs or orgies, darling, their hearts would have stopped.'

'Why don't the rulers take the newspapers to court?'

'The kings of India are much too grand to go to court. Ruling sovereigns can't take the witness stand. That's why they were so upset when the British Empire repealed its Press Act. Now, come on, darling, let's see if your dancing has improved since yesterday.'

As spring approached and the noise of nesting birds drowned

the sound of Bapsy's dance records, the Prime Minister brought a painting of Maharajah Sirpur sitting stiffly among the hundred other Indian kings who had been present at the opening of the Chamber of Princes.

Sir Akbar had barely left the room before Lady Modi shrieked, 'Darling, who is his tailor? That tunic fits like a dream. He can't possibly still have his clothes made in Hyderabad. Everyone there is imitating the Nizam's current passion for Savile Row. Do you know, the Nizam has built a dressing room one mile long for his European clothes? With lifts to take the suits up and down?' She fixed Jaya with an accusing stare, incredulity creasing her small features. 'A mile long, darling. That is the entire length of the imperial route the British are building for the Viceroy in New Delhi at this very moment.'

Several times Lady Modi left Sirpur, returning in a flurry of dogs with a new person in her entourage. Standing on the marble steps of the Wales Palace, Jaya waited for the cigarette holder to appear above the running board of the Rolls-Royce, and tried to guess who would be added to her household this time.

She had already acquired a White Russian refugee, Countess Skorkov, who taught her French and in Lady Modi's absences doubled as a dance instructress, although Jaya insisted she would never allow a strange man, not even the King Emperor himself, to put his arm around her body.

Countess Skorkov was soon joined by a French girl, Annie, who was to be a lady's maid for Jaya. Annie moped in Jaya's dressing room, changing dance records on the Victrola, and only laughed when she overheard Jaya practising French in front of the bathroom mirrors.

Furious that an untouchable foreigner had usurped her role, Chandni threatened to return to Balmer. It had taken a whole week of persuasion before Chandni finally relented, insisting on ostentatiously washing the wooden doors of Jaya's puja room because she had seen the untouchable foreigner lean against them while peering at Jaya's altar.

Still, Jaya was forced to banish Chandni from the room whenever Annie plucked her eyebrows into the thin line recommended by Lady Modi or manicured her nails into the long, pointed shapes fashionable in Europe, unable to endure the monotonous insults Chandni showered on the sharp-featured French girl. From the next room she could hear Chandni abusing the handbags, the high-heeled shoes, the French perfumes with which Jaya was being transformed into a godless stranger. Indifferent to Chandni's jealousy, Annie sauntered in to place another dance record on the turntable, smiling into Jaya's face above her tweezers when the infuriated Balmer maidservant shook her fists until her clacking ivory bangles drowned the music. At night, Jaya was hardly able to enter her rooms through the smoke of burning incense sticks with which Chandni was trying to overwhelm the French scents Annie, and Lady Modi's maid Chantal, gleefully sprayed over all her garments.

Once Lady Modi appeared in triumph with an Italian pastry chef she had stolen from Flury's Tea Rooms in Calcutta. When Jaya asked his function, Lady Modi flung her hands into the air. 'To teach you about food, darling. I couldn't find a Frenchman. Also, Marco says he knows how to play tennis. He cost a fortune, so please try and learn something.'

Spring was heating into summer when Prince Pratap returned from Delhi. He raised an approving eyebrow as Jaya entered the White Drawing Room, her softly draped crimson sari sweeping below her high heels, a handbag held securely in her unpainted hands. She saw the grudging admiration in his eyes when she poured drinks for Lady Modi and himself as easily as a mem-sahib. But the person he kissed in congratulation was Bapsy, and Jaya almost dropped the slice of lemon dangling from the silver tongs at his rejection.

To distract Prince Pratap from his wife's pain, Lady Modi asked, 'Are the newspapers in British India really calling the Nizam of Hyderabad "the little Tsar", darling?'

Prince Pratap ran long fingers over the Alsatian lying at his feet. 'Yes, and the Maharajah of Alwar a sadist.'

'But Alwar and Hyderabad finance the universities which produce the Indian nationalists,' Jaya blurted before she could stop herself. 'Many nationalists took sanctuary in their kingdoms from the British Empire. Why don't the nationalist newspapers write about that?'

Her husband looked surprised at her temerity. 'Because a lot of other rulers are throwing their critics into jail.'

Lady Modi laughed gaily. 'He's only teasing us, darling. The royals and the nationalists are great friends after Delhi.'

'My dear Bapsy, the nationalists believe every piece of fantastic gossip that is being printed about us in the British Indian press. A number of Indian rulers are already preparing for revolutions.' He turned to Jaya at last. 'Your own cousin, Maharajah John, has incarcerated half the population of Balmer and closed the science college your father founded. Says it's a nest of Bolsheviks.'

'Oh, darling, that's too fantastic. Bolsheviks, indeed. He must be mad.'

'If he's mad, Bapsy, so is the Empire. Everyone in Delhi was talking about one kind of revolution or another.' Michel opened the doors, and Prince Pratap helped Lady Modi to her feet. 'The Viceroy has officially asked all Indian rulers to capture any suspected Bolshevik agents and hand them over to the British police.'

As they entered the dining room, Lady Modi lightly drew Prince Pratap's attention to the floral arrangements, and Jaya was grateful for the hours she had spent placing the overblown tea roses and gladioli into vases. While Lady Modi and her husband speculated on the possibilities of revolution, Jaya kept an anxious eye on the servants serving lunch, relaxing only at the pleasure in Prince Pratap's voice when he commented on Marco's cooking.

'By the way, Princess, in Delhi I played polo with a British major who claims to be a friend of yours. Not a bad player, and apparently an expert on Bolsheviks, after the years he's spent on the North-West Frontier.'

'Hukam?' Jaya looked up from the plate where she was boning her smoked hilsa fish with practised ease.

'He was quite a hero in the Afghan War, but he's just resigned from the Army and joined the Political Service. Victor asked him to come to Sirpur and find our Reds.'

Draining his wineglass, he waved it at the Frenchman. 'I think his father was Tikka's tutor, but I don't suppose Major James Osborne will recognise you now.'

The mirrored surface of the table reflected the plucked eyebrows arched above Jaya's green eyes, the lacquered nails extending beyond her slim, unpainted fingers. The first kind words Prince Pratap had spoken to Jaya suddenly displeased her. He was right. The Angrez boy would not recognise the child he had known in Balmer.

29

When it was confirmed that the Prince of Wales would be visiting Sirpur on his tour of India, an excited Maharajah Victor proposed building a new palace to house him, but Sir Henry Conroy threatened to use his powers as British Resident to cancel the royal visit if Maharajah Victor wasted money on new construction.

The disappointed ruler asked Jaya and Prince Pratap to move into the City Palace so the heir to the British Empire could be accommodated in the Wales Palace, built when his grandfather visited Sirpur as Prince of Wales.

Gratified by the dramatic change in Jaya's appearance, Prince Pratap invited her to occupy the suite adjoining his own chambers at the City Palace, and a gleeful Lady Modi helped Jaya move into the City Palace, before departing to summer in Kashmir.

In spite of Lady Modi's parting reassurances, Jaya often excused herself from the evening entertainments in Maharajah Victor's splendid chambers, unable to endure her own jealousy as she speculated on which of the mem-sahibs laughing by the crystal fountains was intimate with her husband.

She tried not to resent Prince Pratap's cruel discretion in indulging his nocturnal activities elsewhere in the many palaces of the City Palace, and she could not prevent herself from waiting sleeplessly for sounds of his return, although she knew she would not hear him until she was sitting at her morning pujas.

During the day Prince Pratap was a charming and attentive companion, teasing her into learning to drive the red Bugatti parked in the driveway, and encouraging her to become involved in the arrangements for the Prince of Wales's visit.

She often accompanied him on his inspections of the stables and the elephant corrals. Once he invited her to the City Palace menagerie, laughing when he saw her surprise at the bricks hanging from the tails of three enormous Bengal tigers. 'It's an old trick to hang weights to a tiger's tail so that when it is released into the jungle and shot by our royal guest, the pelt will be longer.'

Preparations for the royal visit were even taking place in the palace boatyards. Jaya stood at the open windows, through which the hot river breeze only added to the summer oppression, listening to the deep horns of the barges bringing lumber to the sheds.

Prince Pratap dismissed the urgency in the boatyards. 'Sirpur once sent naval missions as far as China. But that was a thousand years ago. Now Victor wants to show Sirpur's ancient river navy to the Prince of Wales, heir to the greatest naval power on earth. It's too embarrassing.'

After repeated requests, Prince Pratap agreed to drive his curious wife down to the sheds. 'But I am warning you, Princess. His Highness Maharaj Dhiraj Sir Vikramji Bahadur, Raj Pandava, Dost-Alam, Raj Pahar, Grand Commander of the Star of India, Knight Commander of the Indian Empire, Maharajah of Sirpur, more commonly known as Victor because he was godson to the Queen Empress of India, has let his passion for films go to his head. He is now a Hollywood maharajah.'

Lifting her high heels over the planks of wood littering the ground, Jaya followed Prince Pratap into the boatyards. Behind the massive hulks of wooden vessels, carpenters furiously planed fresh beams for mastheads. In the summer humidity, their perspiration rolled onto the wood shavings curling around their bare feet. In another shed, tailors sat in circles, their needles moving rapidly through white silk sails. At the farthest shed, the smell of boiling tar added to the suffocating atmosphere created by open furnaces.

Prince Pratap waved a bored hand. 'God knows how much all this is costing. My grandfather built a bridge across the Brahmaputra River and had his Prince of Wales declare it open so the whole of India knew about the achievement. And in those days the Empire did not allow rulers to raise money outside their kingdoms. If Victor wants to waste money, instead of parading a tenth-century navy in the twentieth century, he should get some aircraft.'

That year the monsoon wreaked itself on the capital with more than customary fury, and Maharajah Victor's drawing room emptied of Europeans making desultory plans to play tennis in the indoor courts, to be replaced by Armenian and Jewish bankers from Calcutta as Maharajah Victor raised loans to repair the capital and refurbish his navy. To mollify his younger brother, the Maharajah also decided to purchase three Sopwith Camel aircraft as a symbol of Sirpur's commitment to modern progress.

As the date of the royal visit drew closer, telephone lines were installed between the Wales Palace and the City Palace. The palace clerks rushed around overseeing the refurbishing of the railway cars, the fleet of palace Rolls-Royces, the state carriages. In the boatyards the ancient vessels were nearly reassembled and Prince Pratap's aircraft were on their way from London. Watching the feverish activity, Jaya began to wonder if the only thing that impressed the British Empire was motion.

When the three aircraft arrived, the ground beyond the garden houses of the merchants was levelled for a landing strip. Sheets of corrugated iron were hammered onto bamboo scaffolding to create hangars, and Prince Pratap, watched by curious children, spent his days unpacking the wooden crates with John MacGregor, a stocky, ginger-haired engineer who had come with the machines from London.

In the riverside tea stalls there were furious arguments between tribals in animal loincloths and disdainfully superior British Residency clerks in three-piece suits as to whether the gods would permit mere mortals to fly.

On the day the aircraft were finally assembled, the entire population of the capital massed around the hastily constructed flying strip to watch MacGregor and Prince Pratap test the planes. A group of boys shinned up the pole that supported the wind sock for a better view. Prince Pratap ran towards them shouting, then laughed as he walked back to his aircraft. He was still laughing when he raised his thumbs to the palace servants nervously turning the iron crank on the nose of the plane. The engine caught and the dignified retainers jumped back, and the crowd cheered with derisive pleasure as they ran awkwardly after their saffron turbans, blown across the field by the rotating propeller.

The fragile aircraft taxied down the grass, gaining speed. When it pulled into the air, people ran screaming onto the grass. Jaya had to press her hands to her ears to stop herself from joining in the deafening cheers as the shaking machine looped through the cloudless sky.

John MacGregor shouted over her cupped hands. 'I'm testing the next aircraft. Would you care to come along as a passenger, Princess?'

The crowds watched her being helped up the struts of the aircraft by the Angrez aviator. Jaya was aware of the wind clearly outlining her body under the thin sari, and her thick hair falling in dishevelled clumps from under the leather flying helmet.

Her self-consciousness evaporated in exhilaration the moment the small craft pulled away from the ground and straightened out over the river shining silver in the brilliant noon sunlight.

She could see the small squares of green rice fields, separated by tiny groves of coconut trees, stretching toward the Sirpur foothills.

The Scotsman was shouting into the rubber speaking tube. Jaya opened the flap of her helmet to hear him more clearly, and loose hair whipped around her face. 'Take the controls, Princess.' MacGregor pointed to the wooden stick in front of her. Jaya pulled. The plane rose sharply into the air, driving her body back into the seat.

'Not that hard, Princess.' Jaya waited until the instructor had levelled the aircraft, then tried again. Soon she was laughing with the excitement of controlling the plane, so sure of herself that she even leaned over the side to wave to the cheering specks below.

When the airplane rolled to a standstill, she climbed out and ran toward Prince Pratap. 'Mr MacGregor let me have the controls, hukam. Did you see me fly?'

'Well done, Princess.' The boredom was audible in his voice, and Jaya stared at the flying helmet in her hand, crushed by her husband's indifference.

BY WINTER the bamboo scaffolding that had covered the capital for weeks had been removed, revealing the freshly painted houses. Dahlias and canna lilies bordered every avenue. White balconies rose above brilliant bougainvillea topiary shaped in the Sirpur crest, the elephant of war and the snake of purity.

Lady Modi was ecstatic at the elegant appearance the city had presented as her car rolled down the newly tarred streets. 'Darling, the Prince of Wales will be so impressed. God knows he needs spoiling after the rough reception he is getting in British India. Isn't it extraordinary how quickly things change? I mean, only ten years ago we were all so thrilled by the Imperial Durbar when his father was crowned Emperor of India. And now the glamorous Prince of Wales is being met by silent crowds wearing black armbands and Gandhi caps. The British are so furious with the demonstrations they have even invented a pole with an iron hook to pull off the Gandhi caps.'

Lady Modi kicked off her shoes and settled herself on Jaya's bed. 'Anyway, the Viceroy is still trying to give His Royal Highness a taste of imperial spectacle. Peasants are standing every hundred yards down the railway tracks holding huge torches to light the night in case HRH happens to look out of the window. Rather romantic, don't you think, darling?'

Jaya tried to calculate how many hundreds of thousands of torchbearers would be required to keep the spectre of Indian disenchantment with the British Raj at bay.

'The trouble is,' Lady Modi observed, 'Indians are no longer in awe of the British Empire. They are enthralled by Gandhi's loincloth. After all, what is a mere heir to an empire compared to a Mahatma, a Great Soul? I only wish the nationalists weren't so serious. The imperialists do seem to have all the fun.'

As though echoing Lady Modi's sentiments, Prince Pratap devoted his energies to ensuring that the Prince of Wales would have fun in Sirpur. Tribal headmen crowded into his study to discuss the arrangements for the elephant hunt, when the Prince of Wales would see wild elephants being tracked and lassoed through the ten-foot-high grass.

Lady Modi was taken to see the drugged Bengal tigers asleep in their cages, bricks hanging on the ends of their tails. At the polo ground, Prince Pratap indicated the returfed field. 'Dickie Mountbatten learned to play polo when the royal party visited Jodhpur last month. Now he's besotted by the game. I suppose we'll have to play an exhibition match with him.'

'Naturally, darling. You and Victor do have the highest polo handicaps in India.'

'Not much point in having a high handicap if you fall off your horse.' Prince Pratap frowned. 'I only hope Victor manages to stay sober for the royal visit. Have you noticed how much he is drinking? I keep telling him Cora Hart is exactly like all his other showgirls, but he won't listen.'

In the City Palace there was widespread concern that Maharajah Victor might betray himself during the royal visit. His eyes were bloodshot and puffy, as though he had been drinking through the night while the rest of Sirpur slept. Jaya wondered if Maharajah Victor had wearied of courting the British Empire's approval with his displays of loyalty and chosen to take refuge in drink and the harmless images on a screen, finding them the most desirable of the unrealities which assaulted him every day.

In the evenings, Jaya sat in the gardens of the Purdah Palace trying to disguise her boredom while Lady Modi and the Dowager Maharani competed over the extravagances being showered on the Prince of Wales by the Indian kings.

'Well, Ma-sahib, what do you think of Udaipur's efforts to upstage Jaipur's elephant fights by setting three hundred leopards to fight three hundred wild boar for the Prince of Wales's entertainment?'

'That is nothing. When this boy's grandfather came to India as Prince of Wales, the Maharajah of Nepal put a guard of ten thousand soldiers, two thousand elephants and three thousand cavalry at his personal disposal. And in Sirpur, the Prince of Wales shot six tigers in a single day.'

'Well, in Bikaner the royal party killed eleven thousand grouse in one day, Ma-sahib. The British are saying Bikaner is Maharajah only by the Grouse of God.'

'You may think this is all a joke, Bapsy. But when this boy's grandfather came to India, Englishmen used to beat Indians to death for daring to enter their rooms with shoes on.' The Dowager Maharani sniffed in outrage. 'Such airs, from people who do not even know the left hand is unclean! The Prince of Wales himself wrote to Rani Victoria that the British Residents extorted fortunes in gems and pushed the rulers about with their hands.'

Pulling at her hookah, the Dowager described how the earlier

Prince of Wales had made rulers promise to prevent their wives from committing sati. 'A waste of time. The rulers may have promised, but their wives did not. When Nepal died, his three wives burned themselves on his funeral pyre. They had written to Victoria that their honour demanded it.'

'That was in 1876, Ma-sahib. It's different now.'

The Dowager Maharani ignored the interruption. 'My life is my husband's gift of honour to the British Raj. I did not commit sati, and so I have lived to witness the shame of having my grandsons stolen from me and made into Englishmen themselves. Dreaming only of white women.'

Lady Modi tried to stem the flow of bitter memories. 'Darling Ma-sahib, do stop fussing, or I won't bring you any gossip from the Viceroy's Valentine Ball in Delhi for the Prince of Wales.'

'Is it true that my grandsons are also attending the ball?'

Lady Modi nodded, and the old woman laid bent fingers on Lady Modi's knee. 'See they don't make fools of themselves over some white woman in the presence of the Viceroy, Bapsy.'

Jaya gazed bitterly at the ivory-coloured jasmine blossoms filling the warm air with their heavy scent. Even the Dowager Maharani knew that Prince Pratap still preferred mem-sahibs to his wife. She vowed that as soon as the Sirpur princes and Lady Modi departed for Delhi, she would move into the Purdah Palace, leaving her handbags, her high-heeled shoes and her entourage of foreigners behind.

30

ONLY A MILE of bamboo groves separated the Purdah Palace from the rest of the City Palace, but the hectic preparations for the Prince of Wales seemed distanced by centuries from the wide verandah open to the river breezes.

At dusk, as flocks of birds shrieked their way to the trees beyond the harem walls, the purdah women tied garlands of fresh jasmine buds around their wrists and exchanged gossip about the day's small events until the heavy iron bell rang from the Dowager Maharani's chambers. Filing into the puja room, they circled the image of the Goddess with lights, while the Dowager invoked the curse of the Goddess on the actress who was stealing the Maharajah's sanity with this new witchcraft that reproduced her image in Sirpur when she was on the other side of the world.

Jaya sank gratefully into the familiar routines of seclusion. Every morning she sat with the palace women, cutting vegetables into the elaborate animals for which the Sirpur cuisine was famous, before placing the tiny menageries on green plantain leaves for the maid-servants to carry to the kitchens.

Sometimes a brocade screen was set up in the Dowager's durbar room. The purdah women scurried in and out of the room making sure that the Prime Minister's favourite drink of chilled pomegranate juice was in its silver decanter and the coals in his hookah alight. The cries of the Abyssinian eunuchs echoed down the corridors: 'Be vigilant! Be vigilant! The Prime Minister of Sirpur approaches!' and the women disappeared in a clash of anklets and glass bangles, slamming the wooden doors of their chambers shut as Sir Akbar took off his shoes.

Separated by the screen, the Dowager Maharani and Sir Akbar pulled at their hookahs and discussed the kingdom's affairs, their conversations full of long pauses, as if their shared silences communicated their thoughts better than words.

Soothed by the gentle monotony of the harem, Jaya almost forgot that she did not herself belong to the Purdah Palace until the Prime Minister sent for her. Watched by sympathetic purdah women, she loosened her hair again and painted her nails with crimson varnish. Instead of spraying herself with Bapsy's perfumes, she defiantly circled her wrist with a thin garland of fresh jasmine buds.

The drawing room was already crowded with guests when the Lancers separated their lances. Jaya moved through the crowd that surrounded the Prime Minister, clasping her hands in greeting. Sir Akbar bowed before her. 'Please return to your apartments, hukam. The Maharajah has requested your assistance with last-minute details for the royal visit.'

Jaya lowered her hands, and her velvet reticule slipped from the bend of her elbow. Before she could bend down, a large hand closed on the small handbag.

'Marriage obviously suits you, Bai-sa.' Jaya blushed in confusion as she accepted the handbag from the unintroduced stranger in the khaki uniform, medals covering his broad chest. But the voice was remotely familiar, as if she had once heard it in a higher register. 'Have I changed so much, Bai-sa?'

The repetition of her childhood title pulled at Jaya's memory. She looked up. Thick black lashes framed the deep blue eyes, above lips turned in a half-embarrassed smile. Major James Osborne shook her fingers, and the handbag once again slipped to the ground. He almost fell as he scrambled for it.

Jaya hid her smile at his muttered apologies. 'Have you been in Sirpur long, James-sahib?'

'Almost two weeks. Upcountry, seeing if anyone was upsetting the tribals. When I heard you were living in the harem, I was afraid I might not meet you at all, Bai-sa. Tomorrow I leave for Delhi to accompany the Maharajah and the Prince of Wales on their journey back to Sirpur.'

'I understand you are here because you are an expert on Bolsheviks, James-sahib. Are there many in India?'

He watched the round figure of the British Resident move towards them. 'Everyone blames the Bolsheviks for India's troubles, though with their civil war and the famine in Russia, they are hardly in a position to start a revolution here, Bai-sa.'

'I wouldn't be surprised if Gandhi were a Bolshevik.' Sir Henry Conroy's lead-grey eyes were cold in the shining folds of his face. 'How else do you explain the violence when the Prince of Wales arrived in Bombay? Thugs beating up anyone who wasn't wearing a black armband, mobs burning and looting shops, setting Union Jacks on fire.'

'Gandhi's volunteers tried to stop the violence, sir.'

'Rubbish, Osborne. The man's an anarchist, unleashing dangerous passions that will turn this whole continent into a sea of blood. Only we British can control India. That's something these nationalists should understand.'

James Osborne looked away in embarrassment as the doors to the banquet room opened. The British Resident grunted in irritation. 'Well, at least Maharajah Victor had the good sense to invite you back for the Prince of Wales's visit. I, for one, will be relieved to have a Bolshevik expert in Sirpur while His Royal Highness is here.'

James Osborne offered Jaya an arm, his mouth turned in that half-shy smile again. Grateful for Lady Modi's deportment lessons, Jaya placed her hand on the khaki sleeve.

'Are you married yourself, James-sahib?' she asked as they entered the banquet room.

'I've only just left the Army, Bai-sa. I shall have to become British Resident to some grand kingdom like Sirpur before I can afford a wife.'

Conscious of James Osborne seated at her side, Jaya was unable to concentrate on the conversations about the royal visit. Without looking at him she could feel the changes in the Angrez boy, the way the slim body had filled out into a man's frame, yet kept some part of its vulnerability under the military carriage. Deep lines scored the skin on either side of his mouth, and Jaya remembered he had been in battle, on one front or another, for the last eight years.

She felt his breath on her skin. 'Tikka would be very proud of you if he saw you now, Bai-sa.' He bent forward and gripped her wrist, crushing the jasmine buds with the pressure of his fingers. Afraid his gesture might have been seen by a courtier, Jaya pulled away.

RELIEVED TO learn James Osborne had already left Sirpur, Jaya joined Sir Akbar on a tour of the public rooms to make sure everything was in order before Lady Modi and Prince Pratap reached the capital that afternoon.

Sir Akbar raised an eyebrow when he saw the men struggling with pulleys to lift a polished chandelier back to the ceiling of the Durbar Room. 'I can't understand all this expenditure and excitement. After all, the House of Sirpur is two thousand years older than the British throne.'

In the ballroom, Mr Sengupta, lately arrived from the Calcutta Light Operatic Society, was conducting the Sirpur orchestra. A pock-marked violinist waved his instrument in the air, and Mr Sengupta rapped his baton on the music rest to silence the violinist before turning to the other musicians, berating them for failing to insert enough passion into the tango.

The Prime Minister brushed a discreet hand over his ears. 'I have always believed that dancing girls should dance and the rest of us should watch.' The pale hands removed a nonexistent feather from the severely cut Indian frock coat, as if dismissing the present as an aberration of taste. 'And you are planning to dance with His Royal Highness, hukam?'

'If my husband insists, I shall have no choice.'

The Prime Minister's cane echoed on the parquet floor of the ballroom as they retraced their steps to Jaya's apartments. 'I understand that you studied Rajniti, Princess. You may find it easier to place your hand on the Englishman's arm if you remember Kautilya's maxim "When you cannot defeat your enemy by force of arms, defeat him by friendship."'

'I learned another version, Sir Akbar: "If you cannot kill your enemy with your sword, then place your arm around his shoulder in friendship and kill him with your dagger."'

'Exactly so, Princess.'

Puzzled, Jaya watched the upright figure moving through the

gardens towards the administration buildings, the peacocks side-
stepping from his precise advance as though conscious of his authority.

LADY MODI was waiting in Jaya's apartments. 'Darling, I can't
tell you what an event the Valentine Ball turned out to be.
Cupid was working overtime. The Viceroy had Edwina Ashley, the
richest of those Bright Young Things, staying with him – you
know, those wellborn English girls who hang around bars and
black men, darling. And guess what?'

Lady Modi's ability to make everything sound like the titles in
Maharajah Victor's films swept Jaya into her enthusiasm. 'Dickie
Mountbatten asked her to marry him, right in the middle of the
Valentine Ball. The Prince of Wales is to be the best man at their
wedding. It's all still a terrific secret.'

She kicked off her shoes. 'Unfortunately, that very same day
Cora Hart had cabled Victor that she is prepared to marry him
if she is installed as full Maharani of Sirpur.'

'But she can't be a full maharani, Bapsy. The British Empire ·
forbids it.'

Lady Modi stretched across Jaya and crushed her cigarette into
the ashtray. 'Everyone knows that, darling, but with all the romance
in the air at the Valentine Ball, Victor just lost his head. As soon as
he learned about Mountbatten's engagement, Victor went straight
to the Prince of Wales and told him he was going to marry Cora
Hart.'

Jaya stared in shock into Lady Modi's wide eyes. 'If the Viceroy
finds out, the Maharajah may lose his throne.'

'Now, don't get excited, darling. Luckily, the Prince of Wales
regards Victor as a friend. HRH read Victor a long lecture about
duty and not letting personal desires get in the way of public
responsibilities. He told Victor it was highly unsuitable, rather as if
he were to marry a divorcée or a Roman Catholic. But we will have
to keep an eye on Victor. If he gets stinking drunk during HRH's
visit, anything could happen.'

Prince Pratap appeared in the doorway. 'Come on, ladies. We're
going for a drive. His Royal Highness may speak to you about the
arrangements, Princess. Unless you have seen them, you will be

tongue-tied like all the other royal women he's encountered in the last months.'

The streets were already crowded with people, infected by the air of holiday. The Sirpur Lancers were riding six abreast down the central avenue of the new city, horse hooves clattering on the road, pennants waving in the breeze. In the park alongside them, a brass band in white uniforms and gold-braided caps rehearsed 'God Save the King", watched by a group of bare-breasted tribal women who were laughing raucously as they passed a cask of coconut toddy among themselves.

Excited urchins flung flowers at the Rolls-Royce as Prince Pratap honked the car horn at the bicycles, cars, carts – all flying the Sirpur flag and the Union Jack – seething on the streets.

'Look at that, will you?'

Lady Modi and Jaya craned to follow his pointing finger. Cloth banners blazoned with florid calligraphy stretched across the crowded bazaars. *Give Our Love to Mummy. Good for Mummy. Your Mummy Is Our Mother.*

Lady Modi sank back into her seat. 'Darling, I had no idea your subjects felt so strongly about Queen Mary.'

'Those are antiques from the last royal chukker – when the Prince of Wales visited Sirpur in 1876. The Mummy in question was my brother's godmother, the Empress Victoria.'

On the river, the Sirpur flotilla shone in the evening light, gold leaf glittering on the wooden masts of the ancient vessels. Prince Pratap slammed his fist against the dashboard. 'God knows what HRH is going to make of this. It's like some native Henley. Film stars and riverboats – really, Victor has no sense of occasion at all!'

Jaya visualized Maharajah Victor's gentle face and bloodshot eyes as he moved like an unconvinced actor in the baroque trappings of his own history, and prayed he would do nothing to endanger his throne during the Prince of Wales's visit.

31

'How do I look, darling?' A large diamond pendant caught mauve chiffon pleats high on Lady Modi's shoulder. The fabric bunched awkwardly over a lace-collared blouse, and the entire garment was tied so high on Lady Modi's small waist that it looked more like an ill-fitting Edwardian dress than an Indian sari. Chantal was still curling the ends of the shining helmet of hair into tight curls.

'The trouble with having been in school abroad is that whenever I dress like an Indian I look so unconvincing,' Lady Modi observed ruefully.

The mirror reflected Jaya's sari sweeping over her feet in graceful folds and the classic cut of her unadorned blouse. Seeing the chestnut hair being teased into reluctant curls, unlike the hair falling in a black curtain to her own knees, Jaya suddenly understood that the lessons she had learned with such impatience in Balmer – the rangoli classes which had taught her the aesthetics of colour and form, the lectures of the Balmer purdah ladies – were all part of a civilization that was sure of its own permanence. She firmly peeled the gloves off her hands.

'Don't lose them, darling,' Lady Modi warned over Chantal's curling tongs.

'I don't need them, Bapsy.'

Lady Modi gave a little scream. 'You can't possibly meet the Prince of Wales without them.'

'He is our guest, Bapsy. Surely our traditions will please him more than his own.'

'But the British think their traditions are the only ones worth having. They make the rules. After all, darling, it is their Empire.'

Before she could remonstrate further, an aide bowed at the door. 'We must leave immediately for the Wales Palace, hukam. The ruler's train has arrived.'

A marble pergola had been built beyond the oleander pathway at the Wales Palace. Turbaned retainers were waving cloths to prevent the circling birds from soiling the red carpet that stretched from the cupola to the end of the pier. From under bright awnings, rows of Sirpur nobles and their wives bowed as Jaya walked to the pergola with Lady Modi.

A band was playing in the new wooden bandstand, its white paint shining in the sun. A regiment of Sirpur Lancers marched down the path, oleander blossoms falling on their starched turbans. They came to attention beside the pier, snapping their heavy steel lances to their shoulders as the boom of cannon fire shook the marble pergola.

The crash of cannon was followed by the hollow notes of conch shells as the priests of Kamini Temple performed a puja to make the visit auspicious for the Maharajah.

Across the river from the merchants' houses, flags lifted in the breeze to show the Sirpur crest and the feathers of the Prince of Wales. Below them, lumber barges, tribal canoes, motor launches bumped against each other in the muddy water, as if everyone possessing a boat were waiting to join the Maharajah's procession.

Jaya looked at the official programme lying on her lap. Each ceremony seemed to contradict the last: the conch shells of the priests were followed by a march-past of the Sirpur Infantry. Through her binoculars she could see the Prince of Wales sitting with the Maharajah in an open Rolls-Royce. They disappeared from view, and the programme informed her they were now mounting elephants to ride in state through the old city.

Cheering echoed down the riverbanks. The nobles and their wives shifted excitedly under their awnings. Around the curve of the river three catamarans appeared, their wooden hulls almost too small for the huge silk sails blazoned with the Sirpur elephant and snake billowing from their gold-painted masts. Behind them a flotilla of painted wooden vessels moved in formation, hulls deep in the muddy water, silk sails ballooning above their prows.

At last the heavy royal barge came into view, a three-decked galleon propelled by oars pulled by unseen rowers so that golden combs seemed to be cutting through the sluggish water. On its prow a painted snake wound around a wooden elephant trumpeting into the water. As the royal barge moved forward, hundreds of boats crowded into its wake, chopping at the water until it swirled in muddy ripples towards the riverbanks.

Lady Modi peered through her opera glasses. 'Darling, it's too wonderful. The Prince of Wales and Victor are sitting on red thrones, and there's Dickie Mountbatten with the Resident.'

Reverberating engines drowned the music from the bandstand. Jaya looked up. Three aircraft were flying towards the river.

They spiralled towards the royal barge, strutted wings shaking with the impact of their loops. Grey smoke streamed behind them as the aircraft sketched the Prince of Wales's feathers in the cobalt-blue sky. Firecrackers exploded from the riverbanks. Boat horns, drums, flutes, anything that could be pressed into service as noise created a wall of sound over the river. Jaya could barely hear Lady Modi shouting above the cheering spectators. 'Darling, you have to admit the Sirpur brothers really know how to put on a show. Bet HRH never saw anything like this before.'

The flotilla of ancient vessels moved slowly down the river, sun striking like a mirror off the gold leaf of the royal barge, in strange contrast to the European dance tunes sounding from the bandstand. On the riverbank, the howdahed elephants were swaying towards the City Palace. Lady Modi asked restively if there was time for a drink. But the nobles were rising to their feet and applauding.

Prince Pratap was walking down the path between the olean-der bushes, his flying helmet replaced by a turban. He waved in acknowledgement of the cheers and sat down in the cupola as the royal barge turned towards the pier.

Maharajah Victor and the Prince of Wales were visible on their red thrones. 'Like bloody Cleopatra,' Prince Pratap snorted in derision as the band struck up the opening chords of 'God Save the King'.

The Prince of Wales stepped onto the red carpet and the Sirpur Lancers presented arms. Jaya was surprised at how small the English Prince appeared next to the slender figure of the Maharajah. His bare head only reached the Maharajah's shoulder. She remembered Tikka's description of his father, the King Emperor, riding to his coronation, so small that no one had seen him properly.

'Come along, Princess.' Jaya followed Prince Pratap to the pier, where the Prince of Wales was reviewing the rows of Sirpur Lancers wearing the medals they had won in the Great War.

The Lancers marched away, and Jaya nervously folded her bare hands in front of her face. She was surprised when the Prince returned her traditional gesture of welcome. 'Victor has been describing your feats as a rider and a pilot, Princess.'

'I have been up in an aeroplane, sir. But I cannot fly one.'

'I'm told it's only a matter of time. And I know your father was a great polo player. Perhaps you can give a few tips to my cousin.'

A tall young man stepped forward. Behind Mountbatten's shoulder Jaya watched the Angrez attendants talking to the Prince. She was fascinated by James Osborne's servile attitude and the unctuous demeanour of the usually frigid and arrogant British Resident, Sir Henry Conroy. For the first time Jaya understood Gandhi's genius in challenging this alien Empire with the very elements that terrified the Angrez, poverty instead of power, humility instead of exclusivity.

CONVINCED THAT she had gained a perception which had not occurred to the others, Jaya moved through the welcoming ceremonies and the lunch that followed with a serene ease, as if she were acting a role that already belonged to the past.

Driving back to the City Palace, Prince Pratap congratulated Lady Modi. 'The Princess is making quite an impression, Bapsy. I even heard Mountbatten remarking to Metcalfe that it was a pity the Princess couldn't play polo with the men.'

'I'd rather play polo with the Angrez than dance with them, hukam.'

Prince Pratap laughed. Impatient with her husband's patronizing, Jaya added, 'I'm sure I am as good a player as any of them. At lunch, the Prince of Wales told me that when Mountbatten played with the Jodhpur team, he didn't hit the ball once in the first three chukkers.'

Prince Pratap took her arm and pulled her around to face him. 'My grandfather had to impress the Prince's grandfather by swearing my grandmother would not commit sati. But if you were to play polo with us, could the Empire doubt Sirpur's commitment to progress?'

Jaya freed her arm. 'In exchange, hukam, you will excuse me from the ball.'

Prince Pratap slammed the car door. 'Out of the question. You are Victor's hostess.'

'Then let me say I do not dance.'

Jaya saw the combative gleam in his eyes, as if her exhibition of courage were eroding the barrier between them. 'It's a bargain, Princess. Play polo and you don't have to dance.'

'At last. A round to you, darling,' Lady Modi whispered. 'I just hope you know how to play the silly game.'

Jaya silently beseeched the elephant-headed God Ganesh to protect her from her folly. She had only three days in which to practise, while the royal party was away, shooting their drugged tigers.

A FINE MIST of spiderwebs covered the bushes when Jaya rode on-to the polo ground. Despite the early hour, gardeners were hacking at the grass with scythes. Above the royal pavilion, the Prince of Wales's standard and the Maharajah's flag were already tied to the flag posts.

All day she hit the polo ball with her mallet, getting used to striking it sideways instead of head-on, as she did when she was tent-pegging. At the edge of the field, clerks of the Household Administration supervised the cleaning of the wooden benches that flanked the royal pavilion, and cotton carpets were unrolled in front of the refreshment tents.

On the third morning, the sun threw the shadow of a cantering horse and rider in straight lines across the bright cobwebs, and James Osborne pulled his horse up next to Jaya's. Reaching into the leather pouch slapping against his saddle, he threw a white ball onto the ground.

'Come on, Bai-sa. The Prince of Wales has shot two tigers and watched an elephant roundup. Now he's eagerly waiting to see how you play tomorrow.'

Osborne rode down the polo ground, correcting her each time she hit a ball directly. 'Hit it under your horse's neck, Bai-sa. Like the Americans. Add your body weight to the blow.'

Perspiration rolled down Jaya's body, soaking her clothes until the thin linen shirt clung to her body. Each time she spurred her horse into a gallop, the heavy hair which she repeatedly wound onto the top of her head fell like a blanket over her shoulders; but in her anxiety to play well, she was unaware of Osborne's eyes on her as she pushed her hair away from the breasts thrusting against her sweat-soaked clothes.

When she returned from the polo ground Lady Modi was reclining on Jaya's bed in front of a tray with an ice bucket and a bottle of gin. 'Well, darling – to go straight from purdah to a polo game in front of the Prince of Wales! As for that poor English officer getting sunstroke out there . . . My dear, you are about to become a legend.'

Jaya circled her long hair around her aching forearm, shaking off the sweat as she entered the bathroom. Chandni splashed water over her naked body. 'Think what people will say at the sight of a royal princess flaunting herself in front of the Angrez,' Chandni hissed. 'You will create a scandal. The Dowager Maharani will certainly put an end to this foolishness.'

When the Abyssinians ushered Jaya into the old woman's presence, the Dowager Maharani waved a crippled hand, dismissing the attendants. 'You have done well, child. Anything we can do to distract the Prince of Wales is important. I shall be watching you tomorrow. Victor is not playing polo, but he will not have the courage to broach the subject of that American actress if I am present at your game.' In sudden agitation, the old woman threw the mouthpiece of the hookah away from her, and it clanged loudly against the crystal base. 'You are young, child. You belong to a world that I no longer understand. Tell me what magic these foreigners possess. How have they so corrupted my grandson's soul that he is prepared to place a white whore on the most ancient throne in India?'

The Dowager's question lay like a shadow across Jaya's mind as she sat astride her horse, waiting for the polo match to begin. The Sirpur nobles crowded into the stands next to the royal pavilion. Around the polo ground, the cotton carpets were invisible under the mass of people and shouting guards pushed children back from the turf, where they could be mowed down by galloping horses.

A company of Sirpur Lancers trotted down the field. Behind them Maharajah Victor and the Prince of Wales waved from an open state landau. The Sirpur trumpeters played a fanfare as the ruler dismounted with the Prince of Wales. There was a momentary lull in the cheers when the Maharajah Victor presented the Prince of Wales to the Dowager, hidden under waves of white veils. Prince Pratap galloped onto the polo ground, shouting over his shoulder, 'Come on, Princess, let's have some fun.'

The trumpet sounded for the beginning of the first chukker. The Master of the Horse threw a white ball between the milling horses. There was a loud clash of polo mallets, and the players chased the white ball spinning down the centre of the field. Jaya hung to one side, aware of the crowds pointing at her as Prince Pratap let the other riders accelerate towards the ball before pressing his heels into his own mount to effortlessly overtake them and send the ball spinning between the white posts, so certain of himself he never looked back to see if the red flag had gone up confirming a goal.

Suddenly he hit a swinging backhand that sent the ball racing down the ground towards Jaya. She dug her heels into her horse, the fastest polo pony in the Sirpur stables. The speed of her mount made her laugh out loud with exhilaration as she followed the bouncing ball. Seeing James Osborne and Mountbatten bearing down on her, she felt her exhilaration boil over into a fierce competitiveness that she had never before experienced. She gripped the mallet harder in her hand and bent over her horse's head, whispering encouragement into the flattened ears. The ball was only yards in front of her, but the hoofbeats of the other horses were so close she could hear them thundering louder than her own mount's, and she shouted to her horse, as if all the humiliations that had been heaped upon her father's family and her husband's could be wiped out in a single goal. The white ball bounced awkwardly in front of her. Leaning over her horse's neck, she smashed the ball toward the goal mouth. James Osborne galloped at her. She crashed into his horse's shoulder with the full momentum of her own mount. 'That's a foul, Bai-sa!' Osborne shouted angrily as a red flag waved in front of the goal mouth and the cheering spectators fell back from her foaming horse.

Twice more in that chukker Jaya managed to connect with the ball. Once she even created an opening for her husband. He yelled his thanks as he galloped James Osborne off the ball and scored a goal. When they were changing horses, Prince Pratap put his hands around her waist and lifted her into the saddle, pulling free the end of the plait which had hitched itself under her thighs. 'Having fun,

Princess?' Jaya saw the Prince of Wales clapping and waved at him gaily, as if her husband's fleeting gesture of intimacy had melted away the Dowager Maharani's premonitions.

The trumpet sounded the end of the game, and two Sirpur Lancers marched forward to place a table holding a large trophy and a line of eight silver cups in front of the royal pavilion. The Prince of Wales accompanied Maharajah Victor onto the polo ground, where Jaya was standing with the other players, half-hidden by her husband.

'I'm sure my cousin will be grateful for this further example of your wonderful Sirpur hospitality, Pratap, although I thought it was a trifle obvious.'

'I don't know what you mean, sir.'

'You clearly held the Princess back out of consideration for my cousin's pride.' The Prince of Wales held out his hand. 'Congratulations, Princess. Your goal was without question the best goal in the game.'

AT THE BANQUET, as too many guests congratulated her on the polo game, Jaya felt as if the only people visible in the vast dining room were herself and the Prince of Wales. She was relieved when the doors of the banquet hall were flung open and Mr Sengupta's orchestra swung into a fox-trot under the chandelier shining above the candlelit, flower-flooded ballroom.

Prince Pratap pulled back her chair, whispering into her hair, 'Since you're not dancing, stay close to Victor. Make sure he doesn't get so drunk he says something indiscreet.'

Jaya obediently sat on the couch with Maharajah Victor, watching the mem-sahibs fluttering their fans as they tried to attract the attention of the royal party. The Prince of Wales's equerries flirted with the Sirpur ladies, unsure what to do with their hands when they led the ladies onto the dance floor and the ladies lifted their saris, exposing their bare waists to the embrace of the Angrez.

As Maharajah Victor rose to join the Prince of Wales, James Osborne bowed in front of Jaya. She looked at the braided epaulets shining on his shoulders and was swamped by homesickness. The last time she had been carefree was when the Angrez boy and her brother had been friends in Balmer Fort, playing cricket in the nets below the Round Tower and excitedly discussing the King Emperor's coronation in Delhi.

'Well, your husband certainly made monkeys of us in front of the Prince of Wales today, Bai-sa.' Osborne began to relive the game, and Jaya recognised something she had never seen before: that anger between their races which had once governed his father and now seemed to govern him, as if he resented her husband's excellence even more than he resented his failings. In only ten years, she and the Angrez boy had both changed too much, as though reflecting the changes in a world that once had seemed so permanent.

A hand closed over her wrist. She heard a glass bangle breaking in his white glove. 'What is it, Bai-sa?' The anger had gone from his face. She felt herself being pulled into the deep blue eyes looking at her with gentle concern.

'We have not spoken about Balmer, James-sahib. You are leaving tonight. We may not get another opportunity to talk of old times.'

'I'm in the Political Service now, Bai-sa. Who knows? One day I might even be sent as British Resident to Sirpur.'

Mr Sengupta's orchestra indicated that the Prince of Wales was leaving. James Osborne rose hurriedly to his feet as the Prince of Wales paused before Jaya. 'We have had a wonderful time in Sirpur, Princess. I told your husband that he must bring you to visit us in England.'

A fleet of Rolls-Royces was parked in the drive, white tyres shining in the darkness. Turbaned chauffeurs stood next to open doors, and a motorcycle escort waited for the Maharajah to make his farewells before gunning their engines.

'You see how easy it is, Princess?' Prince Pratap whispered as the Maharajah and the Prince of Wales took leave of each other. 'A year ago I was forbidden to travel abroad. Now the Prince of Wales himself is insisting that I should. He wouldn't have done that if you had been hidden in the Purdah Palace, covered in henna.'

Car doors slammed, and the motorcycles roared in front of the departing Rolls-Royces. 'Since you seem to have received the royal seal of approval, I suppose it's safe to display you in Calcutta, after Bapsy has had a few weeks to show you the ropes. But now, if you'll excuse me, I'm going to enjoy myself at last.'

The Prime Minister bowed before Jaya. 'Shall I see you to your apartments, hukam?' She nodded unhappily. In silence she followed

226

him past the lotus lake. The mournful melodies of the flutes from the barges floated in the night air, louder than the receding sounds of dance music.

A nightjar broke from the bushes, screeching into the darkness. As if the disturbance had reminded him of something, Sir Akbar stopped. 'A polo mallet can sometimes be as useful as a dagger. You have studied Rajniti, even if Prince Pratap has not. Such knowledge would give a wife great power over her husband if she used it intelligently, hukam.'

32

THE TRAIN pulled alongside the platform of Calcutta's Howrah Station. Jaya saw the vendors, displaying cane baskets filled with wooden toys, clinging to the iron bars of the still-moving train window, and she knew they had arrived in the metropolis that was called the second city of the British Empire.

On the platforms, passengers tried to keep pace with the red-coated porters swinging through the crowds, and imperious mem-sahibs shouted instructions in incomprehensible Hindustani to the porters trying to lift heavy cabin trunks onto their heads.

An Anglo-Indian ticket collector in a shiny black suit and solar topi was demanding tickets from a confused family clutching crying babies. Behind him, a board covered with shiny paper pinwheels separated Jaya from Lady Modi, teetering determinedly on high heels behind the porters.

By the time Jaya reached the sleek black Daimler, Lady Modi had already made herself a martini from the bar enclosed in the wooden panelling behind the chauffeur's seat.

The Daimler rolled down the bridge that spanned the Hooghly River. 'Makes the Sirpur Bridge look like a toy, doesn't it, darling?'

Outside the stone buildings in Dalhousie Square, discreet brass plaques winked in the sunlight. 'Those are the offices of the big British Raj fortunes. And that's Writer's Building, where Indian clerks count the British Empire's money.'

The car turned down the Esplanade. Neat flower beds bisected the streets. Inside the traffic circles the bronze statues of British statesmen raised imperious forefingers at the vehicles hurtling around them.

A trolley car rumbled slowly on its steel tracks in front of the wide green acres of the Maidan, passing a row of rickshaws filled with dark-skinned women in European clothes. 'Anglo-Indian girls, darling. Fathered by Englishmen working on upcountry tea estates. Of course, those same Englishmen are more discreet in Calcutta. At night they go to the brothels on Cryer Street, and in the daytime' – the cigarette holder waved at a row of white stucco buildings with pillared porticos – 'they drink at the Bengal Club or the Calcutta Club – two of the many clubs in Calcutta with signs saying "Dogs and Indians not allowed".'

The high grey arches of a cathedral rose above the streets. Behind the cathedral a white marble dome glistened in the afternoon sun. 'The Victoria Memorial, darling. Built in memory of Victor's godmother, Queen Victoria. The Sirpurs contributed handsomely to it, of course.'

'Do you think the British Empire has built anything in India out of love instead of power, Bapsy?'

Lady Modi looked at Jaya curiously. 'What an odd question, darling. Of course not.' She pointed at a shallow moat surrounding the green lawns of a whitewashed building. 'And there's the fountain of their power. Fort William.'

Small bronze cannon broke the symmetry of the low brick walls. Above the main verandah a Union Jack fluttered in the breeze. Jaya thought it was the least impressive fort she had ever seen, as the Daimler crossed the bridge into Alipore and moved towards the Calcutta Zoological Gardens and the imposing lawns of Government House, where the Viceroy stayed when he visited Calcutta.

Then they were turning into the drive of Sirpur House, a two-storey marble bungalow looming above the English oak trees that shaded the drive.

Jaya entered the black marble hall of the Calcutta residence of the Sirpur rulers, and for a moment she thought she had wandered into a museum. Stuffed tigers and leopards peered through red glass eyes from under a sweeping staircase. The walls were covered with tiger skins and antlers, a procession of slaughter broken only by portraits of Queen Victoria, King George and Queen Mary. On either side of the staircase, busts of the Empress Victoria and the Emperor George reflected dimly in the black marble floor, and tuberoses spilled from huge vases, their heavy perfume adding to the oppressive atmosphere.

Lady Modi laughed at Jaya's expression. 'This is to impress the British with Victor's loyalty and expertise in the jungle. It's all they really want to know about him. Now, darling, don't take forever with your pujas. We're expected at Flury's for tea.'

She led Jaya up the staircase, and Jaya's spirits rose again when she saw her white-and-gold apartments and the sunlight pouring in through French windows, dispersing the gloom of the black hall below with its mementos of death.

AT FLURY'S Tea Rooms, it was obvious from the frigid greetings of the owners that they still had not forgiven Lady Modi for stealing their pastry chef, Marco, to teach Jaya tennis. Lady Modi swept past them, weaving between the small tables towards a banquette where two Indian women dressed in silk shifts, cloches and pearls were sitting with their backs to the glass panes that gave onto Park Street.

Lady Modi had scarcely completed her introductions before her cigarette holder was waving at a glamorous redhead examining a pastry trolley. 'To your right, darling. Anita Delgado, the Spanish Maharani. She used to be a flamenco dancer until she married the Maharajah of Kapurthala.'

Jaya examined the creamy skin and dark eyes of the slender Spanish woman dressed in a sari as Lady Modi whispered, 'She's just commissioned a life-size portrait of herself in the nude to be hung in the palace where the entire population of Kapurthala can feast their eyes on it.'

'What nonsense, Bapsy.' Jaya didn't know whether to laugh or be angry at the absurdity of Lady Modi's suggestion.

'It's probably true, darling. It's the sort of thing that always happens when East meets West. I suppose it's just as well that the British Empire insists marriages between Indian rulers and foreign women can only be morganatic, and their children can never sit on the thrones. Drink your chocolate and guess what the Spanish Maharani's companion did before she became a maharani herself.'

Jaya peered over her cup. Talking to the flamenco dancer was a pretty, plump woman, blond hair escaping in thin streaks across her rouged cheeks.

'A hot-air balloonist!' Lady Modi announced gleefully. 'She used to throw flowers to the crowd from the gondola of a balloon. Maharajah Jind looked up and fell madly in love. Now she's his Maharani. I can't think why the British think we're backward. And any of those three Armenians could be yet another Maharani of Nepal.'

A trio of dark-haired women, chiffon dresses clinging to their bare white shoulders, were giggling among themselves, not once looking in the direction of their escorts. 'The Maharajah of Nepal has tried to make love to all three of them. As a result of his attentions, their husbands don't speak to them any more. He sent the girl in the middle a whole basketful of rubies as a compliment to her beauty.'

Lady Modi's companions explained that Calcutta, as the British Empire's second city, attracted nearly as many refugees as London: White Russians; Armenians who had fled the pogroms of the Ottoman Empire; Polish and Hungarian nobles with nowhere to go after the disintegration of the Hapsburg Empire. As the ladies chattered on, Jaya's eyes wandered over the glass cases filled with cakes, thinking of the Indian wives waiting in their purdah chambers, fearing to even speak their husbands' names, while those royal husbands married dancers and acrobats from Europe.

Lady Modi gave a small scream, and Jaya jumped. 'My God, darling, it's the silver swan!' Jaya looked through the window. A Rolls-Royce even more strangely shaped than the Dowager Maharani's car was sitting outside on the pavement. Silver feathers swooped over its trunk. A long silver neck stretched above its windshield.

'A mad Armenian refugee who made his fortune promptly celebrated his wealth by ordering that. It lays the most enormous golden egg.'

The other ladies assured Jaya that it was true. 'In fact, there was a riot the first time his car laid its golden egg on the street. Everyone tried to get it, so the police have restricted him to laying eggs in his own drive.'

Jaya watched the people collecting on the pavement and felt she was in some dream world where cars laid eggs and Indian women dressed as Europeans while European women not only dressed as Indians but were themselves maharanis.

IN SIRPUR HOUSE the aides informed Jaya that Mrs Roy was waiting in her apartments.

Jaya ran up the marble stairs, eager to be reassured of reality by the gentle voice and impatient intellect of her old tutor. Pressed against the coarse cotton sari as Mrs Roy folded her in an embrace, Jaya felt the alienation of the day slipping away.

Mrs Roy stepped back and for a long moment examined Jaya through rimless steel spectacles. Opening a paan casket and choosing the ingredients she knew Jaya liked, Mrs Roy handed a paan to her charge.

Jaya shook her head. 'My husband has forbidden me to eat betel leaf. It makes my teeth red and he says I look like a peasant.'

A familiar flash of anger crossed Mrs Roy's sharp eyes. 'White teeth will not make your skin white, Bai-sa. Nor French perfumes and eyebrows plucked like a European woman's. The British have taught your husband to hate himself. Do not become like him or you will belong nowhere.'

Jaya averted her eyes. 'I don't want to become like him, Mrs Roy. I just want him to treat me as a wife.'

'I warned you, Bai-sa. It takes courage to fight for your rights. Read the words of our great poet Tagore: "Where the mind is without fear and the head is held high, to that dream of freedom let my people awake." Every Indian should learn those lines.'

Jaya hid her smile at Mrs Roy's undiminished nationalism. Lady Modi appeared at the door, and the two women examined each other with transparent hostility.

As if that momentary encounter had been a silent challenge, a duel developed between Jaya's two mentors and they vied to show her a Calcutta differing from the other's as much as Mrs Roy's austere homespun saris differed from Lady Modi's cigarette holder and pearls.

If one evening Lady Modi took Jaya to see Esmé Moore, the Anglo-Indian girl who was the current toast of Calcutta, kicking her long legs under her feather boa, the next evening Mrs Roy took her to the Indian theatre to hear classical actors declaim long Sanskrit speeches on moral war through their painted masks.

If Jaya had spent the previous day buying French chiffons in New Market, Mrs Roy drove her to the schools on the outskirts of the city where rows of young nationalists sat behind wooden spinning wheels, spinning raw cotton into thread for their Gandhi caps.

If Mrs Roy took Jaya to badly ventilated restaurants that served Indian cuisine, Lady Modi responded by taking her to Calcutta's sprawling Chinatown to eat with chopsticks and see the old men asleep on their wooden benches, long opium pipes falling from their mouths.

Jaya began to believe there were two cities, separated from each other by the white stucco clubs and pillared offices of the British Empire, and every evening when she was driving back to Sirpur House she looked at the unimpressive walls of Fort William and wondered how the British controlled the chaos of this volatile metropolis with their Union Jacks and their certainty of race.

British Empire, and every evening when she was driving back to

33

EXHAUSTED BY the conflicting demands made by Mrs Roy and Lady
Modi, Jaya was relieved to learn that Prince Pratap and Maharajah
Victor were at last on their way to Calcutta for the Derby.

The Calcutta Derby was one of the most important events in
the Indian racing calendar, and the city had already begun filling
up with princes famous for their racing stables – the Aga Khan;
the Maharajahs of Bikaner, of Rajpipla, of Gwalior, of Mysore, of
Cooch Behar, of Dungra.

The Viceroy had arrived from Delhi for the Christmas season
to take up residence in Government House, down the road from
Sirpur House. Every evening, bands played Christmas carols outside
the Viceroy's residence, and troops of ragged Indian Santa Clauses
begged outside his wrought-iron gates at dusk, coughing into their
dirty white cotton wool beards as the fog enveloped them. Late at
night, Jaya heard the honking of car horns as British guests left the
Viceroy's parties and Christmas pantomime.

But when the Sirpur brothers finally reached Calcutta, Jaya
seldom saw them. They disappeared in the mornings to the Royal
Calcutta Turf Club with the trainers and the jockeys responsible for
the Sirpur horses, returning drunk late at night to be helped up the
marble staircase by waiting servants.

It was Lady Modi who told Jaya that Prince Pratap had been to
the Globe Theatre to see the dancer Esmé Moore at least a dozen
times. 'I believe Pratap and Hari Singh of Kashmir are having quite
a battle for her favours.'

Jaya tried to hide her bitterness at the revelation as Lady Modi jumped from her chair. 'Look at the time, darling! Tiny will be sitting in Firpo's wondering what has happened to us.'

In the car, Lady Modi explained that Firpo's was the oldest European restaurant in Asia, built at the same time as the Suez Canal. 'It's our Maxim's, darling. And after the Long Bar in Shanghai, the Venetian Bar at Firpo's is the longest bar in the world. Absolutely everybody lunches at Firpo's, even though no one expects letters from England to be delivered there any more.'

A small crowd milled at the staircase. Lady Modi darted through it exchanging kisses while Jaya stood motionless in a corner of the foyer, unaware that her own stance was as intimidating as she had once found the Maharani's or that people were falling back to allow her to follow Lady Modi up the stairs into the Venetian Bar.

'How is the fearless Princess?' Jaya smiled as Tiny Dungra's ungainly form struggled to rise from behind the table, remembering the laughter of the Balmer purdah ladies when they had seen him enter Maharajah Jai Singh's durbar.

'I wasn't at all surprised when I heard about your polo game. Pratap has always been able to make women do the most outrageous things.' Tiny Dungra sank down on the small gilt chair next to her as Lady Modi disappeared into a group of friends. Behind him was a mural of Venetian gondolas moving down a blue canal, and Jaya was reminded of the paintings on the outer walls of the Balmer zenana.

'How is my mother, hukam?'

Instead of the pity Jaya had expected, Tiny Dungra's expression softened with respect. 'My father gave her some land. She sold her jewellery, and from the proceeds she has made a school, a dispensary and an ashram for the needy. Actually, she is considered a saint in Dungra. We call her the Sati Mata.' Jaya remembered the cobra coiling above the iron trident and the ascetic's deep voice warning the Maharani of her destiny.

A commotion at the entrance to the bar distracted Dungra. Esmé Moore, the dancer from the Globe Theatre, was standing at the door. Jaya's skin burned with anger when she saw the gentlemen at the bar craning around their companions to watch the long-legged girl, dressed in a clinging pink silk shift that seemed to add a glow to her slightly dusky complexion, move through the crowded room. A hat covered her tight black curls, dropping a veil over her wide

235

eyes, allowing her to appear demure even as she acknowledged the men rising to greet her from every table.

Tiny bent forward. 'You know I handle your investments now, Bai-sa. I had hoped Pratap would make more of your marriage. As he hasn't, let me remind you that he gets a handsome annual payment from Balmer for your dowry. On no account tell him about your private fortune, or he will fritter it away on some woman – and then your financial affairs will enter the British Political Office's secret files.'

'Do the British have a secret file on Sirpur, hukam?' Jaya asked in alarm, wondering if the Empire knew that Prince Pratap did not spend his nights with her.

'Of course. That's how governments are run. We bribe their people, they bribe ours, and everybody keeps track of everybody else – though the Sirpur brothers are so indiscreet, their lives are public knowledge anyway.'

Lady Modi was waving from the doorway of the restaurant. Tiny Dungra led Jaya into a high-ceilinged room reproduced in the fourteen-foot-high mirrors hanging on the walls. An orchestra dressed in white tailcoats was playing dance tunes that Jaya recognised from Lady Modi's collection, and a Christmas tree threw coloured lights onto the wooden dance floor. Indians and Englishmen leaned forward with unselfconscious ease to make themselves heard over the music. Jaya could not believe that only three hundred yards away, British clubs carried signs saying DOGS AND INDIANS NOT ALLOWED.

'Such a lot of people are looking at you, darling. They must be talking about the Prince of Wales's visit to Sirpur.'

At Jaya's frown, Lady Modi pointed in irritation at two demure Bengali girls, dressed in traditional saris, seated at the table behind her. 'Cheer up, darling. You're not the only daring woman in India. Do you see those girls? The younger girl plays polo with her own women's team in the public maidan. And the one sitting opposite you was the first Indian, man or woman, ever to go up in an aeroplane.'

Jaya looked around the mirrored restaurant. The Maharajah of Kapurthala was sitting with his Spanish Maharani, the flamenco dancer. At another table, the Maharajah of Jind was showing a menu to the blonde hot-air balloonist. At the doorway, a jovial-

236

looking man was laughing with the dancer from the Globe Theatre.

Lady Modi bent towards Tiny Dungra. 'Look at Esmé Moore flirting with the heir to the Kashmir throne. I'm sure she's hoping to be the next Maharani of Kashmir. Poor Pratap. He will be furious if she succeeds.'

Lowering her eyes, with a bright red fingernail Jaya scratched her rage on the white tablecloth.

At Sirpur House an envelope addressed in Mrs Roy's familiar handwriting lay on her dressing table. Jaya tore it open and found a note pinned to the newspaper clipping: '*My dear Bai-sa. This letter appeared in* The Bombay Chronicle *yesterday. I thought you might find it of interest.*'

Printer's ink smudged Jaya's fingertips as she unfolded the clipping.

The Status of Indian Women:

A Tale of Woe. By One of Them.

It will seem strange that a person from my class should seek the help of the public – and that through the agency of a daily paper; but there are limits to human patience and suffering. It is said that even the proverbial worm will turn, and we the women of the ruling Princes of India are surely more sentient than the proverbial worm.

For generations we have quietly suffered untold and unbelievable wrongs. Our grandmothers put up mildly with insults and humiliations. They allowed themselves to be treated like pet dogs. Our mothers cried and killed themselves when the agony was unbearable. But the new generation has started to protest.

Why should we not protest? We are also human. Even we dare to dream.

Persons of my class are married off when they are quite young. I did not understand what marriage was except that in future I had to stay with strangers. But I was old enough to understand that the Prince who married me belonged to a big house, and I did dream dreams of splendour.

One day the news came to me that there were other women with whom the Prince spent weeks. I was overwhelmed with shame, and

237

dared not look into the faces of my servant-women. When the Prince came to me, he was absolutely brutal. He told me things I refused to believe.

God alone knows what has happened to our Indian Princes. Why are so many of them running after baby faces? Why have they become so recklessly careless of their name and reputation?

It is obvious that some of them go to Europe so that they may indulge in licence without check. They are neglecting their State affairs. The subjects of the Princes are raising their voices in complaint, but how are our grievances to be redressed?

We are treated like chattels. We are taught to be slaves. Our duty is merely to satisfy the whims of our masters. We are deprived of our self-respect. Our existence is a mere cipher. We are the toys of our master. He may dress us or tear our clothes away.

I have been made to pocket insults, and they say that self-respect is a commodity unknown in the Palace.

I want my status to be regularly defined. I want to fight for the many voiceless women who are being ill-treated.

You politically minded men will say there is morbid exaggeration in my account – but will you not listen to the tragic appeal of your Indian sisters?

We have no rights.

I want my rights.

Looking down at her lacquered nails, Jaya recognized the helpless self-loathing in the letter. She turned back to the clipping.

NOTE FROM THE EDITOR: It is generally surmised that the writer is a Maharani, the wife of a Prince of the highest rank, once considered very enlightened and progressive, but who has latterly spent much time on the Continent.

34

'I WANT YOU to meet the nationalist leaders who are trying to help women like the princess who wrote to *The Bombay Chronicle*. I particularly want you to meet India's greatest poet, Rabindranath Tagore. Do you know about him?'

There was the same impatience in Mrs Roy's question as there had been when she questioned Jaya as a child. When Jaya shook her head in defeat, Mrs Roy frowned. 'But Tagore is the only Indian to have won the Nobel Prize for Literature, Bai-sa. He was also knighted by the British Empire. After the massacre in the Punjab, he returned his knighthood. Now he has started a university where Indians can learn the progress of this century without forgetting their heritage. The same dream your father had for the science college which Maharajah John has closed down. And which you seem to be forgetting.'

Embarrassed by the accusation implicit in Mrs Roy's lectures, Jaya accepted an invitation to attend a music evening in Mr and Mrs Roy's garden house on the outskirts of Calcutta.

While she was dressing, Jaya saw the pig-pearl Arun Roy had given her all those years ago, nestling at the bottom of her jewel case. In a sudden nostalgic impulse she put it around her neck, remembering how the lawyer's gift had made her feel they shared a guilty secret which he had not yet revealed.

A chauffeur with a cotton Gandhi cap on his oiled hair drove Jaya through the broad imperial avenues into the narrow lantern-lit streets of Indian Calcutta. They left the outskirts of the city, and now only the black water of the river was visible beyond the dark rice fields.

The car drove through an avenue of coconut trees and braked in front of the high pillars of a red brick mansion. Mr Roy ran down the steps. Jaya could see Mrs Roy's thin body, lit by electroliers, waiting on the wide verandah

Mrs Roy led Jaya down a corridor lined with heavy wooden cupboards. Felt hats, rolled black umbrellas and three-piece suits were hanging inside them. 'This is where our husbands take off their European clothes. In British India, Indians are not allowed to dress in their own clothes when they visit government offices, but our older ladies will not allow the men into the main house until they have taken off their uniforms of slavery.'

Wondering if she would be meeting these stern old ladies, Jaya began to feel self-conscious about the French chiffon sliding over her shoulder. Laughter sounded below the balustrade. Two bare-foot boys were struggling to free a torn kite from the wooden eaves above the verandah. Jaya remembered the photograph albums, the gentleness in Mrs Roy's voice when she had spoken of her family, and understood what it must have cost her tutor to be exiled from this bustling world to a silent, empty house in a desert kingdom.

The verandah opened onto an enclosed lawn. A group of people were sitting on wicker chairs. Sure that all nationalists would be as stern in their pursuit of freedom as she had always found her tutor, Jaya was astonished at the laughter, the ease with which the men in their cotton caps and the women in their homespun saris joked with each other.

'Tagore,' Mrs Roy whispered as a man with a white beard and the kindest eyes Jaya had ever seen approached them between the shoulder-high bronze candelabra.

Someone called his name. The poet waved and turned back to Jaya. 'That is Motilal Nehru. He used to be very European until Gandhi inspired him to become an Indian. Then he threw his decanters, his Savile Row suits and his French shirts into a huge bonfire. What do you think of that, Princess?'

Jaya pulled her French chiffon sari tighter over her head, and under the white beard, the poet's lips opened in laughter. 'No, child, I do not believe in bonfires. Today we throw silk shirts into the flames; tomorrow we will burn books, perhaps even human beings.

Destruction, like imitation, stems from fear, and a colonized people must lose their fear. Have you met the Nightingale of India, Sarojini Naidu? She is fearless.'

The poet led her towards a plump woman in a brilliant scarlet sari, surrounded by a group of laughing men and an Englishwoman.

Mrs Naidu took Jaya's hands in her own, exclaiming on Jaya's beauty. A hawk-nosed man introduced himself as Sapru.

'I met your father in Patiala years ago, Princess. At the first secret meeting between the rulers and ourselves, to discuss means of putting an end to the British Empire's power over India.'

Jaya tried to hide her concern at the Englishwoman's presence as the lawyer described the resolutions that had been passed in Patiala. Seeing Jaya's unease, Mrs Naidu's plump body shook in amusement. 'Don't be afraid, Princess. Annie Besant is a pillar of the nationalist movement.'

'An Angrez is a nationalist?'

'Surely you know the nationalist movement in India was founded by the British?' Jaya threw Mrs Roy an accusing glance as Mrs Naidu drew her closer. 'Ideas have no nation, child. Annie Besant belongs to a long line of English people who have always said Indians must govern themselves. So how can we hate the British? We only want to free ourselves of slavery and become self-governing. Like Canada and Australia.'

Then she was laughing again. 'But it is too beautiful an evening to discuss politics. Come, let's sit in the Music Room and listen to an evening raga. Mrs Besant will sit between us, and for a night she will help us forget the injustices of the British Empire.'

Beyond the lawns, the musicians were already tuning their sitars in the Music Room, but on the dark grass, the bare torsos and marble clothes of European statues mocked the Indian melodies floating across the night.

Jaya hung back, intimidated by the writers and painters and lawyers crowding into the chamber. They gave no indication of the months they had spent in British jails as they settled on the carpets, their energetic conversation filling the room.

Incense spiralled towards the musicians' platform. Jaya watched Mrs Naidu lean back against a bolster cushion, her eyes closed in pleasure as she listened to the Raga Durbari, the evening raga of the king. Beside her, the poet brushed his white beard with his long

241

fingers and smiled at the Angrez woman.

Suddenly Jaya felt trapped by the nationalists, as if the unhappiness of the anonymous princess who had been driven to write to the newspapers, or her own experiences, were restricted to royal India. She stepped outside, gulping the night air, with its heavy scent of frangipani, into her lungs as if she had been underwater.

A fog was rolling in from the river, obscuring the heads of the marble statues on the lawn. Jaya thought the pale, headless figures seemed confused, as if frozen in an unfamiliar present like herself.

A tall man, a beige shawl thrown over his shoulders, was walking through the mist. The folds of his dhoti opened like a fan across the grass. He put a hand on her shoulder. Jaya moved, unresisting to the pressure of his fingers.

The light from the Music Room shone into her eyes, making the tall figure an indistinct shape in front of her. 'Why are you out here? Doesn't the music please you? And wearing my gift, Bai-sa.'

Hearing the laughter in Arun Roy's voice, Jaya's hand went up to cover the pearl on its ornate golden chain. She did not know how to tell him that it was a talisman of her childhood, when the future had seemed comprehensible.

'A married woman, and yet you shy away like a girl, Bai-sa.' The voice became serious. 'Is all well with you, Bai-sa? Is your husband kind?'

The gaiety of Jaya's stay in Calcutta trembled like a soap bubble around her, threatening to burst if she allowed Arun Roy's seductive concern to touch her.

As a child she had stared at the concubines, wondering what it was like to adorn oneself night after night for a man, knowing he might never come. Now she was familiar with the bitter defeat of preparing for each night as though it were her wedding night, while her husband took his pleasure in the arms of women like Esmé Moore.

Jaya walked backwards into a pillar. The lawyer closed the space between them, enclosing her rigid body within the folds of his shawl. She felt like a deer paralysed in the glare of headlamps, as if Arun Roy's gaze saw every humiliation hidden in her soul, knew her desolation as she waited without hope for her husband while the scented candles in her chambers sputtered into pools of melted wax and Chandni removed the wilted flowers, averting her face from Jaya's despair.

242

'I asked, is your husband kind, Bai-sa?'

This time Jaya could not stop the tears from welling into her eyes. She fought back the desire to throw herself into the beige shawl and tell the lawyer of the way she decorated herself each night for love, and how each night she was betrayed.

The lawyer smiled. Bending forward, he pressed his lips briefly to hers. Jaya's body froze against the pillar as his moustache brushed her skin, and the sound of the sitar seemed unnaturally loud in her ears.

Long after the lawyer had taken off his slippers and entered the Music Room, Jaya stood pressed against the pillar, feeling herself an adulteress in a marriage that had not yet been consummated.

35

PRINCE PRATAP was standing at the bottom of the staircase, his hand resting on Queen Mary's marble head, when Jaya descended for the Calcutta Derby, her red-and-indigo sari reflected in the glass eyes of the lunging tigers.

Outside the iron gateways of the Royal Calcutta Turf Club, cars were backed up against each other. Race-card vendors dodged the Turf Club guards advancing on them with raised lathis, and crowds ran across the broad avenues to the picket fences ringing the racecourse where touts stood on wooden crates, fingers moving with lightning speed as they accepted bets and shouted changing odds.

Boys beat at the windows of the Rolls-Royce, waving yellow race books at Prince Pratap's immobile profile as irate chauffeurs fought to open doors to allow figures in wide straw hats and morning suits, or saris and turbans, to dismount from their vehicles.

Prince Pratap steered Jaya through the iron gates, and the noise diminished to genteel laughter. A well-built older man with a sweeping white moustache and a magnificent diamond flashing from the aigrette of his turban waved at them. 'Excuse me, Princess. There's Maharajah Bikaner. I must greet him. I was his aide in Europe and America.'

Prince Pratap and the Maharajah of Bikaner followed a French jockey into the paddock, enthusiastically discussing the Sirpur horses with him in French, as Lady Modi joined Jaya.

'Darling, you look quite breathtaking. What made you think of red and indigo?'

'My husband wanted me to wear the Sirpur colours today, Bapsy.'

'But, darling, you're not a jockey. Women should only wear shades that flatter them. I can't understand it. Pratap turns traditional at the most extraordinary times.'

'And after the Derby, Maharajah Victor has invited the three rulers who lead the Chamber of Princes to dine at Sirpur House. Bikaner. Alwar. Patiala.'

Lady Modi's eyes widened with interest. 'Well, Bikaner is the most impressive. That's him in the paddock with Pratap. He represented India at the signing of the Versailles Treaty at the end of the war, and then at the opening of the League of Nations. As for Alwar – both the British and Gandhi have called him the most intelligent ruler in India, but I think he has gone mad. I've been told he thinks he is an incarnation of the god Krishna at the moment.'

The brown eyes closed mischievously. 'But the one you have to watch is the Maharajah of Patiala.' She tapped Jaya's wrist. 'Never, never let Maharajah Patiala know you find him attractive, darling, or he will abduct you the way he abducted the Viceroy's daughter.'

Jaya grimaced in disbelief, but Lady Modi insisted. 'It's absolutely true, darling. Patiala kidnapped the Viceroy's daughter and held her in his harem for a whole night. Of course he never touched her, but think of the delicious scandal. And then there are those scandalous cricket matches. Patiala is one of the finest cricketers in the entire British Empire. You can imagine how wonderful he looks in his cricket whites, a magnificent six-foot-seven giant crowned with a jewelled turban, holding a puny bat in his huge hands. But when he invited the British Government for a cricket match at his summer palace, he and all his players wore long Edwardian dresses to tease the British. Actual frocks, darling. Just think of those splendid bearded Sikhs rushing around the lawns of Chahil Palace in Simla, picking up their hems like a bunch of genteel Englishwomen. Bizarre, darling. It's the only word for him.'

'But Maharajah Patiala is a major figure in the Chamber of Princes. My father attended secret talks which he organized with the nationalists years ago.'

'Well, of course, darling. You can tell from his behaviour that he is not frightened by the British Empire. But do be careful. He has more than five hundred women in his harem, and the largest collection of pornography in the world. He's not called Bhupinder the Magnificent for nothing.'

Jaya followed Lady Modi into the Sirpur box. On the benches below the boxes of the Indian rulers, the officials of the British Empire stiffly acknowledged each other's importance, as if aware of the necessity to show the measured dignity of the British Empire before the chaotic Indians watching the Calcutta Derby, while their mem-sahibs moved in self-conscious hierarchy down the lawn.

Beyond the Members' Enclosure, Anglo-Indian men in shiny suits showed race cards to women in clothes that were a little too colourful, hats that were a little too large, in the attempt to imitate their imperial masters across the picket fencing that separated the Turf Club members from the public.

A bearer placed a silver ice bucket with a bottle of champagne at Lady Modi's elbow. Over his shoulder Jaya saw a group of glamorous Anglo-Indian girls pushing their way to the front of the picket fencing, shouting with laughter as they waved at the Members' Enclosure. Two Englishwomen, their rigid backs and disapproving faces reinforcing their haughty demeanour, moved away from the fence.

'Mrs Faith's girls, darling. This is their weekly entertainment. They love embarrassing their pompous British clients in front of their upright wives. Can't say I blame them.'

Jaya gripped Lady Modi's arm anxiously. On the lawn Prince Pratap was laughing with a group of pretty young English girls.

'They're just the Fishing Fleet, darling. Debutantes who didn't manage to land a husband during the London season. They come to Calcutta in the winter season looking to marry an owner of a tea plantation or some dashing army officer who is a younger son of some well-known English family. Poor darlings, doomed to become mem-sahibs, using racial superiority to make up for their leathery complexions and their disappointed lives. Look down there.'

Lady Modi pointed discreetly at a woman walking towards the boxes, her slim body clearly revealed by the cream chiffon swirling around her limbs with every step. 'It's the Maharani of Cooch Behar – the one who eloped from her own wedding.' Someone called the Maharani's name, and she half-turned. Large eyes, hooded by heavy eyelids, looked around lazily. The small mouth opened in a pout of recognition, then people surrounded her and she disappeared from view.

Maharajah Victor entered the box and sat down at Jaya's side. 'The Sirpur colours seem to belong on you, Princess. I often think you are the only one of us who knows who you are.'

'But you are the Maharajah, hukam. You are Sirpur.'

He looked at her and Jaya was shocked at the unhappiness in his eyes. 'Only by birth and the tolerance of the British Crown, not because I believe I am a king. I am acting and actors should be allowed to marry actresses.'

The horses for the Derby were cantering down the course towards the starting gate. Behind the racecourse, the white marble dome of the Victoria Memorial glittered in the afternoon sunlight.

Riding four abreast, the Viceregal Lancers trotted down the racecourse, scarlet uniforms with gold breastplates, and gold and scarlet turbans brilliant against the white marble. The crowds surged forward. From an open carriage, the representative of the King Emperor of India raised a hand to the million subjects climbing the fences for a better look.

The Viceroy walked up the red carpet, stopping for a moment to speak to an enormous man and his wife. 'The Aga Khan, darling,' Lady Modi whispered. 'The children of his European wife will be allowed to inherit the title. But I don't suppose the Aga Khan really counts to the British Empire, since he hasn't even got a country.'

The cigarette holder pointed at a man in a long coat with a stiff hat on his head. 'Now, that man, Hyderabad's son, is about to marry the daughter of the Ottoman Emperor. But the poor old Ottoman Emperor lost the war, so he just sits in the South of France, while the Aga Khan gets all the attention.'

In the distance a gun fired. There was a roar from the people pressed against the white fences as the horses pounded past them, dust lifting on the track. Jaya raised her binoculars. The Aga Khan's horse, the Maharajah of Rajpipla's horse and the Maharajah of Gwalior's horse were running neck and neck as they rounded the turn. A length behind the front-runners Jaya saw the indigo and red quarterings of the Sirpur colours. The French jockey, obeying the Maharajah's prohibition against using whips on the Sirpur horses, was vigorously slapping the horse's rump with the flat of his hand. Half a furlong from the post the Sirpur horse lengthened its stride.

Jaya held her breath, praying the Goddess would give the horse strength to win and convince her husband she was lucky for his family. Only feet from the finishing post the Sirpur horse managed to pull in front of the other horses, thundering past the scoreboard.

Betting slips inundated the touts. People crowded into the box to congratulate the Sirpur brothers. Prince Pratap rose lazily to his feet. 'Come along, Princess. Victor wants you to lead the horse in. He thinks your wearing the Sirpur colours did the trick.'

The French jockey cantered back down the track, and Maharajah Victor handed Jaya one of the reins. Applause rolled down the wooden benches as she led the winner onto the gravel pathway, wind lifting her hair like a black wave against the glistening horse. 'You're doing wonders for our tarnished reputations, Princess,' Prince Pratap observed above her head.

At the Turf Club restaurant, the Sirpur staff had already set up the champagne buckets around their table. Lady Modi ran up the steps. 'Darling, Indira Cooch Behar says you are the most beautiful thing she's ever seen. Imagine if Jaya had listened to you, Pratap, and cut off that magnificent hair.'

More people joined their table, and Prince Pratap's mood improved as they whispered congratulations on his wife's beauty into his ear. He kept a hand on Jaya's arm, seeming to read her every thought, so that a slight movement on her part sent a Sirpur servant scurrying for her shawl or a cummerbunded club servant to refill her glass. His lazy solicitousness melted Jaya's resistance until she began to hope the hypocrisy that had governed their marriage was about to end.

The hope became stronger when he kept an arm possessively around her shoulder as they stood at the paddock for the horse auctions. It became a certainty when he encouraged her to bid. But when Jaya thanked him, she saw the long eyes half-closed against the smoke from his cigarette as he examined someone behind her.

Jaya looked over her shoulder. The Anglo-Indian dancer from the Globe Theatre was beckoning her husband and Prince Pratap's hand was still around her shoulder. She clenched her teeth with the effort of not flinging it away.

Waiting for Chandni to prepare the bath, Jaya relived her latest humiliation, more acute than any other because she had allowed herself to believe that Prince Pratap at last wished to accept her as his wife.

She took out Mrs Roy's clipping and read again the anguished letter of the anonymous princess, remembering the huge dowry payments her husband had demanded before he had consented to their marriage; his insults when they first met; the wearying months in which she had remodelled herself to win his favour only to have her efforts mocked by the parade of women whose company he preferred to hers.

Sir Akbar had hinted at the power she could possess. She had not then understood that the Prime Minister of Sirpur was reminding her that her traditional marriage was an alliance of power. Swearing to somehow make her husband pay for her humiliations, she entered the Durbar Room to greet Maharajah Victor's royal guests.

A slender man, moving with an athlete's ease, entered the room, a facsimile of the god Krishna's crown tied on his turban. Jaya bowed to the Maharajah of Alwar and saw the white gloves covering his hands. Behind him, a gigantic Sikh filled the doorway, almost blocking out the light from the hallway beyond. Jaya knew this was the Maharajah of Patiala even before the aide finished reciting his titles. Behind them came Maharajah Ganga Singh of Bikaner.

As Jaya touched the feet of the Rajput king who had represented the kings of India at Versailles at the conclusion of the Great War, she saw Prince Pratap embracing the heir to the throne of Kashmir, the rotund Hari Singh. Tiny Dungra was with them.

Jaya made her obeisance to the assembled rulers and withdrew to the verandah. Through the open French windows she could hear the rulers toasting the winner of the Calcutta Derby.

Maharajah Victor bowed. 'It is a great privilege to win the Derby. But an even greater privilege to have the spokesmen for royal India in the Chamber of Princes in my house.'

'I wonder how long the chamber will last,' remarked the Sikh Maharajah, towering above the religious crown that was tied over Alwar's turban, 'if we continue provoking the British Empire. Is it wise to insult the King Emperor himself by wearing gloves when you meet him?'

'Wiser than abducting the Viceroy's daughter,' Alwar countered.

The Sikh king laughed, the warm, rich sound swelling up from his massive torso and pouring through the tightly rolled beard. Alwar pulled at the gloves on his hands. 'Anyway, what does it matter? After all, they are both untouchables. King George understands my reluctance to touch him personally. He even removes leather furniture from the room when he receives me in Buckingham Palace, since he knows cow hides are anathema to Hindu rulers.'

Bikaner stroked his sweeping white moustache with long fingers. 'Whether the British are untouchables or not is irrelevant. But the power of the British Empire is supremely relevant. Gloves and kidnapped girls will not change that.'

Alwar turned his crown in Bikaner's direction. 'How many insults must we endure before the British Empire honours our treaties? Even the Chamber of Princes is only a bribe to buy our silence.'

Listening to their anger, Jaya recognised the helplessness of these rulers. If her self-respect was mortgaged to a husband, their self-respect was mortgaged to an empire.

'It is up to us to convert the bribes of the British Empire into weapons to safeguard our own interest,' Bikaner replied. 'And we must forge closer links with the nationalists. After all, we are Indians, not Englishmen.'

'We are neither, hukam. We are ruling kings. Why should we exchange our dependency on the British Empire for a dependency on the nationalists when they revile us in their newspapers, ignoring the financial and moral support we have given them, at great jeopardy to our own thrones?'

Maharajah Victor gently broke into Alwar's passion. 'And even when we defend ourselves within the Chamber of Princes, the rest of India does not hear us because the Empire insists that our deliberations be kept secret.'

The doors opened. A group of men stood in the light thrown by the chandeliers in the marble hallway. Maharajah Bikaner led a perplexed Maharajah Victor towards them. 'I asked some of the nationalist leaders to join us, Victor. I'm sure you will find what they have to say interesting.'

As they came closer, Jaya realised in surprise that she had met them before at Mrs Roy's garden house. The poet Tagore was smiling under his white beard at the hawk-nosed lawyer Sapru. Behind them, Arun Roy adjusted his beige shawl over his shoulder.

She flushed in the darkness of the verandah, remembering the touch of his lips on her own.

Maharajah Alwar strode towards them. 'Gentlemen, we hear you are about to pass a resolution supporting revolution in the Indian kingdoms?'

Sapru, the patrician lawyer, faced Alwar's rage. 'We gave you fair warning when we met clandestinely in Patiala seven years ago that our fight was to raise the condition of all Indians, not just to get rid of the British Raj. We told you then that you must have representative government. Your personal expenditures must be controlled. Your courts and your newspapers must be free from interference. Your people have begun demanding those basic rights now, and you are throwing them in jail or confiscating their property.'

'Do you nationalists exercise more control than we do, gentlemen?' the Maharajah of Patiala asked cynically, bending his towering frame towards Sapru. 'Your nonviolent mobs attacked and sometimes killed those who did not boycott the Prince of Wales in Bombay.'

Tagore, the gentle intellectual who was the conscience of Indian nationalism, now moved towards the circle of men whose aggressive postures reflected the heat of their arguments. 'Come, Your Highnesses. We would have the British Empire over a barrel if our assemblies and your Chamber of Princes were to form a federation of interests. Instead of fighting each other, let us fight to achieve a federation that will rid us of the British Empire.'

Maharajah Bikaner gave him a grateful glance. 'That is what we are trying to do. But there are over five hundred kingdoms recognized by the British Empire. Some of them still live in the tenth century and will resist any suggestion of reform. You must be patient with us and control your own demagogues as we will try to control ours.'

The mouth under Bikaner's sweeping white moustache stretched in a tired smile and the poet sighed under his beard, the same colour as Maharajah Bikaner's moustache. 'Two things create demagoguery in India, Your Highnesses. Religion and ill-digested idealism. Let us insist on the counsels of reason or we will all perish.'

The wide doors at the side of the room opened. The Sirpur servants bowed, their hands almost touching the ground. Observing the precedence imposed on them by the British Empire's gun salutes, the rulers walked past the servants into the banquet room, courteously followed by the nationalists.

As the rulers and nationalists disappeared through the doors, Prince Pratap turned to the heirs of Kashmir and Dungra. 'All this talk achieves nothing. The thing that really matters is money. If you have enough money, you can keep both the British Empire and the nationalists happy.'

Hari Singh of Kashmir slapped him on the shoulder appreciatively. 'And still satisfy the needs of one's greedy women friends.'

On the verandah Jaya flushed with rage, thinking of the sums Prince Pratap must have showered on the Anglo-Indian dancer from the Globe Theatre.

36

IN THE City Palace, the Prime Minister and the British Resident were waiting to present the Maharajah with the budget for the new year.

The budget revealed the Prince of Wales's visit had overstretched the Sirpur treasury to a dangerous degree and Sir Akbar and Sir Henry Conroy were both adamant there were not sufficient funds for Prince Pratap to travel abroad. A furious Prince Pratap watched Maharajah Victor sail for Europe alone.

The Prime Minister's continual reminders of the state of the Sirpur treasury led Prince Pratap to escape to Calcutta as often as he could. Jaya wondered if she should tell him, despite Tiny Dungra's warnings, of her private fortune. Her generous impulse evaporated when she learned that her husband was visiting Esmé Moore, the dancer from the Globe Theatre.

The next year, Jaya hardly saw her husband. He spent the summer months in Kashmir with Esmé Moore.

By winter, he had exhausted his credit with the Calcutta bankers. Returning at last to Sirpur, he instructed Jaya to prepare for a journey. 'These damned fool bankers want me to start selling jewels, like some tradesman. There's nothing for it but to go to dusty old Balmer and ask Maharajah John for an advance on your dowry payments.' Remembering the harsh penances imposed by the desert on her own people, Jaya told herself she had been bred to an endurance which could yet conquer her husband.

The Rolls-Royce bumped over the stone ramparts leading to Balmer

Fort; breaking in front of the zenana, Jaya saw the Baran and the purdah ladies waiting behind the carved walls. She answered their overlapping questions, forgiving the fear that had led them to treat her like a prisoner in her last days in Balmer. From the moment she left Balmer in a mirrored palanquin, she too had experienced the helpless dependency that governed these women's lives.

At the Temple of the Balmer Maharanis, the zenana women circled her head with offerings to the Goddess, intoning auspicious mantras, as Rani Man Singh pushed sweets into Jaya's mouth.

Jaya averted her eyes, trying to forget how viciously Rani Man Singh's hands had forced the ivory bangles over her swollen wrists at the time of her marriage.

As soon as the puja was over, Jaya informed Rani Man Singh that she was visiting the concubines' quarters, to see Kuki-bai.

'That is out of the question, Bai-sa. It will be an insult to the Maharajah.'

Without turning her head, Jaya silently walked down the pathway. The shocked purdah ladies parted, allowing Chandni to follow.

'Sometimes you become just like your mother, Bai-sa.' Chandni's voice echoed in the stone stairwell leading to the lower fort, and Jaya felt a stab of longing for the Maharani as she inhaled the rich smell of grain and vegetables seeping from the padlocked storerooms.

The high wooden doors of the harem swung open, revealing arched doorways crowded with white-haired women. Jaya returned their greetings unsure if the sputtering light thrown by the oil lamps made the women seem thinner and dirtier than before. Then Kuki-bai's hands were stroking her face and she was enclosed in familiar clove-scented clothes.

She followed Kuki-bai through the deserted painted courtyards. But when they reached the octagonal chamber where the young concubines should have been splashing in scented water or drying their hair on the malachite terraces, a musty smell came through the open door. The green terraces were thick with dust, and the pool was empty of water, chipped tiles lying loose in its hollow basin.

'Maharajah John has liberated the concubines. He told them to return all their jewellery and possessions and go home. Most of them were left as babies outside the walls of the zenana during the famine and have no families.' Kuki-bai's voice resounded in the deserted chamber. 'They pleaded to stay. He threw them out anyway. Now they sell themselves in the bazaars, to drunks who want to sleep with a king's woman.'

Kuki-bai led Jaya into a small stone-walled cell with a wooden cot in a corner. 'This is where I live.' Jaya leaned against the damp wall, remembering Kuki-bai's painted chambers in the zenana, the silver bed and the tiny bells tinkling in the breeze that blew through the vetiver screens. Kuki-bai sat down heavily on the wooden cot, pulling her small painted feet under her. 'At least the Raj Guru was able to persuade Maharajah John to keep the older concubines, for fear of people's anger. But we are just a lot of inconvenient old women now, Bai-sa, waiting to die so that our progressive Maharajah can draw the curtain over history.'

Jaya took the old concubine's hands, averting her eyes from the scalp visible through the sparse white hair. Kuki-bai freed her hands impatiently and leaned back against her tattered bolster cushion. 'Do you think these usurpers can defeat me? I, who have danced on the tusks of an elephant carrying the Lion of Balmer? Now tell me, child, does your husband ever leave such a beautiful girl in peace?'

Jaya examined the walls, pretending not to have heard. Kuki-bai bent forward in concern. 'Is your husband too demanding, child?'

'He will not touch me.'

When Kuki-bai said nothing, Jaya shouted, 'Do you understand? I disgust him. He will not touch me!' The humiliations of the last five years exploded inside her as she flung herself into Kuku-bai's lap and sobbed her anguish into the scented skirt.

Kuki-bai said nothing until Jaya's passion had spent itself. Then she gently dried Jaya's tears with her veil. 'Your husband will come to you, Bai-sa. You will bear his son. It is written in the horoscopes cast at your birth.' She ran her fingers through the long hair that had knotted itself around Jaya's shoulders. 'I may never see you again, child, so remember my words.'

Ashamed of her loss of control, Jaya took Kuki-bai's small body tenderly between her arms as though she were enclosing a rare treasure. 'Of course you'll see me again.'

Kuki-bai shook her head. 'I do not think the Goddess wills it.

255

But when your courage fails you, child, remember that the blood of the Lion of Balmer runs in your veins. Now go, before Rani Man Singh's jealousy revenges itself on the zenana.'

Jaya backed out of the cell, looking at the shrunken old woman but seeing Kuki-bai balancing on Moti's tusks, describing the mudra of the warrior to the entranced children beneath her elephant.

AFRAID OF compromising her husband's delicate negotiations, Jaya spent the day riding alone around the Fort. The mahouts greeted her vociferously, and when she fed Moti handfuls of cane sugar the tusker wrapped his trunk around her. Held high in the air, she saw Tikka's wooden cricket pavilion still standing under the yellow stones of the Round Tower.

At the fort zoo she dismounted and leaned against the fence, listening to the cry of peacocks as a tiger appeared from behind a bush to sun itself on the broken boulders. At the sudden noise of hoofs the tiger took fright and retreated. A Lancer galloped up. Surprised at the conspiratorial note in the Lancer's voice, Jaya rode after him to the Fort Temple.

The Raj Guru came out of the temple, his austere clothes spotless and uncreased, his thin features almost revealing pleasure.

He took her into the inner temple, where she had once stood with Tikka's sword between her hands. Major Vir Singh was sitting cross-legged on the stone floor, his waxed moustache quivering with amusement. 'We hear you are a polo player now, Bai-sa. I hope you did not discredit me in front of your husband.'

Jaya stared at the ground in embarrassment. 'You don't understand, Major-sahib. It was a difficult situation, it was –'

'Rajniti, Bai-sa?' the Raj Guru asked in his hoarse whisper.

Jaya looked up in surprise. 'The Sirpur Prime Minister suggested the same thing.'

'Rajniti is uppermost in all our minds these days. Did you know that Major Vir Singh was dismissed from his command of the Balmer Lancers within days of your departure as a bride? And that I myself am under constant observation?'

'But that's impossible! You are the teacher of the Balmer kings. You are the highest authority in Balmer.'

'You have forgotten your first lesson, Bai-sa. The people are the highest authority in the land. First there is Praja, the people; only then is there need of the Raja, the servant-king. A decision taken by the elders of five villages can overturn the laws promulgated by a king. It was always thus until the king looked to the British Empire for his power, not to his people.'

Major Vir Singh pulled at his moustache. The waxed hair still snapped back against his cheek. 'Do you remember when your father held a durbar for the village headmen, urging them to send representatives to the State Secretariat? Now the Secretariat councils have been dismantled. Your father's colleges have been closed, Balmer's newspapers banned. Maharajah John persecutes the people. Any voice that is raised in protest is silenced by jail and the confiscation of property.'

'The Maharajah has profaned his dharma as a servant of the people. Therefore, the people must fulfil their own dharma. They must serve themselves.'

Major Vir Singh interrupted the Raj Guru's harsh whisper of anger. 'Throughout royal India, dissatisfied subjects are forming People's Councils. The Raj Guru and I are the leaders of the People's Council in Balmer Kingdom.'

'The People's Councils will now have to learn the four arms of kingship. Tell me, Bai-sa. Can you still recite them?' the Raj Guru inquired.

'*Saam*, a king must serve his people's needs. *Daan*, he must provide for their welfare. *Dand*, he must punish injustice. *Bhed*, he must protect the kingdom with treaties and alliances.'

'Let us hope the People's Councils forming all over royal India do not confine their activities to *Bhed*, to scandals and intrigues. Let us hope they first try *Saam*, *Daan*, *Dand*.'

Major Vir Singh rose to his feet. 'We have kept the Bai-sa too long. The Maharajah's entertainments will begin any moment, and her absence will be noticed.'

Jaya touched the Raj Guru's feet and followed Major Vir Singh outside. Major Vir Singh cupped his hands to help Jaya mount her horse. 'By the way, Tikka's friend, the Angrez boy, has dinner in my house whenever he tours Balmer.'

'Is James Osborne a good officer, Major-sahib?'

Major Vir Singh smiled. 'He is an excellent rider and an honourable man. If you put a turban on his head and a sword in his

257

hands, he could almost pass for a Rajput.'

'That's what the purdah ladies used to say, Major-sahib, but they thought it was the colour of his eyelashes.'

IN THE OUTER courtyard of the Balmer Fort, people were already seated for the evening entertainment. Prince Pratap stirred as Jaya sat down at his side. He gave her a triumphant smile. 'The deed is done, Princess. We'll be in London by summer.'

The bards dexterously set up a bamboo frame for their cloth paintings. Jaya watched them, afraid that Mrs Roy's warning had come too late and that she had already ceased to know who she was or where she belonged. On the very spot where her marriage pavilion had stood, instead of the simple cushion of the traditional Balmer gaddi, Maharajah John was sitting on an ornate silver chair upholstered in red velvet, his foot resting on a padded footstool, like a sahib.

The outer walls of the zenana glistened in the light of new gas lamps, but there were no bright paintings by folk artists on the walls to tell her of the changes in the kingdom in the five years she had been gone. Now the stone walls were covered with a shiny green paint that reflected light back onto the ramparts, and gas flames hissed inside their steel frames, making the ancient courtyard look like a deserted city bazaar. Jaya's heart ached as she observed the changes in her father's fort, and she wished she had never returned to Balmer to witness the shattering of her childhood world, or seen the pillars of her father's reign leading the people against their ruler.

A group of musicians danced through the stone gateway, their silver jewellery glistening in the light of the gas lamps. An old man, his white beard swept backward over his thin shoulders, his jacket flaring out from his waist to reveal the dagger tied above his waist, stepped forward to declaim:

'Queen Pushpavati

'The greatest queen in India

'Famed for her prowess with a sword

'Who could draw a bow almost as well as a man

'Who rode at the side of her husband in pursuit of the cheetah . . .'

The gas lamps threw shadows on the rolling cloth paintings. Jaya closed her eyes and imagined that she was sitting on a carpet with Tikka in front of Maharajah Jai Singh and the Maharani.

Drums echoed as the assembled bards recited the royal infant's birth, and Jaya wondered if Kuki-bai was right, if she would/ever have a child by the man drowsing next to her.

37

As THE DEPARTURE for London drew closer, Jaya became fearful that some demonic power destroyed those who associated too closely with the West, and she fasted and elongated her pujas with renewed fervour, hoping piety would somehow insulate her from the terrors of crossing the dark waters.

Lady Modi was shocked by Jaya's appearance. 'Darling, no one telegrammed me saying you have been ill. Or are you expecting a child?'

Jaya embraced the confusion of pearls and leaping dogs, assuring Lady Modi that she was in perfect health. Lady Modi pulled Jaya onto the sofa. 'Now, darling, I don't mean to be cruel, but you do look an absolute fright. Everyone is going to be in London this season for the Great Empire Exhibition. Do you realise that you have a reputation for being beautiful to maintain?'

Jaya angrily tossed Lady Modi's vermouth into the rosebushes. 'Parties, impressions. That is all you and my husband seem to care about, Bapsy.'

'Perhaps you think you should be riding into battle with a lance in your hand? Do drop your sentimental nonsense and face the facts, darling. The era of warrior kings ended half a century ago. Haven't you wondered why most of the nationalist leaders are lawyers? This is the era of negotiations, not heroism, darling.'

Lady Modi put a cigarette into her holder, filling the air with the scent of Turkish tobacco. 'I bet you have neglected to order something special for your presentation to King George and Queen Mary.'

Jaya followed the fragile figure from cupboard to cupboard, chastised when Lady Modi rejected the rows of saris as being inadequate.

At last Lady Modi held up a tissue shot with gold and green thread. 'With the Sirpur emeralds I think this will do nicely. Now, what colour gloves should you wear?'

She looked at Jaya sternly. 'You can't get away from wearing gloves at a Court Presentation, darling. And I must get Countess Skorkov to teach you a court curtsy. Since you are being presented at the second court, I'll find out whether you are required to wear a tiara, and order one from M. Cartier before you arrive.'

'Why must I wear a crown and curtsy? Even tribals wearing animal skins are treated with respect at our durbars.'

'Oh, darling.' Lady Modi fell into the billowing saris, and the uncomprehending maidservants joined in her infectious laughter. 'I can't imagine what King George and Queen Mary would do if they were faced with someone wearing a loincloth. Faint dead away, I expect.'

Even after Lady Modi left, Jaya was inundated with notes on scented paper issuing additional instructions.

Chandni professed astonishment at the preparations. 'Such a lot of trouble for these untouchables, hukam?'

'Stop using that word, Chandni. Someone in London might understand what you are saying.'

Chandni shrieked and covered her face with her veil. 'I beg you, don't take me to London, hukam. The Angrez will pollute me. If maharajahs can be corrupted by the touch of the Angrez, how will I, a poor maidservant, fare in the land of the shameless, hukam?'

In the end, Chandni was persuaded to accompany her mistress if there was sufficient Ganges water travelling with them. Annie packed dance records between thick sheets of cardboard so Jaya could continue practising the tango on board ship, while Chandni had her wrist tied with sacred thread against the evil eye of the foreigners. In a welter of individual preparations, Jaya and her household boarded the train for Bombay.

THE HUMID sea breeze carried the smell of vegetation and open

261

gutters to the passengers throwing paper streamers from the decks. Chandni and the other maidservants stared in awe at the P. & O. liner towering above them, until Prince Pratap clapped his hands and sent them scurrying aboard after the aides, to stand at the railing looking down on the crowds with the same astonishment with which they had looked up at the ship.

A naval band in starched white uniforms was playing familiar dance tunes. Jaya tapped her painted fingernails on the railing as she watched a small woman, her nine-yard Maratha sari swept up between her legs, walk determinedly towards the water, followed by a line of shaven priests.

Prince Pratap groaned when he saw the little figure throwing marigold garlands into the sea. 'That's the Tiger Queen of Baroda. A crack shot, and Queen Mary's dearest friend in India. Now she's going to do her pujas, and the Captain will have to delay weighing anchor for at least another hour.

'Oh, God, and there's the Begum of Bhopal.' Preceded by aides, a plump woman was mounting the steps, her body covered in a heavy white cloak, the latticed face flap swinging with the motion of her ascent.

'Isn't that Hari Singh of Kashmir? What luck! I didn't know he was travelling on the same ship. At least the journey won't be a complete bore.'

For the first half of the voyage, Jaya felt that she had returned to purdah, so strictly did the routine of the men differ from that of the women. Sitting at her pujas at dawn, she could hear ringing bells and chanting voices, from adjoining rooms, indicating that the other royal women were also at their pujas, and all down the thickly carpeted corridor, incense smoke escaped from under cabin doors.

A curtain had been stretched across one side of the upper deck. Despite their emancipation from the veil, the royal women collected behind the curtain after their prayers to sit on their crested deck chairs, their maidservants squatting at their sides, staring at the endless blue water. Jaya rested her head on the embroidered snake of Sirpur, listening to the royal ladies making plans to see each other again in Deauville or comparing notes to discover if they would be taking the waters at Baden Baden at the same time.

Sometimes there was a disturbance at the curtains and the maidservants peered through the cloth, bringing back messages that one ruler or another wished his wife to join him. Occasionally Jaya was invited to watch Prince Pratap play deck tennis with Englishmen in white trousers and blazers, straw hats protecting their skin from the fierce sun. At night, at the Captain's table, the royal ladies, so garrulous in the privacy of their curtained enclosure, sat woodenly in front of their food while their husbands flirted with European women and led them onto the dance floor.

Only the Tiger Queen of Baroda lowered her book at exactly the same times every day, until all the ladies knew when she was required to assist her husband with his files and when she would be promenading on deck.

'I remember seeing your husband during Queen Victoria's courts, Princess,' the tiny but formidable Tiger Queen said, raising her eyes from her book. 'When the Empress asked for the Baroda heir, my sons pushed my five-year-old daughter forward. Pratap laughed so loudly I thought he was going to be sick. Fortunately, the Empress wasn't offended.'

Two sisters, married to the same Maharajah of a powerful Himalayan kingdom, were listening to the conversation. The younger maharani looked up with bright blue eyes. 'The Emperor never gets offended like his officials, hukam. See, my sister and I are married to the same man. Our father got drunk, and when our husband asked for one daughter's hand, my father said, "Why one? Take both." We were babies at the time of the engagement, but the Angrez officials make us feel like we have done something wrong. Only King George and Queen Mary don't mind.'

The other sister moved her chair forward, stuttering enthusiastically. 'And then – in London – at a dance in Buckingham Palace – the King Emperor asked me to dance with him, hukam. I explained it was not our custom to be touched by men other than our husbands. The King wasn't angry even. He appreciated my position, hukam.'

The younger maharani interrupted her sister. 'Only our husband doesn't appreciate our position. He wants us to wear lipstick in Europe, but at home he wants us to wear the veil.'

The Begum of Bhopal was facing the ocean, the chattri of monarchy shading her head. She turned heavily in her deck chair, and the other women, merely wives of rulers, fell silent in deference to the single ruling sovereign in their presence.

'I have always found the veil a most useful device.' The Begum's deep voice carried in the respectful silence. 'True, my grandmother pulled the veil from her face at her coronation so the people could look upon the face of their ruler. And she bared her face when she galloped at the head of her troops to liberate besieged British families during the Mutiny. But those were extraordinary times. These days I find the veil gives me a necessary distance from the meddlings of outsiders.'

The ladies nodded in agreement, knowing that the meddling outsiders of whom the Begum spoke were the officials of the British Empire.

When the ocean liner reached Marseille, royal retainers scurried down the planks with urns of Ganges water for their Hindu rulers, and the Begum of Bhopal's attendant held the Koran, wrapped in a velvet cloth embroidered with the ninety nine names of Allah, high above his head so it would not be profaned by waving parasols.

A row of squat black Renault cars was waiting beyond the docks for Prince Pratap's entourage. The cars sped through the sprawling city, tyres screeching as they halted outside the railway station. Jaya got out of the car to find her Balmer maidservants, their Rajput veils too bright in the soft European light, holding on to Annie, her French maid, like frightened children.

Hours later, the train pulled into a tiny station with a single track. Prince Pratap entered Jaya's compartment. 'Bring anything you might need for a puja.' Jaya followed her husband, pausing briefly to comfort the frightened maidservants squatting at Annie's feet on the platform.

The black car drove away from the station into a pastoral setting of fields and low-roofed country cottages. At the foot of a hill, the road gave way to a bumpy dirt track which led into a treeless landscape of deep ditches. Occasional patches of grass and tiny white daisies lent brief colour to the denuded earth.

The aide manoeuvred the Renault through a ditch, flinging Jaya forward. She clutched her husband's shoulder. He turned around. Jaya sat back quickly, frightened by the expression in the sloping eyes as he pointed at the shell craters. 'This was called the Devastated Area. The only time there was a real cavalry charge in the entire war, and already we were too late. Our poor horses looked like toys in front of the tanks.'

A small marble pavilion, incongruously Indian, stood in the

264

middle of the scarred countryside. Jaya climbed behind her husband to the pavilion. A stone was embedded in the marble, shaped like the image of the Goddess in Kamini Temple. Carved into the white marble were the names and ranks of the Sirpur Lancers who had fallen in battle.

'Eight Balmer Lancers died in the Battle of Cambrai, Princess. Your cousin has had no monument built for them, so perhaps you would like to do your pujas here.'

Jaya smeared sindoor on the image of the Goddess. A breeze blew the red powder onto the names engraved in the white marble, reminding her of the blood running into the fork of her elbow when she had stood in front of Tikka; of the nagara drums thudding from the elephant gates of the Fort as the Balmer Lancers had trotted down the ramparts, marigold garlands catching on the pommels of their saddles.

The sun moved behind the hill, throwing shadows across the scarred landscape. Prince Pratap suddenly pulled Jaya into his arms. 'It was such a terrible slaughter. The graveyards stretch for miles. But for many of us, including Tikka, it was the only time in our lives when we were permitted to be men. Living without pride is not a pleasant business, Princess.'

'An unwanted wife shares that experience, hukam.'

The fingers loosened around her shoulders, and Jaya bit her tongue, wishing she had kept silent, as a mocking smile once again twisted her husband's lips. 'Well, we have done our duty. Let's get back to civilization.'

IN PARIS, it was as if Prince Pratap wanted to put as much distance as he could between himself and his wife. Jaya stayed in the suite at the Ritz, looking at the cars disgorging elegantly dressed people who smiled at the flashing bulbs of waiting cameras before doormen ushered them through the doors of the hotel. Infrequently, she sat silently at crowded restaurant tables while Prince Pratap laughed with his guests.

Sometimes, when mounting the steps to a restaurant, the folds of her sari lifted in one slim hand, her dark hair swirling around her body, she saw the flash of a camera in front of her eyes. But it was not until Prince Pratap took her to lunch at Maxim's that

Jaya understood Annie's boasts to the Balmer maidservants that the French newspapers were writing about their mistress.

Maharani Cooch Behar acknowledged Jaya's bow. 'So I meet the Black Lotus, at last. Why have you been hiding her from us, Pratap? Though of course I noticed you at the Calcutta races last year, my dear.'

'I thought I'd wait for Queen Mary's approval.' Prince Pratap lifted Maharani Cooch Behar's hand to his lips. 'By the way, Indira, who is that poor creature?'

A small Indian man in a close-collared suit was sitting at a table by himself, staring unhappily at the wine waiter. Maharani Cooch Behar raised her hand and he nodded sadly, allowing the waiter to fill his wineglass.

'My cook, darling. I'm developing his palate. How can he produce French cuisine unless he learns about wine?'

'He is only going to get indigestion from your outrageousness.'

'I'm hardly outrageous, darling. I don't run around with a pair of hooded cheetahs like that absurd woman in Sussex. I only have this to keep me amused.' She reached into her handbag and put something on the white tablecloth.

Prince Pratap stared in disbelief at the wrinkled legs moving over a silver knife. 'Do I see emeralds embedded in that turtle's back, Indira?'

'It's brought me such luck at the casino I thought it should have a few gems of its own.' The hooded eyes widened innocently. 'Don't you think that's only fair, Princess?' Jaya giggled, and Maharani Cooch Behar reached across and patted her hand. 'At last, someone has brought a smile to the lips of the Black Lotus. The newspapers say the Black Lotus never smiles, Princess. But you have a lovely smile.'

She turned back to Prince Pratap. 'I believe you travelled to France with Hari Singh of Kashmir. What is he planning to do now, Pratap?'

'What do you mean, Indira?'

'Don't be coy. We all know he is being blackmailed by a French couple for having a liaison with the wife.'

Prince Pratap shrugged. 'If the blackmail situation is not resolved satisfactorily, the British are threatening to force Kashmir to choose another heir.'

Rubies from the Maharani's bracelet tinkled against her wine goblet as she raised her glass. 'To British justice. The Prince of Wales has affairs with married women only. But the heirs apparent of Indian kingdoms must lose their thrones for the same penchant.'

38

_____

ON THE CHANNEL crossing, Jaya stood on deck, watching for the white cliffs that guarded the heart of the British Empire. She could almost smell the pages of Tikka's books through the salty breeze, see the illustrations of sahibs and mem-sahibs in flowering gardens always lit by gentle sunshine.

The London she had imagined was cruelly contradicted by the reality beyond Lady Modi's embrace. While the maidservants chattered excitedly about the tall buildings and the double-decker buses, Jaya stared out of the car window at the men with amputated limbs sitting behind cardboard boxes into which infrequent passersby threw coins.

'Darling, what did you expect? The war ended only five years ago. Half the factories and mines have closed down and there are no jobs. Everybody is terrified that if things don't improve soon the Communists will take over. That's why the Socialists won the elections – and, darling, the most extraordinary people have become Socialists. Curzon's daughter, the Countess of Warwick, half the Bright Young Things because they think it's fashionable. Even the last Viceroy of India is a member of the Socialist cabinet. By the way, his wife, Lady Chelmsford, will be presenting you at Court. Now, did you bring every single thing I told you to pack for the Presentation, darling?'

ON THE DAY Jaya was to be presented, Lady Modi arrived with

a French hairdresser to arrange Jaya's coiffure. Under Lady Modi's sharp eyes the hairdresser experimented with Jaya's hair, dipping the ends in a solution which promptly turned the gleaming black hair bright red.

Chandni snatched the hair out of his hands and shook it angrily in Jaya's eyes. 'Why are you allowing a strange man to touch you in this way, hukam?'

Lady Modi banished Chandni from the room as the hairdresser cut the reddened ends off with a pair of scissors. The objecting maidservant backed into the doorway, suspiciously watching the Frenchman's every move. He lacquered Jaya's heavy hair down with beer, then sprayed gold dust over it. The weight was so uncomfortable that Jaya could hardly move her head.

'Endure it, darling. When Pratap and Victor take you to Claridge's after the supper at Buckingham Palace, the society press will be waiting for you. They always notice the tiniest flaw.'

Jaya fidgeted as the maidservants dressed her for Buckingham Palace. Chandni straightened the folds of her sari again. 'You'll tear the tissue unless you stand still, hukam. And I hope it won't fall off when you curtsy like a servant in front of the king of the untouchables.'

Jaya stood anxiously in front of the mirror, staring at the reflection of the slender, dark-skinned woman enclosed in sheets of jet-black hair powdered with gold dust. A diamond nose ring glittered against the aquiline nose; green eyes looked out in panic above the dark throat encircled with emeralds of such depth their green was known as the colour of desire.

Taking her gloves, she descended the stairs to join Maharajah Victor and Prince Pratap, then stopped, intimidated by the elegance of the Sirpur brothers. Long gold brocade tunics made them seem even taller. Gauze sashes emphasized their lean waists. Tight silk pyjamas enclosed their calves, pleating like cloth anklets above their jewelled slippers. Maharajah Victor wore the crimson turban of Sirpur sovereignty, a huge diamond encased in the coils of a ruby snake clasping its aigrette. In his gloved hand he held the ceremonial Sirpur sword. Prince Pratap's turban pulled at his temples, making the long eyes slope upward so that he looked more Mongolian than Indian. In his hands was the sword Jaya had carried at her marriage.

Maharajah Victor bowed. 'You look magnificent, Princess. But the gloves are a mistake. Leave them behind.'

'Bapsy says I must wear them, hukam. And I'm so worried my foot will catch in the back of my sari when I make my curtsy.'

Maharajah Victor looked annoyed. 'You will not be curtsying to Their Majesties.'

'What will I do instead?' Jaya was alarmed that Maharajah Victor's contempt for court protocol might create problems for the ruler.

'You will behave in a manner appropriate to a Sirpur princess and use our traditional greeting, as you did when the Prince of Wales came to Sirpur. I am astonished that you even considered anything else. Can you imagine my grandmother the Dowager Maharani curtsying to anyone?'

Curious crowds lined the streets outside Buckingham Palace, and voices shouted the identities of the passengers in the cars. Someone yelled, 'The polo players!' as the Sirpur Rolls-Royce, flying Maharajah Victor's flag, went through the iron gates of the palace.

Jaya turned to look at the hats and umbrellas waving behind them. 'How do they know who you are, hukam?'

'The newspapers, my dear. They may never have seen a game of polo, but they know all about our handicaps.'

The car pulled up at the private entrance through which the Indian sovereigns were received privately by the King Emperor. The Sirpur brothers got out, and Jaya shrank back into the suede upholstery, terrified at being left alone in the very centre of the Empire as the Rolls-Royce drove to another doorway.

Jaya's courage returned when she saw an Indian woman lifting her sari off the stone steps.

The royal ladies who were to be presented were waiting in an antechamber. Lady Chelmsford introduced Jaya to the Duchess of Devonshire, the Mistress of Robes. The young Indian woman who had preceded Jaya into the palace was struggling with her gloves, trying to fold them into her handbag.

The Duchess of Devonshire said kindly to her, 'I'm afraid you can't carry a handbag when you are presented, Princess.' The young woman gave her a frightened look and tried to close the clasp over the crushed gloves. The Duchess repeated her observation more slowly.

Panicking, the Indian woman stuffed the gloves down further. Pale fingers moved in the air above the handbag, and enunciating distinctly, the Duchess said, 'Tut, tut! Tut, tut!'

Almost in tears, the Indian woman turned to Jaya for an explanation. When she at last understood what the Duchess was trying to say, she pulled out the gloves, whispering, 'I thought she wanted to dance.'

The heralds announced the entrance of the King and Queen. Jaya followed Lady Chelmsford to the door of the Throne Room. Her hands were perspiring. She wiped them surreptitiously on the tissue sari as she stared at the jewels and decorations sparkling on the gowned ladies, the diplomats, the officers standing in rows under the chandeliers.

On the dais stood the King Emperor, a small man with a thick beard cut close to his face. The figure whose name she had heard spoken fearfully since she was a small child reminded Jaya of a rather sad dog. She could more easily imagine his wife at the Imperial Durbar in Delhi. A silver gown moulded Queen Mary's body. Diamonds glittered in her hair and around her throat and wrists. The Prince of Wales and his younger brothers flanked the King and Queen. Behind them, Jaya was comforted to see Maharajah Victor and the Maharajahs of Alwar and Patiala on the royal dais.

Lady Chelmsford placed a card on the platter presented by a footman. The card was passed from one functionary in knee breeches and court dress to another until it arrived at the foot of the dais, where the Lord Chamberlain, covered with chains and ribbons, read out Jaya's titles.

Conscious of the watching eyes, Jaya followed Lady Chelmsford the length of the Throne Room to be presented to the Emperor of India. A smile lit up his sad face when she folded her hands in an Indian greeting, but Queen Mary's eyes went up and down her hair and sari. There was silence in the Throne Room. For a long moment, Jaya thought everyone in the chamber must be holding their breath, as she was doing under that expressionless scrutiny. Then the Queen smiled. The Prince of Wales nodded. The Presentation was over.

Jaya allowed herself to be led through the rows of people, almost fainting with relief when she saw Prince Pratap standing behind her chair.

For three hours a line of women were led to the dais, their names announced by the Lord Chamberlain before they sank in deep curtsies to the royal couple, feathers quivering on top of their heads. Watching the long ceremony, Jaya wondered how the wounded soldiers and the destitute widows she had seen in the streets of Britain's capital could hope to gain entrance to this gilded chamber.

At last Queen Mary curtsied and King George went through a door behind the dais, followed by the Indian kings. Everyone in the Throne Room began talking at once, their voices loud after the silence of the presentation ceremony. People waited for those who were dining in Buckingham Palace to file through their midst. Jaya moved closer to Prince Pratap, embarrassed by the audible remarks on her beauty as she walked through the glittering human corridor.

'I hope Alwar took his gloves off before shaking hands with King George,' Prince Pratap observed in a low voice as a footman led them to a supper room. 'After all, he is one of the three spokesmen at the Chamber of Princes. And just pray the Prince of Wales has not told the King about Victor wanting to marry Cora Hart.'

The other guests were moving around the buffet tables in the supper room. Jaya picked at the food on her plate, unable to dispel the spectre of abdications hanging like a sinister presence over the brilliantly lit chamber.

But when Maharajah Victor joined them after dining with the King and Queen, he seemed more lighthearted than Jaya had ever seen him.

'Queen Mary was very gracious about you, Jaya Devi. Even His Highness Alwar remarked what a credit you were to the image of Indian women.'

'Did Maharajah Alwar take off his gloves before greeting the King Emperor, hukam?'

Maharajah Victor shook his head. 'But at least Alwar didn't make any insulting remarks about the presence of the Beefeaters.'

Outside Claridge's Hotel, a battery of flashbulbs exploded in Jaya's eyes. Reporters surrounded her, demanding her impressions of the Presentation and scribbling her formal, monosyllabic replies onto their pads.

Prince Pratap rescued Jaya, angrily leading her through the revolving doors of the hotel into the restaurant.

Maharajah Victor was leaning towards a woman in a low-cut satin dress. The fabric clung to her small breasts so that they were clearly outlined as she threw her arms around him. The pouting lips were familiar, but for a moment Jaya could not place the features, accustomed as she was to seeing the blonde curls and small face enlarged across the screen in the cinema at the City Palace.

Maharajah Victor introduced Cora Hart, and a small hand, fingers turned limply downward, extended itself to Jaya. Other people joined the table. Between the waving cigarette holders, waiters refilled champagne glasses and removed plates as Maharajah Victor, a smile of adoration on his face, expansively sent for a succession of dishes that Cora Hart wanted to taste. When she suddenly announced a desire to dance, the party piled into cars, demanding to be taken to the Embassy Club.

Inside the Embassy Club, another chair was added to the already crowded table. Hari Singh of Kashmir squeezed himself between Prince Pratap and Lady Modi as Maharajah Victor led Cora Hart onto the small dance floor.

The Prince of Wales was escorting his own companion onto the floor. Hari Singh laughed loudly. 'At least we Indians have taken precedence in something. My lawyers are referring to me as Mr. A., but if Mrs Dudley Ward's husband blackmails HRH the way my little French couple are blackmailing me, I suppose the Prince of Wales will only be Mr B.'

39

THE BALMER maidservants were outraged when Cora Hart moved into the house in Belgrave Square. Every day they crowded at the windows to watch the aides following the American girl, their arms filled with bandboxes and packages from her daily shopping expeditions with Maharajah Victor.

Maharajah Victor was always at Cora Hart's elbow at the races and the polo matches, unashamedly attentive to her demands in the long evenings, which always ended in embraces on the dance floors of the same nightclubs.

Prince Pratap managed not to address a single word to Cora Hart, and most of Maharajah Victor's friends treated the film star as if she were invisible, until Jaya reluctantly found herself befriending the American girl.

When Prince Pratap learned that Maharajah Victor had invited Cora Hart to Deauville, he stormed into Jaya's room. 'Are you mad to make this girl feel at home? Victor has already bought her everything from the most expensive jewellery and fur coats to a racehorse. Now he's thinking of buying her a villa in France. She's so stupid she probably thinks being Maharajah of Sirpur is just a more glamorous version of being a Hollywood film star.'

'You are too harsh, hukam.'

'I have more experience of these little gold-diggers than you. Tell her about Kamini Temple, and the cobras in the bamboo thickets in the City Palace, and the tribals. Explain that she will never be presented at the British Court, that her half-breed children

274

will never have any rights on the Sirpur throne. Tell her the truth, for God's sake, before my brother loses his throne!'

In Deauville, Jaya did not have the heart to start the campaign Prince Pratap had demanded. Maharajah Victor, happy for the first time in Jaya's experience, headed the Sirpur polo team in victory after victory, and his polo players toasted Cora Hart, claiming she had brought Victor back from the dead.

At the casinos, the Maharajah stood behind Cora Hart at the roulette tables, motioning to the aides to fetch more chips whenever her counters dwindled – as if glad, each time she lost a fortune, to have the privilege of giving her another, indifferent to the glances exchanged between the other Indian rulers at his infatuation.

Jaya moved through the gaming tables restlessly, feeling as if she were in the Balmer zenana watching the purdah ladies play cards to while away their boredom in the hot months of summer. At one roulette table, the beautiful Maharani of Cooch Behar was the centre of attention, the small turtle with the emeralds embedded in its shell crawling in front of her, knocking her neat piles of chips onto the baize cloth. At another table, the Maharajah of Gondal played chemin de fer, watched by a small crowd who knew he had broken the bank at Monte Carlo and hoped to see him do so again.

Tiny Dungra appeared at Jaya's side. 'Do you know what Gondal does with his winnings? Every rupee is spent on hospitals and schools. He never touches the assets of the state treasury, and no one in his kingdom has paid tax in the last fifteen years. Fortunately, I have been as lucky as Maharajah Gondal for you. But I shall need some signatures before you leave Europe.'

A heavy hand closed on her arm, leading her to a table on the terrace. Foam sprayed white against the sand, and the sound of laughter echoed from the beach. A waiter appeared with a bottle of champagne and a tray of small sandwiches. Tiny Dungra ate several sandwiches, as if to fortify himself. 'Sitting here, nobody realises how serious the situation is becoming again. The emperors who fought the Great War are gone. Leaders like Mussolini are rising in their place. Their followers dress like soldiers, and they are hungry for new wars. I want to diversify some of your holdings and invest in the armaments industry.'

Jaya shook her head in violent disagreement, remembering that

275

bleak landscape of trenches and shell craters. Tiny Dungra faced her. 'Victor is squandering money on that little American creature when the Sirpur treasury is already deeply in debt. Your private wealth may soon become necessary to save the fortunes of your husband's kingdom.'

The grim picture painted by Tiny Dungra activated Jaya at last. In the next weeks, she described Sirpur in terms she knew would shock the pretty American girl staring at her with horrified china-blue eyes. Learning that she would never be received by King George and Queen Mary, Cora Hart pleaded headaches whenever Maharajah Victor sent for her. At the polo games, she began flirting with a large Texan whose booming voice carried halfway down the field as he shouted support to the polo team he had brought from America.

She announced her intention to marry the Texan while still residing in Maharajah Victor's house. Jaya stood on the steps watching the servants throw Cora Hart's many recently acquired possessions into the fleet of cars sent by the Texan, her heart aching for Maharajah Victor.

The next day, Maharajah Victor announced he was tired of Deauville and would spend a few weeks in Biarritz. Prince Pratap took Jaya aside to congratulate her. 'Well done, Princess. I've arranged your return to Bombay. Stay with Lady Modi while I help Victor mend his broken heart. And don't worry about him. He'll lick his wounds in Biarritz until he begins to freeze. Then he'll be back in London, wanting to marry Tallulah Bankhead next.'

Obedient to her husband's wishes, Jaya went to take her leave of the ruler. Although it was raining, the Maharajah was walking on the beach. Jaya pulled her sari closer to her shoulders against the wind whipping against the striped umbrellas that forlornly dotted the deserted beach.

Maharajah Victor was kneeling on the ground. He picked up a piece of driftwood, and the hollow filled up with water. The wind screamed past sand too wet to be lifted into the air as the Maharajah walked to the edge of the water. Jaya followed him in silence.

'Isn't that sea the colour of Henry Conroy's eyes?' the Maharajah asked at last. 'I was always terrified of him and my grandmother. My whole life has been controlled by those two people. I'm tired

276

of lying to them. I need a rest from all the lies, Princess. Go back to India, and I'll join you when I am able.'

BY THE TIME Jaya arrived in Bombay, the rumours of Hari Singh of Kashmir's blackmail settlement had already been published in the Indian press. The details were not known, only that Mr A. had made the largest blackmail settlement in the history of the British Empire. Daily newspaper editorials demanded immediate reforms in the Indian kingdoms.

The situation became worse when a dancing girl was found dead in the Hanging Gardens next to Lady Modi's palatial bungalow, and the Maharajah of Indore was accused of the crime.

'But, darling, it's ridiculous. The murder happened in the middle of the night. The only witness is an English officer who says he heard the murderer shout that he was in the pay of the Maharajah of Indore. Have you ever heard of a more trumped-up charge? And it's only twenty years since Indore's father lost his throne, also on a British charge of murder. What's happening to India? Everything seems to have gone crazy.'

The Indore murder replaced Mr. A.'s blackmail payment in the press. Jaya could hardly bear to look at the newspapers in the mornings for fear that Maharajah Victor's presents to Cora Hart might feature in the editorials that were growing stridently more critical of the Indian rulers every day. As if to make her fears worse, the Viceroy refused to grant the Maharajah of Indore's request to be tried by a jury of his peers, and Maharajah Indore was deposed.

Two weeks later, the newspapers were full of British allegations that the Maharajahs of Patiala and Nabha were fighting over a dancing girl and might both be forced to abdicate by the British Empire.

'Darling, this is too much. Patiala can have as many dancing girls as he wants.'

Jaya thought of the imposing figure of the giant Sikh ruler, and then of Maharajah Victor looking at the lead-grey sea, and was frightened thinking of the India that Maharajah Victor would encounter on his return.

She lengthened her pujas, beseeching the Goddess to protect her brother-in-law, but when Lady Modi interrupted her devotions for the first time and Jaya saw the telegram held by the painted nails, her hands went cold with dread.

'The Viceroy has recalled Maharajah Victor from Europe, hasn't he, Bapsy?'

'Oh, darling, I'm so sorry.' Lady Modi took Jaya in her arms. 'Victor is dead. Pratap wants you to wait in Calcutta while he tries to keep the details of the suicide out of the nationalist press.'

Jaya stared into Lady Modi's eyes, remembering how Hari Singh of Kashmir, his voice loud above the saxophones in the Embassy Club, had boasted of his mountain kingdom where saffron grew wild and glaciers melted into mountain orchids, and how Maharajah Victor had laughed at Hari Singh's boast, pulling Cora Hart into his embrace as he described the Son of the Creator, the great Brahmaputra River that blessed his ancient kingdom of Sirpur with its power.

Lowering her head onto Lady Modi's shoulder, Jaya wept for the gentle brother-in-law who had always treated her with tenderness, as if recognizing their mutual displacement, and who had now killed himself, no longer able to straddle his separate worlds.

BOOK THREE

Maharani

40

'WE ARE CROSSING the border into Sirpur,' Prince Pratap's voice announced through the wooden door. Jaya woke abruptly.

Darkness flashed by the iron bars of the train window, broken by the infrequent blur of village lanterns. But there was no strain on Prince Pratap's face to show he had been wearied by the night of fasting and prayers when he entered the bedroom and, indifferent to her presence, stripped naked for his bath of purification.

The sun's first rays glanced off water lying like flat grass over green rice shoots, and Sirus cranes stood awkwardly submerged on single legs in paddy fields tinged with pink. Seeing the familiar landscape, Jaya grieved for the gentle brother-in-law who had died on a wintry beach in Europe, on the day her husband was to take his place as ruler of Sirpur.

Prince Pratap came out of the bathroom. Around his still-wet waist he tied the sign of the highest-born, the unsewn silk falling in ivory folds to his bare feet. The train pulled to a halt and the deep moan of conch shells engulfed the station. Three ranks of the Maharajah's Bodyguard held drawn swords to their faces, saffron turbans creating banks of colour across the whitewashed station buildings. Behind them the Sirpur Lancers steadied the horses shying nervously away from the crowds.

The carriage door was thrown open. The Maharajah's Bodyguard locked their swords at the blades, forming a steel barrier against the cheering mobs flinging garlands at their new ruler. An aide ran into Jaya's carriage. 'Come quickly, hukam. You must leave for the

Kamini Temple before the streets become impassable.'

He cleared a way through the crowds enclosing the Rolls-Royce like a gigantic fist, and the chauffeur inched the car out of the bazaars, with tinsel arches and silk banners sagging across their narrow streets, towards the Kamini Temple.

Enclosed by muslin screens, the Dowager Maharani was waiting with her harem ladies to witness the coronation. The old woman pointed through the muslin at a square object covered with red silk, and Jaya heard the awe in her harsh whisper, 'The Sirpur gaddi.'

Only a fragment of the original gaddi formed the present Sirpur throne, the other disintegrated fragments consigned to the Treasury in the City Palace. Still, Jaya felt her skin turn clammy at the Dowager Maharani's words. So ancient and so holy was the Sirpur gaddi that a ruler could sit on it only once in his lifetime, at the moment when he joined his name to the names of those ancestors who had fought at the side of the god Krishna himself.

The Raj Guru entered the temple, the conscious dignity of his measured gait reinforced by the slow thud of the nagaras announcing to the crowds swarming into the temple forecourts that the anointing of their new ruler had commenced. Prince Pratap approached the Raj Guru. For a moment Jaya saw the scar from an old polo accident on Prince Pratap's naked back, then he was engulfed by priests.

The Raj Guru began the recitation of the Sirpur lineage. Names fell over the hushed chamber. The first kings of Sirpur were known by single titles: the Virtuous, the Just, the Courageous, the Bountiful. These gave way to delineations of power: King of the Seven Rivers, Sovereign of the Lower Mountains. The most recent names had the longest titles – the elaborate additions unable to disguise the leaking power of the rulers, until Maharajah Victor's titles suggested only impotence, though he was called Grand Commander of the Star of India and Knight Commander of the Indian Empire.

The Raj Guru raised the symbols of monarchy to remind the new ruler of the significance of each icon. Holding the Sirpur sword in his hand, he declaimed, 'This sword is the final power of the sovereign, the symbol of justice. But there is no justice without dharma, and the dharma of a king is righteous service to his people.'

In a motion so sudden Jaya did not see it, he slashed the flesh of his thumb and smeared three long lines of blood across Prince Pratap's forehead. Blood from the slashed thumb still dripped onto the floor as he recited the blessing which acknowledged Prince Pratap as Maharajah of Sirpur. The ancient words cut through the crowded chamber, rendering the bare-torsoed priests irrelevant, as if the accretions of the temple served only to expose the clarity of dharma:

'Take heed, O sovereign. First, there is the people.

'May you be zealous in performing your duties.

'May you give in just measure.

'May you be humble in the presence of the wise.

'May you be learned.

'May your presence have dignity.

'May your zeal be tempered by humanity.

'May your union with the people be as the union between the Goddess and the Ascetic.'

Raising their conch shells, the priests blew a single note that swamped the chamber as though sucking a tide through the stone pillars. In the temple forecourts, down the crowded hillside, the people of Sirpur prostrated themselves as their new ruler mounted the gaddi.

'Maharajdhiraj Pratap Singhji, Dost Alam, Raj Pahar...' The chanted titles went on and on, drowning in the thud of nagaras and the crash of cannon, and Jaya pressed her hot face against the stone floor, willing her husband to touch her and keep his ancient line unbroken.

FOR THE NEXT month, delegations from every part of the kingdom came to offer the new Maharajah the gold coin of their fealty. Maharajah Pratap touched the coins with his fingertips, and his satisfied subjects took them home, to place on family altars next to the coins touched by Maharajah Victor.

Occupied with her own ceremonies, Jaya hardly saw her husband. In the evenings, a steady stream of Sirpur ladies, accompanied by their children, poured into the City Palace to pay their respects. The patient tribal women who had travelled for days to call on the new Maharani had to be seen. During the days, she organised the move from the Wales Palace into the opulent suites of the City Palace.

A distracted Maharajah Pratap called on his wife, almost forgetting to hand her the diamond necklace he had brought as a gift. Jaya overlooked her husband's preoccupation, knowing the Viceroy of India had consented to preside over the ceremony by which the British Empire formally recognized Maharajah Pratap's ruling powers.

Jaya realized the Viceroy's visit to Sirpur was a singular honour, bestowed in recognition of the Sirpur ruling family's unwavering loyalty to the British Empire. Learning of the Viceroy's decision, a number of Indian rulers had asked to attend. The leaders of the Chamber of Princes, the rulers of Patiala, Bikaner, Alwar, wanted to use the occasion to press the Viceroy to accept the demands being made in the Chamber of Princes by royal India.

A single unpleasant incident marked the month of celebrations. 'Lift censorship on our newspapers, hukam!' a group of writers shouted in the Durbar Hall, their angry voices ricocheting in the shocked silence of the crowded room.

'Let your reign usher the twentieth century into Sirpur!'

'Stop the police from monitoring our contacts with the nationalists in British India!'

The Maharajah soothed the writers with assurances that his reign would be marked by neither secrecy nor repression. The next day, accompanied by his Maharani, he left for Sirpur's northern borders, to accept the allegiance of his tribal subjects.

FOR A FORTNIGHT Maharajah Pratap's entourage travelled up-country, abandoning cars for barges to cross the marshy upper reaches of the river, then mounting elephants to penetrate the dense jungles of the Sirpur foothills.

Every day more tribals attached themselves to the Maharajah's procession. Sometimes the tribal men went hunting for deer. When they returned they skinned off the pelts with their long knives, and Jaya watched the tribal women turn the slaughtered animals on spits in ditches dug during the night, before slinging the cooked carcasses onto poles to carry on their naked shoulders.

Once the women pumped milk from the dugs of a slain tigress, shouting that the tiger's milk would give Jaya a strong son. Jaya reluctantly drank the milk, wanting to ask the women what she should do to make her husband love her, even as her stomach churned at the thought of the tiger cubs huddled in a bamboo thicket calling for their dead mother.

As the procession approached the Himalayas, the foliage gained a sinister brightness. The Brahmaputra River, closer to its source in the melting ice lakes of Tibet, flowed with transparent fury down perpendicular waterfalls, and the tribals themselves, with their feathered headdresses and animal-skin loincloths, seemed possessed of a mystic connection with nature absent in the soft creatures who lived on the fertile rice plains around the capital.

At night, drunk and abandoned on chandan toddy, they danced for the Maharajah and Maharani. Bodies glistening in the firelight, they performed the tiger mating with the elephant; the lotus with the snake; even humans with the Goddess, as if they were so close to the gods they could not be profane.

It was dusk when the elephants broke through the heavy forest into a clearing near a lake sacred to the tribals. Grass huts mounted on stilts were visible in the twilight, and woven banners indicated the lineage of the tribal clans.

The rulers were led toward animal skins spread out on the red earth, over a mud path clogged by lotus plants stretching long stalks out of the clear water.

Behind the skins, a two-storey wooden hut raised on high stilts stood with monumental solidity in the wilderness, curtains of freshly strung jasmine blossoms and mountain orchids hanging from its beams. The tribals disappeared, leaving Jaya sitting in silence on the animal skins next to Prince Pratap.

As night descended, it was as though the centuries of evolution had left no mark on Sirpur. Fireflies swept in huge waves above the lake, their intermittent flashing reflected in the black water until the clearing, with its simple grass huts, ceased to be a makeshift camp, and became instead a circling wheel of light and darkness.

Lanterns dipped up and down in the night. Jaya stared into the jungle. Rows of men and women were dancing down a path, to the insistent beat of the oval drums that hung from the shoulders of the tribal chiefs. Bare bodies seemed to snap in half as each wave of dancers reached the water's edge and whiplashed back into the centre of the path. Clacking sticks and bronze anklet bells crashed on the red mud, the rhythm of drums and feet growing more urgent as they approached the Maharajah.

Toddy bags were flung from one dancer to another, hands leaving waists to pour liquor down throats, ankleted feet never missing a beat. Drumbeats pounded in the dark, shaking the thin stilts of the grass huts, and Maharajah Pratap was lifted off the tiger skin, his red turban disappearing into a sea of feather headdresses.

A painted toddy bag was thrust at Jaya. She choked on the fiery chandan. She was whipped away in the dance, her body sliding against sweating breasts. The toddy bag was thrust at her again and again. Lifted by strong naked arms, instantly drunk on the raw country liquor, Jaya could no longer tell whether she saw stars spinning in the sky or fireflies swimming in the black water.

The tribals backed away, leaving her in the clearing, her hair loose and dishevelled around her body, facing Maharajah Pratap, his crown and turban gone, his silk dhoti spattered with red mud.

Lanterns swung in a slow arc and the tribals linked arms to dance around the rulers, at first slowly, then with increasing abandon until the thudding feet resonated in the night like blood pumping through an artery or the pounding of the Tandava, the heartbeat of creation, a sound so insistent it had awakened the great Ascetic from his trance to dance across the constellations.

As though compelled by that relentless rhythm the Maharajah enclosed his wife in his arms. Powerful muscles pressed against Jaya's wet skin as he led her to the bamboo ladder propped against the high hut shrouded in jasmine curtains. On the red mud below, bronze anklets thudded to the momentum of the drums, and Maharajah Pratap thrust himself into his wife's body with such savagery that it seemed he was the Ascetic fragmenting the body of the Goddess with his rage, until her glass bangles smashed into the jasmine garlands and blood stained the crushed petals.

41

WHILE SIRPUR prepared for the arrival of the Viceroy of India, Jaya wept that Maharajah Pratap would not touch her until inebriation turned what should have been a husband's tenderness into a captor's assault.

After long days spent with Sir Akbar and Sir Henry Conroy planning the Viceroy's visit, followed by evenings spent with the foreign guests who had begun arriving in Sirpur for the investiture celebrations, Maharajah Pratap appeared in his wife's bedroom and drunkenly plunged himself into her body as if she were a concubine brought to him for the night. The urgency with which he fulfilled his needs left Jaya bitterly regretting an intimacy which soiled her as his remoteness had never done.

She could not count the times she had stood on her balcony watching the muddy water trickle past the crocodiles sleeping on the white sandbanks of the summer riverbed, or the black monsoon clouds scudding like herds of angry elephants over the flooded river, waiting to hear her husband's footstep outside her door. Now she dreaded the sound of that footstep.

She had little knowledge of what a marriage bed should be, only that on the two occasions when she had seen her parents touch each other, each moment had been gentle with tenderness. Lying on sheets soaked with her husband's sweat, Jaya clung to those images, wondering that Maharajah Pratap could not hear the silent screaming in her mind. But sometimes, while her husband laboured above her, the shadow of other men slipped unbidden into her mind,

James Osborne's arms around her shoulders, Arun Roy's lips against her skin, and for a moment her rigid body softened under her husband's.

She half realized that the more Maharajah Pratap prostrated himself before the British Empire, the more he hated his wife as the symbol of that empire's power over his private life, and she distanced herself from the energetic preparations for the Viceroy's visit.

JAYA'S INSULATION from outside events was shattered by the arrival of the Indian rulers.

Sitting on the verandah of the Wales Palace, the visiting maharanis expounded angrily on the scandalous manner in which the British Empire was dethroning India's kings.

'The Angrez are trying to drive a wedge between ourselves and British India, so they can keep their empire. After all, if royal India and British India were to stand together, we could throw out the British in a minute.'

'And where did the filthy propaganda in the nationalist press come from if not from the British Empire's secret files?'

'Soon every strong ruler will be dethroned on one pretext or another.'

An older maharani stopped smearing lime paste on her betel leaf and looked up in disgust. 'The British pretend such innocence, but this Jewish Viceroy who has stolen Indore's throne and now wants to steal Patiala's – this Lord Reading, who has been sent to us because he is supposed to understand our Oriental ways better than an ordinary Englishman – he has all the cunning of his race.'

A bright-eyed younger maharani from a Rajput kingdom lowered her voice conspiratorially. 'Do you know the real reason why Indore lost his throne?'

The other ladies stopped cracking betel nuts and inclined towards her over their paan caskets.

'Petty revenge. Lord Reading has taken Indore's throne because when the Viceroy and Vicereine visited his kingdom, Indore told the Viceroy, "My treaty makes me subservient to the British Crown. But the Viceroy's wife is merely another Englishwoman. You cannot expect my wife, a ruling queen, to wait at an Englishwoman's car door." '

The assembled ladies gasped in shocked admiration. Pleased with the effect her story had elicited, the maharani continued: 'As for Patiala and Nabha, this is Britain's dirtiest game so far. The Angrez are still despised in the Punjab because of the Amritsar massacre. These two kings were asked to mediate between the Sikhs and the British. Now the British fear their influence is too widespread, and . . .'

Servants entered with trays of savouries, and the maharanis fell silent. Beyond the oleander bushes, the throbbing of steamer engines drifted across the water as Jaya reminded herself to study the sheets of typed instruction that had been left in her apartments by Sir Akbar to ensure that she did not commit some small error which could be read as an insult – or worse, an act of sedition – by the hawk-eyed officials in the Viceroy's entourage. The servants bowed out of the verandah, and the maharanis resumed their discussion.

'Chee! The British Empire says Patiala and Nabha are about to start a war over some dancing girl with blue eyes and auburn hair, and their people will suffer untold hardships if the two maharajahs do not abdicate immediately.'

'That is British gratitude for you. Dethrone Patiala, now that he has brought peace to the Punjab.'

Jaya thought of Lady Modi's stories about the five hundred women in the giant Sikh king's harem, the cricket match in which he and his nobles had worn long frocks to shock the British Governor. She could not imagine that a king who had dared to abduct the Viceroy's own daughter could be intimidated into giving up his throne.

As if reading her thoughts, one of the maharanis said, 'The British will never rob Patiala of his throne. Patiala challenged the Viceroy, saying, "Let's see who speaks for the people of Patiala – their king or an Englishman. If my people are suffering, I will leave Patiala voluntarily and walk barefoot from my kingdom to the holy city of Amritsar to do penance at the Golden Temple of the Sikhs. And you, Viceroy-sahib, will have a revolution on your hands before I have gone fifty miles." '

THE DOWAGER Maharani pointed at the floral arches supported on wooden replicas of the Kamini Temple, studded with shields from the Palace Armoury. 'They say the Viceroy has more power than the King of England. I hope all this will please him.'

Through the window of the Dowager Maharani's Rolls-Royce, Jaya watched the people massed on the streets of the capital. The crowds seemed denser, if possible, than on the pilgrimage days to the Kamini Temple, the decorations more elaborate than they had been for the Prince of Wales. Bright green banana leaves and paper Union Jacks framed the garlands strung across the balconies, as if each building on the Viceroy's route were vying with its neighbours to provide an auspicious aspect for the Englishman.

More crowds lined the railway tracks, waiting to see the Viceroy of India's white train enter the capital for the first time in the kingdom's history.

A red carpet ran down the centre of the platform where the white train would stop. Under a canopy to the left of the carpet sat the Indian kings, jewels flashing in the morning sunlight. Facing them were the ministers of the Sirpur court and the British Resident, Sir Henry Conroy, and his officials.

The Maharajah himself was seated on a silver chair at the far end of the carpet. The famous Sirpur aigrette, a diamond enclosed in the coils of a ruby snake, crowned his turban. Rows of pearls circled his throat. The Sirpur sword hung from his emerald belt.

The shriek of a whistle announced the approach of the Viceroy of India's white train, and Jaya gripped her protocol notes so tightly that black print streaked her perspiring palms.

White faces watched through the carriage windows as the Viceroy's Household Guard jumped onto the platform in a blur of scarlet uniforms and gold cummerbunds, to lower the red-carpeted stairs on which the Viceroy and Lady Reading would descend onto Sirpur soil.

The visiting maharanis studied their programmes, caustically noting that no fewer than eighty-six officials and personal staff were accompanying the Viceroy, although he was stopping in Sirpur for seven hours only, before moving to Shillong to pursue his favourite sport, golf, at the highest golf course in the world.

'He also thinks he is a great shot now, although he never even sat on a horse until he was appointed Viceroy of India at the age of sixty.'

290

A tall figure dressed in a cotton suit appeared at the doorway of the viceregal carriage. Jaya just saw the high forehead and dark eyes above the long nose before the Viceroy placed his hat on his head.

He descended the steps, and the Sirpur cannon fired the thirty-one-gun salute that heralded the presence of the proconsul of the British Empire. The Maharajah rose from his silver chair. The crash of gunfire shook the station buildings as the two men walked towards each other down the red carpet, their advance precisely negotiated between previous Sirpur kings and the British Government.

The cannons fired their last salvo, and rows of schoolchildren began singing the national anthem of the British Empire. Behind them, the trombones and trumpets of the Sirpur Palace Band shone against green uniforms epauletted with gold braid. The two rulers stood motionless, even as the cymbals clashed with too much force and the children shouted the final bars: 'Send him vic-tor-yus, Hap-py and glor-yus, Long to reign ov-rus, God Save the King.'

The Sirpur Lancers who had fought in France and Mesopotamia marched towards the Viceroy as the purdah screen slid open and an Abyssinian whispered in Jaya's ear.

The Prime Minister was waiting in the car. 'Remember, hukam, Lady Reading came to India a simple woman. In fact, Maharajah Bikaner told me just last night that she eats her cheese with a knife.' The pale hand removed a nonexistent feather from the severe tunic coat in a gesture that Jaya recognized as indicating Sir Akbar's intense disapproval. 'Unfortunately, the splendour of India has made her more royal than Queen Victoria herself. She is very unhappy her husband is going back to England next month. She wanted to be Vicereine for another five years, at least. She will not tolerate any mistakes.'

Jaya looked at the sheets in her hand, although she knew the protocol by heart, and Sir Akbar smiled at her anxiety. 'Gun salutes, national anthems, the reckless squandering of history for a few favours of recognition. Where does it all end, hukam, when the ruler of the oldest line in India is unable to reign until the Angrez declare him a king?'

'Should I look at the Banquet Room again to make sure everything is all right for the lunch?' Jaya asked as the car rolled through the gateway where the Maharajah's elephant would enter the City

Palace. Rows of howdahed elephants waited in the courtyard and people crowded together on the high walls with flower garlands in their hands.

'The Maharajah visited it himself this morning, hukam, and Michel will see to the last details. Lady Reading is a great party-giver. Her costume balls in Simla are legendary. Durbar-sahib wanted to make sure there were no errors for her to gossip over when she returns to England.'

Jaya remained silent. Letters and telegrams from all over the world had been flooding the Sirpur post office to congratulate the new Maharajah on his accession. She had been shown none of them. Now his French valet had been delegated to arrange the banquet for the Viceroy, as if the Maharani of Sirpur were unequal to the task.

Jaya stood at the portico of the Durbar Hall, trying to calm herself for the Vicereine, as a Rolls-Royce flying the Union Jack entered the courtyard. One of the maharanis in the East Verandah had said, 'Be careful with Lady Reading, hukam. My husband's secretary, Mr Forster, wrote a book while working for us in Dewas, *A Passage to India*. It has been very well received abroad. But the Vicereine didn't like it at all. She said it gave a bad impression of the British. And the Viceroy said, 'That's what comes of chiefs having the wrong kind of Europeans around them.'

Jaya slowly descended the stairs so that her foot would reach the ground as the car braked. The Vicereine stepped out. Jaya could not believe this frail, middle-aged woman was so suffused with her own importance that she could have been responsible for deposing the King of Indore until the Vicereine put out a gloved hand, the wrist dangling so limply it indicated her sense of superiority more emphatically than any words.

She wearily preceded Jaya up the marble steps as if bestowing a favour. In the Durbar Hall, Lady Reading hardly glanced at the famous frescoes on the wall as Jaya made stiff conversation about the weather.

Gunfire heralded the approach of the Maharajah's elephant. Relieved that she had not said anything to offend the Vicereine, Jaya led her to the courtyard, where the other maharanis were already seated.

The Maharajah's mounted bodyguard trotted into the courtyard, and the crowds on the walls flung their flowers on the caparisoned elephant entering the golden gate. The elephants lining the court-yard raised their trunks to shower rose petals onto the ruler and the Viceroy as they stepped to the ground.

The two men approached the red cushion at the side of the silver chair blazoned with the Viceroy of India's crest. The Vicereine and other European women sank in curtsies when the Viceroy passed them.

'Your Highness, the Maharajah of Sirpur.' The Viceroy's clipped English voice silenced the murmur of the crowds crushed on the courtyard walls. 'The eventful moment of your installation as Chief of Sirpur State has arrived. It is my privilege, as representative of the King Emperor of India and the Government of the British Empire, to place you on the gaddi of your ancestors and invest you with the powers of a First Class Maharajah of a kingdom honoured with a twenty-one-gun salute.

'For yourself, to the instincts of a proud lineage you have added the wider experience of a great empire, first gained by your educa-tion at Eton College and Cambridge University, later by your long residence in Europe, both in time of peace and during the dark years of the War.

'It is customary on such an occasion for the representative of the British Empire to read the new ruler a homily. But you are no boy on the threshold of man's estate, and there is no need to warn you against intriguers and sycophants.

'Be always careful of the various departments of your admin-istration. Employ the best men, pay them adequately, insist on efficiency and do not be led by any mistaken feelings of kindness into retaining a bad man. Be liberal in your programme of public works, and husband the resources of your ancient kingdom well.'

Jaya stopped listening to the address, infuriated by the Viceroy's tone. Did the Viceroy not see how much had been spent on his visit to Sirpur? Did he not know the biggest expense incurred by an Indian kingdom was the expense of winning the approval of the British Empire? Or the shadow Britain cast between a ruler and his people? She was sure the Viceroy and his wife would not refuse the jewels and gifts that would be pressed on them as they departed for the golf courses of Shillong in the white train with the eighty-six attendants.

The Viceroy led Maharajah Pratap to the red cushion and seated him on the gaddi. The crowds on the courtyard walls cheered. The Vicereine brushed her ears with gloved hands, and the visiting maharanis eyed each other knowingly at the gesture of irritation as Sir Henry Conroy handed the ruler the Seal of State and the keys of the Sirpur Treasury that had been kept in the British Residency since Maharajah Victor's death.

Maharajah Pratap rose. The Vicereine shifted in her chair as Maharajah Pratap's tributes to Lord Reading and herself went on. Jaya watched her angrily, until she heard the note of excitement in Maharajah Pratap's voice. 'It was Great Britain that persuaded my grandfather to lay the railway lines which now connect us to British India. Then my late brother acquired a fleet of aircraft which won the appreciation of the Prince of Wales. I shall lay new airfields which will permit the speedy dispatch of business, connecting the most remote areas of the kingdom to the capital in a manner that could not have been dreamed of only ten years ago.'

Jaya could see the expression of fatigue on the Prime Minister's fastidious features and knew he was already calculating the cost of the ruler's enthusiasm to the Sirpur treasury.

But the Viceroy seemed pleased with the ceremony, and at the luncheon he complimented Jaya on the arrangements.

When the last covers were removed, the visiting maharajahs rose to their feet to toast the new ruler. Knowing Patiala's throne was in jeopardy, Jaya was surprised to see the Sikh king lift his glass and face the Viceroy.

'Your Excellency.' Patiala's voice was loud in the banquet hall. 'We have today seen a moving ceremony, the installation of an Indian king on the gaddi of his ancestors. An Indian king who rules, as is all too often forgotten, an independent country. At this happy moment, may I remind you that our treaties are made with Great Britain, not with British India.

'Yet British India's officials concern themselves with our internal affairs and threaten us with impunity when we object. The Chamber of Princes, a gathering of independent kings in its way not so different from other international bodies, cannot be convened except at the convenience of British Indian officials, sometimes twice in one year, sometimes not at all. The content of our speeches is decided and controlled by British officials. In matters of common concern,

British India will not allow us to hold joint consultations with other Indians. The Chamber sessions may not be reported in the press. Thus, our reputations are recklessly smeared and we are denied the means of redress.

'We, the ruling Princes of India, have been Great Britain's most loyal supporters in war as well as peace. There is no ruler sitting at this table today who has not lost valiant citizens on the Empire's battlefields. We ask you to reassure us of our constitutional guarantees, as the bond of Great Britain's good faith.'

No surprise showed on the Viceroy's face during Patiala's speech, and the glass in the Englishman's hand remained steady as he lifted it in response to the Sikh king's toast. 'Your Highnesses,' he said, 'when addressing a gathering of India's senior rulers, it is fitting that I repeat the views I have already expressed to the Nizam of Hyderabad on the relationship between the Indian states and the British Crown.

'The sovereignty of the British Crown is supreme in India, and therefore no Ruler of an Indian State can justifiably claim to negotiate with the British Government on an equal footing.

'Our supremacy is based not only upon treaties but exists independently of them.'

The rulers flinched at the baldness with which Reading's words destroyed the fundamental agreement between royal India and Great Britain.

After the luncheon, the Vicereine planted the first sapling in the new park that would bear her name, Lady Reading Park. Jaya saw the maharanis whispering behind their hands, and she was relieved that Lady Reading could not understand how the Viceroy was being abused for betraying the trust of the Indian kings.

'If our treaties are meaningless, the Viceroy can take our thrones at any time, claiming he is preserving the peace and good of India.'

'The Angrez are worse than moneylenders. They steal everything we have and still say we are in their debt.'

42

WITH THE DEPARTURE of the Viceroy of India, Jaya found herself once again vulnerable to Maharajah Pratap, violated by the very act that should have been proof of love. Every morning she dutifully recited prayers for her husband's long life, and tried to rid herself of the uncleansing memory of his embrace.

When he had finally taken her in his arms in the wooden hut with its curtain of flowers, the moment had carved away the memory of his other women as the long knives of the tribals sliced the skin from an animal, and she had hoped her empty life would overflow with the abundance for which all wives prayed. But night after night she watched him blow out the scented candles as though he could not bear to touch her until he could no longer see her, as if the night soiled him as it did her, and her humiliations hardened into a rage that mirrored her husband's.

She remembered the long years she had waited for him to consummate their marriage. Now only the necessity of an heir forced her to admit the ruler to her rooms, and when the palace doctors confirmed at last that she was with child, she moved into the Purdah Palace, eager to be away from the ruler.

The excitement of the purdah ladies in her confinement erased the indignities of Maharajah Pratap's conjugal visits. At dusk Jaya sat on the balcony listening to the purdah ladies sing of her unborn child's heroic ancestors, soothed by their serene voices, until the memory of her husband receded like a garish picture. When Sir Akbar sent news that Maharajah Pratap had left for Europe in the company of the dancer from Calcutta, Esmé Moore, Jaya was almost relieved.

The Dowager Maharani opened the storerooms where the traditional playthings for an heir to the throne were kept. 'Choose toys for a son. So much kicking can only mean a boy.'

Cradles, frames for the unborn child's horoscope, small puja objects with which he would perform his first prayers, brocades for his first tunic coat, and aigrettes for his first turban were piled high in the chambers.

Jaya took out a globe made of ivory and gold, enamelled with scenes of tiger hunts and war. The Dowager rattled the globe in Jaya's ear. 'See, this one still has earth in it. He must learn about earth, water, light, air – the four elements that make up the world. What is a ruler who does not understand the fundamentals of nature?'

Jaya rolled the smooth object in her hand, rounded so an infant would not cut himself.

'And this is to teach him about the heavens.' The Dowager Maharani held up a necklace of cabuchon gems so the sunlight caught its colours. 'The nine gems that represent the planets, which govern the moods and changes of our lives, as the tides govern the sea.'

As the child grew in her womb Jaya spent hours in the storerooms, choosing little – but dreaming, in the afternoon sun, of the baby.

IN APRIL, a son was born to Maharani Jaya Devi. Holding the squalling infant in her arms while the Dowager Maharani's stiff fingers swept the long hair matted with sweat from her face, Jaya felt she belonged to Sirpur at last. She had kept the Sirpur line intact, and the knowledge filled her with unfamiliar security.

While Maharajah Pratap travelled back from Europe, the overjoyed Dowager Maharani celebrated the birth with appropriate ceremony. At dawn and at dusk, firing cannons drowned the clanging of temple bells, announcing the birth of the kingdom's heir. Prisoners were released. New clothes were distributed to the people of the kingdom. Twice a day the poor were fed under vast tents put up in the main courtyard of the City Palace.

When the wives of the Sirpur nobles circled her son's head with coins to deflect the evil eye, Jaya felt the celebrations were as much a recognition of herself as of her child.

On her husband's return, Jaya drove to the City Palace, staring proudly into the bright eyes of the baby held close to her breast. Enveloped in her own world, she was only amused by Maharajah Pratap's charming apologies at not being present for the birth of his son.

But when he bent forward, Jaya turned her head so that his lips only brushed her cheek. She smiled at the crying baby as she pulled down her sari to feed him.

'Stop that!'

Jaya looked up in surprise from the infant suckling at her breast.

'The Maharanis of Sirpur employ wet nurses. I will not have my wife feeding a baby like a peasant woman.'

'Hukam.' The blood rose to Jaya's face. Maharajah Pratap had already robbed her of the dignity of being a wife. Now he was stealing the rights of maternity. She lowered her eyes so he would not see the silent anger breaking in waves against the respect for a husband which had been ingrained so deeply by the prayers and ceremonies that had marked her whole life.

With an iciness she had not known she possessed she sat at his side in the Durbar Hall while the wet nurse fed the baby in her apartments, listening to the list of guests prepared by Sir Akbar for the child's name ceremony.

Her fury at her husband's crude display of power briefly evaporated when Tiny Dungra reached Sirpur.

'Your mother is thrilled at the news of her grandson.' Dungra circled the baby's head with a crimson purse filled with gold coins and handed the purse to Chandni. 'When my father was dying, he asked for your mother's blessing, and now that I am ruler of Dungra, her presence in the kingdom is a great comfort to me.' He settled his large frame into an armchair. 'But I don't think the British were comforted to see Pratap playing in London when their own people are starving.'

'Is there famine in England, hukam?'

'A famine of jobs, Bai-sa. Men who survived the war cannot feed their children because they cannot find work. Last month, in despair, they marched on London, only to be met by bullets. There is even talk of revolution in England if the situation does not improve.' He reached across and took the baby's small hand in his own. 'In your private moments, persuade Pratap to cultivate the nationalists. If England collapses, our future lies with them.'

'At this moment my husband seems interested only in pleasure, hukam. Even his son takes second place.'

Irritation exploded from the large frame. 'Pratap is a charming man, but like the other Sirpur rulers, he cannot endure reality. And the reality is this, Bai-sa. Last month, the People's Councils formed a Reformist organization in Bombay to push for revolution in the Indian kingdoms.'

Jaya hugged the baby, knowing the Sirpur family's strength came from its close links with the British Empire, carefully cultivated over four generations.

The shouts of a Household Guard signalled the Maharajah's approach. Dungra rose to congratulate Maharajah Pratap. 'We rejoice in the birth of your son, Pratap.'

'And my Resident tells me he wants to go home next year, Tiny. A second reason for rejoicing.'

'This is no time for making jokes, Pratap. The new Reformist movement is a real threat to our futures. And now the British Empire is sending Indian officials in place of Englishmen to our kingdoms. Some of these Indians hate us more than the British ever did. At least Sir Henry is someone you know. His successor may prove much worse.'

'Don't get excited, Tiny. The ever-efficient Sir Akbar has a list of successors, stolen from the British Residency by our spies. He'll manage to find someone sympathetic to Sirpur. Come on, I want to show you the two new aeroplanes that have just arrived from England. They are being unpacked in the hangars right now.'

IN OCTOBER the name ceremony took place in the courtyard where Maharajah Pratap had been invested with his ruling powers by the Viceroy. Once again eager citizens sat on the high walls, watching the priests perform the pujas for the heir to the Sirpur throne.

The Raj Guru carried the child to the sacred fire. Grains of rice were placed in the small hands. The crowds shouted with pleasure when the infant's hands opened at just the right moment to allow the grains to fall into the fire. Ganges water was sprinkled on the baby's body; sindoor was rubbed over his forehead. Raising his voice, the Raj Guru announced that the new prince of the Sirpur family would be called Arjun.

Pleased that the baby had not cried once through the long prayers but had stared with his big eyes at the flames leaping up whenever the priests ladled butterfat into the fire, Jaya thought it fitting that her son should be named after the great king whose chariot had been driven by the God Krishna.

Two DAYS later Lady Modi arrived in the Wales Palace, hardly visible behind a parcel in distinctive Cartier wrappings. She leaned forward to kiss Jaya and the parcel crashed onto the marble floor.

'I can't believe I hauled the damned thing across the world only to have it break into a thousand pieces just as I was going to present it.'

Jaya embraced Lady Modi. 'I don't need a present, Bapsy.'

Lady Modi drew back, a shocked expression on her doll-like face. 'It's not for you, darling. It's for your son. A picnic hamper with gold-rimmed glasses and an extremely dashing cocktail shaker and monogrammed plates and cutlery and . . .'

'He's hardly six months old. What on earth is he going to do with a picnic hamper?'

'Well, you can never tell. Children are always starving.'

'Shall I send for him, Bapsy?'

Lace gloves fluttered in the air like disturbed butterflies. 'Absolutely not, darling. You know I have no feeling for infants.'

With a sigh of resignation Jaya sat down to listen to the latest gossip from Europe, watching the waving shadows dapple Lady Modi's porcelain skin while her dogs chased each other through the oleander bushes.

Pursued by the distracted Chantal, the dogs bounded up the stairs and leapt onto their mistress's lap.

'Scott-Ward, Ali! Sit down!' Lady Modi hit the Borzoi with her glass. The stem smashed against its diamond collar, and she fell back into the sofa, defeated. 'Hope they bleed to death!' she moaned faintly from the cushions as servants rushed in to clear the mess. 'Make me another drink, darling. I turn to ice just thinking of how these filthy beasts are going to behave at the Nawab of Junagadh's wedding.'

Jaya swirled vermouth in a glass and tossed it into the flower bed. 'He won't even notice them among his eight hundred dogs. Which poor girl is the Nawab marrying this time?'

'That's the whole point, darling. He's not marrying a girl. He's marrying his favourite dog.'

Jaya nearly dropped the glass. 'The ruler of Junagadh is marrying a dog?'

'Oh, darling, don't be ridiculous. The Nawab's favourite bitch is being married to a dog.' The brown eyes widened with excitement. 'Haven't you seen your invitation? It's going to be the social event of the season.'

'I don't know what you are talking about, Bapsy. I don't receive invitations to dog weddings.'

'I knew it!' Lady Modi said morosely. 'I knew that coward Pratap would make me break the news to you. Now, darling, please don't get on your high horse, but I can't tell you how serious we all had to be in Europe this summer, what with the General Strike in London and all those peculiar people marching about in uniforms in Baden Baden and Naples. And you've just had a baby. We all need some fun.'

She appealed to Jaya with large eyes. Taking their cue from their mistress, the dogs turned to stare at Jaya, red tongues dripping saliva onto the floor. 'It's going to be a terribly grand wedding, darling. Even the Viceroy has been invited. People are taking odds he will attend. You know how the English feel about animals.'

'The Viceroy will probably have Junagadh's throne for daring to send him an invitation. It's only been six months since the British dethroned the rulers of Indore and Nabha.'

'Unlike his predecessor, the new Viceroy, Lord Irwin, was born and remains a gentleman.' A manicured nail tapped Jaya's knee to gain her attention. 'Now listen carefully. The bride-to-be is called Roshanara – the light of the Nawab's eyes. This pampered creature who sleeps between satin sheets, eats from jewelled bowls and is kept in a manner which is quite beyond *comme il faut*, is to be given in holy matrimony to a golden retriever called Bobby. Such a masculine-sounding name, don't you think, darling?'

Lady Modi clapped her hands in delight, and the dogs at her feet barked. She looked down at them. 'Wouldn't it be nice if my awful animals died in Junagadh? Whenever one of the Junagadh dogs dies, it is given a full state burial, with a band playing Chopin's funeral march.'

DESPITE JAYA'S fervent appeals that her husband not lose his dignity by attending the marriage of a prize bitch, Maharajah Pratap was adamant that Jaya accompany him to Junagadh.

In their anxiety to prevent the visit Tiny Dungra and Sir Akbar let their masks of formality slip.

'Two British Commissions are touring India right now. The Butler Commission is re-examining our relationship with the Crown. And the Simon Commission is studying the possibility of offering self-government to British India.' Dungra could not conceal his out-rage. 'Other Indian rulers are doing their best to impress the Butler Commission with their sobriety in order to counteract the threat of the Reformists. And you, Pratap, choose this moment for attending the marriage of a bitch.'

Maharajah Pratap exchanged glances with Lady Modi, who began giggling behind her gloves. The Prime Minister frowned. 'It is vital that royal India show itself in the best possible light to both the Empire and the nationalists at this time, hukam. And your presence in Junagadh will certainly be reported to the Empire by Sir Henry.'

Maharajah Pratap brushed aside the Prime Minister's words. 'Now that my dutiful wife has presented me with an heir, the British Empire approves of me. That old stick-in-the-mud may have ruined Victor's life, but Sir Henry Conroy is not going to destroy mine. By the way, I hope you're making sure that Osborne is Sir Henry's successor.'

Maharajah Pratap lifted Lady Modi's fingers to his lips. 'Apparently Tikka's friend, James Osborne, made a favourable impression on Sir Henry during the Prince of Wales's visit, so I've told Sir Akbar to make sure the damned fellow is sent here. At least he plays decent polo. And you love presenting polo cups, don't you, Bapsy?'

43

THE SIRPUR Alsatians leaped at the iron bars of the window as the train pulled into a small station on the boundary of Junagadh kingdom. Jaya ignored them, resigned to the agitated dogs after travelling two thousand miles with them across India to the coast of the Arabian Sea.

Maharajah Pratap descended onto the red carpet. A band was playing the Sirpur anthem, but the music was inaudible through the din of barking dogs. Jaya thought the Alsatians were responsible for the deafening noise until she stepped onto the platform where Maharajah Pratap was inspecting the Guard of Honour and saw hundreds of dogs tied to the railway railings.

'Hope you brought some earplugs, darling,' Maharajah Pratap shouted as the car pulled away from the station. 'Those hounds are the bridegroom's party. They're coming with us to the capital.'

A sea breeze blew through the windows as the car approached a balustraded marble wind palace that seemed too delicate to withstand the sea stretching beyond them. The dogs leaped out of the car and circled the Prime Minister of Junagadh, sniffing at his knees. He watched them with an indifference born of long practice.

'You have time to change before we board the train for the capital, Your Highnesses. The other rulers are already taking refreshments.'

A group of princes were sitting on the verandah of the wind palace. Jaya glanced at them in surprise. Known for their insistence on precedence, too proud to attend the Chamber of Princes when the very future of their kingdoms hung in the balance for fear of

303

sitting next to a ruler they considered inferior, they had consented to be members of a dog's wedding party, their destructive haughtiness forgotten as they sipped whisky sodas in the afternoon sun.

Lady Modi led Jaya up the staircase. 'You maids will have to help me dress. I didn't bring Chantal.' She ran lacquered fingernails through her short hair. 'I suppose I'll have to curl my hair myself, but surely your women can manage my tiara.'

'Bapsy, you're an Indian. You can't dress like a mem-sahib in a conservative kingdom like Junagadh.'

'Conservative?' Lady Modi squealed in disbelief. 'What are you talking about, darling? The man is giving a state wedding for a dog. Now, remember to simply drip jewellery, darling. For the photographers.'

Fearful of what the new Reformist organization would say about her husband's presence at this wedding, Jaya reluctantly changed into an ornate sari. Her maidservants were monopolized by Lady Modi's anguished cries. 'Where's my rouge? My hair looks simply awful. I'm going back to Bombay immediately.' At last Lady Modi was ready, a hip flask bulging from the beaded handbag hanging from her elbow.

In the foyer the assembled rulers leaned on their swords, their brocade tunics and turbans fastened with royal aigrettes glistening in the afternoon sunlight as the palace doors were flung open and a fleet of expensive cars inched into the drive.

At the railway station, dogs were being herded, yapping and growling, into train compartments. The Sirpur Alsatians, followed by the whimpering Scott-Ward and the snapping Ali, were pushed into a carriage. Lady Modi crowed at their misery. 'Silly animals. They should be mad with excitement. They'll never see so many dogs again in their lives. Darling, look! The bridegroom himself.'

A red palanquin was lowered to the ground. Children ran between legs, shoving past their elders to watch the bridegroom being pulled out of the palanquin by liveried servants.

The retriever had golden anklets on all four paws. The crowd pressed forward to see the emerald and topaz necklace swinging from the retriever's neck. Guards beat back the mob to allow the snarling retriever to be dragged towards the nuptial carriage, almost invisible under garlands of flowers.

Lady Modi grabbed Jaya's elbow. 'Oh, my God, darling. We had better call the whole thing off. Someone has tried to cut the bride-groom in half. Probably after the poor dog's jewellery. The Nawab is quite unpredictable. If that damn dog dies before the marriage, he's capable of throwing us all in jail. Even the Viceroy won't be able to get us out.'

Maharajah Pratap separated himself from the rulers walking in front of the ladies. 'Control your hysteria, Bapsy. The dog is only wearing red silk pyjamas.'

Lady Modi reached into her bulging handbag and extricated a lorgnette to stare at the retriever. 'But why? They spoil his ensemble.'

Maharajah Pratap leered at Lady Modi. 'To make sure Bobby does not violate Roshanara before the wedding.'

In the carriage champagne bottles were already cooling in silver buckets. Spying Maharajah Pratap and Lady Modi toasting each other near the windows, the other rulers crowded into the compartment until there was no room to move. The carriage lurched, and the rulers fell onto each other as the train pulled out of the station in a cacophony of barking dogs.

It was night by the time the train reached the capital of Junagadh kingdom. Swaying in front of the window, a ruler announced sadly that he could see an enormous reception committee awaiting them. The other rulers groaned and straightened their brocade tunics. Maharajah Pratap suggested they arrange themselves in order of precedence, so they could dismount with a semblance of order.

'Excellent idea, hukam!'

'Now who can remember how many gun salutes he has?'

'Send for the Viceroy. Only he knows for sure.'

Laughter rocked the small compartment as Maharajah Pratap, senior among the assembled rulers, descended to be greeted by the Nawab of Junagadh.

The Junagadh cabinet flanked their ruler. Behind them, kennel boys restrained dogs of every known breed, each animal weighted down with jewellery. Gems sparkled and shook in the bright station lights as howling dogs responded to the cannon salvos calculated to the status of the rulers descending onto the red carpet. Over the firing cannon and the state anthems, Lady Modi shouted, 'Conservative or not, darling, you must admit the Nawab simply reeks style!'

The golden retriever was lowered to the platform, whining unhappily at the roar of barking that greeted his appearance. With grave formality the visiting Indian kings watched the Nawab shower gold coins onto the retriever's head. The dog ducked and growled, but the imperturbable Nawab pulled the retriever to inspect the Household Guard. The Guard presented arms, their hands slapping against the wooden butts of rifles with such precision that the frightened bridegroom raised a leg and soaked his silk pyjamas.

Ignoring the mishap, the Nawab dragged the dog between the lines of soldiers as the assembled rulers solemnly fell into step behind him. The band played a fanfare and the kennel boys turned, pulling their barking charges forward to join the procession.

Cameramen lined the platform. Phosphorus flashes exploded in the station. Almost blinded by the flashes, Lady Modi smiled at the press photographers. But the journalists were already running towards the ceremonial elephant, where the Nawab was mounting the steps that led to the golden howdah.

The struggling retriever was forced down on a cushion beside him. Inclining his head with regal dignity to the crowds on the platform, the Nawab waited for the visiting rulers to mount the silver howdahs behind his tusker while the bejewelled canines, in a welter of raised legs and bared teeth, were shoved unceremoniously into vehicles.

Jaya pulled Lady Modi into the curtained palanquin strapped to the purdah elephant. With a screech of relief Lady Modi sank onto the cushions. 'My God, darling. What a smell. Don't they ever air these things?' She pulled her hip flask from her handbag. The elephant rose to its feet, flinging her against the side of the howdah. She wiped furiously at the gin running down the embroidered skirt. 'Damn the Nawab and his stupid dogs. Why didn't he put us in a car? It's all very well laughing, darling, but do you realise this man has built three fully equipped hospitals for his dogs and none for his people? He should have been king of a dog kingdom. His eight hundred animals have fans to keep them cool in the summer and fireplaces for the winter. They have their own retainers who feed them from gold and silver dishes. But his subjects – who are only human beings – have nothing. Perhaps they should practise sitting on their hind legs and begging when he whistles. Might improve their lot.'

Raucous singing interrupted her tirade. Cheered by the sound of festivity, the mercurial Lady Modi opened the curtains again. Rose petals fell on her hands. 'Oh, darling. Dancing girls. And all the buildings have been outlined in fairy lights. Look at the crowds. They obviously love the Nawab for being so mad.'

Firecrackers exploded in front of the elephant. The animal veered to one side, rocking the howdah. The experience so unsettled Lady Modi that she lay back on the silk cushions silently sucking at her hip flask as the elephant plodded through the narrow streets.

A blaze of lights lit up the curtains of the howdah as the long line of elephants swayed into the palace. The attending rulers dismounted to enter the Durbar Hall, ceremonial swords held against the dull gold of their brocade tunics.

Eunuchs escorted Jaya and Lady Modi into the harem enclosure, where the light shining through the carved walls threw prismatic patterns on the veils of the sequestered ladies. Jaya looked through the stone apertures. In the arched doorways, kennel boys pulled at the leashes of the bridegroom's companions, and barking shook the glass prisms of the chandeliers until they hit against each other. Under the main chandelier a figure shrouded in a heavy red-and-gold veil moved restlessly on a cushion.

Flashbulbs popped, their sudden incandescence rendering the richly patterned carpets dingy for a moment as the photographers pushed against each other for a better view of the golden retriever entering the Durbar Hall. A thin court minister struggled to control the overexcited animal straining at the lead.

The marriage of the two dogs, Roshanara, veiled and covered in gems, to Bobby, shivering in his wet silk pyjamas, was conducted with all the ceremony that would have accompanied the marriage of a royal princess. A court minister solemnly read out a list of the wealth Roshanara was bringing to the marriage. When the last item, a golden palanquin, was described, he leaned over to the bridegroom and warned that all these items would be returned to the bride if he dared to terminate the marriage. The golden retriever wagged his tail at the admonishment.

At the end of the ceremony, the visiting rulers circled the dogs with gold coins, and their aides placed gifts in a large basket. The Nawab raised an eyebrow in pleasure as jewel cases piled up in the basket.

The doors of the Durbar Hall were flung open and excited subjects rushed into the room. The Nawab sat impassively on his gaddi watching queues of men circle the heads of the dogs with money, before flipping it onto the carpets until paper currency covered the floor like confetti.

The strains of Mendelssohn's wedding march were faintly audible over the barking of dogs being dragged away to be fed. The Nawab rose to his feet. Pulled by their attendant ministers, the bride and bridegroom entered the banquet hall for the nuptial dinner.

An enormous rectangular table for the two hundred guests dominated the banquet hall. In the centre of the rectangle, dancing girls sang and danced for the dogs.

The Nawab sat on a gold chair between the newly married couple. High on her haunches on a velvet cushion, the bitch stared lugubriously at her master through the gauze veil sliding down her left ear. Each time her veil slipped beneath her head the Nawab adjusted it, as if fearful for a daughter's reputation. The golden retriever ignored the guests and whirling dancing girls to wolf the food on the thali in front of him, raising his head only once, to bark when an aide entered the room and bowed by Maharajah Pratap's chair.

As the rulers were leaving the banquet hall, Maharajah Pratap thrust a telegram into Jaya's hand, and Lady Modi craned over Jaya's shoulder.

'NATIONALISTS SUPPORTING REFORMISTS WITH FOLLOWING RESOLUTION. QUOTE. THIS CONGRESS URGES ON THE RULING PRINCES OF THE INDIAN STATES TO ENACT LAWS GUARANTEEING ELEMENTARY AND FUNDAMENTAL RIGHTS OF CITIZENSHIP, SUCH AS RIGHTS OF ASSOCIATION, FREE SPEECH, FREE PRESS AND SECURITY OF PERSON AND PROPERTY. THIS CONGRESS ASSURES THE PEOPLE OF THE INDIAN STATES OF ITS SUPPORT IN THEIR LEGITIMATE AND PEACEFUL STRUGGLE FOR THE ATTAINMENT OF FULL RESPONSIBLE GOVERNMENT. END QUOTE. REQUEST YOUR URGENT PRESENCE IN DELHI TO COUNTER POSSIBLE THREAT TO OUR THRONES. PATIALA, BIKANER, ALWAR.'

Lady Modi's cigarette holder tapped the paper. 'Thank God the Viceroy declined his invitation to the wedding, darling. That would have been altogether too much for the nationalists.'

44

'WHOLE DAMN CITY was to have been white marble like the Taj Mahal, until the money was siphoned off for the War,' Maharajah Pratap observed as the car pulled into the wide avenues of the new capital of British India. 'But I see that even without the marble, the British are raising quite an imposing city by taxing us further.'

Jaya looked at the black goats stretching to reach saplings protected by barbed wire, unable to understand why her husband thought the new capital of the British Raj imposing.

New Delhi had none of the solidity and grandeur of Calcutta, the old capital. Barebacked masons squatted on the swell of the hill, mortaring slabs of red sandstone to the walls of the Imperial Offices, sweat rolling off their backs despite the winter cold of February.

An overloaded truck rumbled down the avenue. A burly Sikh contractor leaned through the window, shouting instructions to the village women hoisting cane baskets filled with bricks onto the veils knotted on their heads, hardly able to make himself heard above the yells of half-naked children running in and out between the concrete pipes lying at haphazard angles on the roadside.

A group of men wearing white Gandhi caps and carrying black flags appeared at the bend of the road. The truck braked. The impatient contractor jumped down, and the demonstrators struggled to keep their banners from falling onto his head, as Jaya read the slogans on the banners.

GIVE INDIA DOMINION STATUS NOW
SELF-GOVERNMENT FOR INDIA

'The nationalists expected that Indians would be invited to sit on the Simon Commission which will decide whether British India is ready for self-government,' Sir Akbar explained from the front seat. 'But the Empire has chosen to appoint only Englishmen. And the Indian rulers have asked a British lawyer to speak for them before the Butler Commission, hoping that the voice of Sir Leslie Scott will carry the weight no Indian ruler's voice seems to do.'

The chauffeur steered the Rolls-Royce past the demonstrators into an avenue lined with the town establishments built by the Indian kings. Flags hung limply above Hyderabad House, Jaipur House, Alwar House, Kashmir House, Bikaner House, Patiala House, indicating the presence of those rulers in Delhi.

Maharajah Pratap laughed. 'My fellow princes are clearly unnerved by the nationalist resolution to support the Reformists. I can't recall when so many of us graced the Chamber of Princes.'

'They should be, hukam. Until now, the Reformists were only frustrated individuals in separate kingdoms, but with the support of the nationalists, the Reformists will become a continent-wide movement, and the British Empire will be forced to listen to their demands.'

The car eased through the gates of Sirpur House. The pillared verandah of the three-storey mansion was crowded with subjects waiting to petition the ruler.

Two newspaper editors from Sirpur pushed their way past the crowd. 'Hukam, have you heard the news? The Simon Commission has been met with black flags and riots in Bombay. British houses have been burned down. The police fired on the demonstrators. People were killed, many more injured.'

'Why have white men been sent to decide whether we are competent to govern ourselves?' shouted a young journalist from Sirpur. 'Are we prisoners, on trial for the right to be free?'

'Do you see how India is changing, hukam?' Sir Akbar whispered as he opened Jaya's door. 'Our newspapermen do not feel insulted that their ruler must appear in front of the Butler Commission to plead for the rights he was guaranteed by treaty. They only see themselves as Indians, insulted by the white skins of the Simon Commission. The Maharajah should pay some heed to the power of the Reformists, now that the nationalists are supporting them.'

The gardeners crowded around Jaya with garlands. Over their shoulders she saw the Maharajah of Bikaner's private secretary follow her husband onto the verandah. The Prime Minister hurried after them, afraid the ruler might send an irresponsible message to the Chamber of Princes. Jaya quickened her own pace when she heard the urgency in the private secretary's voice.

'For the first time, the senior nationalists wish to initiate a public dialogue with royal India. The Committee of the Chamber of Princes – the maharajahs of Bikaner, Patiala, Alwar – wish to call on you as soon as possible, hukam. They feel we must placate the nationalists before the Reformists spread more disaffection in the kingdoms.'

'Then the sooner we all meet, the better, I suppose. Tell Their Highnesses I am available to them immediately.' Looking bored, Maharajah Pratap followed Jaya into the drawing room.

Polo trophies glistened in the glass cabinets under the full-length portraits of the Sirpur rulers hanging on the walls. A painting of Maharajah Victor astride his favourite polo pony dominated the wall above the fireplace. Maharajah Pratap grabbed a whisky and soda and raised his glass to the portrait. 'We should have stayed in Junagadh, Victor. Dog eats dog in the British Empire. In Junagadh, dogs only marry each other.'

Through the open door Jaya saw Chandni descending the staircase with Prince Arjun. The baby's wordless chuckles echoed in the marble hallway, and a fat wrist tied with a black thread to ward off the evil eye waved in the air. Forgetting her dignity, Jaya ran up the steps.

Folding the child in her embrace, Jaya entered the puja room to lay gold coins and flowers at the feet of the small idol of the Goddess. The baby swept the bright marigolds to the ground. Clutching at her necklace, he gurgled, 'Amma,' and Jaya felt her limbs grow weak with tenderness, hearing her son call her mother for the first time.

Jaya collected the coins to distribute to the maidservants waiting at the doorway of the puja room. The baby pulled a shining coin free of her hand.

Chandni tried to open the small fist, crooning. 'Ganga/Jumna, give it to me. Be a good child, Ganga/Jumna.' The baby's mouth opened in laughter and he nestled against Jaya's body, the bright sun lighting his face. 'We call our little ruler Ganga/Jumna, hukam. See how his eyes change like the holy rivers of India, the Ganga and the Jumna.'

Jaya looked down. Prince Arjun's eyes were lightening and darkening in the sunlight, sometimes a restless black like his father's eyes, sometimes a still green like her own.

Jaya hugged the small body. In her rooms, she played with the son she had not seen for weeks, rolling the ivory globes inlaid with scenes of war along the marble floor.

Above the baby's gurgling she heard impatient voices carrying up the staircase. Handing Prince Arjun to Chandni, Jaya ran down the stairs and edged into the drawing room.

The agitated rulers ignored her. Patiala's large frame dwarfed her husband. 'The nationalists are prepared to drop their support for the Reformists if we agree to certain reforms and join them in a Federation. The Empire has promised to grant the nationalists self-government if they succeed in creating a Federation between royal India and British India.'

Maharajah Bikaner pulled at his white moustache with grave deliberation. 'We have never been in such a powerful position before. We can seize the initiative if only we have the will.'

'Do you understand what Federation would mean, Pratap?' Jaya noticed that unlike the last time she had seen Alwar, standing on the dais in Buckingham Palace when she was being presented to the King Emperor of England, today he was not wearing his crown of divinity. 'No British Residents spying on us in our own kingdoms. No breaking of treaties. No preferential tariffs so that British goods can sell more easily in our kingdoms. We, the monarchs of India, are even prepared to form a political party, and join hands with every moderate nationalist leader.'

Maharajah Pratap grimaced in disgust at Alwar's passion. 'A political party, Your Highness? That is just a polite name for a trade union. Are you seriously asking the kings of India to behave like coal miners?'

'A trade union, a political party – what does the name matter if we achieve our ends?' Maharajah Bikaner demanded. 'At the moment we have a single goal: to destroy the Reformists. We have resolved in the Chamber to have a free press. An independent judiciary. A clear-cut division between our own expenses and the state treasury. Without such changes, the nationalists will never control the excesses of the Reformists.'

Behind Jaya, an aide whispered that a maharani was waiting to meet the heir to the Sirpur throne.

Jaya reluctantly departed to greet her visitor, the first in a succession of maharanis to call on her.

Each call followed the same pattern. Prince Arjun was brought by the maidservants to be displayed to the visiting maharani. Between compliments the more devout maharanis recited mantras for the child's protection, then inquired after his horoscope and which planets had been in the ascendant at the time of the birth. Jaya knew these mothers were already planning alliances between their infant daughters and the future Maharajah of Sirpur.

The child was taken away by the bowing maidservants. The ladies nibbled on their savoury pastries and, with every appearance of indifference, interrogated Jaya as to Maharajah Pratap's stand on the reforms promised by the Chamber of Princes.

Jaya would answer diffidently, uncertain whether her husband was taking the momentum of national events seriously, since he spent his days at the Flying Club, circling Delhi in his aircraft.

Maharajah Pratap made a brief appearance at the puja to celebrate Prince Arjun's first birthday, but when he saw the maharanis dismounting from their cars, followed by royal infants held in maidservants' arms, for the birthday feast, he left abruptly.

As the servants circulated among the guests with iced sherbets, Jaya overheard one visiting maharani announce to another, 'We have always had British Residents in our country. Then last year the Empire sent an Indian official. Well, hukam, they say the newly converted Muslim takes the name of Allah a hundred times more frequently than the born Muslim. This Indian Resident inquires into every aspect of my husband's government, demanding to see files that are none of his business. He even reports on how much my husband spends on his wives.'

A flutter of apprehension passed through Jaya. An Indian Resident would be appalled by the revenues being poured by her husband into an airline that could not aid Sirpur in any way, beyond convincing the British Empire that its ruler was progressive.

For months Sir Akbar had been stressing the need to find a new Resident sympathetic to Sirpur. Each time, Maharajah Pratap put the file aside as soon as Sir Akbar left the study.

As the days passed and still the Maharajah did not pursue the

313

matter of the new Resident, Sir Akbar tried to push the issue to a conclusion by inviting Major Osborne to Sirpur House.

Jaya was not surprised when an embarrassed aide bowed outside her chambers. 'Major Osborne has arrived, hukam. I telephoned the Flying Club. Apparently His Highness is up in his aeroplane and they do not know when he will return.'

Major Osborne was standing at the fireplace, examining the portrait of Maharajah Victor. At the aide's cough he turned and strode towards Jaya, his hand outstretched. 'I was admiring Maharajah Victor's mount. The Sirpur brothers have always been such fine judges of horseflesh.'

Jaya was surprised at the tremor of excitement that passed through her when the Angrez boy took her hand in his. She lowered her eyes, afraid he could still read her mind as he had done when they were children. 'My husband has been unavoidably detained, James-sahib. He asked me to make his apologies and wondered if he might arrange another meeting.'

'I'm afraid that's impossible, Bai-sa. I leave for Bombay tomorrow to prepare for the Butler Commission meetings on the status of royal India.'

'His Highness wished me to emphasize how happy he would be if you were to succeed Sir Henry Conroy as the British Resident in Sirpur.'

'That's not up to me. The Political Office in Delhi makes those decisions, Bai-sa. And with Lord Irwin as the present Viceroy, the Political Office is taking the new appointments very seriously.'

'Surely such important appointments are always taken seriously?'

Osborne walked to the window. 'They should be. After all, we represent the British Crown in a foreign country. Unfortunately, the envoys to the Indian kingdoms are the only British ambassadors who can hold their posts indefinitely, unless some scandal forces their removal. And yet a ruler's ignorance is often compounded by the ignorance of his Resident. The officers of the Indian Civil Service, who govern British India, are so highly trained they are called the heaven-born and are supposed to be the finest administrators in the world. But the men who represent the British Empire in the Indian kingdoms have no training in diplomacy or administration, although they exert as much power as the ruler himself – perhaps even more, since they can recommend a ruler's abdication.'

Jaya heard the shock in his voice, as if he were still surprised to discover those truths which had governed her whole life, and she wished she could see the Angrez boy's eyes.

'If the rulers who form the Committee of the Chamber of Princes can enforce reforms in the five hundred kingdoms governed by men less enlightened than themselves, there will at last be an Indian Federation.'

Jaya was astonished. 'You sound as if you support Federation, James-sahib.'

'Of course I do, Bai-sa. Many of us who love this great country want Federation, including the present Viceroy of India, Lord Irwin. He too is an enlightened man. Unfortunately, there are many unenlightened Englishmen in royal India, who know Federation means the end of their power. They may encourage the rulers to resist the reforms without which Federation will not be possible.'

Suddenly Jaya was overcome with an acute longing for the Englishman's presence in Sirpur. His clarity reminded her of the ambiguities that governed her own life, and she could feel her loneliness flooding into the room.

Trying to keep the desperation from her voice, she asked, 'Would you come to Sirpur if the Political Office appointed you, James-sahib?'

Osborne laid a hand on her shoulder, and Jaya felt herself being drawn into his steady gaze. 'How can you ask, Bai-sa? You know I would. Especially now that there is an heir to the most ancient throne in India. May I pay him my respects?'

He laughed as Chandni entered the room with Prince Arjun. 'I can see this child is going to be raised just like Tikka, Bai-sa. Carried everywhere by the maidservants, his feet never allowed to touch the ground until he can sit on a horse.'

Jaya placed the baby on the carpet. Prince Arjun began crawling towards Osborne's chair. He suddenly pulled himself upright and took three unsteady steps towards the Englishman, before falling in an awkward heap to the floor. The Englishman swept the child up before he could cry, and carried him to the window.

Jaya looked at the powerful arms of the Englishman around

315

the small round figure of her son, sunlight changing the colours of their eyes, and in a guilty corner of her mind she wondered what her life would have been, married to a man like James Osborne.

45

WHILE THE RULERS argued in the Chamber of Princes about implementing reforms in their kingdoms, Jaya wilfully absorbed herself in the pleasures of maternity, determined to forget the commissions with which the British Empire was adjusting its imperial power to the changing mood of Indians.

But Maharajah Pratap insisted she accompany him to the dinner meeting with the nationalists. 'I warn you, Maharani-sahib, it's going to be a dull evening. Not one of them has a sense of humour.'

Jaya remembered Mrs Roy's garden house and how the people her husband was dismissing as humourless had oppressed her with their very lightheartedness.

Sir Akbar leaned forward, his hand gripping the gold knob of his cane. 'I don't think the evening will call for humour, hukam. You will be meeting two of the most formidable men in British India, Sardar Patel and Mohammed Ali Jinnah.'

Maharajah Pratap raised a languid eyebrow. 'Should I be frightened, Prime Minister?'

'Not frightened, hukam. Wary. Sardar Patel, who speaks for the Indian National Congress, the major nationalist party, is known as the Iron Man of India. He does not threaten. He acts. As for Jinnah, the President of the Muslim League, he is reputed to have the most acute legal mind in the subcontinent. Unfortunately, that brilliant mind has been sharpened to a dangerous edge by bitterness.'

'Why is he bitter?'

Sir Akbar turned to Jaya, pleased by her curiosity. 'Jinnah was once President of the Indian National Congress, hukam. And a great president. Under his leadership, Hindus and Muslims briefly buried the religious enmities that divide our great subcontinent. When he was ousted from prominence by the ambitions of younger men, he left public life and practised law abroad. Now he has returned, as President of the Muslim League. With the brilliant and bitter Jinnah as spokesman for India's Muslims, the Indian National Congress will find it hard to ignore their demands.'

Maharajah Pratap was already bored. 'Let's get the damn thing over with,' he said, preceding Jaya into the car.

The car drove through the wide avenues of the new capital and entered the teeming streets of old Delhi. 'Sir Akbar fusses too much,' Maharajah Pratap remarked. 'We merely have to show the nationalists that we are not backward, and your presence at such an important meeting will prove I'm not one of those silly fools who get hitched to dancers and balloonists.'

Jaya huddled in her seat, frightened by her husband's nonchalant conviction that the nationalists would suspend their call for reforms in Sirpur simply because the ruler chose to be accompanied by his wife.

A large family house in the old city suggested that Maharajah Pratap was to be surprised by the conviviality of the evening. He flirted with the younger women of the household as they ushered him through the gentlemen's courtyard into a drawing room already filled with rulers and British Indian leaders.

The plump woman whom Jaya had met years ago in Mrs Roy's house in Calcutta broke from the circle. 'My dear child. This is a surprise. Were you brought here by your old tutor?'

Jaya blushed as Mrs Naidu's attention focused all eyes on her. There was laughter from the rulers that Sirpur's wife should be so well known to the Nightingale of India.

Jaya noticed that the only persons who did not join in the laughter were a dark man with a white shawl draped down one shoulder like a Roman toga, watching the exchanges from a corner, and a spare figure in an impeccably cut English suit, a monocle fixed in one eye, leaning against the fireplace.

Jinnah let the monocle drop, as if signalling an end to the banter. 'Now that we are all assembled, I have only one question. When will the rulers make a reality of their proposed reforms?'

318

'We have managed to pass a motion declaring we will pursue reforms,' Bikaner replied.

'Motions are mere lip service, Your Highness. Enforce your reforms, or the British will deny us freedom.'

'Give us time,' Patiala demanded.

'You have run out of time,' Jinnah announced coldly from the fireplace. 'History has already left you behind. We are all that stands between you and bloody revolution.'

For a moment, the imposing Sikh king and the austere Muslim lawyer stared at each other with undisguised hatred.

Through clenched jaws Patiala said, 'Mr Jinnah, you speak of history as if you had just discovered it, but we deal with its reality every day. In your India the Muslims and the Hindus have not yet come to terms. In royal India we must agree on five hundred different sets of historical fears, a fact ignored by the Reformists you so irresponsibly support.'

'Gentlemen, make no mistake,' the man in the togalike shawl cut into the argument, the implacability in his voice making Jaya understand why Sardar Patel was called the Iron Man of India. 'The royal states will be eliminated if you delay self-rule in India.'

At Patel's words the urbanity slipped even from Maharajah Pratap's features, and the tension in the room became feral. Faces appeared at the doorways, drawn by the raised voices.

'Gentlemen, gentlemen,' Sarojini Naidu lifted a plump hand with surprisingly delicate fingers. 'Remember we are only spokesmen for the aspirations of those we represent. Mr Jinnah speaks for India's fifty million Muslims. The rulers speak for a hundred million subjects of royal India. We speak for two hundred million Indians who embrace the idea of freedom unencumbered by religious loyalties. Whatever fears divide us, we share a common aspiration for liberty. Let us fight to have the British Empire accept an All India Federation in which we will jointly govern British and royal India.'

'The National Congress insists on elementary and fundamental rights of citizenship in royal India,' Sardar Patel repeated, 'before it can join a Federation with the princes.'

'The Muslim League demands those rights,' echoed Jinnah.

Although the two men had made identical demands, Jaya noticed they did not look at each other as they preceded the rulers from the room.

Maharajah Pratap was silent on the drive back to Sirpur House. Jaya was relieved that the meeting had shaken him from his indifference to political events.

Suddenly his mouth opened in a yawn. 'Just imagine. After all this, I still have to present myself in Bombay to the upstanding Englishmen of the Butler Commission. I think I'll go to Calcutta for a little interlude from the tedium of politics.'

Jaya castigated herself for having believed her husband could be impressed by the unforgiving leaders of British India, and she stared through the windows at the crowded bazaars of the old city, fearful that Maharajah Pratap's indifference would offend the stern sahibs of the Butler Commission, and endanger her son's future.

46

JAYA'S PLEASURE in watching Prince Arjun grow from a baby into a small boy, constantly escaping the maidservants to stagger down the corridors of the City Palace, was no longer enough to protect her from the events outside the kingdom.

In the mornings, while her son pulled at the cords of the mosquito net falling over the bed, Jaya studied the stridency of the Sirpur newspapers. Bold headlines announced the reforms the Indian rulers had promised their people in the Chamber of Princes. On the same front pages, with an obviousness that needed no editorial emphasis, other headlines reported that in numerous Indian kingdoms the voices demanding reform had been silenced by imprisonment or exile.

The Prime Minister returned to Sirpur but the ruler was not with him. At the Purdah Palace, Sir Akbar pulled his chair closer to the brocade screen and apprised the worried Dowager Maharani of the latest events.

'A British lawyer, Sir Leslie Scott, was hired to speak for the princes before the Butler Commission, hukam. Even with his advice and the urgings of the senior princes, it is clear that many rulers have no intention of implementing the proposed reforms.'

The Dowager Maharani spat into her spittoon. 'Forgive an old woman's ramblings, Prime Minister, but I am confused. Only eighty years ago the British Empire stole the power of our people and called it progress. Now they want to give that same power back to the people in the name of progress?'

Sir Akbar shook his head, forgetting that he could not be seen through the brocade curtain. 'The situation has passed beyond kings and empires, hukam. The Reformists have decided to take their war to the heart of the Empire. They intend to start a campaign in London.'

The Dowager Maharani's harsh voice carried through the curtain: 'Are the rulers of India going to join battle with a group of disgruntled subjects in full view of the British Empire, Prime Minister?'

'They have no option, hukam. The Reformists hope their campaign will force the Butler Commission to demand reforms in royal India. Maharajah Pratap is preparing to leave for London. The other rulers feel his popularity in England will be useful in this campaign.'

Hot breezes carried dust from the dry riverbed through the windows, and a brilliant sunset lit the faces of the Dowager Maharani and Sir Akbar, marking the lines on their faces like scars recording their too-frequent defeats in the defence of the kingdom.

Jaya stared at them, thinking of the ammunition the Reformists would take to London in their battle against the Indian kings.

What would the British people make of the stories of murdered courtesans, and kings fighting over the favours of dancing girls? Of the Maharajahs married to balloonists and flamenco dancers? These self-indulgent men could put her son's throne in jeopardy.

In the months that followed, the newspaper reports from London only increased her apprehension. On the inside pages Jaya found the dignified speeches made by the leaders of the Chamber of Princes.

At a crowded press conference, the Maharajah of Patiala had said: 'I ask whether there be not room within the wider confines of India for two sister polities, in one of which the democratic, and in the other the monarchic, principle is embodied. In my judgement, they can coexist and work together for the common good of India. To forget the persistent regionalism of our people which finds expression in the Indian states is an error which has spelled disaster for India in the past.'

Ignoring Patiala's statement, the front pages of the British newspapers chose to concentrate on his splendour.

On his arrival in England the Maharajah of Patiala took over
the entire fifth floor of the Savoy Hotel, comprising thirty-five
suites.

July 26. A special banquet was held in honour of the Indian Princes at Buckingham Palace. Among those present were the Maharajah of Kashmir, the central figure in the Mr A. blackmail case, and the Maharajah of Patiala, who is rumoured to spend £31,000 a year on his silk underwear.

Each time Jaya saw the lurid headlines that drowned the rulers' statements, she knew the Reformists were winning their war against royal India, and she was frightened that some extravagant act would draw the attention of the Reformists to Maharajah Pratap, as she had once been frightened that the actions of his brother, Maharajah Victor, would attract the disapproving notice of the Viceroy.

ON PRINCE ARJUN'S second birthday, the Dowager Maharani took her great-grandson to be anointed in the Kamini Temple. The little boy stood between the arrogant figure of the Raj Guru of Sirpur and the crippled body of the old Dowager, staring at the shaven-headed acolytes crowding the sanctum, the colour of his eyes changing from green to black in the light of the flickering clay lamps, as the priests chanted mantras for his long life.

But when the Dowager Maharani thrust her hand into the stone image of the Goddess, he ran to Jaya, hiding behind her legs from the old woman advancing on him, red liquid dripping from between her stiff fingers.

Jaya held him still until the Dowager had anointed him with the blessing of the Goddess. The thick red liquid dripped from his forehead onto his tear-stained cheeks. Jaya remembered the liquid dripping onto Cora Hart's photograph, staining the blue eyes crimson, and she was overcome with dread for her son, caught between the demands of the Reformists and the oppressive rituals of his ancient kingdom.

The summer months dragged on like a fever that would not break. The heat seemed to fog Jaya's mind. She stood on her balcony staring at the sandbanks of the fallen river, wondering if the Reformist campaign would render the emerald calm of the rice fields and the sluggish river illusory, like the pastoral backgrounds the court artists had painted in Balmer at the time of the Great War.

The abstractions of her fear gained harsh focus with Tiny Dungra's telegram, urging the need for her presence in London. 'PRATAP EXPERIENCING SERIOUS DIFFICULTIES WITH TRAVELLING COMPANION, ESMÉ

MOORE. BLACKMAIL INVOLVED. SUCH AN INDISCRETION COULD NOT HAVE HAPPENED AT A MORE INOPPORTUNE TIME.'

Jaya crushed the telegram between her hands, enraged that her husband had chosen to flaunt his half-breed mistress in London when he knew the eyes of the British Empire were on India's kings.

Dungra's message changed Jaya's perceptions of Sirpur. The restful rice fields now seemed a sinister green, the jungles bursting through the red mud symbolic of insatiable desires. She watched the muddy water moving past the white sandbanks and thought how it reflected the deceptions of Sirpur itself, its torpor only concealing its lust. In another few weeks, the monsoon rains would swell that trickle of water until it swallowed the city and the serene villages lining the riverbanks.

Lady Modi wrote from Bombay offering to sail to England with Jaya. At the bottom of the scented page was a postscript. *Suggest you first call on Madame Enid at 14 Cryer Street, Calcutta. You may learn more about the situation. Esmé Moore worked in her establishment before she became a dancer.*

47

THE GARDENERS were waiting under the oak trees of Sirpur House with their usual garlands, but no tuberoses cast reflections in the black marble hall of Sirpur House, the only indication of the suddenness of the Maharani's arrival in Calcutta.

Equerries followed Jaya up the stairs. 'We have sent a message to Cryer Street, hukam. You are expected there this afternoon.'

Jaya lay down on her bed, exhausted by the overpowering humidity. The gold and white apartments that had once represented freedom from the strictures of royal India no longer comforted her. Dusty sunlight filtered through the muslin curtains, and the cries of a distant spice vendor broke the gentle silence of late morning. 'Cumin, mustard, coriander. Seeds, leaves and powders,' the litany of names rose above the lawns as Jaya closed her eyes. But sunlight still seeped through her closed eyelids, and the high cry became menacing, as if warning that her son's future rested on her.

Jaya's long hair lay like a hot towel on her wet skin as the car drove down the crowded street to where Madame Enid's establishment turned wooden shutters to rickshaws and shouting pedestrians.

A fishmonger waved a dirty cloth at swarms of flies circling the prawns that lay on blocks of ice in front of him, trying to sell his goods before the fierce sun turned them into foul-smelling waste. He dropped his hands in surprise when he saw the unlikely figure dressed in a sari moving towards the entrance of the brothel, her head shaded by a lace parasol.

The smell of stale cigar smoke overwhelmed Madame Enid s shuttered salon. Motes of dust whirled through the air like moths disturbed by the unaccustomed activity of the afternoon as Madame Enid led Jaya to an ornate sofa covered with lace antimacassars.

A young girl, barefoot, her thin legs sticking awkwardly from under her dress, offered iced tea. Reaching for the glass, Jaya wondered if this child was being reared to the profession, like so many other girls born to parents who had, for a brief moment under noisy fans between damp sheets, halted the war of the races, and she averted her gaze from the black eyes staring longingly at her parasol.

In a voice still heavy with sleep, Madame Enid said, 'You must not be too angry with Esmé Moore, Your Highness. She has her dreams. They all do. Look at this child. Her mother was raped by an English overseer. The baby was bought by a Pathan pimp, and when it seemed she might grow up pretty, she was sold to me. Your husband is such a glamorous man. A ruler who treats my girls as though they were princesses. And sometimes they behave like princesses.' She whispered into the child's ear. The child nodded and ran from the room.

Minutes later a figure in a silk peignoir appeared at the doorway. Under the high cheekbones a deep cleft indented the finely boned chin. Small teeth bit the full lower lip in apprehension, but the tense muscles in the long neck could not disguise the elegance of the girl's carriage or distract from the shoulder blades sweeping out like wings below the straps of her dress. Madame Enid beckoned to her. The girl came as far as the piano, hiding behind a vase of dying bougainvillea blossoms.

'Velma, tell the Maharani why you have never let Maharajah Pratap touch you.'

The girl shook her head, her long chestnut hair sweeping in a circle around her slender shoulders.

'Come here, dearie,' Madame Enid insisted.

The slender figure advanced reluctantly. 'I always take care of him, Your Highness. Even when he is drunk, I sit by his bed, making sure no one disturbs his sleep.'

Madame Enid refused to let the subject drop. 'Tell the Maharani why you will have nothing to do with His Highness, Velma.' The girl glanced in fear at Jaya through long eyes, then turned and fled from the room.

Jaya's hands were slippery with perspiration. She wiped them on her sari. When she looked up, the girl was standing at the doorway again.

The girl walked towards Jaya, her eyes expressionless. 'The first time His Highness called for me, he was lying on the bed. These were on his feet.'

She thrust a pair of slippers in Jaya's face. A snake and elephant were embroidered on the black velvet. 'When I saw the Sirpur crest, I realized that your husband was my brother.'

The girl threw the slippers on the floor, and Jaya covered her mouth with the edge of her sari, trying not to vomit.

Madame Enid was describing how her girls watched their clients to learn manners which might equip them for the outside world, creating new identities for themselves. Jaya hardly heard the words, her eyes fixed on the ancient crest which the Sirpur ruler, aping his British masters, had chosen to wear not on his turban, but on his feet. She felt sick with shame that a whore had respected that crest more than the ruler himself.

'Esmé Moore wanted to be in films, but your husband persuaded her to become his mistress with the promise of marriage. Do you know what such a promise means to these children?'

Jaya swallowed the bile in her mouth, unable to take her eyes from the velvet slippers, wishing she had never had a son by the husband waiting in London. On her way out, she handed the child who had served tea her green parasol, ashamed when the child dipped in an awkward curtsy.

48

SALT WATER SMASHED against the concrete pilings as Jaya's car inched towards the docks, its windshield wipers helpless against the heavy monsoon downpour.

A steward preceded Jaya down the deck. Under the wooden awnings protecting the upper deck, Jaya huddled closer to the glass windows of the cardroom and saw a group of men in sombre, close-collared Indian jackets seated around a table.

Something crashed in Jaya's stateroom. The steward backed away as a dog with a diamond collar jumped on him.

'Scott-Ward! Get back here, you stupid animal!' Lady Modi appeared in the doorway. 'Darling, I hope you've brought some suitably funereal clothes. The entire Reformist committee is travelling to London with us, and there's nothing we can do about it. The *Hyderabad* is the last ship out of Bombay for weeks.'

She put her arm around Jaya's shoulder. 'I'm sorry about Pratap, darling. But don't worry. We'll work something out.'

'We'll have to, Bapsy. My husband thinks his connections with the British Crown will save him, no matter how irresponsibly he behaves.'

'That's the trouble with terribly good-looking men, darling. They become irresponsible because everyone spoils them so.'

The glass panes of the porthole rattled as the wind beat against them. Jaya stared at the dirty green waves heaving helplessly against the ship, feeling as if she had also become impervious to the waves of tradition that demanded only obedience from a wife. 'I do not care about my husband's looks. Only that his irresponsibility could disinherit my son.'

Lady Modi recoiled from the expression on Jaya's face. 'But, darling, Pratap is the Maharajah. You have no powers.'

'Not yet, Bapsy.'

'What do you mean, darling?' Suspicion and nervousness made Lady Modi's voice squeak.

Fury at the generations of silent complicity that had built edifices of respect around such men as her husband shattered Jaya's inhibitions. 'He can't touch his own wife until she is turned into a toy who no longer represents a woman. Or until he himself is so drunk he can no longer pass for a man. He shrinks from the sight of his wife giving breast to his son, but not from wearing his ancient crest on his feet to visit a brothel. Is this the conduct of a husband? Of a king?'

'Darling, I did my best to help you become acceptable to Pratap. I don't see what more you can do. After all, you have no rights beyond those he gives you.'

The blunt observation deflated Jaya's anger. She sat down on the bed, watching in defeat as the maidservants set up the small altar in the corner of the cabin, placing the Maharajah's portrait next to the idol of the Goddess.

The monsoon seas kept passengers in their cabins. Reacting badly to the tossing ship, Lady Modi did not see Jaya locked in her stateroom, staring at the portrait of her husband as she planned their encounter. Or know that with an aching sense of loneliness Jaya had decided that Lady Modi's counsel, limited to social proprieties, could no longer assist her in the battle against Maharajah Pratap.

It was not until the ship reached the becalmed waters of the Red Sea that Lady Modi felt well enough to lunch in the dining room. At the back of the room, the men Jaya had seen when she boarded ship were sitting in austere isolation, dressed in cotton dhotis and high-necked jackets, their socks incongruously visible above their leather shoes. A group of mem-sahibs watched them disapprovingly from the Captain's table.

Lady Modi sighed. 'I don't know what's happened to everyone. No one laughs anymore. And I'm sure those badly dressed people over there have never had any fun in their whole lives.'

Jaya turned to examine the insignificant men who threatened the kings of India. A familiar figure, his shoulders draped in a white shawl, had joined them.

Lady Modi squealed in delight. 'Darling, it's Arun Roy. Did you arrange this in Calcutta?' She waved her cigarette holder to attract the lawyer's attention, and Jaya lowered her head in embarrassment as he approached the table. 'Arun, darling, what are you doing with those awful people?'

'Those are the best legal minds in India, Bapsy. Hired by the Reformists to wage their campaign in London.'

Lady Modi pursed her lips in disapproval. 'If you can call gutter gossip a campaign.'

'Is an unwholesome interest in the rulers' private lives worthy of the men who want to be the leaders of India?' Jaya demanded.

As always, Arun Roy's mouth lifted in a smile when he addressed her. 'The scandals are being used to illustrate how India's rulers abuse their power while their subjects suffer in silence. You should know that, Bai-sa. After all, you attended the wedding of a dog in Junagadh. Do you know what the Viceroy said when he visited Junagadh a few weeks ago? "All power should rightly be accompanied by a sense of responsibilities." '

'There are a lot of Indian rulers who don't abuse their power, and do have a sense of responsibility,' Lady Modi insisted. 'The Maharajahs of Jodhpur and Jaipur, for instance.'

'Do you know how many slaves there are in Jodhpur, Bapsy?'

'Slaves?' Lady Modi shrieked. 'There aren't even slaves in America anymore.'

'On the contrary, in those bastions of Rajput chivalry where our beautiful Bai-sa was born, whole communities are bought and sold like animals – the Darogas, the Chakars, the Huzuris, the Chelas, the Golas.' Jaya was reminded of Mrs Roy's eyes, so unforgiving behind her rimless spectacles, as Lady Modi fumbled with her champagne glass, intimidated by Arun Roy's passion. 'The men sitting at that table tried to organize an antislavery movement in royal India. They were treated as criminals by the Indian kings. And the great British Empire called them seditious. But frankly, the slaves are only an extreme example of the conditions under which everyone in the Indian kingdoms lives – unprotected by laws, subject to their rulers' whims.'

'That is not true,' Jaya argued.

'You know it is, Bai-sa. Do men like your husband really think the British Empire will last forever, to protect them from the anger of their people?'

As he walked back to his companions, Lady Modi whispered ruefully, 'Politics just ruins everything. It's still a full week before we reach London. We could have had such an amusing time.'

Unable to endure Lady Modi's observations any longer, Jaya excused herself from the dining room and went out onto the deck.

The thought of the best legal minds in India engaged in battle against her husband and the sight of the grey-green waves splashing against the ship turned her stomach queasy. She gripped the wooden railing for support.

A hand closed on her elbow. 'Are you all right, Bai-sa?'

She nodded weakly.

'Don't look at the water, Bai-sa. In this heat it makes the head swim.'

But Jaya was afraid to turn and face the lawyer's probing eyes, as she had once done on the dark lawn of Mrs Roy's house, with the fog rolling over the heads of the marble statues and the raga echoing from the Music Room.

Arun Roy put his arm around her. 'I know why you are going to London, Bai-sa.' He tightened his grip, and she could not stop her body from trembling under his fingers. 'Your husband's situation is an open scandal to those who follow such matters in British India.'

This time Jaya could not control her tears. Arun Roy stroked her long hair as her tears splashed off the wooden railing into the swirling water below. 'You were so fearless in the jungle, Bai-sa. Galloping on a wounded boar with a lance almost too large for your hand to hold. You are only in another, more unpleasant jungle. Don't lose your nerve now.'

She stepped back in shame and he walked away, calling over his shoulder, 'But I hope we find ourselves in the real jungle again, Bai-sa. Nature is less treacherous than men.'

49

When the Sirpur aides bowed Jaya into the rooms at the Ritz Hotel, Maharajah Pratap was leaning against the French windows that opened onto Green Park. Jaya saw his expression, and her anger was mixed with regret. Anxiety did not sit well on her husband's handsome face.

She joined him at the windows, silently watching the ladies walking in the park, umbrellas held above their heads to protect their complexions from the hot July sunshine.

The Maharajah tapped his glass against the windowpane, as if continuing a conversation. 'Turning down fifty thousand pounds is quite a gamble for someone like Esmé Moore, but the Viceroy can't invoke his ban on her, and she knows it. After all, I can have as many wives as I want, and since she is an Indian, her children will have a claim on the Sirpur throne.'

Jaya remembered the child staring at her parasol and felt a guilty admiration for the dancer. 'What possible pressure can she bring on you to marry you, hukam?'

The Maharajah tossed back his drink and collapsed, coughing, into an armchair, still elegant against the shiny chintz. 'Breach of promise, my dear. Photographs, letters proving she broke her engagement to a wealthy Iraqi Jew because I promised marriage. She has me over a barrel. And she could not have picked a more perfect time to create a scandal. The Viceroy of India himself is on his way to celebrate his father's ninetieth birthday. You know what a Christian Lord bloody Irwin is. I'll probably be forced to abdicate.

I wish old Queen Victoria were still alive. At least you knew where you were with her.'

The top of the decanter fell from his hand as he refilled his glass with whisky. Slopping the liquid on the floor, he moved unsteadily towards his wife. 'What am I going to do? Bikaner and Patiala won't let me attend any meetings until this matter is resolved. I wish the bloody whore would drop dead.'

Jaya backed away from the slanting eyes bloodshot with alcohol and self-pity, astonished that she had ever feared the predator in her husband. This was a spoiled child, dependent on an empire that had conspired to keep him infantile. 'Would you like me to take the matter in hand, hukam?'

'What could you do?'

'Perhaps as a woman I might find some bargaining position.'

Hope gleamed in the bloodshot eyes, and he pulled clumsily at her sari. Whisky soaked the thin silk as his lips moved down her throat to her breasts. She pushed him away, fighting back the waves of disgust that threatened to overcome her self-control. 'There is a price for my services, hukam.'

Sunlight lit his dishevelled hair as he stumbled to the cocktail cabinet. By the time he turned around, he had recovered his composure. 'I see the worm has turned. You were always such a dutiful little Indian wife, constantly doing pujas for my long life.' He lifted his glass to his mouth. 'So what is the price of your husband's honour, my dear?'

'I wish to be named Regent Maharani of Sirpur, in the event of anything happening to you, until Arjun is of an age to take the throne.'

'Power. Of course.' There was genuine delight in Maharajah Pratap's laughter. 'Your price would have to be power.'

Jaya was unbalanced by the accuracy of his perception. After a lifetime as power's victim she wanted to be its executor, and she could taste the longing, even as she remembered that her husband was a fit and active man who would be reigning long after their son became an adult.

'God willing, nothing will happen, hukam.' She was unable to keep the bitterness out of her voice. 'But if it should, I do not think even the kindest British Resident's sympathies will extend to protecting a child against the Reformists or the interests of the Empire.'

333

Maharajah Pratap looked bored. 'We already know how kind the next Resident will be. Sir Akbar sent me a telegram last week. Major James Osborne has been appointed British Resident to Sirpur.' He gave her a knowing smile. 'You seem to manage your life so much better than I do, my dear.'

As JAYA waited impatiently for Esmé Moore to arrive in a London filled with Indians of different political persuasions, she studied the propaganda war between the Indian kings and the Reformists.

The Maharajah of Patiala was the main spokesman for royal India, legends of his sexual prowess and lavish generosity, his skills as a polo player and cricketer and shot, circulating throughout London. Over and over again, Bhupinder the Magnificent had declared in town halls and drawing rooms and board chambers that the Reformists and the British press were fabricating stories too fantastic to merit denial.

Jaya could visualize Patiala entering the crowded assembly rooms, his turban crowning his towering frame, flanked by his equally impressive Sikh nobles, to plead with the genteel British men and women who could influence his future by the power they could exert upon their own government.

In spite of Patiala's appeals, the flood of rumours about the excesses of the rulers was reaching dangerous proportions, and Jaya was terrified that Esmé Moore might sell her story to sensation-hungry journalists seeking to divert their countrymen's attention from the gloom of Britain's economic situation.

When Maharajah Pratap informed her that Esmé Moore had decided to go directly to New York, Jaya set sail for America, anxious to conclude her negotiations and return to London, where the fight for the future of royal India was being conducted in deadly earnest.

The glittering city, with its high buildings, only increased her restlessness. While she waited to be contacted by Esmé Moore, Tiny Dungra was often her escort as oversolicitous friends insisted on showing Jaya the night life and speakeasies of Prohibition New York.

Dungra generated the required excitement as they waited outside innocuous-looking doors to be stared at by unseen figures before being admitted to scenes of frenzied dancing and bourbon drunk from coffee cups. Sometimes Tiny Dungra whispered in Jaya's ear that she was not playing her part correctly. Then, ignoring the eyes that followed her sari, Jaya danced with self-conscious stiffness between the gyrating blondes in beaded, fringed dresses.

In the suite at the Waldorf-Astoria Hotel, Chandni had made friends with the chambermaids. One afternoon, while the noise of New York traffic echoed from the street twenty floors below, Chandni asked shyly if Jaya would consent to meet a black chambermaid eager to speak to a real maharani.

The black girl curtsied. 'I brought you a gift, ma'am. A souvenir of America. It's a book just been written by a Harlem writer called *The Dark Princess*. Shows how all us coloureds, here in America and you in India, got to fight to make the white folks give us our rights.'

Jaya lay on her bed, gravely studying the plot of *The Dark Princess*. An Indian princess had conceived a child out of wedlock with a Negro. When the infant was old enough to assume his ruling powers as a maharajah, the Indian princess married her Negro lover and together they founded a worldwide organisation to oppose imperialism. Jaya laughed out loud at the ominous name of their organisation – the Great Council of the Darker People – but there was bitterness in her laughter. The black flags with which British India had greeted the all-white members of the Simon Commission; the Maharajah of Patiala wooing the English men and women who could influence the Butler Commission to allow him to rule a kingdom that was legitimately his; even her own meeting with her husband's mistress, these humiliations had all been necessitated by imperial ambition.

The telephone rang. Jaya picked up the receiver. In the long silence she knew it was Esmé Moore even before the voice said hesitantly, 'I didn't want to involve you in this, Your Highness.'

Jaya was unable to keep the pain out of her voice. 'I am involved. When can we meet, Miss Moore?'

'I could come now, Your Highness.'

Jaya replaced the receiver, her heart thudding against her rib cage.

Giggling like schoolgirls, the two maids appeared in the doorway. Chandni dropped in an awkward curtsy, while her Negro friend attempted a salaam. 'The Maharajah of Dungra is asking to be announced.'

Relief swamped Jaya. Tiny Dungra would be present when she talked with Esmé Moore. She knew she could depend on Dungra's sophistication and on the passionate sense of duty which made him despise Maharajah Pratap's caprice.

Dungra picked at the hors-d'oeuvre spread on a silver platter as Jaya informed him of her pact with her husband. 'He has promised to make me Regent Maharani of Sirpur if I can stop Esmé Moore from blackmailing him into marriage.'

The large eyes sparkled with amusement. 'I congratulate you on striking such a good bargain, Bai-sa. Your doorbell is ringing. I shall wait inside until you and Miss Moore get acquainted.'

Jaya's hands were wet with perspiration as she opened the door to the elegant but unmistakably half-Indian girl standing in the hall, smiling under her sweeping hat.

Impressed by the dancer's self-possession, Jaya led her to a couch. The girl made pleasant small talk about the weather. Then suddenly, and without any attempt to disguise her loss of dignity, she said, 'He offers me money, Your Highness. What will I do with his money? Set up a brothel?'

'But money will make you independent.'

'If I became his wife I would have more than money. I would have rights.'

Jaya remembered her father's hand crashing down on the clay soldiers that covered the billiard table, and his anguished cry, 'What remains of the four arms of kingship but *Bhed* – the arm of the mistress?' But she knew the fragile creature in the modish clothes would not understand that a kingdom like Sirpur subscribed neither to the old laws nor to the new realities.

'You are wrong, Miss Moore. If I had rights, I would not be talking to you now.'

'I don't want to harm your husband. But I want to wipe out my past. And he promised to marry me.'

'Do you want a family?'

'No, no!' The girl was annoyed at Jaya's incomprehension. 'I don't really want to be a wife. I want to be in films. I know I can be a big star.'

Jaya rose to her feet. 'I have a friend who may be able to help you. In exchange for his assistance, you must return everything my husband gave you.'

'My clothes and jewels?'

'Of course not, Miss Moore. Those are gifts from my husband to you. I was talking about his letters and photographs.'

Tiny Dungra entered the room. Settling his ample form on the sofa, he patted Esmé Moore's knee in an avuncular fashion. 'Fame, Miss Moore. Sometimes a blessing, sometimes a curse. But since you hanker for it, what terms would you consider adequate? A screen test? A small part in a film, to begin with?'

Greed coarsened the girl's pretty features. 'I need something to live on, too. I'm just a poor girl trying to survive on her wits.'

'And doing very well at it, my dear,' Tiny said comfortingly. 'Shall we say an allowance while you are making your way in Hollywood?'

'I don't want anyone to know about Calcutta and Madame Enid. At least three other girls from the Calcutta houses are film stars in Hollywood today. I want to be like them.'

The dancer left with assurances that she would be contacted the following day, and Dungra extracted a sheaf of papers from his case. 'This is going to be an expensive business, Bai-sa. But I suggest you cover the costs yourself, to ensure that Pratap keeps his word about your regency. Actually, it's happened at rather a fortunate time. I was going to liquidate some of your American holdings anyway.'

He handed Jaya a paper for her signature. 'There is a sort of madness here. The stock market is like a bazaar without goods, only dreams. The sale of your land in Florida should cover the cost of Miss Moore's ambitions.'

Jaya returned the signed document.

'Now these, Bai-sa. I think we'll expand your interests in the film industry.'

Jaya looked up in surprise.

'But you have investments in Hollywood, Bai-sa. How else could I have offered Miss Moore a screen test?'

Before departing for Hollywood, the triumphant dancer handed Jaya all of Maharajah Pratap's letters and photographs as though eager to be rid of her past.

Chandni was almost hysterical with relief to learn they were sailing back to London.

'One month we have been here, hukam. Has my skin got darker from being with all my hubshi friends? They say it fubs off, all that black.'

THE DRAWING ROOM of Maharajah Pratap's hotel suite was crowded with rulers. Patiala rose to greet Dungra. 'The Butler Report has just been released. The British have given us nothing, Tiny.'

Jaya folded her hands to a South Indian king as she moved towards her rooms. He ignored her, anger contorting his aquiline face. 'The British Empire has indirectly invited the Reformists to launch agitations in our countries.'

Angry voices carried through the closed doors of Jaya's bedroom.

'England will destroy us from within. After all, how much can it cost the greatest empire on earth to finance Reformist uprisings in our kingdoms?'

'Now Britain will disregard our treaties, claiming it is the popular will of our people.'

Jaya was knocked backwards as the door was pushed open. Maharajah Pratap entered the room. 'Have you got what I want?'

Jaya handed her husband her jewellery case. He arched an eyebrow in feigned distress as he rifled through the papers inside the case. 'I hope you didn't look at the photographs, my dear, but boys will be boys.'

He pulled something from his pocket and waved it in the air. Jaya recognized the Viceregal seal on the heavy envelope. Laughing, he threw the envelope on the bed and left the room.

Jaya sat on the bed, holding the document that recognized her as Regent Maharani of Sirpur. She had expected to be overjoyed at her victory, but the furious voices in the other room reminded her of her own inexperience.

When the strongest kings in India were impotent before the might of the British Empire and the ambitions of the Reformists, how would she hold a kingdom for her son if anything happened to her husband?

On the return voyage to India, Jaya prayed for Maharajah Pratap's long life with more fervour than she had done since she first entered Sirpur as his bride, wishing she could wipe out the last months and become once again an ignored wife.

338

Each time she went onto the upper deck she saw groups of Indians deep in discussion about the Butler Report. Whenever a nationalist leader appeared, he became the focus of attention, as though it were already clear where India's future lay, and she huddled into her deck chair, afraid that an accident of destiny could leave her struggling to preserve her son's throne from the shifting realities of India.

Arun Roy stopped at the side of her deck chair.

'Your Reformist friends must be gloating over their victory, after the Butler Committee's report,' Jaya said bitterly.

He smiled down at her. 'Not at all, Bai-sa. Do you think the British Empire gives anything away? We are all going back empty-handed. The Reformists will be the means by which the Empire foments disaffection, but after the Reform movement succeeds, the kingdoms will not be returned to the people.'

'Where will the kingdoms go?'

'They will be annexed by the Empire, Bai-sa. No more Balmer, no more Sirpur. Just more pink patches added to the map of British India. I warned you, this is an unpleasant and ugly jungle.'

50

IN SIRPUR, mythology drew its customary curtain over history. During the Divali celebrations, the priests held daily readings from the *Mahabharata* at the Kamini Temple, and the names of the Sirpur kings were recited to the satisfaction of every citizen present.

The discreet resolution of his dilemma with Esmé Moore had improved the Maharajah's spirits beyond recognition. In the mornings, from her puja room, Jaya watched the three-year-old Prince Arjun walking next to his father, his head barely reaching the top of his father's shining riding boots. While the Maharajah galloped down the polo field, Prince Arjun was led around the field on a pony by the old groom who had taught the ruler to ride. An hour later the child returned to the palace, and Jaya knew her husband had gone to the airfield to test one of his new planes.

Sir Henry Conroy set sail for England, and the Maharajah's good humour improved further. Now Jaya often found him in his study with Prince Arjun on his knee, telling the child stories about cavalry charges and the tank battle at Cambrai.

But the Prime Minister's relief at James Osborne's imminent arrival was mixed with anxiety, and he questioned Jaya about the Englishman's views on India.

'I have known Major Osborne since I was a child, Sir Akbar,' Jaya reassured him. 'I never found him less than sympathetic to Indians.'

'That was the high noon of empire, hukam. When you were a child, no Indian dared object that white men determined his fate. Today, British India is still shaking from the demonstrations against the Simon Commission. And if Major Osborne were to hear how some of the rulers talk about raising armies against the British Raj . . .'

'Mutiny?' Jaya covered her mouth with her hands, almost afraid to speak the word.

'Yes, Maharani-sahib. The Butler Commission's report was a thinly disguised threat to royal India, and some rulers want to strike at the Empire now, when it is weak. They believe a war would eliminate both the British Raj and the Reformists.'

'Has my husband taken part in these discussions?'

Sir Akbar nodded, and Jaya realised that all the time she had been negotiating to win the position of Regent Maharani for herself, the months when she had felt nothing but contempt for her husband, he had been engaged in plots so dangerous that her own designs to protect her son's future were rendered meaningless. 'They are even corresponding with each other. The Maharajah is attracted by the danger, but he would never fight the Empire. He is too much the Anglophile. Still, discovery of our secret files would certainly expose the Maharajah to the charge of sedition.'

At Jaya's gasp of fear, his face softened. 'These plots will never amount to anything, hukam. If the Indian kings were capable of acting in a concerted manner, they would not be in their present predicament. Instead of hankering after the glories of the battlefield, they should enact reforms and create a Federation.'

'What if the British Raj learns of my husband's involvement? What if they get copies of his correspondence?'

'That can never happen, hukam,' the Prime Minister permitted himself a small smile. 'Unless Britain declares war on Sirpur. Our most secret files are kept in the Purdah Palace. Even the British Empire cannot enter the harems of royal India.'

IN JANUARY James Osborne presented his credentials as Ambassador and Plenipotentiary of the British Empire to the Maharajah of Sirpur. Although the ceremony was conducted with every appearance of a diplomatic exchange, Jaya noticed with alarm that the Residency officials standing stiffly in their morning coats against the painted frescoes of the Durbar Hall were as numerous as the members of the Sirpur cabinet in their brocade tunics and turbans, facing them across the expanse of carpet over which James Osborne was walking towards the ruler.

Ignoring the formality of the occasion, Maharajah Pratap rose from his gaddi to shake Osborne's hand. The handsome profiles and athletic physiques of the two figures bent towards each other, and Jaya allowed herself for a moment to believe that James Osborne would become as trusted a friend of her husband's as he had once been of her brother's. The sword at the ruler's waist, the military medals shining against the Resident's coat reminded her that although one was now a king and the other an ambassador, both men believed their true calling to be war.

At the end of the ceremony the Maharajah and the Resident retired to the ruler's study, deep in discussion of polo ponies, but the Residency officials and the Sirpur cabinet made no move towards each other. Recognizing the hostility frozen behind their rigid expressions, Jaya warned herself that James Osborne was no longer the boy who had once played cricket under the shadow of the Round Tower with Tikka, but the representative of an empire that could destroy Sirpur.

A week later, the ruler was received at the British Residency. Jaya sat beside her husband as the car drove out of the city and into a tree-lined avenue leading up a sloping hillside. On one side of the hill, the Brahmaputra River stretched towards the Himalayan range; on the other, green rice fields rolled towards the plains of Bengal.

The car drove through a wrought-iron gateway crowned by the crest of the British Empire, into gardens given a careless informality by three successive Residents, unmistakably English to any visitor, even if the Union Jack had not hung on the flagstaff outside the pillared bungalow.

James Osborne was waiting to greet the Maharajah. He led them into a drawing room covered in floral prints reminiscent of the flower beds outside.

'Let's see your stables, Osborne,' Maharajah Pratap demanded.

Jaya joined Sir Akbar at the window to watch the Resident and the ruler striding over the grass in the direction of the stables. 'Does the British Resident keep his secret files here?' she whispered.

The Prime Minister lifted his hand in triumph. 'Yes, hukam.

But files and secrets will soon belong to the past. This morning the Chamber of Princes guaranteed reforms in royal India, and the Reformists have dropped their agitation. Messages from Delhi tell me everyone is drunk on the possibility of freedom.'

Seeing Jaya's confusion, he explained: 'The British Empire said the only hitch to self-government was the antagonism between the kingdoms and British India. Now, aided by a sympathetic Viceroy, that stumbling block has finally been removed. When the Simon Commission releases its report, Parliament must offer India self-government. Imagine, hukam, we will be in Delhi to watch the British Empire transfer its power.'

Maharajah Pratap and James Osborne entered the room. The Prime Minister turned, his hand still in the air.

'What is this unaccustomed enthusiasm, Sir Akbar?' Maharajah Pratap asked.

'I was telling Her Highness that if only the Simon Commission keep their word and inaugurate the Federation, India will become a self-governing Dominion like Canada or Australia.' He almost smiled. 'And then Englishmen will have to call us cousins.'

'Does that mean we will have to go to Delhi to attend yet another boring session of the Chamber of Princes?' Maharajah Pratap asked in irritation.

'Yes, hukam. But it will hardly be boring. This is the most important session the Chamber has ever held.'

Jaya was embarrassed when even James Osborne forgot the distance of his office in his anxiety to overcome the ruler's inattention. 'The Prime Minister is right, Your Highness. Lord Irwin deplored the damage that was done by the all-white Commissions sent here by Parliament. For the first time India has a Viceroy who fully supports Federation. Many of us who love this great land would like to see Indians achieve self-government. It would be the greatest legacy Britain could give the subcontinent, an India governed as Britain is governed, by laws enacted by free men.'

Osborne smiled at Jaya. 'As the Maharani knows, I have always held that belief.'

IN PREPARATION for the Chamber session in Delhi, James Osborne called often on Maharajah Pratap.

Watching the upright figure walking down the high-ceilinged corridors of the City Palace, his shoes striking the marble floor with military precision, Jaya recalled how she had once studied his photograph in despair after the Baran had left her room with the painted miniatures of the men who might have owned her future, and how she had longed for the innocence unmarked by defeat that still stamped the Angrez boy's face.

Sometimes he stopped to exchange desultory pleasantries with Jaya about Prince Arjun. Although nothing of significance was spoken between them, Jaya felt comforted by his presence in Sirpur. There was something so clear and direct about the Englishman, so unencumbered by the complicated inferiorities which dragged her husband towards the increasingly thoughtless adventures that imperilled his kingdom.

Once he advised her to discourage the Maharajah from spending so much time flying. 'There could be an accident, Bai-sa. He should not be taking such risks.'

Jaya flushed at the implication that her husband was more interested in his newest aeroplane than in this vital meeting of the Chamber of Princes. 'I can't stop him, James-sahib. Danger is like a drug to my husband.'

James Osborne smiled at her dismay. 'And not to you, Bai-sa? Don't forget, I saw you shoot a tiger.'

Jaya could remember the smell of gunpowder on his skin, the trembling in her legs when she had looked into the deep, changing colour of his eyes, and she turned away, not wanting him to see that she remembered his closeness too well, or that her love of the familiar dangers of the jungle had turned into a fear of the alien dangers of power.

WHEN JAYA had last seen Delhi dust had swirled around the half-completed buildings of the new imperial capital. Now red sandstone battlements enclosed the domed imperial offices on the hill, their massive outline broken by pillared pergolas. The linear mile of King's Way cut true as an arrow through the hill, leading from the great doorways of the Durbar Hall of Viceroy's House to the mighty stone archway of India Gate inscribed with the names of the Indian troops who had fallen in the War.

Flowers bloomed beside the wide boulevard of King's Way, and water tanks led the eye to two enormous fountains, beyond which could be seen the obelisk of the Jaipur pillar rising above the Viceroy's iron gates.

As if the red battlements that dwarfed the fountains were too severe, beside them towered the circular building that now housed the Legislative Assembly and the Chamber of Princes, girdled by the Great Gallery which seemed to hold the aspirations of India's many peoples in its pillared arms as a mother holds her child.

For the first time, Jaya could sense the exhilaration of a world in which Indians might govern themselves, and the city seemed to reflect that spirit. Kings in magnificent turbans and nationalists in white Gandhi caps circulated on the lawns of the town houses of the Indian rulers, excitedly discussing a new India federated between democrats and monarchs.

Maharajah Pratap was a great favourite at these gatherings, his nonchalance lending relief to the seriousness around him. Whenever the nationalists tired of arguing with those rulers who still resisted reforms, they turned to Maharajah Pratap for his good-natured indifference, and Jaya could see the laughter in the Nightingale of India's soft eyes when he winked at Mrs Besant, or charmed the young Jawaharlal Nehru, who now led the Indian National Congress, with anecdotes about their schooldays in England, or melted the cold reserve of Mr Jinnah, who led the Muslim League, by discussing the finer points of London tailors, and Jaya knew everyone forgave him for the hours he spent circling Delhi in his new aircraft instead of exhausting himself with political negotiations.

As India waited for the Simon Commission report on self-government, Sir Akbar escorted Jaya to a session of the Chamber of Princes, first showing her the Legislative Assembly, from which the Viceroy's Council governed British India. Jaya descended the steep steps of the Visitors' Gallery to peer down at the scarlet and gold throne of the Viceroy, raised on a dais between the Englishmen in their three-piece suits who sat on wooden benches on one side of the chamber, facing their Indian counterparts in homespun clothes on the other.

'Of course, the presence of the Indians in the Legislative Assembly is mere decoration, hukam,' Sir Akbar remarked, 'since their counsels are constantly ignored by England. But once the Simon Commission's report is published, all that will change forever.'

Sir Akbar ushered Jaya into the Chamber of Princes. She leaned over the teak railing. Instead of suits or cotton Gandhi caps, the Indian rulers sitting below her were as richly adorned as their chamber, their colourful turbans reflecting the pageantry of the inlaid dome above them, gems flashing on their tunics as they turned to speak to each other.

Lord Irwin entered the room, to take his place on the scarlet and gold throne that dominated this room as another dominated the Assembly. The Viceroy of India motioned to Maharajah Bikaner, and there was silence as the ruler who had represented India at the end of the Great War and the birth of the League of Nations rose to his feet.

Sweeping his white moustache from his lips, Bikaner declared in a ringing voice, 'We the Princes of the Indian States are Indians, and we do most sincerely wish our Motherland and fellow countrymen well. We look forward as proudly as any British Indian to the day when our united country attains the full height of its political stature, as much respected as any other self-governing British Dominion.'

Ruler after ruler rose to his feet to applaud Bikaner's words. Jaya saw the Viceroy smiling and felt she was watching a people's impotence turn into dignity.

As WINTER ended and bougainvillea bushes covered the broken monuments of earlier empires with outrageous colour, the city heated up, and dust storms swirled loose earth around the gardens of Sirpur House.

At last, the Simon Commission report was published. To their horror, the Indians learned that the British Empire intended to retain its power.

Self-government was to be delayed for an unspecified time, Dominion status postponed indefinitely.

Like the weather, the mood of Delhi changed and the city erupted in demonstrations against the British Raj. Each time Jaya drove out of Sirpur House, her young son on her lap, she saw the fury of Indians that Britain had once again broken its promises of freedom.

The increasing heat of the season reflected India's outrage. The boycott of British goods rose to a dangerous level for a Britain endangered by the General Strike and widespread unemployment, increasingly dependent on the revenues and markets of India.

In April, on the very day of Arjun's fourth birthday, the rage of India found alarming expression. While the Viceroy was sitting on his scarlet and gold Viceregal throne in the Legislative Assembly, a bomb was thrown from the Visitors' Gallery into the Treasury Benches, crowded with Englishmen. The bomb was designed to do no damage, but the implication of widespread insurrection shook the Empire.

The man who had thrown the bomb, Bhagat Singh, defended his action in an overcrowded Delhi courtroom: 'The attack was not directed against any individual but against an institution. We are next to none in our love for humanity. We hold human life sacred beyond words. But freedom is the imperishable birthright of all mankind. For this faith we shall welcome any suffering to which we may be condemned.'

The Viceroy immediately censored Bhagat Singh's words. Imperial censorship only ensured that Bhagat Singh's defence was spread by word of mouth throughout the subcontinent, and when he was condemned to be hanged, his name was intoned as a mantra of freedom.

A new chant became the rallying cry of Indians. Any Indian thought to be imitating the British was surrounded by people shouting, 'British toady! Hai! Hai! British toady! Shame! Shame!'

Indian rulers began deserting the Chamber of Princes, convinced their future lay with an immovable Empire.

In an attempt to stop the haemorrhage of rulers from the Chamber, the Maharajah of Alwar ignored the Viceroy's time limit and spoke passionately for seven hours on the many injustices perpetrated by the British Empire on India's kingdoms. His pleas were ignored, and at the Viceroy's request, many Indian rulers jailed anyone who seemed a potential terrorist.

As news of the jailings filtered into Delhi, the capital's anger turned against the kings of India. Their town houses became the focus of violent demonstrations. Maharajah Pratap complained that it took him an hour to reach the Flying Club through the crowds spitting at his British car and beating the shiny black paint of the Rolls-Royce with their fists as they shouted, 'British toady! Shame! Shame!'

Afraid his irritation would make him take greater risks in his aircraft, Jaya pleaded with him to return to Sirpur, away from the fierce heat of the Delhi summer. Maharajah Pratap brusquely told her to cover the roof with vetiver screens and soak the whole house with water if she was feeling the heat.

EVERY DAY the din of shouted slogans rattled the windows of Sirpur House, until Jaya had to hold Arjun in her arms to quiet his fears. By May, Jaya could take the heat and the hatred no longer, and she instructed the aides to make arrangements for her departure.

The mob in front of Sirpur House refused to allow the aides' car through the gates, and the police, led by an enthusiastic Scotsman, began clubbing the demonstrators, until bright blood stained their cotton Gandhi caps.

Through the window, Jaya recognized the two newspapermen from Sirpur as the Maharajah's Rolls-Royce moved down the drive. Jaya was certain her husband was going to the aid of the demonstrators. Cold with disbelief, she heard the car accelerate and the police smashing their bamboo staves against anyone in its path.

She ran downstairs to argue with the police, fearing her husband's insensitivity would create an incident which might have repercussions in Sirpur itself. The constables rudely pushed her aside, and the nationalists being dragged towards the waiting police vans wiped the blood from their faces, shouting their battle cry 'British toady! Hai! Hai!'

All afternoon Jaya waited for her husband's return, praying that he would reach the safety of Sirpur House before nightfall, when the mob at the gates might turn violent and the intervention of the police lead to firing and death.

Chandni banged at the door of her bedroom. 'Maharani-sahib, come quickly! The ruler has been taken to hospital!'

An instructor from the Flying Club pushed Jaya into the Rolls-Royce and Jaya knew it was not the anger of the crowd she should have feared, even before the instructor told her that the Maharajah's plane had crashed.

Aides squashed against her, all protocol forgotten. Other cars careered down the drive, filled with guards and servants. The cavalcade of cars sped down the broad avenue, past Viceroy's House and the green star on top of the Jaipur pillar winking in the flat afternoon light.

Then they were running past the charity patients huddled on the wide verandah in the Indian section of the hospital.

A surgeon came out of the operating theatre, followed by orderlies wheeling a trolley. Jaya stood still in the middle of the running people as an aide lifted the bloodstained cloth from the body.

The bruises had already blackened, and Maharajah Pratap's features were barely discernible through flesh puffed up like a balloon. An aide took her elbow. 'Come, Maharani-sahib. We will take care of the details. You must return to Sirpur House.'

Jaya let the young man guide her through the verandah, her mind numbed by the image of her elegant husband swelling in the heat into a mass of disintegrating flesh.

Crowds circled the car, smashing their fists against the black paint of the Rolls-Royce, shouting 'British toady! Shame! Shame!' The aide pushed Jaya through the mob. She stumbled, and her glass bangles shattered against the car door. Dazed by the noise, she watched the shards of coloured glass falling on the melting tar.

Then reality struck her with unendurable force. She was a widow. Her four-year-old son was Maharajah of Sirpur, and she was guardian of his throne for fourteen dangerous years.

BOOK FOUR

Regent

52

1929

'The embrace of the British Empire is a dangerous thing. It is not and cannot be the life-giving embrace of an affection freely given and returned. And if it is not that, it will be what it has always been in the past – the embrace of death.'

INDIAN NATIONAL CONGRESS

AN AGITATED stationmaster flagged the train to a halt on the outskirts of the railway station. At the next siding British police inspectors were searching a white train. The Sirpur aides jumped down from their compartment as khaki-clad policemen ran past them with drawn revolvers.

'What's happening, Sergeant?' Osborne shouted from the Sirpur railway carriage to the British soldier trying to calm the crowds on the platform.

Seeing the white face under the sun helmet, the soldier cupped his hands around his mouth. 'The damned cowards bombed the Viceroy's train, sir.'

'Were Their Excellencies injured?'

'Thank God for the incompetence of these terrorist swine. The bomb exploded under the wrong compartment.'

Major Osborne swung onto the platform, pushing through the people pressed against the soldier.

'Hato! Hato!' The soldier's swagger stick descended on some-
one's arm. There was a yelp of pain and the Indians fell back.
'These natives don't deserve a Viceroy like Lord Irwin. The man's
a bloody saint – still trying to talk Parliament into holding a Round
Table Conference so that Indians can be heard in England by the
King Emperor himself.'

Osborne motioned with his sun helmet towards the window
where Jaya and Sir Akbar stood listening, and the soldier lowered
his voice grudgingly, as if the other Indians within earshot were
irrelevant. 'But it's true, sir. The Viceroy has got it all wrong.'

A group of coolies swung past, pushing the crowd onto the soldier,
and the swagger stick swept down again. 'Can you imagine this lot
being received in Buckingham Palace? As equals of the Australians
and the Canadians? A bloody good hiding is the only language the
beggars understand.'

Arjun trembled at Jaya's side. She wondered if he was remembering the last time they had been in Delhi: the bomb thrown at the
Viceroy's scarlet and gold throne; the crowds spitting at the Sirpur
car, their faces twisted in anger shouting, 'British toady! Hai! Hai!'

Or the Durbar Room emptied of its European furniture and
Maharajah Pratap's body lying submerged in a blanket of flowers,
only his bruised and battered face visible on the cotton cushion
supporting his broken neck.

Seven months had passed since then, months when she had been
locked in another world of rituals and priests. The child glanced
up, confused by the commotion on the platform. Fear darkened
the large eyes the maidservants called Ganga/Jumna because they
changed colours like the holy rivers of India.

Jaya remembered the fear in those eyes when the maidservants had
cut her heavy hair while trucks rumbled down the drive, delivering
blocks of ice to preserve Maharajah Pratap's body from putrefaction,
and old women shrieked the bleak dirges of professional mourners,
their shrill voices mocking the framed photographs of Maharajah
Victor and Maharajah Pratap, savage reminders that the sophistication of the Sirpur brothers had been a momentary ornamentation
on their kingdom, like a thin patina overlying an ancient bronze.

Unclean by the act of surviving her husband, Jaya had been confined to the airless puja room. The Raj Guru had bowed outside, his
face averted from her polluting shadow. 'Come, Maharajah-sahib.

Your mother cannot be with you at this time. She is unclean.'

The dazed child had followed the priest, and Jaya had known the Raj Guru was already challenging her regency.

For thirteen days she had sat in the puja room while the mourners shrieked their obscene litanies of death in the corridors and the sun beat relentlessly against the windows, filling the small chamber with oppressive heat. On the fourteenth day, after Maharajah Pratap's ashes had been scattered in the river at Benares, she had been permitted to return to her own apartments.

'The power of the priests is too great, hukam,' Chandni had hissed over the water streaming over the marble stool on which Jaya had been bathed since childhood. 'While you are in mourning they will take possession of the kingdom through the child. They say you are an outsider. The Raj Guru is already boasting openly that he will assume the power of the Regency.'

Jaya's toilette had taken only a moment. There were no glass bangles to be slipped onto her wrists, no long minutes spent combing the thick hair that had once fallen to her knees, no sindoor to mark the circle of matrimony on her forehead. She did not even have to cover her shaved head. A widow was not considered desirable, only unlucky.

The Durbar Hall had seemed cold after the stifling puja room. Jaya had stood where her husband's bier had lain, trying to adjust to the unfamiliar spaciousness of the room.

A man in a linen suit watched her from a corner. The curves that had given her slender body a woman's shape were gone. The unadorned neck, lengthened further by the absence of her hair, had seemed too fragile to support the drawn face.

'What have they done to you, Bai-sa?' The gentle pressure of his fingers had passed like a current through Jaya's body, breaking the shell of pollution that encased her, and with a desolation in no way different from her son's, she had wept in the Englishman's arms.

The Prime Minister had hovered at her shoulder, as if debating whether to break the rules of protocol and touch her. When Osborne released her, he had coughed in relief. 'We must return to Sirpur at once, hukam. Unless the Maharajah is crowned, the priests will precipitate a crisis in the government.'

355

ARJUN'S SMALL hands gripped the iron bars of the window and Jaya recalled how his small hands had gripped the bars in excitement when the train rocked over the Sirpur bridge for his coronation, and he had seen the elephants ringing the perimeter of the platform. But Jaya had been filled with dread, seeing the dark clouds that presaged Sirpur's sudden summer storms shrouding the saffron turbans of the Sirpur Lancers in a black mist.

At the precise moment that Arjun's small foot touched Sirpur soil, the elephants had trumpeted in unison, grey trunks weaving like snakes against the sinister sky.

The aides had hastily ushered Jaya through the crowds, removing a widow's unlucky presence from the occasion. Alone on the balcony of the Purdah Palace, Jaya had watched the river's sandbanks turn dark under the lowering sky, wondering if Arjun would be frightened as three millennia of names and titles cascaded over his head. The roar of voices had risen above the hundred and one salvos announcing the coronation of Maharajah Arjun of Sirpur. Rolling thunder had drowned the bursts of cannon fire and Jaya visualized the child alone in a sea of prostrated bodies, mounting the ancient Sirpur gaddi.

The clouds had scudded closer. The threatening storm had burst in a fury of black water. Across the river Jaya had seen the Durbar elephant swaying out of the temple, and on the howdah, the chattri-bearer struggling to keep the canopy of state from blowing forwards over the new ruler, bouncing forlornly with the movement of the elephant.

The silence of the deserted Purdah Palace had been shattered by the returning procession. The Maharajah had entered the zenana, the gold anklet of monarchy dragging at his ankle. Tears had filled Jaya's eyes when she had seen a new gravity in his conduct, as if the rituals of the coronation had weighted him with the knowledge that he could no longer retreat into childhood.

The high voices of the eunuchs had echoed in the corridors: 'Hoshiar! Hoshiar! Be vigilant! The Prime Minister and the Council approach!'

For the first time Jaya had joined the Dowager Maharani behind the brocade curtain, staring at the Chinese ladies crossing bridges to distant pagodas embroidered on the blue silk as the Dowager Maharani's voice, strong with authority, had declared: 'Ministers of Maharajah Arjun's court. You are all aware of the tragic circumstances under which my grandson died in Delhi. Bombs thrown in the Assembly, rulers besieged in their houses, mob demonstrations and the burning of British goods. This chaos was brought about by the Empire's bad faith. Yet until Maharani Jaya Devi's period of mourning is ended, the Seals of State and the keys to the Treasury remain in the hands of the British Resident.' Golden rope struck against the glass base of her hookah. 'I am of the opinion that it is dangerous to leave Sirpur's government in the hands of an Englishman for a whole year at such a critical time.'

Jaya cursed herself for demanding the Regency. How her husband would have enjoyed her present predicament – hidden behind a brocade curtain, unconsulted while the affairs of the kingdom were decided.

'The Raj Guru says that the storm at the time of a coronation is a bad omen, hukam, and the priests must take custody of the child until the year of mourning is over.'

A thin voice, its slight stutter identifying the Minister for Agriculture, had raised Jaya's hopes: 'If Maharani-sahib were to immerse herself in the waters of the holy river at Benares, she would be purified and the period of mourning ended.'

'Is the Raj Guru amenable to such a pilgrimage?' The Dowager's harshness had reminded the Council of the power struggle already joined in the kingdom. Jaya had held her breath, but the rustle of ministers pulling at their hookahs had given Jaya no indication of who had moved into the Raj Guru's circle and who remained with her.

As the Council departed, there had been the click of a box being opened as Sir Akbar's long fingers had dipped into the paan casket. 'Maharani-sahib still has one card. Osborne holds the Seals of State and the keys to the Treasury. He could prevent the –'

'Give the knave the power of the king?' the Dowager Maharani had interrupted angrily. 'Use Osborne and you invite the British Empire to meddle in our internal affairs. We must break the power of the priests through our own devices.'

In the following weeks, Jaya had come to hate the chamber with the Chinese ladies under their parasols endlessly climbing the blue silk walls while beyond the curtain the voices of the increasingly emboldened priests pressed for custody of her son.

357

The priests knew her helplessness, sequestered behind curtains in the Purdah Palace as the young Maharajah sat in the Durbar Hall touching gold coins with his small fingers, unconcerned that the Raj Guru was leaning in animated conversation with the Reformists who had been clubbed by the British Raj's police.

As if he too were watching the increasing complicity between the priests and the Reformists, Sir Akbar had placed himself in front of Jaya's curtain. 'You must take the child out of Sirpur, hukam. In only six months, the priests have spread much ill feeling against your Regency. During your absence, the Resident and I will govern on your behalf; but we cannot control the priests while the ruler is here.'

The silk had billowed with his breath as he edged closer. 'Maharajah Dungra is on his way back to India and urges you to visit him. Your mother has expressed a wish to see her grandson.' A pale hand had appeared at a corner of the screen. 'Dungra sends these to persuade you.'

Jaya had unwrapped the proffered parcel. The Prime Minister was still whispering behind the curtain, but Jaya had been unable to answer through her tears as gold bangles showered into her lap – the symbol of a brother's protection.

THE STATIONMASTER was blowing furiously on his whistle. Arjun jumped up and down at the window, shouting at Major Osborne to hurry. On the platform the soldier wielded the swagger stick like a lance, clearing a path for the Resident.

The train lurched as Osborne reentered the compartment. 'The Viceroy has achieved a miracle by getting the King Emperor to receive Indians at Buckingham Palace. But these terrorist bombs! These unreasonable demands for immediate Dominion status. Don't Indians understand how volatile the political and economic situation in the Empire has become since the Wall Street crash?'

The elation Jaya felt, freed after months of manipulation by the priests, evaporated as Sir Akbar answered, 'India did not cause the crash, Major Osborne, yet Britain has just punished us by doubling tariffs on Indian cloth and many other Indian goods.'

Osborne flushed with anger. 'If it were not for the British Empire, this newly discovered Motherland, for which criminals are prepared to murder innocent men and women, would disintegrate in two minutes.'

Sir Akbar raised an eyebrow at the Englishman's passion, his fatigue conveying the arrogance of his nobility more strongly than words. 'But the Empire changes its mind as often as a capricious courtesan. That is why you have bombs. Last year we were promised Dominion status. This year Britain says we are not yet ready to govern ourselves.'

He gave Osborne a tired smile as the train pulled into Delhi station. 'Of course, if we were to govern ourselves, the British would have to leave the luxuries of India. Perhaps India has corrupted you, Major, and like ourselves, you now fear unity more than you fear division.'

THE CAPITAL of the British Raj seemed festive, as if unaware of the violence that surrounded it. Winter flowers bloomed in well-tended gardens and through the windows of the white stucco bungalows, Christmas trees sparkled with glass ornaments. Under the colonnades of Connaught Place, mem-sahibs hurried from shop to shop, followed by porters balancing cane baskets filled with the morning's purchases on their heads and by children singing carols.

New grass, mown to a flat carpet of green, stretched on either side of King's Way. As the car pulled up the hill, Sir Akbar pointed to the sandstone pillars outside the high-domed buildings which housed the government of the British Raj. 'Read those inscriptions, Major Osborne: To India from New Zealand. To India from South Africa. To India from Australia. To India from Canada. India is called the jewel of your empire. But all those colonies govern themselves. And India does not.'

Enclosed by stone elephants, towering iron gates guarded the residence of the Viceroy. Rickshaws, horse-drawn carriages, bicycles made a chaos of the elegant approach, and the star of Jaipur winked green as if in disapproval on the milling crowds of angry nationalists waiting to bargain for the right to self-government.

Jaya gripped Arjun's hand, tensing with anxiety as the car turned towards Sirpur House. Instead of hostile demonstrations, a row of gardeners waited at the gates with flowers.

The furniture was back in place in the Durbar Room. A fire burned in the fireplace below the portrait of Maharajah Victor astride his favourite polo pony, giving the room the atmosphere of an English country house. It was as if the heat of summer and the dead body packed in ice had never happened.

Relieved that the oppressions of the past no longer haunted the house, Jaya passed the brief stay in Delhi inventing amusements for her son. Gratified when the succession of picnics and visits to the puppet theatres gradually thawed the look of numbness in Arjun's eyes, Jaya began to recover her own confidence.

ON THE FIRST day of the New Year, she stood at the window of the puja room where she had been incarcerated after her husband's death, watching the sky turn purple with dusk.

Dark memories of being wedded to a sword, of a marriage blighted by public humiliations and private bargains, melted into the anticipation of seeing her mother again. In another four months the period of official mourning would be over, and she felt strong, even eager to assume her duties as Regent.

Nails scratched below the closed door of the puja room. Jaya opened the door and Scott-Ward leaped into her arms.

'Darling!' Lady Modi's pearls described an arc around her body. 'You did it at last! Without even telling me.'

'What are you talking about?' Jaya tried to fight off Scott-Ward's attentions.

'Your hair! You've shingled it. My dear, it's breathtaking. You look like Clara Bow.'

'I'm a widow, Bapsy. I had to shave my head at the time of my husband's death.'

Lady Modi refused to be abashed. 'Nonsense. It's that scoundrel Pratap getting his way. Even from beyond the grave. Anyway, isn't all this traditional mumbo jumbo rather pointless when the world is coming to an end?'

'The journey from London couldn't have been that bad.'

'Not the flight, darling. I'm talking about the Crash. All my friends are leaping out of skyscrapers or throwing themselves under trains.' The big eyes looked glumly at Jaya. 'And on top of all that, there is this afternoon's news.'

'Has another stock market crashed?'

'Oh, darling, if only you spent a little more time listening to the wireless instead of at your prayers. Haven't you heard? The National Congress are going to snub the King Emperor. They refuse to attend the Round Table Conference in London.'

'But why?'

Lady Modi drained her glass and handed it to Jaya with a mournful expression. 'They have decided to throw every Englishman out of India. They don't want Dominion status anymore. They want a republic. January 26 is to be Republic Day. We are all to lower the Union Jack, raise the Indian flag and dedicate ourselves to ending the Empire. The cat is really among the pigeons now, darling. Terrorists will be exploding bombs. We will have to burn all our gowns and wear that awful, scratchy homespun cotton.'

She puckered her painted lips in a small kiss. 'But we mustn't be fainthearted. After all, it is the New Year. Let's hope your delicious new hairstyle will set the *ton* for 1930.'

53

*'We stand ... today for the fullest freedom of
India. India submits no longer to any foreign domi-
nation.'*

INDIAN NATIONAL CONGRESS

THOUSANDS OF small mirrors flashed in the corridors of the Maharajah of Dungra's residence, the Shish Mahal, the palace of mirrors, as
Jaya followed Tiny Dungra's ungainly figure, reproduced endlessly in
the mirrored fragments of the lamplit galleries, to the outer courtyard
where a car waited to take her to her mother.

The chauffeur guided the car down an avenue lined with whitewashed bungalows, their pale monotony broken by rows of jaca-
randa trees dropping yellow and purple blossoms into the dust.
'You are a fortunate daughter, hukam. I have seen the Sati Mata
only once, but I felt I was in the presence of a saint. The way she
moves. Her head held so high, as if she sees the face of God before
her.'

Recalling her own awe of that regal carriage, Jaya almost forgot
that she had last seen the Maharani treated as an unwanted burden
in the Balmer zenana, humiliated into seeking sanctuary in Dungra.

The car turned towards a garden banked with hedges of sweet
peas leading to a colonnaded bungalow. Carpets were spread on

the wide verandah to accommodate the waiting people. Despite their numbers, they exuded serenity. There was no misbehaviour from the children sitting gravely by their elders, or wailing from the infants held in young mothers' arms. Everyone, even the children, appeared to be listening for someone's approach, and few turned to look at the car.

An elderly gentleman guided Jaya through the crowded verandah into a large room, where more people were sitting on the floor. But there was a precision in their rows, unlike the press of visitors outside. Right hands spun wooden wheels balanced under crossed ankles. Left hands stretched as if in the motions of a dance, steadily drawing out coarse flax until it became thread, spinning the cloth that Indians were calling 'the livery of our freedom'.

'The Sati Mata says we must strengthen the hands of our own workers by shunning British goods,' the guide whispered.

Jaya turned to hide her shock. Beyond the rows of silent spinners, on the deserted back verandah, a woman wrapped in a coarse cotton sari was rising from the ground.

Without seeing her face, Jaya recognised the dignity of the rising figure, and she ran to touch her mother's feet. A pale hand pushed the sari from Jaya's shorn hair. Jaya grasped the hand, pressing it to her cheek. Ten years had passed since she had seen the Maharani, but the skin was as smooth as when she had been a child.

'I knew I would hold my daughter before I died,' the Maharani said softly, 'but I thought I would hold a bride, not a widow.'

Tears welled in Jaya's eyes. The Maharani did not remind Jaya that Rajput girls never displayed their grief. Instead, the pale hands stroked her cropped hair, as if nursing an infant's fever. 'It is not easy, child. It has never been so. Remember the Sati Mata's words, Bai-sa. The true sati continues to live when her world has shattered around her.'

'I have brought your grandson to Dungra for your blessing, hukam.'

Lines of delight creased the Maharani's fair skin. 'I shall come to the Shish Mahal this afternoon. He must not come here until I explain that people call me Sati Mata and other foolish names from affection, not because I have any powers. But now I must go. The doctors will be waiting.' She laughed at Jaya's expression of alarm. 'We have a dispensary and a nursing home here. On the other side of the compound there are a school and a free kitchen. Tiny manages our funds. The boy is a genius – no matter how much we spend, the money never diminishes.'

Slim fingers tipped Jaya's chin upwards. 'I live by the Sati Mata's mantra now, child. Do you remember it?'

'Of course, hukam. Ram Nam Sat Hai. The Name of God is Truth.'

'Did you know it is also Gandhi's mantra? He calls himself a satyagrahi, a seeker of truth.' The Maharani picked up the papers lying on a low stool. With uncharacteristic impetuosity she folded Jaya in a last embrace before turning towards the crowd of supplicants.

Watching the slender figure disappear into the room of spinners, Jaya felt the moorings that tethered her own past to Arjun's future slipping loose. The Maharani had taught her of the permanence contained within a harem's high walls, how a veil could protect the traditional world from alien events more powerfully than the blade of a sword. But now, when she most needed the Maharani's certainties, the Maharani had exchanged the veil for 'the livery of India's freedom', discarding the traditional world like a worn-out garment.

ARJUN FORMED an immediate attachment to his grandmother, and within days he was inseparable from her, trailing behind her as she visited the institutions, or playing in the ashram stockade where goats, cows and a single buffalo supplied dairy produce for the ashram inmates. It was clear he loved the ashram life, the smallness of its scale so perfectly tailored to a child's view of self-sufficiency.

Relieved that the general turbulence outside Dungra's borders had not shaken the placid rhythms of the kingdom, Jaya grasped at Dungra's suggestion that she familiarize herself with administrative matters.

'Did you study Rajniti, hukam?' she asked as she followed him through the mirrored corridors of the Shish Mahal to his private study.

Tiny smiled, and Jaya was moved by the intelligence in the soft eyes dominating the unattractive face. 'Rajniti is a map to just government, Bai-sa. But to be effective in today's world, my father sent me to learn government under Maharajah Baroda and foreign affairs under Maharajah Bikaner.'

He opened the door into a room lined from floor to ceiling with shelves holding leather-bound volumes of the Dungra gazettes. A large desk covered with files occupied the centre of the chamber. There were no photographs of racehorses on the walls. Only the gold-embossed titles on the gazette volumes glistened in the afternoon sunlight: FAMINE CONTROL 1897–1903. TREATY NEGOTIATIONS. VICEREGAL VISITS. IRRIGATION PROJECTS 1900–1928.

Tiny pulled a volume from the shelves. 'Take this, for instance. Did you know that the ruler of Bikaner was only twenty years old when he conceived the greatest irrigation project in India? The British prevented him from raising enough loans to realize his dream. But if he had succeeded, Bai-sa, your desert, your Abode of Death, could have become the granary of India.'

He replaced the volume and lowered himself into the chair behind the desk. 'The next years will be hard for us rulers, Bai-sa, caught between the Empire and the Reformists. Already the Empire raises more than ten million pounds every year from our kingdoms to spend on British India. As the demands of the nationalists increase, and the situation in Britain grows gloomier, where will the Empire look for funds, except to us? And each time we increase taxes, our own people will be more disposed to join the ranks of the Reformists.'

Jaya felt unspoken prophecies lingering in the air. Determined not to endanger her son's throne through inexperience, Jaya spent her mornings with the Dungra engineers and administrators learning how to govern his kingdom.

Irrigation projects for harnessing the capriciousness of the Brahmaputra River were discussed. A site was located for a new dam, to be named after the late ruler. The long-neglected tribal areas required schools and dispensaries, and the Dungra financial experts suggested means of raising funds.

When they had gone, she sat alone in Tiny Dungra's study, not allowing herself to be lulled to sleep by the bees droning outside the windows and the long columns of statistics and dates blurring in front of her eyes.

But in the evenings, Jaya could almost imagine herself back in the Balmer zenana as she sat with her mother watching parakeets swoop across the sky as sparrows had once swooped towards the bougainvillea bushes below the Maharani's balcony.

'Are your days in Dungra fruitful, Bai-sa?'

'Yes, hukam. His Highness is helping me with administration.'

'Do you remember when I taught you to provision a fort? Provisioning a fort and provisioning a kingdom are not such separate tasks.' In Jaya's mind, the Maharani's words conjured up images of young girls clapping their hands to frighten away the monkeys bounding down the stone stairs, and the rich scent of grain and vegetables as the Household Controller opened the padlocked storerooms of the lower Fort. With sudden fear, she realized that the three people most concerned with Arjun's welfare had all been raised behind purdah. But the Maharani and the Dowager Maharani belonged to a world where accurate information was gained through human contact. Today, machines brought information − conveying facts, but not the ambiguities in a person's eyes or the subtleties of unspoken supplication.

Arjun ran onto the grass, holding a sheaf of green straw high in his hands. Goats butted at his legs. 'The Mahatma also lives in ashram,' Arjun shouted. 'He has hundreds of goats.' Someone called his name, and he raced towards the animal stockade. Jaya watched him, grateful that her son was too young to fear the inexperience of his mother or understand that in his idyllic ashram, Gandhi was searching for a means to unite an unruly subcontinent without bloodshed.

As spring approached, Dungra gained a festive air. The political upheavals outside the kingdom seemed irrelevant as the grain from a good harvest was poured into gunnysacks, and girls whirled in village squares, clashing the lacquered sticks held in their hands to the rhythms of the harvest dance.

Then it was Holi, the festival of colour. The Durbar elephant swayed out of the Shish Mahal, followed by a tank truck from which two rubber hoses snaked their way past the standard-bearers into the howdah. The massive frame of the elder maharajah dwarfed the tiny figure of the younger as the elephant and truck moved slowly down the capital's streets. Arjun directed his hose of coloured water onto the crowds lining the roads, giggling in delight as their white garments turned magenta, orange, bright pink.

Holding bamboo syringes, the crowds sprayed the rulers with cold water and Arjun screamed with pleasure each time a jet of water splashed against his chest. From every balcony, lacquered balls filled with green, blue, yellow powders were hurled down on the Maharajah's procession until truck, elephant and both rulers were invisible in clouds of brilliant colour.

By late afternoon, Holi was over. Unable to participate in the festival, Jaya had waited to drive to the Maharani's ashram, to ensure her white widow's sari would not be sprayed with colour by a stray reveller. But city streets, which should have been deserted, were still crowded with people buying newspapers.

A cow covered with bright red handprints walked in front of the car. The chauffeur braked near a group of students studying a newspaper, colour streaking their faces.

'What has happened?' Jaya called.

'The Mahatma has broken his silence at last, hukam.'

The students pushed the newspaper through the car window, and waited for Jaya to read Mahatma Gandhi's letter to the Viceroy of India.

Dear Friend,

Before embarking on Civil Disobedience I would fain approach you and find a way out.

Why do I regard British rule as a curse? It has impoverished millions by a system of progressive exploitation and by a ruinous and expensive military and civil administration. It has reduced us politically to serfdom. It has sapped the foundations of our culture.

It seems as clear as daylight that responsible British statesmen do not contemplate any alteration in British Policy that might adversely affect Britain's commerce with India. If nothing is done to end the process of exploitation India must be bled with ever increasing speed.

I respectfully ask you to pave the way for the immediate removal of these evils and open a conference between real equals.

But if you cannot ... I shall proceed with such co-workers of my ashram as I can take, to disregard the Salt Laws.

Nothing but organised non-violence can check the organised violence of the British Government.

This letter is not in any way intended as a threat. Therefore I am having it specially delivered by a young English friend who believes in the Indian cause.

Your sincere friend,

M. K. Gandhi

Jaya handed the newspaper back to the students. They interrupted one another in excitement.

'The Viceroy did not even reply to the Mahatma's letter, hukam.'

'His secretary acknowledged the letter, warning Gandhi not to defy the British Empire.'

One of them slapped the bottom of the newspaper, then pushed his head inside Jaya's window, triumph tinged with fear marking his thin face. 'But you didn't read the last item, hukam. Tomorrow, Gandhi launches his Civil Disobedience movement against the British Empire.'

54

1930

> 'On bended knee I asked for bread and I received
> stone instead.'
>
> MAHATMA GANDHI

A MAP of Sirpur was spread on the table. An engineer was bending
forward to explain the markings to Jaya when the study doors were
flung open.

'Darling, what are you doing here when the whole of India
is on its way to the sea?'

The engineer edged nervously past the yapping Pekingese that
was running around a silk-stockinged leg as Lady Modi pulled her
skirt free from Scott-Ward's diamond collar. 'And what are all these
boring papers?'

Dungra's large body filled the doorway, multiplied in the mirrored corridors. 'I see you couldn't keep away from the excitement,
Bapsy.'

'Naturally, darling. There hasn't been anything like it since the
Prince of Wales visited India.'

'Don't tell me you are planning to break the Salt Laws.'

A cigarette holder tapped his arm in reproval. 'There are many
ways to be a patriot, Tiny. I shall watch. But what should we
wear? Pearls seem a little inappropriate for defying the British
Empire.'

'I think I have an extra Gandhi cap. I'll have my valet send it to your rooms.'

Jaya turned away in disgust. In three weeks Gandhi had already walked more than two hundred miles from his ashram towards the seacoast at Dandi where he planned to break the British Empire's laws. Indians had flocked to join the elderly ascetic's march, until his small band of workers had swollen from hundreds to thousands to tens of thousands. As Gandhi approached the Dungra border, Jaya's car had often been delayed by families waving small wooden spinning wheels at each other, travelling on foot or in rickshaws pedalled by thin-legged cyclists to the village where they hoped to catch a glimpse of the Great Soul of India.

Lady Modi saw Jaya's expression. 'Oh, darling, don't be so serious. Gandhi laughs, you know. What's more, he dances. In London, he was terribly keen on the fox-trot; I think he may even have learned to tango. Now do let's hurry, or we'll miss all the fun.'

In spite of herself, the sight of the white Gandhi cap sitting at a jaunty angle on Lady Modi's curls made Jaya laugh out loud as the car sped down the avenues leading to the Dungra border.

On the outskirts of the kingdom the car could no longer move in the press of people. Jaya saw saffron, green and white banners stretched across every thornbush. At the edge of the road, women sat behind spinning wheels, their hands steady as they drew flax into thread. Behind them, crowds knelt on the dusty earth as far as the eye could see. A group of sweepers pushed forward to sprinkle the path with water from the goatskin bags slung over their bare shoulders.

'The Mahatma is coming!'

The sound of distant singing was drowned in the excited shouts of the children perched on the high branches of the mango trees.

'Gandhi-ji is here!'

'We can see him!'

People clambered over one another to throw flowers on the wet mud so that Gandhi's rough sandals would walk only on petals, and the pathway became an avenue of rose and marigold petals as an emaciated figure strode around the bend. A bamboo staff was gripped in one hand, knobby knees protruded under his short dhoti, a thin cotton shawl hung around his bony shoulders. At his side, a plump woman clad in bright silk kept pace with difficulty.

370

'My God, darling. Look at the speed at which the Mahatma's walking. Our poor Nightingale is practically running to keep up.'

Standing in open-topped cars, newsreel photographers swung their cameras onto the babies held up for the Mahatma's blessing, and men and women rushed onto the road to touch their foreheads to the flowers over which Gandhi had walked.

Gandhi's ashram workers gently pushed the crowds back. 'Brothers, sisters, give Gandhi-ji some room. You must not delay him.'

The chaotic supplicants retreated to the sides of the road as a crate was placed on the crushed petals. Handing his bamboo staff to Mrs Naidu, Gandhi climbed onto the crate and folded his hands in greeting above a toothless smile.

'Brothers and sisters, in the name of God I greet you.' The high, nervous voice immediately silenced the noise around him. 'We fear the British Empire has no intention of granting us self-government when even the salt a peasant needs for strength to till his fields under the burning sun is taxed, and any Indian who dares make his own salt is called a criminal by the Empire.'

Angry voices yelled agreement. A thin hand lifted to silence them. 'But we do not hate the British, brothers and sisters. We seek to make them recognize the wickedness of their system through nonviolent protest. As a soldier must learn to kill, a satyagrahi must learn to suffer, to die if need be, to prove the righteousness of his cause.'

The angry shouts turned to passionate promises of self-sacrifice. The high voice continued to goad them. 'When we speak of the evils of the British Empire, let us not forget the even greater evils we have perpetrated upon ourselves. We call our own brothers untouchable. We send children to the marriage beds of strangers. We buy British cloth because it is cheap and force our own workers to starve. We seek oblivion from our misery in drink and drugs while enriching the coffers of the British Empire. These evil practices must end. I ask you, brothers and sisters, to practise hygiene of the body and of the spirit. And when the time comes, I ask you to join me in breaking the Salt Laws of the British Raj.'

Cries of 'Jai Hind! Jai Gandhi-ji!' washed over the bent body descending from the crate. Mrs Naidu handed him the bamboo staff. Cars spun wet mud and flowers under their wheels as journalists from all over the world followed the frail old man and the plump matron striding down the road again, four days' march from the seacoast where Gandhi would challenge the might of the British Empire.

Bullock carts carried younger marchers unable to sustain the punishing pace of the old ascetic's walk, and black umbrellas shaded their heads from the fierce sun that had taken the temperature to over a hundred degrees.

People surged forward to join the march. Lady Modi moved into the protection of Dungra's arms, shouting over the noise, 'Everyone told Gandhi salt was too trivial an issue to merit attention. Can you imagine, darlings? Now Gandhi's journey is being compared to Napoleon's march from Elba.' She stepped gingerly over a pat of cow dung smeared in the path by trampling feet, the silver enamel on her toenails visible through her open sandals. 'Do you think they could be right, Tiny? Could Gandhi become the British Empire's Waterloo?'

IT WAS BARELY midnight when Chandni woke Jaya on the day that Gandhi was to break the Salt Laws. 'The Sati Mata has left for Dandi, hukam. She wishes to pray all night with the Mahatma before he defies the Angrez.'

Jaya's lips moved in automatic recitation of the sati prayers, remembering the last time she had seen the Indian Ocean. Then she had accompanied her husband to the state wedding of a dog. Only five years later, the woman from whom she had learned her sati prayers was at Gandhi's camp, waiting to break the British Empire's laws.

The car drove out of the high gates of the Shish Mahal. Despite the early hour, heat made their clothes stick to the leather seats, and Lady Modi's hair grew damp with perspiration as she drowsed on Jaya's shoulder.

The slate-grey sky was paling into silver as they neared the ocean, where a small wooden dais shook on its roughly constructed supports each time the surf crashed against the sand.

Lady Modi awoke with a start and stared out of the window in disappointment. 'Oh, darling, this is not at all like Napoleon's march from Elba.'

Lines of volunteers were filing out of the grass huts that housed

Gandhi's workers, singing, 'Ram, Christ, Allah. These are Your many names, O God. Whatever Your name, O God, grant us enlightenment.'

Hearing the singing, there was a flurry of activity on the beach. Sleepy journalists jumped into their vehicles and roared over the ivory sand turning rose-pink with the sunrise. Jaya searched for the Maharani, but there were too many women wearing white homespun saris forming a cordon in front of the farthest hut.

A bent figure holding a bamboo staff appeared at the doorway, and a hush fell over the gathering.

The sound of crashing surf seemed to magnify as Gandhi and Mrs Naidu walked through the silent cordon towards the sea. At the edge of the water Gandhi handed his staff to Mrs Naidu and strode into the Indian Ocean.

A solitary old man, he stood in the water as surf surged around his spindly legs and splashed against the threadbare shawl clinging to his emaciated body. The bent figure remained motionless in the spraying foam until the waves receded. Then he knelt and picked up a handful of sand encrusted with sea salt.

Mrs Naidu raised her plump arms. 'Hail, Deliverer!' she shouted, and a smile split Gandhi's toothless mouth.

The two leaders circled the wooden dais. Finding no steps, Gandhi clambered onto the platform and leaned down to grip Mrs Naidu's wrists. Her weight pulled him forward, and he collapsed onto the rickety platform. Mrs Naidu sank heavily onto the sand below him, tears of laughter streaming down her cheeks. Responding to their infectious high spirits, the crowds cheered each time Mrs Naidu's weight pulled the Mahatma down onto the platform, until the old man succeeded in levering the plump figure onto the dais beside him.

Microphones were pushed forward. Gandhi lifted his handful of sand. The high voice, eerily amplified above the crashing waves, declared, 'This is a nefarious monopoly by the British Empire on India.'

Like clouds of gulls, figures in homespun cotton descended on the water. Brown hands scooped into the beach, making it a momentary landscape of small craters as white surf crashed against white cotton, receding to leave thin ridges of white salt on the wet sand.

The Maharani was walking back from the water, the wet cloth of her sari dragging at her ankles. Jaya raced towards her. 'Hukam, what are you doing? Come back to Dungra with me now!'

The Maharani stopped. She lifted a pale fist, and sand and salt fell in thin driblets onto Jaya's palm. 'When famine was destroying Balmer, your father begged Rani Victoria for help. He came back empty-handed. Even Lord Curzon, moved to pity by our misery, pleaded with Britain's Parliament to lift this cursed tax, and the hard-hearted Angrez refused the pleas of their own Viceroy. The Mahatma will make these grains into the weapon that will destroy the Empire.'

'But the British will arrest him, hukam. Will you follow him to jail?'

'I am free to follow the path of truth, even if it leads to jail. You are not, Bai-sa. Go back to Sirpur and guard your son's throne.'

55

'This is an oligarchy of disaffected and seditious clerks.'

WINSTON CHURCHILL

JAYA RELUCTANTLY returned to Dungra to perform the ceremonies that marked the end of her mourning, preoccupied with the thought of her mother sitting at Gandhi's makeshift ashram on the beach at Dandi.

Each afternoon she waited for Tiny to return from his Secretariat with news that Gandhi had finally been arrested, and with him all those who had defied the Empire. Every day Tiny Dungra assured her that Gandhi was still in his ashram, before telling her of the insurrection that Gandhi's pinch of salt had unleashed.

Contraband salt was being sold openly in British India's major cities. All down India's seacoast villagers were wading into the sea with pans to make illegal salt. In Calcutta, the Mayor gave a public speech urging people to stop wearing British-made textiles. He was jailed. In Delhi, fifteen thousand men and women watched the police arrest Pandit Malviya as he bought a handful of salt. At Patna, thousands waited to make salt under the direction of Dr Rajendra Prasad. Mounted police blocked the highway, threatening a cavalry charge, and the men and women who had thrown themselves on the ground in front of the horses were dragged away, only to be replaced by new waves of volunteers.

375

The Viceroy passed a series of ordinances giving the police unlimited rights of arrest, and throughout the subcontinent teachers, housewives, peasants daily goaded the Viceroy by defying his emergency ordinances.

Rigorous press censorship was imposed. Indian newspapers closed their presses voluntarily in mute objection as the British Empire, by imperial writ, withdrew every Indian's right to freedom and property.

'God knows what the Viceroy thinks he's doing,' Tiny observed, relaying the latest news to Jaya. 'The censoring of the native press has only meant that every incident is known throughout India by word of mouth.' The large head shook in despair. 'And yet by the end of this year, we are expected to attend the Round Table Conference in London like gentlemen, as if what is happening in India were only a game of cricket.'

Dungra's reports revealed that the game was turning ugly. On the North-West Frontier, tribesmen formed themselves into a Red Shirt movement inspired by Garibaldi's republican movement in Italy. Although they practised nonviolence, the British Empire ordered one of its most distinguished regiments, the 37th Garwhal Rifles, to fire on them. When, for the first time in eighty years, the Raj's soldiers reversed arms, refusing to obey the command of their British officers, an outraged British Inspector of Police rammed his armoured car into the demonstrators and opened fire with a machine gun, killing seventy people and wounding many more.

Within two weeks the British Raj jailed sixty thousand people, and just as he was about to march on the Dharsana Salt Depot, Gandhi was at last arrested.

Jaya raced through the mirrored corridors to the Maharajah's study. Dungra leaned forward, the chair creaking with his weight. 'It's all right, Bai-sa. Your mother is still free.'

'Has she returned to the ashram?'

'No. Mrs Naidu has taken over Gandhi's march on the Salt Depot. Your mother has gone with her to nurse the casualties.'

'Then I must go and help them. I should leave for Dharsana immediately.'

'Absolutely not. If you are seen at the Salt Depot, you will be stripped of your Regency. Arjun might even lose the Sirpur throne. I have already sent my men there to make sure no harm comes to the Sati Mata.'

'Suppose there is violence? Suppose the police attack them?'

'My men will keep us informed. With the newspapers silenced, who knows how much of this police violence is rumour?'

While they waited for news from Dharsana, Tiny carried on his administrative business, his papers rustling as the wooden blades of the fans stirred the summer air. Each time a secretary entered, Jaya looked up, only to see more buff-coloured files being handed to the Maharajah.

At sunset, an aide ran through the door with a telegram from Dharsana. Tiny switched on the ugly steel lamp. A pool of light fell on the files covering the desk as he tore open the envelope.

In a flat, emotionless voice he read out the message: 'HUKAM, THE ENORMOUS SALT PANS AT THE BRITISH RAJ'S SALTWORKS ARE SURROUNDED BY DITCHES RINGED BY BARBED WIRE. FOUR HUNDRED POLICEMEN UNDER THE COMMAND OF SIX BRITISH OFFICERS STAND GUARD OUTSIDE THE BARBED WIRE. ALL MORNING THE VOLUNTEERS MOVED IN RANKS TOWARDS THE GATES; ALL MORNING THEY WERE SAVAGELY BEATEN BY THE POLICE, ALTHOUGH THEY OFFERED NO RESISTANCE. THE SATI MATA WAITED WITH MRS NAIDU AND THE OTHER WOMEN TO ATTEND TO THE CASUALTIES.

'WE ACCOMPANIED A GROUP OF FOREIGN JOURNALISTS TO THE TEMPORARY HOSPITAL ORGANIZED BY THE LADIES. THE SATI MATA ASKED US TO INFORM YOU THAT ARUN ROY, THE LAWYER, WAS BRUTALLY BEATEN. BOTH HIS COLLARBONES ARE BROKEN BUT HE DOES NOT SEEM TO HAVE SUSTAINED PERMANENT DAMAGE FROM HIS WOUNDS.'

Moths fluttered against the telegram. A large hand waved them away. Watching the small wings disappear into the darkness, Jaya remembered the sky black with roosting birds as Tiny Dungra and Arun Roy had shouted to each other in the Balmer jungle.

'WEBB MILLER, UNITED PRESS CORRESPONDENT, COUNTED THREE HUNDRED AND TWENTY INJURED, TWO DEAD. WE SAW MANY VOLUNTEERS STILL UNCONSCIOUS. TOMORROW THEY WILL APPROACH THE SALT DEPOT AGAIN.'

Day after day Jaya sat in the Maharajah's study, waiting for news of her mother, and thinking of the lawyer lying in Mrs Naidu's hospital with broken bones. She could remember the touch of his fingers on her long hair when she had wept, his voice saying softly, 'This is an ugly and unpleasant jungle,' and wondered if that thought had flashed through his mind when the lathis of the British Raj's police had descended on his body.

Sometimes the heat made her head heavy and she closed her eyes, but the golden titles remained imprinted on her retina: FAMINE CONTROL. BRITISH TARIFFS, TREATY NEGOTIATIONS. VICEREGAL VISITS. When the messages arrived from the Salt Depot and Tiny read them aloud in his flat voice, each message, with sickening regularity, carried the same story of silently advancing marchers and stretcher-bearers taking their wounded to Mrs Naidu's hospital.

It was almost a week before the Maharajah jubilantly announced that the Maharani was on her way back to Dungra. 'The British imprisoned Mrs Naidu, Bai-sa, but my aides took your mother away.'

ALTHOUGH IT was midnight, the ashram had already filled with people waiting to greet the Maharani. Tiny Dungra led Jaya through the verandah onto the ashram lawn, where a fan whirred behind a block of ice. Sitting on cane chairs, the ice-cooled breeze damp against their hot skins, they looked at the moti blossoms pale against black leaves. Jaya listened to the lowing of the buffaloes in the ashram corral, realizing she had forgotten the serenity of her mother's ashram, the stillness that seemed to deny the city around it.

When the Sati Mata reached the ashram, she first blessed the people on the verandahs and in the crowded rooms. At last she came outside to join them on the lawn.

For a long while the Maharani sat in silence, listening to the crickets and the drip of melting ice. Then, as if speaking to herself, she said, 'All my life I have tried to fulfil the dharma of the warrior. The sound of the nagaras has always echoed in my ears. The prayers of the sati queens have always been on my lips. But I became a widow before I understood the true meaning of sati. And I had to go to Dharsana to learn about war.'

She took Jaya's dark hand in her pale fingers. 'I saw the British beat defenceless men with lathis and rifle butts. They did not cringe. They did not complain. But most important, they did not retreat. Their silent courage made them invincible. The British Raj is finished, Bai-sa. I wish your father had lived to see this day.'

56

'We have not the training for organized violence, and individual or sporadic violence is a confession of despair. But if this Congress or the nation at any future time comes to the conclusion that methods of violence will rid us of slavery, then I have no doubt that it will adopt them.

'Violence is bad but slavery is far worse.'

JAWAHARLAL NEHRU

IT WAS JAYA'S last evening in Dungra, but the Maharani spoke only of the Civil Disobedience movement, as if her daughter's departure to govern a kingdom were unimportant, and Jaya could feel the serenity of the ashram being threatened by its founder's fascination with the outside world.

Parakeets streaked the sky with sudden green before settling into the trees, and Arjun's laughter filled the ashram lawns. The sound no longer comforted Jaya. As she touched the Maharani's feet for her final blessing, Jaya felt leaden with the weight of protecting Arjun's future.

That night, there was an urgent knocking at Jaya's door. Chandni ran to the bed, a blurred figure outside the mosquito net. 'Maharajah-sahib has sent for you, hukam.'

'At this hour?'

'It is urgent, hukam. You must hurry.'

When Jaya reached the study, Tiny was shouting into the telephone. He banged the receiver onto its cradle. 'Cancel your journey, Bai-sa. There could be violence at the stations on the way to Calcutta. Two bombs were thrown at the Viceroy in the Delhi Assembly today. One of the terrorists even tried to fire at the Englishmen sitting on the Government benches. Fortunately, the revolver jammed.'

'Who did this, hukam?'

'The Indian Republican Army.'

'Has the Indian Army mutinied?'

'No, Bai-sa. These are students and poets and romantic young girls, who have modelled their Indian Republican Army on the Irish Republican Army in Dublin. But they are based in Calcutta, and the British will crack down on them. There will be more violence.' Concern marked the heavy features. 'Stay here until the situation is calmer.'

Jaya let her eyes wander over the leather-bound gazettes with their gold-printed titles for the last time. Only five months ago she had fled the intrigues of the Sirpur priests, hoping to find sanctuary from politics in Dungra. Now Sirpur seemed to offer escape from the ferment around her.

'I can't delay any longer, hukam. The Maharajah must return to his country.'

THE LONG train journey to Calcutta confirmed Dungra's prediction. Crowds of nationalists waited at every railway station. As steel wheels clashed against sparking rails, they surged forward to press small bags against the train windows, shouting, 'Buy salt for India's freedom!'

Chandni and the other maidservants crowded at the windows, their glass bangles breaking against the bars as they pulled bags of salt into the compartment before the police ran through the crowds and bamboo lathis descended on unresisting bodies.

Through the iron bars of the windows, the maidservants shrilly abused the police. 'Have you no shame, beating children and old women?'

'Why are you taking those men away to jail? Who will feed their families?'

Arjun trembled at Jaya's side as he had trembled when he

saw the Viceroy's bombed white train. Now she kept him away from the windows so he would not see the fury on the faces of the British officers or the confusion that marked the features of their Indian subordinates as steel-tipped lathis smashed against unprotected skulls and blood poured down white clothes.

In station after station bags were pushed at the windows, before warning shouts drew the nationalists back from the train to sink onto the dirty platforms and wait for the policemen to race through the bedding rolls and tin trunks, their khaki uniforms as emblematic of the British Raj's power as the bags of salt were symbolic of India's resistance to that power.

'How can the poor live without salt?' the maidservants shouted through the windows.

'For a pinch of salt the British have thrown the Mahatma into jail, and you follow their orders, you shameless sons of jackals!'

Jaya tried to hush them, afraid the police would burst into the compartment and turn their lathis on the cursing women. The maids refused to obey, shrieking at the policemen as the demonstrators were dragged away, their torn bags leaving thin trails of illegal salt across the station platforms.

Jaya was relieved when the train finally entered Calcutta's Howrah Station and she saw the Sirpur aides running alongside the braking train. 'Where is Sir Akbar?' she called through the window.

'There has been an armed insurrection in the East, hukam. The Indian Republican Army has captured Chittagong.'

'Captured Chittagong?' Jaya repeated like a parrot. 'How can a handful of poets take one of the most important cities in the British Empire by force?'

'The British are not releasing any information, but Mrs Roy received the news by telephone. Sir Akbar has gone with her to find out what has happened.'

Porters tried to mount the steps of the compartment. The aides shoved them aside. 'Come quickly, hukam. There may be trouble at the station.' On the concrete bridge above the platform, the crush of passengers was so dense they could not proceed. The aides pushed Jaya and the young Maharajah to the railing to save them from being trampled. A freight train was being unloaded on the siding below the bridge. Lines of porters were flinging bags onto the platform, and purple stamps were visible on the gunnysacking: MADE IN MANCHESTER, MADE IN LANCASTER.

Four young men carrying kerosene tins ran past the loaders. Shouting to one another to hurry, they unscrewed the tops of their tins and poured liquid over the stacked bales. The smell of kerosene engulfed the bridge. People crushed against Jaya to see what was happening. One man lit a match and tossed it onto the soaked gunny-bags. The bags immediately caught fire. Flames leaped into the air. The young men ringed the fire shouting, 'Bande Mataram! Victory to the Motherland!' On the bridge, people screamed in panic. Arjun pointed in delight at the flames, his small hand waving through the railing at the figures running on the platform below. 'Is this a game, hukam?'

Jaya dragged him away from his fascination with the pandemonium as the police broke through the crowds. Steel tips struck frightened onlookers, but the young men had already escaped into the streets.

The aides forced a corridor through the frightened passengers to the waiting car, the sweet smell of kerosene still strong in Jaya's nostrils as they left the station.

The car entered the lanes of a bazaar, and once again the smell of kerosene lanterns was distinct in the rich odours of the market. Jaya stared at the pyramids of fruit and the bargaining housewives, thinking about her son's question. Was violence and nonviolence a desperate game, a passion that would inevitably spend itself against the might of the largest empire in the world? Or was it significant of a new India? Should the Indian rulers join the nationalists, or should they gamble their treaties on an empire that might fragment into a thousand pieces if it failed to hold its ground now?

Beyond the Bengal Club, with its sign saying DOGS AND INDIANS NOT ALLOWED, the terraces of Fort William were a dark shadow. Jaya thought how deceptively calm the city appeared, as if these buildings with their Union Jacks and their uniformed guards could never be shaken by Indian passion.

A row of gardeners were waiting at Sirpur House with garlands of jasmine blossoms. Servants hurried past them to open the car doors.

'Mrs Roy has sent a messenger for you, hukam. He has been waiting more than an hour for your arrival.'

382

In the Durbar Room, a figure dressed in white clothes was bent over a book. Light fell onto his shining scalp and glinted off the glasses on the edge of his nose, reminding Jaya of Gandhi. The sound of her anklets brought him to his feet.

A smile lifted Arun Roy's thin moustache, then widened into laughter. 'Ah, Bai-sa, what a benighted civilization. What a benighted empire. One has taken your hair, the other has taken mine.' His starched dhoti rustled as he moved to her side to brush her short hair with his fingers. 'You look like a child, but I'm afraid that when your mother shaved my head to treat my wounds at the Salt Depot, she put years on me. My wounds may have healed, but my hair has not.'

'Is it true the Indian Republican Army has defeated the Empire?' Jaya asked as she moved away, hoping her awkward advance through the room and onto the dark verandah did not seem like flight to the lawyer refusing to move from her side.

'A short-lived victory, Bai-sa. The British have already regained the Police Station. Now they are firing on the Armoury, which is defended by a handful of youths who will all be dead or in chains on their way to the Andaman Islands before the night is out.'

'Don't you care if they live or die? Or are you angry that they are violent?'

He shrugged, and the darkness seemed to clothe the shaved head with hair. 'Violence, nonviolence – what difference does it make as long as we gain our freedom?'

A bat's velvet wing brushed Jaya's cheek. She screamed and threw herself forward. The lawyer's arms locked around her as the bat circled the verandah blindly, its flapping wings echoing in the darkness. Then it was gone, and Arun Roy was stroking her hair.

Jaya pressed backward against the wrists that enclosed her waist. Arun Roy refused to release his grip. 'Poor Bai-sa. So many roles to perform, and not one of them allows you to be a woman. But perhaps you do not yet know what it is to be a woman.' He smiled, and white teeth gleamed behind his moustache. 'You are still so young, Bai-sa. Is duty enough? Will you become celibate, like our old Mahatma?'

Jaya's glass bangles clinked as she beat her fists against his shoulders, but she could not stop her body from arching into his, crushing the starched folds of his dhoti.

The doors of the Durbar Room opened, and the lawyer gently pushed her away, laughing at her confusion. 'Was I violent or nonviolent, Bai-sa?'

Jaya tried to recover her composure, refusing to meet the lawyer's mocking gaze as Mrs Roy and the Prime Minister advanced towards them.

'All those poor children are dead, Bai-sa,' Mrs Roy whispered.

Sir Akbar's cane tapped the floor in emphasis. 'The British have retaken Chittagong, hukam. The Indian Republican Army's revolution is over.'

57

1931

'The nauseating and humiliating spectacle of this one-time Inner Temple lawyer, now seditious fakir striding half-naked up the steps of the Viceroy's palace, there to negotiate and parley on equal terms with the representative of the King Emperor . . .'

WINSTON CHURCHILL

EACH NEW INCIDENT in India confused Jaya. For every act of sacrifice there was an act of violence, and she feared both.

From her husband she had learned that danger could become an addiction stronger than the cause that had first inspired valour, an exhibition of manhood when every other form of manhood was denied. Now she was fearful, as Arun Roy had intended her to be, that the long denial of her own womanhood might lead her into similar excess.

Fear made Jaya retreat into Sirpur. But outside events had penetrated the complacent self-regard of the ancient kingdom, casting a shadow over her Regency.

Every day Sir Akbar informed the Dowager Maharani of the latest developments at the Round Table Conference in London, where Indians were pleading their case for Federation before the King Emperor.

'The British commissioned a special oval table, hukam, so that no section of Indian opinion would feel unfavoured.'

The Dowager Maharani grunted cynically. 'After spending a century dividing us, do the British really believe one round table is enough to unite us?'

'They even made a special gold and silver microphone for the King Emperor's address.'

'Hah! If an Indian ruler had done such a thing, he would have been accused of Oriental extravagance!'

'Well, for once the Indian rulers are being praised instead of criticized. Observers are saying, "Things seemed at their worst when the miracle happened and the Princes rose to a great occasion." And Sir Samuel Hoare, Secretary of State for India, said, "The keynote of the Conference was at once struck by the Princes, who one after another declared their faith . . . in an All India Federation. Amongst them were several remarkable personalities. The most notable was Bikaner. When he spoke in almost too fluent English, his fine figure and resonant voice dominated the Committee."'

'But you do not seem happy with the praise being showered on India's rulers, Prime Minister?'

'Gandhi is still in jail, hukam. Without him, the Round Table Conference is meaningless, and the Reformists are using this to attack the Regent.'

Sir Akbar did not add that anxiety about the Raj Guru's spies had led Jaya to receive the British Resident in the Wales Palace, to ensure her conversations were not relayed to the priests of the Kamini Temple.

There, in the first home she had known in the kingdom which she now governed, as the flutes of the river pilots floated across the water and the oleander blossoms turned black in the night, Jaya consulted Osborne about Sirpur's future and about the progress of the Round Table Conference.

His quiet, almost pedestrian assurances exuded a confidence that calmed her anxieties. 'We British are not all monsters, Bai-sa. In spite of attempts on his life, and deep resentment back in England, Lord Irwin is about to release Gandhi and invite him to talks at Viceroy's House. No Indian has ever been received as an equal by the Viceroy. Half of England will call Irwin a traitor. But if Gandhi attends the next Round Table Conference and Federation is granted by Parliament, the Empire may soon be packing its bags.'

Jaya lowered her eyes so James Osborne would not see her

fear of governing Sirpur without his assistance. The volatility of her emotions seemed to reflect the veering politics of India, as if the country, like herself, did not know how to respond to the possibility of freedom.

When the Viceroy released Gandhi, even the Purdah Palace no longer afforded an escape from the accelerating events outside the harem walls. Whenever Jaya called on the Dowager Maharani she found the purdah ladies sitting at the old woman's knees, discussing the reports in *The Sirpur Herald*.

'Mrs Naidu says, "India is blessed with two Mahatmas," hukam: "Gandhi and Lord Irwin."'

'Did you read this morning's paper, hukam? The Viceroy asked the Mahatma if he would like sugar in his tea, but the Mahatma put a pinch of illegal salt in his cup instead.'

'In full view of all the Viceroy's officers.'

'And yesterday, hukam. Did you read how Churchill described the Mahatma to the British Parliament?'

They thrust the newspaper into Jaya's hand. 'This fat Angrez insults the Mahatma, but how bad he will feel when our "half-naked fakir" takes away his empire.'

The ladies fell into one another's arms with peals of laughter. Jaya tried to keep a straight face at their delight, grateful when Gandhi agreed to attend the second Round Table Conference and the purdah ladies lost interest in the events in British India, returning to the unchanged pattern of their sequestered lives.

With the onset of the rainy season, the heavy downpour made the streets impassable. Power lines collapsed, plunging the capital into frequent darkness, and James Osborne no longer visited the Wales Palace. Watching the river toss muddy water against Maharajah Victor's boatyards, Jaya longed for the reassurance of the Englishman's presence.

But it was not until the rains ceased that she received a formal invitation to dine at the British Residency. As the car drove past the subsiding river, Jaya wondered if the Englishman, in the isolation of his embassy, had realized how dependent she had become on his quiet approbation.

Major Osborne received her with a tentative warmth that Jaya could no longer gauge as an indication of his feelings and led her into the drawing room.

The Prime Minister was pacing the floor. Lines of concern marked his high forehead. 'In spite of Gandhi's presence, this second Round Table Conference has been a failure. An ugly battle has been joined between the National Congress and the Muslim League, and it will lead to bloodshed between Hindus and Muslims.'

'Oh, come, Sir Akbar. If five hundred Indian kings could speak with one voice last year in London, Gandhi and Jinnah will surely come to an accommodation.'

At the dining table, Sir Akbar and James Osborne continued their discussion. By the light of the candles flickering in the silver candelabra Jaya silently examined the portraits on the walls. She recalled the Angrez boy's first visit to the Balmer zenana, his embarrassment when she had told him of the paintings of love that had once adorned the walls of the Chand Mahal. Now, like the stillness of the portraits, his quiet voice was reassuring Sir Akbar. 'Gandhi and Jinnah are both patriots. They will not permit the fragmentation of India.'

'I hope you are right, but I think we have only seen the beginnings of Hindu-Muslim antagonism.' Sir Akbar turned to Jaya. 'In the meantime, hukam, we must not permit the fragmentation of Sirpur. The ruler must take the allegiance of his tribal subjects.'

Curiosity lit Osborne's eyes. 'I should very much like to see the ceremony.'

'You would not enjoy it, James-sahib.' Jaya remembered her own shock when she had first witnessed the tribal dances, too raw in their imitation of nature to permit indifference. The unselfconscious abandon of the tribals would shake Osborne's faith in his own mission, make him doubt his capacity, as a British administrator, to civilize the subjects of Britain's great Empire.

'Please, Bai-sa,' Osborne insisted. 'If my presence would not be a burden, I should like to attend.'

TO JAYA'S RELIEF, as Maharajah Arjun's procession journeyed up-country, it was not often that the mask of distant rectitude slipped from the British Resident's features.

Sitting on a camp chair while his staff prepared his breakfast, he read his papers, ignoring the half-naked men and women sprawled on the grass around him, passing toddy bags among themselves or pulling thick cheroots from their hair to fill the air with evil-smelling smoke.

At night he wore a dinner jacket, hiding his expression behind his brandy balloon while the tribals pulled the young Maharajah into their dances. When they released the child, a feathered headdress tied over his turban, Osborne accompanied him to his tented bedroom. Passing by the open window, Jaya would see the Englishman sitting beside Arjun's mosquito net, shining a flashlight into a book.

Once she stood in the darkness for a long while, listening to the clipped voice read aloud the gentle stories with which English children were sent to sleep, calming the overexcited child with tales of frogs and dormice dressed as gentlemen, taking tea in cosily furnished woodland drawing rooms.

As the manner of the journey became more primitive, the Englishman became more rigid in the observation of his own customs, and Jaya found herself increasingly dependent on his rituals, as if his calm could in some way protect her son from the forces lying beneath the surfaces of his kingdom. The shining shoes, the occasional glimpse of suspenders as he turned a page – every detail was so ordered, every gesture so precise, as if confirming the fact that he could not be touched by the strangeness of the tribals watching him eat his English eggs and sausages.

Even when they arrived at the clearing on the lake and Jaya sat beside her son on the animal skin spread out on the red mud, the knowledge that Osborne was sitting behind them somehow dispersed the violent memory of her husband and herself on the jasmine-covered bed.

The tribals danced towards the Maharajah, their ankleted feet thudding on red mud and sending waves of fireflies over the water. But the Englishman's presence, watchful but unengaged, made even the tribals self-conscious. There was a diminution in their singing, and they wavered before pulling Arjun off the tiger skin, as if that one unmoved figure had destroyed the rhythm of their dance.

As the tribals whirled Arjun away to the high wooden hut with its curtains of flowers, Osborne rose from his camp chair, the civility of his words masking a rejection of everything he had seen. 'A fascinating ceremony, Bai-sa. But after all this excitement, it's high time the Maharajah got down to some schoolwork. We shall have to engage a tutor for him as soon as we get back to the capital.'

58

1932

Four Muslim undergraduates at Oxford University coin the word 'Pakistan' as the name to be given to a new homeland for India's Muslims.

The name, and the idea of a Muslim homeland, are dismissed as foolish student daydreams by Jinnah, President of the Muslim League.

ON THE ADVICE of the British Resident, a young English tutor, Mr Stevens, was engaged for Arjun. Enraged that for the third successive reign, the Kamini Temple had been deprived of its traditional role in educating a Sirpur Maharajah, the Raj Guru spread the charge that the British Resident was controlling the new ruler through his mother. In response, Jaya accelerated her development programme, hopeful that rapid construction would allay fears about her Regency.

At night, the City Palace shook with the sound of exploding dynamite as boulders were shattered for dam foundations, and a few miles upriver from the capital, the Maharajah Pratap Dam slowly became a reality. Airfields were laid beyond the Sirpur foothills, so that the tribal areas, isolated for so long, would soon have access to their capital. Arjun and his friends often accompanied the Prime Minister on the flights into the jungle areas, hoping the pilots would allow them into the cockpit when the small aeroplanes banked dangerously in front of the low foothills before descending onto makeshift landing strips on the recently flattened earth.

The results of the development programme soon eroded the suspicions the Raj Guru had raised. Village headmen filed nervously into the Durbar Hall, but forgot the chandeliers and painted frescoes in their excitement at the impact the new projects were having on their lives, and at the end of the audience they surrounded Sir Akbar with an avalanche of suggestions for the Regent.

Under its bending bamboo scaffolding the dam site gradually took on the appearance of an immense cane basket, its walkways crowded with tribal women carrying stones on their heads. In the early mornings Jaya and James Osborne cantered past the river to the dam site, to watch men lashing bamboo poles to the emerging structure.

The Resident used the rides to keep Jaya informed of Arjun's progress. 'At first Mr Stevens found the Maharajah inattentive, and rather spoiled. I suppose that's only natural with all the attention he gets in the Palace, and the fawning of the priests. Then Stevens discovered Arjun's natural aptitude for machines, and now he conducts classes at the airfield, or at the Palace garages and boatyards.'

Jaya laughed, remembering Tikka and his friends sitting around Captain Osborne in the Chand Mahal, envy creasing their features as the Angrez tutor described the aeroplanes and cars they had only seen painted on the outer walls of the zenana.

'Perhaps my son should also be taught in the barracks of the Sirpur Lancers. He loves anything to do with soldiers.'

'He's already quite an expert on Cambrai and Ypres, after all his father's tales,' Osborne agreed. 'But he prefers to discuss military matters with me, since I fought beside his uncle in France.'

On Osborne's suggestion, the cricket pitch was resurfaced and a small pavilion built for the children who came to play cricket with Arjun and Mr Stevens. Often James Osborne joined them for a game.

Jaya found herself resenting the children for having claims on the Englishman, and knew her dependence was becoming dangerous.

Long after her reconstruction programme needed the British Resident's approval, Jaya continued to invite James Osborne to join her in the Wales Palace. Sitting by his side on the wicker sofa, too conscious of his closeness, wondering if the same awareness moved him, she showed him her plans for new schools and roads.

She remembered the Angrez boy's first visit to Sirpur at Maharajah Victor's invitation, and how she had pulled away in the banquet room, afraid the Sirpur nobles might notice his hand crushing the jasmine buds that circled her wrist; or the ball for the Prince of Wales and the sound of her glass bangles breaking in his white glove. Now she longed for him to make some similar small gesture of intimacy.

Even as she castigated herself for her weakness, she could not shake herself of her desire. Of all the links between her past and her present, only Osborne remained. But when they cantered down the river path to the dam site, horses' hooves cutting into cobwebs silver with dew, she could detect no sign of awkward tenderness in the Englishman's manner, no evidence of the familiarity that had always lain beneath the surface of their encounters.

The more she contrived to arrange their isolation from the watching eyes of the City Palace, the more distant and formal the Englishman became, as if the burden of rectitude had passed from her to him.

Even Chandni commented upon the alacrity with which Jaya acted on the Englishman's every suggestion. 'I know the Raj Guru is not to be trusted, hukam. But the Angrez is making the Maharajah into a foreigner. He will become confused, the way your brother was confused by the Angrez' father.'

'The world has changed since my brother's time, Chandni. These are matters you do not understand.'

The maidservant tucked her veil into her waistband and muttered defiantly, 'These are matters I understand only too well, hukam.'

Jaya flushed, remembering her own contempt at the desperate efforts of the Sirpur brothers to gain the approval of the Empire. She had despised their weakness, not realizing how self-indulgence had offered them escape from the constant reminder of helplessness. Now, faced with her own fears, she was wilfully ignoring Osborne's power, converting her fear into an attraction more destructive than escape.

LADY MODI'S sudden arrival in Sirpur further disrupted the serenity of Jaya's world.

Over the mirrored surface of the lunch table Lady Modi swept the Sirpur nobles and their wives along in a tide of gossip. 'Do you remember how I laughed at the very thought of King George and Queen Mary receiving anyone dressed in a loincloth? Well, it happened, darlings. Gandhi actually went to Buckingham Palace wearing a loincloth. I believe Their Majesties just could not take their eyes off Gandhi's bare knees.'

She popped the tiny river fish trembling on the end of her fork into her mouth. 'The magnificence of the Princes dazzled everybody at the first Conference, and Gandhi's knees certainly overpowered them at the second. But all this Hindu–Muslim business ruined the third Round Table Conference. In fact, without the Maharajahs or Gandhi to hold their attention, no one in England is interested in India any more.'

Jaya hid her smile as Major Osborne and Sir Akbar struggled to keep up with Lady Modi's monologue, like swimmers hanging on to driftwood.

'Everyone is talking about the Prince of Wales's infatuation with Mrs Simpson. Am I being tactless, Major Osborne? But it is an open scandal in London now. And Old Mauve-y is so embarrassed.'

James Osborne studied his reflection in the dining table as the Sirpur ladies bent forward over their wineglasses.

'Lady Modi, Lady Modi . . .'

'Everyone knows the future King of England can't marry someone else's wife.'

'But who is Old Mauve-y?'

Lady Modi looked shocked. 'Darlings, you mustn't be so provincial. The new Vicereine, of course. Lady Willingdon.'

'Why is she called Old Mauve-y?'

'Because she has had the inside of Viceroy's House painted mauve. Furthermore, she insists on bouquets of mauve flowers wherever she goes. And not since Lady Reading has any Vicereine so loved ruling India.'

An expression of distaste crossed James Osborne's features, and Jaya wondered resentfully how long Lady Modi would remain in Sirpur, intruding the outside world on their lives.

She tried to avoid meeting James Osborne in Lady Modi's presence, but sometimes when she was sitting with Lady Modi in Maharajah Victor's study, windows open to the boatyards where Maharajah Victor's flotilla of wooden boats still sat on their steel supports, their painted masts and furled silk sails covered in cob-webs, the British Resident called to discuss some administrative matter. Then Jaya knew Lady Modi's large eyes were seeing her too obvious need for the Englishman.

Often Arjun and his friends trailed behind Major Osborne, eagerly demanding to go up in the aeroplanes.

'You are going to have to take that child in hand, darling. He's developing Pratap's taste for excitement.'

James Osborne agreed. 'And with the Hindu–Muslim riots, I would prefer to see the ruler leave India for a while. Perhaps attend his father's old school in England.'

Lady Modi clapped her hands. 'Eton. Darling, what fun. We can go down for picnics, and –'

For the first time Jaya rejected the Englishman's advice. 'Never! I will not let my son become an outcast in his own country.'

Osborne looked surprised at the depth of her feeling. 'But with all this uncertainty, the boy will be better off outside the kingdom.'

'To be as miserable as Tikka was in England?' Jaya asked bitterly.

'The world has changed since Tikka was a boy, Bai-sa. And so have we.' He gave her a tired smile and walked away.

'It's funny how Major Osborne is so offended by your behaviour,' Lady Modi observed softly.

'I have implemented all his other suggestions, Bapsy.'

'Only because you want to please him, darling. Not because you think he is right. He has failed to convert you, and conversion, not seduction, is Major Osborne's reason for being in India.'

'But we have known each other since we were children. He is more than the British Resident to me. He is my friend.'

Lady Modi carefully fitted a cigarette into her holder, averting her eyes from Jaya's desperate expression. 'Even if you are lonely, you would be foolish to forget Osborne's office, darling. Major Osborne has always been attracted to you. I saw that during the Prince of Wales's visit to Sirpur, when the poor man couldn't keep his eyes off you, and I see it now, in the way he controls himself. But in a choice between yourself and his Empire, he will always choose the Empire. If, like Victor and Pratap, you become a creature of the Empire, this friendship can blossom. Otherwise, darling, put your childhood relationships behind you.'

Jaya knew Lady Modi was speaking the truth even as she denied it. 'You are wrong, Bapsy. The Resident is not important. Everything I have done has been for my son.'

'Then forget your brother's experiences and send your son to school in England. Osborne has given you sound advice. Arjun could very easily become a pawn, caught in Hindu–Muslim bitterness.'

LADY MODI'S observation shook Jaya from the reverie of the past years, too soothing in their pattern to permit the intrusion of reality. While she had been immersed in construction projects, hoping to win Osborne's approbation, the religious enmities that had led to the failure of three Round Table Conferences were now vitiating the harmony of Sirpur.

The world Jaya had so painstakingly constructed to keep Sirpur intact from the events beyond its boundaries crumbled when the British Empire seized upon the differences between the Indian National Congress and the Muslim League to delay Federation yet again, and Hindu–Muslim riots flared up throughout British India.

Muslim peasants, suffering from their treatment by Hindu landlords in British India, trickled into Sirpur, seeking charity from their Sirpur relatives.

Hindu shopkeepers fleeing Calcutta, terrorized by the threats of Muslim students, spread their tales of persecution in the Sirpur bazaars.

The quarters of the old city, fashioned through the centuries of floods from each other's ruins until men of all religions prayed in every house of worship, confident their own faith was somewhere represented, were beginning to harden into religious fortresses, and neighbours crossed the narrow bazaar streets to avoid encounters.

To defuse the new religious intolerance so alien to Sirpur's history, Jaya convened meetings with the leaders of the different communities. The ten-year-old Maharajah was frequently called away from his lessons with Mr Stevens to sit on his gaddi in the Durbar Hall, confusion clouding his eyes as he listened to his subjects hurling accusations at each other.

Sometimes a refugee from British India challenged Sir Akbar, insisting a Muslim prime minister could not be objective about the insults endured by Hindus at the hands of Muslims. Then Arjun, with the angry directness of a child, would defend his Prime

Minister's dignity, silencing the room with his incomprehension of religious hatred. Jaya's heart ached as she heard the high voice demand why one god was greater than another, remembering his carefree laughter as he chased the goats at his grandmother's ashram only five years before, and she wondered if she should follow James Osborne's advice and send Arjun away to school in England.

When Osborne informed her that the British Parliament, worried by the scale of religious rioting, had at last agreed to an All India Federation in which Indians would share power with the Viceroy, Jaya thought she detected a note of guilty relief in his voice.

'The rulers are being offered a very powerful position in the Federation, Bai-sa. Parliament's Government of India Act has proposed an upper house in which the rulers will hold half the seats and a lower house in which the rulers will hold one-third of the seats. These two houses together will govern the whole of India, but the kingdoms will remain intact.'

He smiled, and Jaya could feel her resolution to be independent of the Angrez boy melting. 'Now all that remains is for the rulers to implement the reforms they promised ten years ago at the Chamber of Princes. That is the only condition Parliament has demanded before inaugurating the Federation.'

In the troubled year that followed, Jaya learned that James Osborne's description of Parliament's conditions had been too simple. Parliament had permitted each king the choice of joining the Indian Federation: but until the majority of Indian kings did so, Parliament would not endorse the Federation.

Worse, smaller kingdoms had been asked to merge with larger ones – a suggestion intolerable to rulers with historical enmities. Added to such humiliation was the rulers' increasing distrust of the inflammatory speeches of the Reformists, who were now demanding democratic elections in every Indian kingdom.

The increasing chaos in the subcontinent robbed the Indian princes of the courage to play statesman. Instead of enforcing the reforms agreed upon a decade earlier in the Chamber of Princes, many conservative rulers now followed the advice of their equally conservative British advisers, who feared a Federation could mean the end of the British Empire.

Dissension was forbidden, Reformists threatened with jail or exile. As a result demands for elections in the Indian kingdoms grew more vociferous every day.

Although Sirpur's citizens had long had the rights which other royal subjects were demanding, *The Sirpur Herald* gleefully reported Reformist speeches. 'There can be no Federation unless the people of the Indian kingdoms themselves determine whether they wish to remain subjects of autocratic monarchies, or whether they wish to join the Federation that will govern India as free democracies.'

Month after month, Jaya watched the Reformist movement gaining momentum, and she realized how foolish her dependence on James Osborne had been. When the bitterness between the Indian National Congress and the Muslim League had unleashed religious hatred in Sirpur, he had been unable to assist in restoring the renewed fervour of the Reformists, and she was almost relieved when Tiny Dungra's letter offered respite from the tensions in Sirpur, informing her of the Maharani's failing health.

59

1935

*If only half the Indian princes enact reforms the
All India Federation will come into being.*

APPENDIX TO THE GOVERNMENT OF INDIA ACT

TINY DUNGRA himself was waiting at the station to greet his fellow
maharajah. Arjun tried to look unexcited as a twenty-one-gun salute
was fired from Dungra Fort, but everyone on the platform smiled at
the boy's delight when the Dungra Lancers lowered their pennants at
his advance.

As they drove to the Maharani's ashram, Arjun's enthusiastic
monologue amused Dungra. 'Arjun is certainly his father's son,
Bai-sa. Cricket, aeroplanes, Englishmen.'

'And now the British Resident wants me to send him to his
father's school in England.'

Dungra's large eyes looked down at Jaya with compassion. 'The
Resident is right, Bai-sa. The times require our full concentration.
With Arjun away you can cultivate the nationalists more freely.
Invite Arun Roy to Sirpur. You may one day need his assistance.'

Jaya turned from Dungra's glance, sure he could see the colour
rising in her face at the mention of the lawyer.

'Once Arjun's grandmother is gone, Arjun will not need to
remain in India,' Dungra observed as the car entered the ashram.

Dungra fell silent, and dread knotted Jaya's stomach as she
followed him through the room where rows of spinners sat behind

their wooden wheels, drawing their flax out with steady hands until it became thread.

Two women dressed in homespun saris were kneeling on the back verandah. They moved away to reveal the Maharani lying on the floor. Shocked, Jaya realized her mother was preparing for death with the humility demanded by the ancient Hindu scriptures.

The Maharani lifted her head, calling for Dungra in a weak voice.

Dungra bent forward, holding his ropes of pearls so they would not strike the Maharani's body. Jaya's head almost touched Dungra's above her mother's prostrate form as the Maharani struggled to make herself heard.

'Tiny, many years ago it was predicted that I would be called the Sati Mata. Bai-sa knows how I fought the prophecy, claiming I would commit sati rather than accept such a title. But when I understood the true meaning of sati, I accepted that name with pride. Now I wish to claim one honour that is granted to the satis. Do not mourn my passing.'

Arjun ran onto the verandah, hovering beside his grandmother with the restlessness of a child being excluded from a secret. She placed her hands on his head, her long fingers pale against his black hair, and Jaya fought back her tears, remembering the Maharani's hands on Tikka's head the night before he had left for war.

It was as if the Maharani's farewell was coinciding with the end of royal India.

The fiercely independent monarchs who had risked their thrones against the Empire were gone.

Alwar, who had put on gloves to avoid pollution when he shook hands with his King Emperor, had been forced to abdicate.

Patiala the Magnificent, who had threatened to start a revolution if the British Empire attempted to take his throne, was now forbidden by the Empire to leave his kingdom.

Bikaner, who had declared so forcefully in the Chamber of Princes, 'We the Princes of the Indian States are Indians. We look forward as proudly as any British Indian to the day when our united country attains the full height of its political stature,' had returned to his desert kingdom, disgusted by the timidity of his fellow rulers and their dependence on their British advisers.

There were now no giants in the Chamber of Princes capable of persuading fellow rulers to grasp the power held out to them.

WITH THE MAHARANI'S passing Jaya felt her son's last links to a courageous past had been severed for ever. On her return to Sirpur, she found James Osborne waiting in Maharajah Victor's study with news of the latest developments on the Federation. Listening to his reports about the vacillation of the Indian kings, Jaya became fearful that the fate of Arjun's kingdom now rested in the hands of men terrified by the future, and she reluctantly asked James Osborne to make arrangements for Arjun to study in England.

Jaya had barely completed her pujas after the Maharani's death when the earthquakes that had devastated other eastern areas suddenly erupted in Sirpur.

Beyond the placid green rice fields, the foothills hid a landscape of ripped jungle and sudden waterfalls. Wild elephants ran between the uprooted trees, stopping in panic as they reached sheer cliffs from which the red earth was still falling.

All seven aircraft of SirAir were dropping supplies to the tribals marooned in jungle islands, separated by huge landslides. Jaya rose halfway through the night to complete her pujas, so that she would be ready at first light to oversee the emergency measures, travelling on any aircraft that could spare the space.

From the air, Jaya helplessly waved encouragement to the tiny figures standing forlornly next to their collapsed bamboo huts watching as burlap bags were pushed through the small aircraft doorway. As the bags split on impact with the ground, the tribals ran from their broken huts towards the scattered goods, looking half-animal themselves as they gathered up the bags of grain, vegetables, matches that would help them survive until the roads were restored, and temporary bridges slung across new streams to connect them with the rest of the kingdom again.

The cost of the relief measures had created concern in the Sirpur Council, and the Prime Minister warned Jaya of possible trouble.

'The increased taxes are encouraging more people to join the Reformists, hukam.'

'Are our people so indifferent to the plight of the tribals?'

'Not indifferent, hukam. Frightened. Your predecessors squandered treasury funds to impress the British Empire. Now people are clinging to what they own for fear of the future.'

Jaya remained silent. The continuing resistance of many Indian rulers to reforms had contributed to that fear, and every day the Indian kings were accused of robbing India of freedom.

'The Raj Guru has convinced those who are foolish enough to believe him that the earthquake is a result of your decision to send Maharajah Arjun to school in England. He says you have made the Goddess violent and warns that more violence will attend the kingdom if another ruler is defiled by contact with the Angrez.'

Jaya nodded wearily. She had overheard the Sirpur maidservants gossiping in the corridors of the City Palace, reminding one another of the violent deaths of Maharajah Victor and Maharajah Pratap. Aware of the Prime Minister's scrutiny, she sipped her tea thinking of the damage the earthquake had done to Sirpur's famous tea plantations.

A large steel safe was hidden behind a bookcase. The dial squeaked as Jaya turned it, indicating how little it had been used. The heavy door swung open, revealing a pile of green velvet files embossed with the Balmer crest. Jaya handed the files to the Prime Minister. 'These were given to me at the time of my marriage. Please tell me which sales would be most advisable to raise the money required for our relief operations.'

Sir Akbar examined the documents. 'But these are worth several fortunes, hukam. Far more than we require. I see that the proceeds from the sale of land in Florida have already been signed over to Esmé Moore ....'

There was a knocking at the door. 'Sirpur has brought you much grief, hukam,' Sir Akbar observed gently as he opened the door to a Council clerk standing behind the Lancers.

Jaya stared at the envelopes in the clerk's hand. From childhood she had been taught to recognise the heavy crest that concealed Viceregal demands. The strain of the relief measures, the necessity to remove Arjun from the kingdom's intrigues suddenly seemed focused on the envelopes. The Empire had recently removed the Maharajah of Rewa from his throne. Had the Raj Guru succeeded in ending her own Regency, to prevent Arjun from leaving Sirpur?

Sir Akbar closed the door. 'Shall I read the messages to you, hukam?' The barely perceptible note of concern in Sir Akbar's voice,

401

as if he did not wish to draw even his own attention to her moment of weakness, shook Jaya from her panic.

Sir Akbar straightened a fractional crease from his tunic coat before tearing open the telegram. The paper fluttered in his hand, in frivolous contrast to his controlled voice.

' "DARLING, OLD MAUVE-Y HAS JUST CONCEIVED THE MOST DIVINE IDEA. SHE HAS DECIDED TO HAVE A LAST CALCUTTA SEASON. CROWNED WITH A MASKED BALL. THEME IS LOUIS SIXTEENTH. VICEREINE WILL TAKE IT AS A PERSONAL SLIGHT IF PEOPLE DO NOT TAKE SUFFICIENT TROUBLE WITH THEIR COSTUMES. BAPSY." '

The Prime Minister gravely handed Jaya the heavy envelope with the embossed crest. 'And this, hukam, must be the imperial summons.'

SOON OPTIMISTIC MESSAGES reached the City Palace, informing Jaya that with the new funds, the reconstruction of the damaged roads and tribal villages had been completed, and Jaya was relieved that Sir Akbar would not have to handle too many crises while she travelled to Europe to put Arjun in school.

But the flurry of telegrams from Lady Modi expressed an urgency far greater than the news from the earthquake areas.

'PRINCES TERRIFICALLY UNPOPULAR. PLEASE TAKE BALL SERIOUSLY AND MAKE GOOD IMPRESSION ON VICEROY.'

'ONLY FOUR WEEKS LEFT. WHAT ARE YOU WEARING TO BALL?'

Jaya pushed the telegrams to one side, preoccupied with Arjun's departure. Two other Sirpur children were accompanying the Maharajah to school in England, and the laughter of the boys echoed in the palace corridors as they ran in and out of the Maharajah's apartments, preparing for their first journey abroad.

But every time Jaya drove past the cricket grounds and saw the boys playing with Mr Stevens, she was filled with foreboding that her son, like Tikka, would be lost to her once he went away to England.

60

1936

*Elections are called in British India to ascertain the
conflicting claims of the National Congress and the
Muslim League.*

CALCUTTA SEEMED to share the urgent superficiality of Lady Modi's
telegrams. The lunches at Firpo's preceded by frenzied exchanges in
the Venetian bar, the polo games, the boat regattas all mirrored the
ostentation of the Viceroy's presence in Calcutta, as if an insistent
frivolity could disperse the strident demands for freedom from the
men and women demonstrating on the streets outside.

No one discussed the British Parliament's sops to Indian nationalism, only whether the Prince of Wales would continue his infatuation
with Mrs Simpson.

The boys responded to the city's mood with enthusiastic delight.
When Jaya took them to the Eden cricket grounds, they did not
notice how frequently the car was stopped by silent nationalists
holding placards demanding immediate self-government for India,
and when Mrs Roy described nationalist fury at the Empire's
unworkable formula for Federation, they ran from the room.

On the night of the ball, Lady Modi and Jaya appeared in
ball gowns, masks held below their powdered wigs as horses' hoofs
clattered on the drive. The boys crouched against each other, trying
to hide their laughter when Tiny Dungra helped the ladies into the
carriage, his bulging calves visible in silk stockings, his foaming lace

403

cravat drawing further attention to his thick neck and protuberant belly.

Jaya struggled to control the rustling skirt of the ball gown as the carriage entered Government House.

The Viceroy's Lancers were immobile on their horses, black silhouettes against the pale blossoms of the lawn, the darkness leaching the colour from their brilliant uniforms.

'Darling,' Lady Modi whispered behind her fan. 'Is it just the lights or is the scarlet livery of the Viceregal staff now a sort of mauve?'

Beyond the Lancers, bronze torches lit figures in French court dress approaching the staircase, ignoring the incongruity of the turbaned staff, as heralds shouted their titles.

Lady Modi's voice rose in excitement. 'And regardez! Old Mauve-y has got herself up as Marie Antoinette.'

Jaya followed the pointing fan. A large-boned middle-aged Englishwoman was indeed masquerading as the Queen of France, and one Indian ruler after another, dressed as French nobility, was bowing before her, all of them unconcerned that what they were enjoying as a charade was the truth of their existence.

In the ballroom, the conversations of the rulers reflected the same complacency: 'Hukam, will we see you at the Berlin Olympics?'

The Maharajah of Kapurthala enthusiastically described the order he had received from Mussolini when he had visited Rome the previous summer. 'Perhaps the German Chancellor will give me another.'

'I accompanied my parents to Austria last summer,' the Maharani of Cooch Behar observed as her eldest daughter was led onto the dance floor by a British officer. 'We heard unpleasant stories about the Brown Shirts beating up Jewish shopkeepers, gypsies, anyone who belonged to another party or religion. Aren't Mussolini's Black Shirts doing the same in Italy?'

'No, no, hukam. The Fascists in Italy are saving their country from Communism. Don't forget, Communists slaughtered the Tsar, and if it weren't for Mussolini they would probably have killed Victor Emmanuel by now. With my own eyes I saw them try to kill the King of Spain, throwing a bomb at the poor man's wedding procession.'

He turned towards the Vicereine, his ease with his costume

proclaiming him the only Francophile among the Indian rulers.

Jaya was grateful for the mask that hid her expression as she moved through the ballroom. Elaborately gowned Indian women, held in the arms of British officers wearing powdered wigs, were swirling towards the tailcoated orchestra. Jewels glittered under the chandeliers. Beauty spots dropped onto the marble floor. People tapped one another's shoulders with their fans, and there were muted exclamations of delighted recognition.

Jaya watched the Vicereine turning on the dance floor with the Maharajah of Kapurthala, wondering if the Vicereine's costume would prove prophetic for the British Raj. By the time Arjun was old enough to dance at such a ball, would the grim realities of the subcontinent, still held at bay by bronze torches and Viceregal Lancers, have submerged Government House?

Through the weeks of Christmas parties and polo matches that followed the ball Jaya was unable to rid her mind of the image of the Viceroy's wife dressed as the French queen who had been beheaded by a desperate people.

But grandeur and frivolity seemed to have slowed the clocks. At the racecourse, the boys clapped with excitement when they saw the Viceregal Lancers in their scarlet and gold uniforms trotting past the picket fences in front of the Viceroy's gilded carriage. To Jaya, the Lancers' perfect formation had the symmetrical fantasy of mechanical toys, and the applauding crowds were like children, their destructive instincts briefly checked by curiosity.

She remembered the Indian rulers who had accompanied Junagadh's golden retriever to its wedding, their haughty disdain of political reality when the Reformists were demanding revolution in India's kingdoms. Now the Viceroy, with equal wilfulness, was re-creating the court that had preceded the French Revolution at a time when Indians were demanding revolution in the British Empire.

Even when Lady Modi burst into her apartments with the news that the King Emperor was dead, Jaya did not feel as if an auspicious new era were beginning.

Lady Modi pressed a glass of champagne into her hand. 'Think of the fun! The dashing Prince of Wales has become King of England. India will finally have a playboy for an emperor. And we are being sent a gentleman as the new Viceroy. Darling, do look happy. The

Willingdons are leaving India. We can stop ordering those awful mauve bouquets at last.'

ON REACHING LONDON, Jaya realized Lady Modi's optimism had been misplaced. The capital of the British Empire was not celebrating the reign of a playboy emperor. Friends briefly expressed their delight at seeing Jaya in London after an absence of eight years, then returned to the topic that preoccupied London. Would King Edward VIII, in his determination to marry Mrs Simpson, precipitate a constitutional crisis that might lead to the end of the Empire?

Listening to the worried speculations of her English friends, Jaya remembered the fury of the maharanis who had attended her husband's investiture at the scandalous manner in which the British Empire was using women as a pretext to remove rebellious Indian kings from their thrones. Those kings had been given no occasion to explain themselves as King Edward VIII was explaining himself now to Members of his Parliament.

The turn of events, no longer limited to harmless scandal, had even frightened Lady Modi. 'But, darling, I don't understand why the King is so determined to marry Mrs Simpson. At the Valentine Ball in Delhi, he read Victor the riot act for wanting to marry Cora Hart. And she hadn't had two previous husbands. I don't know what the world has come to if we can't trust the King of England to behave correctly.'

Jaya said nothing. The last time she had been in England, it had been the Indian kings who were accused of squandering their kingdoms on women – the campaign so effective in her husband's case that in defending his reputation she had ended as Regent of his throne.

Indians also came to the house in Mayfair. They hardly spoke of Mrs Simpson, preoccupied with the electoral battles being joined in India.

'This election has hardened the attitudes between the Hindus and the Muslims.'

'Have there been more religious riots?'

'Yes, hukam. The situation could easily get out of control.'

'Jinnah is being called Quaid-i-Azam, the Great Leader. It is the Great Leader fighting the Mahatma, the Great Soul.'

406

Relieved that her son was away from the dangerous developments in the subcontinent, Jaya toured the city with the boys. Their impetuous pleasure in every new experience, travelling by Underground, visiting the Tower of London, losing themselves in the maze at Hampton Court, convinced Jaya that it had been the right decision to bring Arjun to England.

But Lady Modi refused to be distracted from Edward VIII's equivocations. 'It is ridiculous, darling. The man has been king for six months now. When is he going to make up his mind?'

'Cheer up, Bapsy. If he goes, the Duke of York will become king and we will have another King George and Queen Mary to rule over us.'

'But the Duke of York is such a meek little man,' Lady Modi objected. 'He stutters, darling. His reign would be the death of panache.'

While Lady Modi continued to speculate on whether Edward VIII would give up his throne for Mrs Simpson, Jaya concentrated on school uniforms, grateful that her friend's obsession blocked out other, more frightening news as the word 'dictator' became a common one in the newspapers, and Italy bombed Ethiopia, and Hitler's troops marched into an undefended Rhineland, and war broke out in Spain.

Jaya tried not to cry when she left Arjun at school, and he began the inevitable schoolboy negotiations for food parcels to be sent on a regular basis from Fortnum's. Arjun seemed oblivious of her emotions, showing only the briefest panic when the chauffeur steered the Rolls-Royce over the cobblestones of Eton High Street.

'I'll be home soon, hukam,' he shouted, running after the car. 'Make sure the cricket pitch is kept in good condition.'

On the return voyage, Lady Modi tried to distract Jaya from her anguish at Arjun's absence. 'We should have a wonderful winter season to cheer you up. Like the old days, with Pratap and Victor. Polo games. Dances. Get a good band up from Calcutta.'

But every evening Lady Modi disappeared into the crowded state room, waiting for the next bulletin on King Edward VIII's decision about Mrs Simpson.

Two days before the ship docked in Bombay, posters were nailed on the wooden walls around the decks, advising the passengers that the King himself would be making an address to the British Empire that afternoon.

A larger radio was moved into the main saloon, and long before the broadcast every chair in the room was taken. Latecomers crowded at the windows, their faces tilted towards the loudspeakers relaying the radio message to the outer deck, where the humid air now carried the pungent smell of the East.

The voice that Jaya vaguely remembered from fifteen years ago, when he had visited Sirpur as Prince of Wales, began to speak. Lady Modi cried into her lace handkerchief. Jaya looked around. Emotion marked the features of the gentlemen. Every woman in the crowded room was weeping.

Jaya alone remained unmoved as the man who could have been Emperor of India said, 'I cannot carry the heavy burden of state without the help and support of the woman I love.'

61

1937

The rulers continue to delay Federation, and political agitations are launched in a large number of Indian kingdoms.

WITH ARJUN gone, Jaya performed the tasks of government like a devotee tending a temple from which the idol had long since been removed. The scurrying maidservants, the Lancers lining the marble corridors, seemed to be ghosts, inhabiting an unreal world, and her longing to hear Arjun's sudden laughter make the painted frescoes of the Durbar Hall into a backdrop for children's games was now mixed with an awareness of how insubstantial a kingdom became without a king.

On the rare occasions when James Osborne called, she could see a confusion in his eyes, as if Edward VIII's public betrayal of his office had robbed the Resident of his customary assurance. Jaya wondered how he must have felt all those months when the figurehead of his empire had wavered between duty and desire, as she herself had once done until Lady Modi had warned her that Osborne's belief in the proprieties of the British Empire would never permit the merging of the two.

Now, under the gaze of the Empire's subjects, the King of England had behaved as the British Empire had always accused the Indian rulers of doing, broadcasting to the very people who the British Raj maintained were not yet competent to govern themselves that he preferred personal fulfilment over public office.

Osborne appeared embarrassed when he conveyed the Viceroy's strongly worded advice that any further delay by the Indian rulers in joining the Federation would have serious consequences for royal India.

'The Viceroy is even sending personal emissaries from Delhi to push the rulers to a decision.'

But no sooner did one group of rulers agree to reforms than another group of rulers attacked the reforms as an encroachment on their sovereign power, and in Sirpur, the newspapers had become strident in their demand for elections in the Indian kingdoms.

The frequency with which Sir Akbar's thin fingers dusted imaginary lint from the elegantly tailored tunic coat was sufficient warning of trouble even before he brought news of the agitations that were threatening to get out of hand in Mysore, Jaipur, Rajkot, Kashmir, as revolution rocked the most powerful thrones in India.

'But Sirpur has reforms,' Jaya told Sir Akbar in despair. 'The kingdom supports the Federation. Every freedom that British India enjoys is enjoyed by our citizens. Why are the Reformists disturbing the kingdom's peace?'

'It no longer matters whether individual rulers have enacted reforms or not, hukam. The Reformists can smell power. Maharajah Arjun should remain away for as long as this madness continues.'

Jaya's heart froze at the thought that another year would pass before she saw her son's eyes changing with the light as he begged to be allowed to fly into the tribal areas.

She stood at the balcony as the sun set like a crimson canopy over the river and the lanterns outlined the dark shapes of the river barges, thinking of the Indian rulers she had met in Europe – their unhurried elegance in the casinos, their indifference to the wars shaking Europe as they sat in their spas sipping their whiskies, the rhythms of their desultory conversations like the monotonous clicking of lizards basking in the sun.

She wistfully remembered Lady Modi's shipboard plans to recreate the world in which Maharajah Victor and Maharajah Pratap had governed, with its polo matches and midnight games of hide-and-seek. But all that now remained of that world was the Dowager Maharani. The old woman's mind wandered often now and she was unable to rise from her bed to attend the evening pujas.

When the Dowager Maharani heard that Arjun would not be returning from England for another year, she became incoherent with rage. It was several minutes before Jaya realized that the old queen was locked in past nightmares, afraid again of losing Maharajah Victor to the power of the British Empire.

With the onset of the monsoons, the Dowager Maharani's arthritis became so severe that Jaya moved into the Purdah Palace. Sitting by the vast mahogany bed, its clawed feet resting in brass water containers against the snakes that might suddenly slide in from the purdah gardens, Jaya listened to the Dowager Maharani's rambling stories as incense from the evening puja floated down the marble corridors.

Jaya was almost relieved when the Abyssinian eunuchs came to her chambers in the middle of the night with news that the old woman was dying.

The ceremonies that followed the Dowager Maharani's death kept Jaya in the harem until the thirteen days of pujas were over and the ashes in the simple clay urn were taken away by the priests, to be immersed into the river at Benares.

When Jaya returned to the Wales Palace, Sir Akbar and James Osborne were awaiting her on the verandah. 'The Viceroy sent an emissary to Sirpur, hukam, while you were in the zenana,' the Prime Minister said.

Jaya was shocked at Sir Akbar's appearance. His body seemed to have shrunk inside his tunic coat, and his words were hesitant, as if the Dowager Maharani's death had left him stranded in an alien time. 'I assured him that Sirpur would use every means to urge other rulers to join the Federation. But the British do not seem to understand that ruling kings are not likely to listen to the words of a mere regent maharani.'

He stood uncertainly in front of Jaya, then, supporting himself on his gold-knobbed cane, he began walking down the path between the oleander bushes. A blossom dropped on his shoulder. He stopped, as if confused by his surroundings. Jaya's heart ached, seeing the blossom still stuck to his coat and the hand not rising to remove it.

Osborne cleared his throat. 'Sir Akbar did not mention that the Viceroy has given the Indian rulers an ultimatum, Bai-sa. Either half the rulers join the Federation by September 1939, or royal India loses the chance of sharing in the governing of India.'

Jaya glanced at the strong profile and was pleased to see it had regained its certainty in the weeks that she had been in the Purdah Palace. 'Isn't it strange, James-sahib. I swore I would never expose my son to the humiliations that affected my brother, my husband, my brother-in-law. Yet the situation here is so bad that I haven't seen him for almost two years now.'

Osborne said nothing, but his silence reminded her of the long years of friendship between them. Even when they were children, their shared silences had always conveyed more than words, and she knew the Englishman understood her anxiety that the complicated patronization of the British Raj might corrupt her son until he too became a creature of the ruling race, either in his extravagance or in his self-destructiveness.

James Osborne turned, anger darkening the blue eyes until they were almost the colour of steel. 'Don't you Indian rulers ever tire of self-pity, Bai-sa? The Viceroy has exhausted every avenue in urging you to save yourselves from dying in the past you all love so well. Now he has been forced to give you an ultimatum. But ask yourself this, Bai-sa. How long do you think your Regency will last if Gandhi's or Jinnah's followers enter Sirpur?'

He slammed his glass down on the table. In his uncharacteristic rage Jaya recognized fear. She had seen her father and her husband respond with equal frustration to events over which they had lost control, their fury hiding their despair, and her entire experience had attuned her to recognize the futile gestures of power when power itself was leaking away. As she watched the Englishman striding down the oleander path where the band had once played for the Prince of Wales, she knew she had no choice but to invite Arun Roy to Sirpur.

62

1938

'*The Indian rulers must seize power now, when it is being offered freely, or they may soon find themselves at the mercy of "dictators".*'

SIR MANUBHAI MEHTA TO THE CHAMBER OF PRINCES

ONLY THIRTEEN years had passed since the Viceroy of India had visited Sirpur, but now the capital's balconies were hung with green, saffron and white bunting, and people pressed against one another to catch a glimpse not of the Viceroy's white train but of Arun Roy's white Gandhi cap.

Jaya read through the lawyer's crowded schedule, thinking how quickly things had changed. When she became Regent Maharani, she could not have believed it would some day be as necessary to impress a nationalist as it had once been to impress the Viceroy of India.

A roar of applause, as loud as the cannon fire for the Viceroy, greeted Arun Roy's appearance at the door of the train compartment. For a moment, Jaya did not recognise the silver hair covering the head she had last seen shaven, or the silver moustache pulling at the sides of Roy's mouth, giving his face an uncharacteristically morose expression as he acknowledged the cheers. But his lips lifted in a smile of pleasure as the car drove through streets filled with waving spectators.

During his weeklong tour of Sirpur, crowds followed the lawyer everywhere, waiting as he inspected the completion of the Maharajah Pratap Dam, pressing gifts on him each time he visited another building in the network of new schools and dispensaries.

Jaya was relieved when Roy's congratulations on the work being done in the kingdom were expressed with a distant formality that gave no indication that they had known each other before.

On an inspection flight of the irrigation projects now stretching like a cobweb over the country, Jaya pointed with special pride to the airstrips that connected the farthest parts of the kingdom with its capital.

'I'm very impressed, Bai-sa,' the lawyer shouted over the noise of the propellers. 'But I have been travelling India for a year and a half, making speeches, organizing workers. Your subjects want me to make a speech in Sirpur. Before I start again, can't we get away from the crowds for a short time?'

Preoccupied with impressing the nationalist, Jaya had forgotten the signs of fatigue she had first noticed in the man. 'Forgive me,' she said, embarrassed. 'Tomorrow we are visiting the tribal areas. I'll make sure you are not disturbed by admirers.'

For the first time in the week he had been her guest, Arun Roy allowed a note of familiarity to enter his voice. 'Don't forget to arrange a visit to the jungle, Bai-sa. Who knows, we might find another pig-pearl together.'

In the City Palace, hasty preparations were made for the lawyer's request. News was sent ahead to the tribal chiefs, and Sir Akbar insisted that the lawyer's visit be kept as private as possible. 'Arun Roy won't understand the tribals, but if the aides accompany us, they might say something to turn Roy against our interests. When Roy makes his speech in the capital, he must support your Regency.'

The Jeep cut through thick grass, bumping over the rough track that led to the foothills at the boundary of the tribal areas. Clouds of red dust obscured the huts raised on stilts, and the lawyer held a handkerchief to his moustache as the car halted in front of the cane mats spread out under a banyan tree, glowing red in the light of the setting sun.

At Sir Akbar's stern rebuke, the tribals expressed surprise. 'These arrangements are not for the visitor.'

'We want to hold an assembly with our Maharani.'

Kerosene lanterns were brought into the clearing, and the tribals sat cross-legged, facing Jaya across the cane mats. Insects flapped against the sputtering flames until the smell of kerosene mixed with the smell of burning wings.

The lawyer leaned against the trunk of the banyan tree, listening to the half-naked men interrupt each other.

'What are they saying, Bai-sa?'

'They want to know what an election means. They are asking about the students who come to see them, demanding changes in government.'

'And what do they say about the chances of finding a tiger tonight?'

Waving their cigars in the air, the tribals excitedly described the pugmarks that had been sighted that day. Jaya translated, and Arun Roy looked pleased. 'You must take the first shot, Bai-sa.'

'But I will not be with you.'

The lawyer frowned. 'It is hardly hospitable to leave me alone in the jungle in the middle of the night without anyone who can understand what I am saying.'

Jaya looked in desperation at Sir Akbar. The Prime Minister's age prevented him from spending the whole night high on a platform waiting for a tiger to appear through the undergrowth. Why hadn't he foreseen this problem when he had insisted that no aides accompany them? Sir Akbar gave a barely perceptible nod, and Jaya turned back to Arun Roy. Lamplight threw shadows across the lawyer's eyes. Fireflies seemed to coat his silver hair with silver dust. Seeing his smile, Jaya felt her throat turn dry.

The tribals were still asking about elections in Sirpur. The sweet smell of kerosene filled the humid air, like the smell of kerosene at the station in Calcutta, and Jaya remembered James Osborne's question 'How long do you think your Regency will last if Gandhi's followers enter Sirpur?'

IN SILENCE Jaya climbed into the howdah lashed on the back of the kneeling elephant. The shikaris loaded the guns behind Arun Roy as the grey beast rose to its feet.

'Step lightly, my little one. Go gently as a dancer,' the mahout chanted to the elephant plodding through the dark.

Swaying with the motion of the elephant, Jaya felt the mahout's song blurring her present with her childhood, and her apprehensions melted into the night.

'Gently, my beloved. Step lightly, my dancer,' the mahout whispered as he guided the elephant through the thick blackness of the jungle, and the darkness sighed with the sound of night animals running from the elephant's approach.

Jaya climbed from the howdah onto the high platform from which they would keep vigil for the tiger. The mahout reached forward to free her sari, caught on a thorn branch, waiting until she had settled on the mattress next to Roy before whispering that he would be near the water hole a mile away.

The jungle closed on them as the chant of the mahout and the sound of the elephant's flapping ears grew distant. The lawyer extinguished the sputtering flame of the lantern.

Jaya stared at the night sky, so low the stars seemed caught on the branches of the tree. Arun Roy's lips brushed her neck, and his fingers stroked her hair. Jaya was afraid to breathe, but on the platform high above the night animals, enclosed by leaves like black stains against the thick branches of the tree, she felt the lawyer's tenderness burning away the violent humiliations of her past, allowing her to repossess her soul each time her name was whispered into the darkness.

Hands loosened the folds of her silk sari. The breeze was cool against her bare limbs as his mouth moved down her body as gently as the leaves falling with the gusts of wind. She felt herself expanding to contain not just Arun Roy's desire, but the jungle itself, seething with its predators and prey. The soughing of the high elephant grass enveloped the machan, as soft as the rustle of Roy's falling clothes, then she was in his arms, her thick hair like a garment between his hands and her naked body.

In the morning, the shouted apologies of the shikaris set flights of birds exploding into the thin light streaking the sky. 'If the honoured visitor would care to try again tonight, we can send beaters out all day to ensure that the tiger remains nearby.'

All day Sir Akbar toured the area with Arun Roy, showing him the bridges that had been built across the deep ravines created by the earthquake, and the rock walls which now supported the hillsides until the newly planted saplings could spread their roots wide enough to hold the earth against the fury of the next monsoons.

At sunset the lawyer silently assisted Jaya onto the elephant, taking pleasure in their mutual complicity as they entered the jungle and the voice of the mahout sang softly to his beast.

Jaya felt secure in Roy's embrace, sure that when the elephant reappeared through the grass, barely visible in the darkness turning grey with morning light, they would be dressed and appear to have spent the night watching for the tiger. She even knew that on their last night he would contrive to shoot the tiger, at whose absence the tribals had begun expressing disbelief instead of dismay.

On their return to the capital, Sir Akbar congratulated Jaya on the success of their tour. 'We can count on Mr Roy to defuse the Reformist movement with his speech.'

SIR AKBAR could not hide his consternation as the car stopped behind the bandstand, where a row of speakers shifted in their steel chairs. Crowds still moved towards Lady Reading Park, even though the congregation that already packed the arena was now spilling onto the road.

'I had no idea the Reformists had made such an impact on people's thinking, hukam. Thank God Osborne is in Delhi. It would not have been healthy for the British Resident to see the size of this gathering.'

Students fiddled with a microphone, and the park echoed with amplified voices as one speaker after another informed the crowd of the shooting of Arun Roy's brother by British police, of the years Arun Roy had spent in Japan to avoid the Empire's suspicions, the injuries he had sustained while trying to take over the Dharsana Salt Depot.

At last the editor of *The Sirpur Herald* led Arun Roy up the wooden steps of the bandstand. A roar of adulation rose from the thousands of people on the grass.

The lawyer's voice cut across their cheers. 'Brothers and sisters, Jai Hind! Victory to India! For years we have begged the rulers of India to give their subjects the simple dignities which differentiate a man from a slave. Denied those dignities in British India, we looked to the kings of India to show the British Raj the meaning of justice. But the rulers of India ignored our pleas.

'Now the Viceroy has given the rulers until September 1939 to agree to a Federation or jeopardize India's right to govern herself. Is this justice, brothers and sisters? Must we be condemned to slavery because five hundred foolish men and women, lost in dreams of harems and shikars and foreign cities, cannot see that human beings have a right to be consulted about the conduct of their own affairs?

'True justice lies in the claims of the majority. I say to you, the princes of India have forfeited their chance to share in the governing of India. By their refusal to enact simple reforms, they continue to keep millions of Indians in chains. Demand elections in every Indian kingdom. Let history say it was the subjects, not the kings, of royal India who freed every Indian from the shackles of slavery.'

Cheering engulfed the park as the lawyer shouted, 'Brothers and sisters, join our march to freedom. Jai Hind! Victory to the Motherland!'

Lonelier than she had ever felt before, Jaya stood in the study where Maharajah Victor had once re-created an ancient navy to impress the Prince of Wales. Where her husband had planned an airline to win the approval of the Viceroy. Where she had spent long nights studying budgets and development plans to impress James Osborne.

The doors behind her opened. 'Your subjects were very generous in their applause, Bai-sa. They would not let me go, plying me with questions about the future.'

'I hope you were able to answer them satisfactorily. After all, you are a lawyer, and we are only foolish men and women lost in dreams of harems and shikars.'

Arun Roy parted the thick hair that dipped inward to Jaya's waist, pressing his lips against her neck. She swung around.

He smiled at her. 'Why are you angry, Bai-sa?'

Jaya slapped the smiling face with all the frustration that seethed inside her. 'Did you forget that you were a guest in my kingdom? Or did you always intend to insult the salt you have eaten? To take me in your arms, knowing you would use your power to discredit my son's throne and destroy all the work I have done!'

Roy caught her hand, and the smile no longer reached his eyes. 'No bargain was struck between us, Bai-sa. You came to me of your own free will. Did you think your beauty would prevent me from telling your subjects the truth?'

418

63

September 1939

> 'War has broken out between His Majesty and Germany. The compulsion of the present international situation requires the suspension of all preparations for Federation.'
>
> THE VICEROY OF INDIA, LORD LINLITHGOW

BOLD HEADLINES in *The Sirpur Herald* made it impossible for Jaya to forget the lawyer. As if Arun Roy had somehow become the embodiment of their own aspirations, Sirpur's newpapers reported every speech Roy made throughout India, voicing the rage of the National Congress.

'If the war is to defend imperialist possessions, then India can have nothing to do with it. A slave India cannot help Britain.'

'By entering India in this war without consulting Indian opinion, the Viceroy of India has demonstrated conclusively that Britain retains her dominance in India.'

'How long must the poverty-stricken millions of India pay the costs of Britain's wars?'

Emergency Council meetings, to calculate the costs of the war to Sirpur, forced Jaya to suspend her rage and acknowledge the truth of Roy's speeches. Over the last fifty years, Britain's imperial adventures in China, South Africa, France, Mesopotamia, Afghanistan had bankrupted Sirpur. In the years of peace, there had been the visits of the Prince of Wales and the Viceroy, further draining an exchequer already precarious from punitive British tariffs.

'What about my son, Sir Akbar? Should I send for him?'

'There is no urgency, hukam. The British are calling this a phoney war. The Maharajah of Dungra and Lady Modi are leaving for Europe in the winter. Let them bring the boys back. At least the ruler will have a pleasant journey home.'

Arjun's letters from England made no mention of the war, only that Bradman was captaining the Australian cricket team on its tour of England in the summer, and that he had seen the new film *Gone with the Wind*, which starred a beautiful new actress born in India.

Jaya could find no parallel between this war and the long preparation for the Great War that had taken her brother's life. She remembered the telegraph keys clacking in the King's View, relaying news of the mobilization of imperial armies. But the new war, too sudden and too distant, was only being used to settle the bitter feuds of British India.

As Hitler's armies marched into Poland, every member of the Indian National Congress resigned from government in protest against India's being forced to enter another world war, and the jubilant Jinnah declared the resignations of his opponents 'a Day of Deliverance for the Muslims of India'.

Enraged by Jinnah's growing popularity, angry editorials in *The Sirpur Herald* suggested that Sirpur's Muslims preferred the Great Leader of the Muslim League to Gandhi, the Great Soul of the National Congress.

At the City Palace, Jaya's meetings with the Prime Minister were frequently disturbed by Muslim delegations from the old city.

'The newspapers are creating suspicion against us, hukam.'

The words were addressed to Jaya, but the old men with their hennaed beards were speaking to Sir Akbar, hoping to gain a sympathetic ear from their shared faith.

'Is it our fault that Jinnah is being hailed as the saviour of India's Muslims?'

'The fight between the Muslim League and the National Congress is a fight to govern British India. We live in Sirpur. What have we to do with it?'

420

Despite the unreality of the war, James Osborne came to the palace to invoke the treaty made a century ago between a trading company that had become an empire and the three-thousand-year-old kingdom.

Eager to honour the treaty with anything but human lives, Jaya offered the Empire all seven of Sirpur's aeroplanes. James Osborne was cutting in his rejection. 'This war is being fought five thousand miles away in Europe. What good can seven light aircraft do?'

Remembering the long years he had spent on the battlefield when hardly more than a boy himself, Jaya forgave him his uncharacteristic curtness. Even in his impatience, the Englishman still symbolized order in the maelstrom of Indian politics, steadfastness after Arun Roy's betrayal.

'At least Sirpur is a willing partner to the war effort, Major Osborne. Unlike the National Congress.'

Osborne shrugged in irritation and left the study. Sir Akbar rose to take his leave, and Jaya noticed how fatigued he always seemed since the Dowager Maharani's death. At the door, he hesitated, as if he had forgotten something trivial. Jaya watched him with concern, wondering if the Muslim fears expressed every day at the City Palace were taking too high a toll on his energy.

He walked back and handed Jaya a file. 'I think you should read this, hukam.'

'What is it?'

'The British Resident's secret reports to the Political Office in Delhi.' He closed the door softly behind him as Jaya turned to the first page.

'The Regent Maharani seems to be very close to the National Congress leader, Arun Roy, at a time when it is hazardous to the Empire's interests. Ignoring convention, the Regent Maharani invited the nationalist leader to spend three days with her away from the court. Risking public scandal, she also accompanied him alone at night into the jungle. Her intimate association with a man like Arun Roy imperils Britain's interests in Sirpur.'

Jaya slammed the file shut, rage and shame overwhelming her. She thought of the details the spies must have provided, implied so strongly between the lines of the report, and imagined Osborne in his Residency, with its overstuffed sofas and flowered cushions, listening with cold attention to the men in his pay. Who had sat beneath the platform in the jungle? Who had reported her movements to the Empire?

She forced herself to reopen the cardboard cover, but the print seemed to crawl over the pages, and she could not stop herself from dwelling on the pleasure the Residency clerks must have taken in recording Major Osborne's views on their typewriters. Or the image of the fastidious Sir Akbar reading the report.

'The Regent Maharani is also known to have been present at a large meeting in the capital at which Roy attacked the British Empire and its constitutional guarantees. I am anxious to be relieved of my post and to rejoin my regiment. But I must impress upon the Political Office that the Regent Maharani, a woman of great charm and seeming compliance, is possessed of that peculiarly native ability to dissemble while appearing to act on advice. My successor must monitor her associations closely, with a possible view to recommending her removal from the Regency if she persists in her nationalist friendships.'

Jaya threw the file against the wall, breaking a framed photograph of herself leading a horse. Shards of glass fell on the floor as they had fallen when the Dowager Maharani had smashed Cora Hart's photograph in the Kamini Temple, and she watched the falling splinters helplessly, wondering if her defeats in the defence of her son's kingdom would lead her also to trust only a stone image in a cave.

64

1940

*'Pakistan, a homeland for the Muslims, is the
avowed aim of the Muslim League.'*

MOHAMMED ALI JINNAH

'HITLER HAS overrun France, hukam. A massive evacuation of Allied troops is taking place at Dunkirk. Every boat, every fishing craft, is being used to ferry soldiers away from the German tanks.'

Jaya's heart lurched. 'But my son is sailing from London next week.'

'The Maharajah of Dungra will manage a passage home somehow. As long as the boys are with him they will be safe.'

The overwhelming reality of the war reduced every personal consideration to the ridiculous. The weeks inched past and still there was no news from Maharajah Dungra, only the radio broadcasts as Winston Churchill became Prime Minister of a wartime cabinet in a country preparing for invasion.

As if Britain's vulnerability had made Britain great again in India's eyes, the whole subcontinent now rose to the Empire's aid. Despite Churchill's determined resistance to Indian self-government, from two hundred thousand men under arms the number of Indian volunteers jumped to two million men, twice the number that had fought in the Great War. The German air attack on England moved even the National Congress to join the war effort, and the Nizam of

Hyderabad donated an entire squadron of fighters to Britain's air force.

When at last news arrived that Maharajah Dungra and the boys had boarded a ship leaving for India, Jaya's joy catapulted her into the wartime euphoria that had overtaken the rest of the subcontinent.

'My son must take a march-past of his troops before they leave for the battlefields.'

Ignoring James Osborne's repeated warnings that Rommel was a tank commander and there would be no cavalry in the desert campaign, Jaya dispatched ministers to Delhi to arrange stabling for the Sirpur horses.

The Sirpur Lancers brought out their battle fatigues, eager to campaign on ground already familiar to them from the last time they had fought in Mesopotamia, under the command of Maharajah Pratap.

Delayed by the necessity of sailing around the Cape of Good Hope in order to avoid German submarines, Arjun did not arrive in Delhi until November, only days before the troops departed for the war.

After the emotional reunions, Lady Modi took Jaya to one side. 'The boys have been badly frightened, darling. The Germans are rounding up every Jew they can find. In Paris, Maharajah Kapurthala's daughter sold all her jewellery to buy the lives of her Jewish friends, and she managed to smuggle some of them onto our ship. But we have just received news that she has been taken to a concentration camp herself.'

Dungra shook his massive head in despair. 'Our Lancers must be left in no doubt that in this war the enemy is not an empire, but armies that put women and children and priests to the sword.'

'The same thing could happen here, hukam,' Sir Akbar said in a low voice, as if he could no longer absorb the chaos around him. 'At the Fort in Lahore, the very place where Nehru announced that India would become a Republic, in front of a hundred thousand followers, Jinnah has announced a separate country for the Muslims.'

A SLIGHT WIND carried the warning of winter over the fortresses of the British Raj's capital as eighteen cavalry regiments awaited inspection by the Commander-in-Chief of the Indian Army.

There had been the same crispness in the November air when the Balmer Lancers performed their farewell manoeuvres for Jai Singh before departing for Europe. Now Jaya watched the British Commander-in-Chief riding past the motionless riders silhouetted against the circular building of the Indian legislature, where bombs had been thrown at the scarlet and gold throne of the Viceroy of India.

Arjun saluted the Sirpur Lancers, bringing his hand to his forehead with such force that he momentarily lost his balance, but Jaya realized the lance and the curved sword were for him already as meaningless as the weapons that decorated the City Palace walls.

The Lancers wheeled into formation, their burnished belts and brilliant turbans and the glistening coats of their horses shining in the morning sunlight as they turned towards the massive archway of India Gate on which were inscribed the names of the Indians who had already died for Britain in other wars.

The clatter of horseshoes echoed on the metal road of King's Way as the cavalries regrouped for the charge. A single trumpet sounded from India Gate, and three thousand riders, lances upright, swords drawn, pennants flying from their standards, galloped down the bright grass.

They reined to a halt in front of the stand, lances steady above their mounts. In the silence that followed the charge, the Commander-in-Chief's voice seemed unnaturally loud. 'Men of India's Cavalry. You have had the privilege of belonging to a special family, the Indian Cavalry. Beside you stand three regiments from royal India. You have taken from them the great traditions of India's Lancers – dash, gallantry, and above all, a willingness to engage the enemy without counting the cost.

'Eighteen regiments of the Indian cavalry must shed their horses today. Although you will now be confined to armoured brigades and tanks, I know the spirit of India's Cavalry can never die. But I regret that it is I who must give you this command.

'Men of India's Cavalry, for the last time, make much of your horses.'

The riders dismounted, legs swinging back over their saddles as if in a single gesture. No longer an impressive military formation but again individual men, they stroked the soft noses of their mounts in the customary gestures of esteem that distinguished the Lancer from the foot soldier.

Jaya felt tears on her cheeks, remembering Tikka's letter from the Devastated Area, his disbelief as a cavalry charge turned into a tank battle, and the gun turrets shining too brightly in the freezing winter sun made a mockery of his mounted Lancers.

WITH THE Sirpur Lancers at war, the kingdom's days revolved around the news bulletins. As the telegraph had once dominated the King's View, now the powerful radio transmitter in Maharajah Victor's study became the focus of the City Palace. During the broadcasts, Jaya barely listened to the tallies of destroyed tanks and aircraft and ships. This was not warfare as she had been raised to understand it. The strength of a man's sword arm, the rituals that purified the warrior before he rode out to engage the enemy had become meaningless. Even the thudding of the nagaras at dawn and sunset, reminding the people of Sirpur that their Lancers were on the battlefield, seemed thin and unconvincing against the music from the gramophones in the bazaars and the honking of rubber bicycle horns.

Arjun was interested only in the air battles, questioning Major Osborne about Spitfires and Messerschmitts as Tikka had once run behind Major Vir Singh asking about the firing capacity of Maxim and Gatling guns.

'I must learn to fly.' The changing colour of Arjun's eyes added urgency to his excitement. 'Can you imagine an Indian king with his own Fighter Command?'

Preoccupied with raising the funds required by Sirpur's treaties with the British Crown, Jaya allowed Arjun to take flying lessons and wished she could find similar means of distracting the British Resident from his concern over his country's desperate war.

Sometimes she escaped to the Purdah Palace, where the lives of the harem ladies had not been touched by submarines and armoured cars. As dusk darkened the balcony and the haunting melodies of the river pilots' flutes floated across the water, Jaya watched the ladies wind fresh jasmine garlands around their wrists, and thought of Major Vir Singh describing the weeks it had taken for the Balmer Lancers to arrive in China. Was that only forty years ago? Arun Roy's admiration of the Japanese bombs that had defeated the Tsar's armies. Was that only thirty years ago? Tikka's letters from

France describing the toy aircraft of the Kaiser's forces. Was that only twenty years ago?

The inventions that had been experiments in the Great War had become familiar weapons in this new war, transmitting destruction with terrifying rapidity across the world, until the pace of human action no longer restrained the foolhardiness of human courage.

Throughout the subcontinent, the war effort and a distrust of the war vied for supremacy, and with increasing concern Sir Akbar and the British Resident discussed a war that was going badly not only for the Allied troops but also for the Empire.

India had previously paid Britain for every railway line and telegraph post, every British clerk and soldier used on Indian soil. Now, with half a million Indian soldiers serving overseas and Indian industries working around the clock to satisfy the demand for guns and tanks, Britain was for the first time in sterling bondage to her greatest colony.

To ensure the continued cooperation of Indians, Churchill dispatched Sir Stafford Cripps, Leader of the House of Commons and a member of Britain's wartime cabinet, to offer Indians the chance to frame the Constitution of India themselves. Convinced that Churchill was playing for time to appease the American President Roosevelt in his known sympathy for India's independence, the Indian National Congress launched a Civil Disobedience movement, demanding that full ruling powers be granted India immediately or war production would be brought to a halt. The Viceroy responded by jailing prominent nationalist leaders.

Anti-British sentiments were at their height when Japan attacked Pearl Harbor, and James Osborne at last received permission to rejoin the Army.

'Major Osborne!' Arjun's voice trembled with envy. 'Will you be fighting the Desert Fox?'

'No. I have been posted to Calcutta. Supplies and Communications.'

Arjun's excitement gave way to disappointment. 'But you won't see any action in Calcutta.'

'I hope you are right, Your Highness.' On Osborne's face Jaya saw a fatigue similar to her own, as if they both were incapacitated by the speed with which machines had accelerated the end of familiar worlds, and she almost forgave him his secret files.

65

1942

'The crisis in the affairs of India arising out of the advance of Japan has made us wish to rally all the forces of Indian life to shield their land from the menace of the invader.'

PRIME MINISTER CHURCHILL TO THE
HOUSE OF COMMONS

INDIA HAD BARELY absorbed the news that the United States of America had entered the war when Japanese aeroplanes began bombing Indian ports.

'Does this mean the Sirpur Lancers will be brought back from the Middle East, Sir Akbar?' Arjun asked eagerly.

'I am certain of it, Your Highness. The Empire will need to protect its eastern colonies from Hirohito's advance.'

As Sir Akbar had predicted, within weeks, the Japanese took Malaya and Singapore by land, effectively sealing off the rice basin of Burma to an India desperately in need of food for the armies being withdrawn to defend the eastern front.

The Japanese increased their air attacks on the important Indian ports of Chittagong and Calcutta in an attempt to gain Burma, and American troops arrived in India to assist in the Allied defence of Britain's eastern empire.

American and British flyers appeared in Sirpur. The network of airstrips Jaya had constructed in Sirpur to bring the tribals closer to the capital provided access to the eastern front, and all available aircraft were being commandeered to lift stranded British civilians from Burma.

Jaya had little patience with Arjun's constant demands to be allowed to fly with the Sirpur pilots into Burma to help with the evacuation. Middlemen were coming in droves to buy up Sirpur's grain for the expected massive influx of armies required to make a stand against Japan. Day after day the paddy fields were denuded, as peasants sold their crops at inflated prices and gleefully watched the grain being loaded onto the river steamers.

To convince Arjun that he must be present when she and Sir Akbar tried to persuade the village headmen to keep some of their crops against the next harvest, Jaya showed him a report from Calcutta. '*The food position is growing more and more serious each day. Tens of thousands have died, and millions have been rendered homeless. The disaster is really terrible.*'

But the sixteen-year-old ruler spent his time at the airfield, trailing behind the American pilots with their decorated helmets and their swaggering walks and their infectious laughter, listening avidly to stories of the Japanese advance.

At the durbars he infrequently attended he squirmed restlessly as the farmers argued with Jaya.

'The traders from Calcutta have never offered such high prices before. We have become rich overnight.'

'How will you eat if the next harvest is bad?'

Sir Akbar's frustration made his speech blunter with every durbar, as if propriety could no longer contain the madness. But the opportunity of making quick fortunes had blinded Sirpur's farmers to the shortages and political unrest sweeping the subcontinent, and Arjun remained mesmerized by the stylish bravado of the American pilots, rolling dice and drinking in the hangars before they taxied off in SirAir's insubstantial aeroplanes towards the treacherous foothills that separated Sirpur from Burma.

As the spectre of famine swept eastern India, worsened by fears of Japanese occupation in a war that was not of India's choosing, the National Congress launched a Quit India Movement, urging all Indians to cease cooperating with the British war effort immediately.

A terse letter from Mrs Roy described the velocity of events in British India as violence and sabotage erupted everywhere. 'Calcutta has become a madhouse. Young men queue in front of British recruiting offices while starving peasants flood into the city. The Viceroy has given orders for the machine-gunning of students from the air in Bihar and Bengal to stop the Quit India movement. This, when the Japanese are bombing Chittagong every day and have attacked Calcutta at least four times in the last week. The only people who know what they are doing are the traders.'

News arrived that the Sirpur Lancers were returning from the Middle East to join in the campaign against Japan, and at last Arjun lost interest in aeroplanes. Now he spent all his time burrowing in the vaults in the Purdah Palace for medals and other decorations to pin on the chests of his soldiers.

On the journey to Calcutta, where the Sirpur Lancers were expected, whenever the Sirpur train was stopped to permit the passage of munitions and food trains, Arjun strode down the platform shouting questions at the men in khaki uniforms hanging out of troop trains, hardly noticing the famished peasants lying next to the tracks, too weak to move while bogeys laden with grain rolled past them to feed the Allied armies.

But shock froze Arjun's features as the car drove through the city he had last seen celebrating a vicereine's fantasy. Painted tree trunks mounted on the wooden wheels of bullock carts were pointed menacingly towards the sky, to convince Japanese pilots that the city bristled with anti-aircraft batteries.

The fake aircraft batteries made death too theatrical. Its true squalor was visible in the children with distended bellies wandering among the corpses that lay on the streets while soldiers with handkerchiefs tied over their mouths swept dead bodies up like garbage, and women with dying babies pressed to their emaciated bodies held up their hands with an ancient hopelessness to the smartly uniformed troops in the vehicles speeding towards Fort William.

James Osborne was waiting to clear the car past Fort William's military guards. On the terraces British officers were drinking under garden umbrellas, their laughter giving little indication that they were aware of the horror beyond the low walls of the Fort.

Arjun enviously examined the medals pinned across James Osborne's uniform. 'Much better than the ones I have for our

Lancers. Do you know where the Sirpur Lancers go from Calcutta, Major Osborne? Or is that a military secret?'

'The Lancers aren't coming back. General Slim has opened a new front in Southeast Asia. It will be from there, not India, that the Allies will launch a counterattack on Japan.'

'But what about all the food commandeered to feed the Allied armies?' Sir Akbar asked.

'The Government has sold it back to the traders.'

Jaya stared at Osborne in disbelief. Gunnysacks filled with grain were already piling up on the grass of the Botanical Gardens, the sweet smell of fermenting grain stronger than the scent of flowers in the humidity. In the streets outside starving villagers were drinking water from running gutters and picking through garbage heaps. The traders would sell on the black market the grain the imperial armies no longer required, while people died in the hundreds of thousands.

Seeing her expression, Arjun said angrily, 'Britain can't be held responsible for everything. It's fighting a war.'

Jaya was suddenly afraid for her son. How could he govern, if he could not recognize fear? Arjun had not come back from England humiliated, like Tikka. He had come back with an Englishman's certainty, the very assurance that had once made her so dependent on Osborne.

On the way back to the station a crowd spilled onto the road, forcing the chauffeur to brake near a cinema covered with posters for the new Disney animation film *Bambi*.

Jaya had difficulty directing Arjun's attention away from the wide-eyed fawn to the people being separated by shouting hawkers into three groups, like animals being culled in a herd. 'Look at that café next to the cinema. Those people are being charged one price to see the food. A higher price to smell it. And a third if they have enough money to eat it. This will happen in Sirpur if our farmers are not stopped from selling their grain.'

THE FURY of the monsoons protected Sirpur from the famine swamping surrounding territories in a miasma of death. But Arjun was unconcerned that the swollen river was flowing too fast to allow the steamers and boats owned by Calcutta's insatiable traders onto its water, or that the new Viceroy, General Wavell, was at last controlling the black-marketing of food with the ruthless efficiency of an army commander.

The knowledge that the Sirpur Lancers were now fighting in the jungles of Burma, so close to Sirpur, had driven the seventeen-year-old Maharajah into a frenzy to join them. When a letter from Fort William informed Arjun that James Osborne was joining the Sirpur Lancers battling with the Seventh Army in the hilly jungles and swamps of the Arakan, Jaya saw in her son's eyes the kind of madness she had seen in Tikka's. Too many tales of his father's courage, too many stories of his uncle's glorious death charging the Turkish garrison at Aleppo, had made him believe he could not achieve manhood without engaging in battle.

Travelling restlessly through the country, his jeep cutting deep tracks down a farmer's patiently constructed mud embankment as he roared into the tribal areas, elephant grass whipping against his face, Arjun made speeches in support of the war.

Sometimes he took off in a SirAir plane without informing anyone. At night when he strode into the City Palace, Jaya knew from his flushed expression that he had been circling the hills where he believed the Sirpur Lancers to be fighting, dropping bales of propaganda leaflets sent from Calcutta.

Jaya said nothing, but her heart stopped each time he left the palace, and she prayed the Japanese fighters with the red suns blazoned on their wings would engage the Royal Indian Air Force, not Arjun's unarmed civilian craft with its senseless weaponry of words.

Clutching at anything to distract her son, Jaya permitted the Raj Guru to make a public occasion of the Maharajah's eighteenth birthday. The Goddess was once again undergoing her mysterious confirmation of fertility, but war had prevented pilgrims from reaching Sirpur. For the first time in Jaya's memory, the Kamini Temple celebrations were devoted entirely to the ruler and his subjects, as if the kingdom were reaffirming its belief in a permanence that had outlasted three thousand years of human history.

Farmers and city merchants jostled against half-clad tribals on the stone steps that led down to the cave, eager to smear themselves with the red liquid welling between the stone lips of the stone idol, before the moan of conch shells announced the ruler's approach.

Cannon fired when the Raj Guru placed a tikka of monarchy

on Arjun's forehead and handed him the ceremonial sword. The celebrating crowds milled on the steps of the Kamini Temple, waiting to follow the ruler's elephant to the City Palace, the crash of cannon fire inflaming their fevered mood as Sir Akbar handed Arjun a paper. A triumphant smile lit the ruler's face, and he mounted the steps to the howdah. Balancing precariously on the back of the painted beast, he drew the Sirpur sword from its emerald-studded scabbard, raising his arm so that the blade was visible to the cheering, blood-marked crowds.

'People of Sirpur!' Arjun shouted. 'The Prime Minister has just informed me that the Japanese Army has entered India. At this very moment, enemy forces are only two hundred miles from our own borders. The Armoury at the City Palace will be opened. By tonight, be prepared to join the Sirpur Lancers in the defence of our kingdom.'

Nothing Jaya or Sir Akbar said could deflect the wild enthusiasm of the crowds running to the Palace Armoury in search of weapons. It was as if the mythology that had always cast its shadows over Sirpur's history were once again enacting its confusing charade.

At midnight, swaying on an elephant under the red umbrella of sovereignty held over his head by a palace groom, Maharajah Arjun left the City Palace. Shortage of gasoline had forced his troops to leave their palace cars behind and travel on horseback. Kerosene lanterns lit the path for his infantry, the spurting flames shining dimly on the spears, lances, ancient guns found in the Palace Armoury and now held proudly to the shoulders of half-clad tribals marching next to Household Guards in ceremonial uniforms.

The pounding of the Sirpur nagaras shook the whitewashed walls of the palace as the ruler's elephant swayed through the gates, and Jaya would have laughed if she had not wept at the shabbiness of her son's war.

66

1944

> *'American public opinion cannot understand why, if the British Government is willing to permit the component parts of India to secede from the British Empire after the war, it is not willing to permit them to enjoy what is tantamount to self-government during the war.'*
>
> PRESIDENT FRANKLIN DELANO ROOSEVELT

WITHIN TWO WEEKS the Sirpur pilots were unable to track the Maharajah's movements through the heavy jungle.

When the radio announced that the Seventh Army was cut off from reinforcements and making an isolated stand against Hirohito's forces at Kohima, Jaya prohibited the Sirpur pilots from following Maharajah Arjun's suicidal journey into battle.

Uncertain if her son was dead or alive, Jaya's nights were filled with strange dreams of Arjun's exhausted arrival behind the Seventh Army's ranks with his cavalcade of horses and elephants and tribals.

She wondered how the Sirpur Lancers were surviving without supplies. Were they again making jam jars into missiles to hurl against the most disciplined forces in the world? But this time the young prince who could not bear to be deprived of war was not her brother but her son, searching for troops cut off from all aid, so he could join a battle to which he had not been invited, the half-understood warrior ceremonies of his childhood, the stories of his father's valour, turned into a necessity to bloody himself on the battlefield.

'This war has been an unmitigated disaster for India, hukam,' Sir Akbar observed bitterly. 'Between two and three million people dead of starvation. Self-government postponed indefinitely, making Hindu-Muslim hatreds more savage than they have ever been. And now ninety thousand Indian troops have been taken prisoner on this front, hukam. They are being forced to work like animals to build rail links through Burma so Emperor Hirohito can occupy India and we can exchange our slavery to the British for slavery to the Japanese.'

Refugees flooded into Sirpur. Jaya could not tell whether they were nationalist soldiers who had refused to fight for the Empire or whether they were simply men exhausted from surviving journeys through unmapped jungles. Some said they thought they had seen Maharajah Arjun's bizarre procession winding towards the Seventh Army's position. Others looked at Jaya uncomprehendingly, as if they could not believe that any civilian would willingly become a camp follower to this war.

At last Sir Akbar brought news that the Seventh Army had contained the Japanese attack and was fighting pitched battles to recover Rangoon. Only when Rangoon was retaken did Jaya learn that Arjun's army had managed to join the Sirpur Lancers months earlier.

A month later a Dakota aircraft landed on the capital's airstrip. The door of the aeroplane swung open and crowds converged on the aircraft, cheering their ruler's return.

An uneasy silence fell over the airfield when a form covered with a blanket was thrust through the doorway. Jaya stared at the body swinging with the motion of the listing stretcher as two tribals negotiated the steep angle of the steps leading from the aircraft to the ground.

James Osborne appeared in the doorway. 'It's all right, Bai-sa. Just a leg that needs resetting, and bad malaria.'

For days Jaya sat beside her son's bed, worrying about the wound that had reopened in the badly set leg, barely able to see his form through the thick mosquito net as she listened to his incoherent ramblings about his grandmother's ashram, or England, or the leeches in the jungles beyond the Kohima hills.

The young Maharajah's fever seemed under control, only to erupt again without warning, and when James Osborne joined her at Arjun's bedside to tell her of the progress of the war, Jaya woodenly expressed the appropriate responses, her eyes never shifting from her son's body, indistinct behind the mosquito net, wishing Osborne would leave. The Englishman's presence brought an alien energy into the bedroom. Even when he whispered news of Germany's surrender, she was only concerned that he might wake the drowsing boy with his voice.

Gradually the leg healed, leaving Arjun weak but restless. Jaya untied bundles of miniatures and held them to his half-focused eyes. He responded as Tikka had once done, querulously demanding to see pictures of pointed lances that pierced a leaping tiger's heart, as if the artist's skill could exorcise his own nightmares.

When the fever finally broke, Arjun moved into his father's rooms, windows open to the hot breezes blowing over the sandbanks of the riverbed, and received his court.

The members of the Council pressed the ruler to give James Osborne an early date for the investiture ceremony.

'The war in Europe has ended, hukam.'

'You should assume your ruling powers.'

Arjun rejected their advice. 'I will not walk to my investiture with a crutch. I'm going to London first for an operation. Anyway, Emperor Hirohito has not yet surrendered. The Viceroy will not be free to come to Sirpur.'

'Lord Wavell is busy trying to find some accommodation between the National Congress and the Muslim League so India can be self-governing,' Sir Akbar informed him severely. 'I assure you the Viceroy is not going duck-shooting in any Indian kingdom right now.'

But the idea of entertaining the Viceroy preoccupied Arjun as the war had once done, and he showed little interest in the political battles being fought between the Muslim League and the National Congress for control of British India.

He spent the monsoon months making and discarding plans for Lord Wavell's visit, and at night, as black clouds descended on the riverbed until jagged lightning slashed their heavy bellies to release torrents of water into the raging river, he sat by the radio, waiting for news of Japan's surrender.

'An atom bomb!' Arjun's eyes changed colour with excitement when the radio broadcast news of an American weapon that had destroyed two Japanese cities, sucking houses and humans into a pillar of fire so fierce it had melted everything for miles around.

'An atom bomb!' Arjun repeated the words as if they gave him pleasure, and Jaya felt old and tired. Only weeks before, he had demanded to see the weapons of single combat. Now he was excitedly discussing the statistics of an awesome new destruction with Sir Akbar, and she thought of her father's moustache falling like a broken wing onto his white tunic as he told the Balmer Raj Guru that machines had ended the dharma of the warrior, and with it the dharma of the king.

67

1945

*'The more I see of these Indian politicians, the
more I despair of India.'*

LORD WAVELL, VICEROY OF INDIA

THE VICEROY'S office regretted that Lord Wavell, in the difficult
process of transferring the power of government to Indians, was un-
available to invest the Maharajah with his ruling powers.

The speed with which events were moving even made it impossible
for James Osborne to accompany Arjun to London. The day after
the Maharajah and his aides left for England, Osborne was called
to Delhi.

'The Empire seems in such a mad hurry to get out of India,
it is now making decisions about the Indian kingdoms,' Osborne
observed when he took his leave of Jaya.

'But our relations are not with the Empire,' Jaya objected. 'They
are with the British Crown.'

The blue eyes held Jaya's gaze with a sternness that frightened
her. 'Parliament has to deal with rationing and bombed-out cities
at home. It doesn't want to get involved in legal arguments with
five hundred independent kingdoms in India.'

'Throughout the war, you demanded we honour the treaties you
are dismissing so casually now. How can the British Crown ignore
us?'

438

'I warned you, Bai-sa. The rulers have delayed too long.'

Jaya could not forget James Osborne's ominous remark. Every day the speeches of the nationalist leaders were printed in all their length, and the rulers of India were not even mentioned, their own indifference to changing reality rendering them mere decorations in the fight for India.

Not knowing if events would render Arjun's investiture irrelevant, Jaya studied the Empire's negotiations with India's two major political parties with desperate intensity, wondering if she would be able to hold Arjun's kingdom for even the few months it would take him to recover from his operation.

The tragedy of an offer delayed too long was the absence of an authority into which the power of the British Empire could safely be placed. Jinnah remained intransigent in his demands for Pakistan, while Nehru maintained that only the National Congress spoke for India.

To break the deadlock between the National Congress and the Muslim League, the British Parliament proposed an interim government in which the two parties would rotate power. The National Congress refused to share equal power with the Muslim League, and a frustrated Viceroy swore in an interim government without Jinnah.

'Britain is washing its hands of us, hukam,' Sir Akbar said, turning on the radio with uncharacteristic ferocity. 'If Britain's Parliament, in its haste to get out of India, is prepared to ignore the Hindu–Muslim bloodshed of the last months and leave Jinnah out of the government, I assure you it will not hesitate to throw royal India to the wolves.'

On the river, fishing craft were being tossed up and down by muddy waves. Jaya could see the brown bodies of fishermen struggling with their tangled nets as Jinnah's voice vibrated the radio: 'The two parties with whom we bargained held a pistol at us, one with power and machine guns behind it, and the other with noncooperation and the threat to launch mass civil disobedience. This situation must be met. We too have a pistol. Today we have taken a most historic decision . . . We have said goodbye to constitutions and constitutional methods.'

'What does he mean, Sir Akbar?'

'I don't know, hukam.' Sir Akbar studied his hands as if surprised

439

by the wrinkled skin. 'When I came to Sirpur as a young man, the world was simple. All of us, Hindus and Muslims, nationalists and rulers, wanted the same thing – to live with dignity, free of Britain's interference. But I am too old to understand this new India or the greed of leaders snarling over the corpse of a nation that has not yet been born.'

Jaya turned away from Sir Akbar's despair. Anarchy seemed poised to overtake the subcontinent, but letters from London had reported the success of Arjun's operation. Only weeks remained before she would at last relinquish the burden she had so wilfully demanded from her husband.

68

1946

'The time has come for the Muslim nation to resort to Direct Action to achieve Pakistan.'

MOHAMMED ALI JINNAH, PRESIDENT OF THE
MUSLIM LEAGUE

THE HUMIDITY of August made the heavy stone buildings of Dalhousie Square appear to sweat, and the Calcutta streets were unusually empty as Jaya, accompanied by the Prime Minister and the British Resident, drove to the airport to receive her son.

Arjun ran down the steel steps to show the success of his operation. Sunlight glanced off the high cheekbones below the sloping eyes, and for a moment Jaya thought he was his father, so much did the tall figure in the blazer resemble Maharajah Pratap.

James Osborne pretended interest in Arjun's descriptions of evacuated children returning to their families and debris being cleared from London's bombsites. But, like Sir Akbar, he was staring out of the car windows at the barricades that had been raised across the streets while they had been at the airport.

The car stopped as an empty drum was rolled across the tarmac and a shopkeeper directed children in torn cotton shorts to pile steel pipes and splintering wood planks onto the road. The activity finally attracted Arjun's attention. 'What is going on?'

'There is to be a huge rally tomorrow demanding a separate

nation for the Muslims. Muslims from all parts of the country are attending, and the Hindus are erecting barricades to prevent more Muslims from coming into the city during the night.'

Sir Akbar forced the words through clenched teeth, and Jaya was ashamed that the Muslim aristocrat should need to explain the ugliness of mob religious feelings to her son.

At Sirpur House, the priests anointed Arjun's forehead. As soon as the formalities of the ruler's return had been observed, the servants surrounded Jaya.

'There are no police or security guards anywhere in the city, hukam.'

'Our Sirpur traders are barricading themselves in their shops.'

Jaya turned to Sir Akbar. 'I'll go to Mrs Roy's house. They will definitely have news of any expected disturbance.'

James Osborne hurried into the study to telephone Government House. Apprehension coloured his voice when he returned. 'I don't think you should go, Bai-sa. The Army has been confined to barracks. The National Congress government insists that an imperialist army must no longer be a force in India.'

'I shall be safe out of the city. But something should be done for our subjects here.'

Osborne left for Fort William to find out details of where trouble was expected. Sir Akbar suggested that he and Maharajah Arjun warn the Sirpur merchants and traders in Calcutta to take precautions against sudden outbursts of mob passion.

Arjun placed an arm around Jaya's shoulder as he led her to the car, and she caressed his cheek. 'What a homecoming for you, child.'

'I am not a child any longer. You can't protect me from the realities of India.'

Jaya realised he had spoken to her as if she were the child. The very barriers that she had constructed for his protection had kept her from knowing him, and she determined to correct the omission before he became so preoccupied with government that there would be no time.

In the great park where the rally was to be held, the massive monolith of Ochterlony's needle seemed to pierce the sunset heat, but the usually crowded thoroughfares bordering the park were deserted in the humid haze of the August dusk as a handful of workers completed wooden platforms for the speakers who would protest the exclusion of the Muslim League from India's new government.

The eerie silence in the narrow lanes of the city bazaars, as empty as the broad boulevards of imperial Calcutta, suggested violence, and only when the car left the city and entered a country avenue lined with coconut trees did Jaya relax into her seat.

The chauffeur suddenly accelerated. People were running onto the road to stand in the car's path, hands folded in supplication. The smoky grey light as dusk turned into night could not disguise the stains spreading across their torn clothes.

'Stop the car!' Jaya commanded.

The chauffeur gunned the engine again. 'I cannot protect you single-handed, hukam. There is a mob running through the trees.'

Clouds of dust rose under the screeching wheels as the chauffeur swerved. Hemmed in by tree trunks, the car sped through the landscape of darkness. Jaya looked back. Flames were visible in the distance, and the sound of screaming pierced the night.

Mrs Roy ran down the steps as the car braked outside the pillared house, her thin frame bent by a weight greater than age.

'Thank God you reached here safely. Hindu–Muslim clashes are taking place throughout the city. There is no question of your returning to Sirpur House until the situation is under control.'

She led Jaya past the cupboards filled with the Western suits and hats onto the lawn. Beyond the marble statues, the doors of the Music Room were open to the breeze. Streamers of river mist drifted through the empty chamber where no musicians tuned their instruments to soothe the fears of the men and women sitting on the grass, worriedly discussing the future for which they had fought for half a century as it became a present that already carried the smell of blood.

Their voices carried to Jaya in the darkness. 'When Jinnah was President of the Indian National Congress, he was the first architect of Hindu–Muslim unity.'

'Twice Muslim fanatics tried to assassinate him for his religious tolerance. That he, of all men, should be prepared to tear this great civilization in half for religion!'

'Mrs Naidu says, "Jinnah is like a fallen Lucifer – and young Nehru is dangerously extreme in his judgements." '

Mrs Roy pulled a shawl closer around her shoulders, shivering as much with her thoughts as with the dampness carried by the fog. 'Do you know what else Mrs Naidu said, Bai-sa? "Our anxiety to be free from the Empire has prevented us from examining the demons within our own souls." She is right. The demons in our own souls will destroy us. I'll show you where you will stay while we wait to hear if we have succeeded in butchering India.'

Jaya could hear the heartbreak under her tutor's rage. Mrs Roy had always been so impatient of confusion, so sure of justice. Now her dream of justice was turning into a nightmare.

Mrs Roy entered a room with crimson marble floors, its darkness deepened by the heavy mahogany bed in the centre of the chamber, and turned on the lamps. Sudden light glinted off the steel rims of her spectacles as she sat down heavily on the bed. 'The world is too full of politics. Speak to me of something else, Bai-sa.'

The night seemed suspended in waiting, and on the lawns, below the marble statues, Muslim and Hindu servants sat silently on the grass, too frightened to speculate about the fate of their families as news filtered in of the panic and violence that had overtaken the largest city in India.

Major Osborne telephoned at one o'clock in the morning. 'Barricades are going up everywhere, Bai-sa. Whole parts of the city are in flames.'

Each time Osborne rang that night, people crowded behind Jaya begging her to ask if he had visited this area or that, to see if it had been spared the arson and killing.

With every call Osborne's voice sounded more tired. 'The savagery of the killings, Bai-sa. Everyone has weapons – guns, knives, kerosene cans. The Maharajah and Sir Akbar are bringing all the Sirpur subjects back to the safety of Sirpur House. Since there doesn't seem to be any anti-British feeling, I am going to the rally tomorrow to see if I can learn how long this will go on.'

All through the night people who had managed to flee Calcutta trickled into the riverside house, seeking sanctuary from the mobs. By dawn there was a full-fledged camp on the lawns.

The Music Room was turned into a makeshift hospital. Wounded children lay on the marble floor, staring at the chandeliers shrouded in muslin dust covers hanging high above them, and flinching at the sound of sheets being torn into bandages.

The menfolk sat on the grass, sweating in the heavy stillness of the atmosphere, as though even the river breeze had been halted by the madness that was inundating the city sprawled across its banks.

'Our whole quarter was burned to the ground. We could do nothing but run ourselves.'

Mr Roy looked at the hem of his dhoti. 'Are the Hindus or the Muslims doing the killing?'

The men at his feet laughed bitterly. 'Can you tell from a murderer's eyes what his religion is, baba? These are murderers, drunk on blood.'

James Osborne telephoned in the evening. 'The rally was packed with armed hoodlums waiting to start trouble. I barely managed to get away before the mobs began moving towards the streets beyond New Market to set shops and houses on fire. The Army has been called out at last.' There was a crackle over the telephone line, and he shouted to make himself heard. 'But the Sirpur subjects have not indulged in the madness. The sight of their Hindu king and their Muslim prime minister saving lives together has reassured them.'

Two days passed before James Osborne rang again. 'I have been helping the Army clear the city of its corpses, Bai-sa. Despite the curfew, there are fresh bodies everywhere. The stench of rotting flesh is so strong the soldiers are calling it the City of the Dead. Sixty thousand people dead and the murders have not yet stopped, although the Muslim League has now been included in the government. I'm coming to collect you in an Army jeep, Bai-sa. The Maharajah wants you here, under his protection.'

'Where is he now?'

'Helping the traders collect their things. Everyone is being brought back to Sirpur House in case the violence starts again. You'll have your hands full when you return – it's like a refugee camp here.'

The calendar above the telephone showed that it was August. Jaya shielded her eyes like a superstitious child. Two years ago this month, her son had been fighting Japanese troops and she had not known whether he was alive or dead. Last August the Americans had with a single atomic bomb destroyed Japanese cities as large as San Francisco, where the leaders of the world were now inventing their new weapon of peace, the United Nations. Next August, what fresh insanity would be unleashed on a world impatient for novelty?

She returned to the Music Room and spooned gruel into a

445

young child's mouth. The boy opened his lips obediently, large eyes watching her with no expression, as if his experiences had robbed him of the capacity to distrust. But he did not swallow, and the gruel ran down his chin.

Mr Roy sat next to her. 'Let me do this, Bai-sa. Major Osborne has arrived.'

Jaya walked from the darkness of the Music Room into the sudden light, blinking at the whiteness of the statues against the green foliage. James Osborne ran towards her, and for a confused moment she thought he was a moving statue.

He led her to a military jeep still painted in its wartime camouflage. The coconut palms were as still as lamp posts in the heavy humidity as he drove down the mud road. Jaya was grateful for the open jeep and the wind blowing her heavy hair away from her hot skin. 'Have all our people reached the safety of Sirpur House?'

Osborne nodded. 'Arjun and Sir Akbar went back to make sure they had left no one behind.' His knuckles were white against the steering wheel. Jaya laid a hand briefly on his, and the gesture seemed to reassure him. 'As they were returning to Sirpur House, a Hindu mob gathered around the car, demanding to know why a Hindu king was travelling with a Muslim. Sir Akbar's tunic must have alerted them. Arjun shouted that Sir Akbar was the Prime Minister of Sirpur, but they dragged the old man out of the car and ripped off his clothes to see if he was circumcized. The mob rocked the car to prevent Arjun from getting out. He still managed to open the door. But it was too late. They had already cut off Sir Akbar's manhood.'

Osborne stopped the jeep. Jaya was surprised that she felt nothing, knowing what the Englishman was going to say. She stared into his eyes, noting the way the colour of their irises was darkening.

'Your son died like a true warrior, Bai-sa.'

'Savaged by a bloodthirsty mob, trying to protect the dignity of his Prime Minister? You call that war?'

She smashed her clenched fist into his mouth. Blood dribbled from James Osborne's lips. With academic interest she watched it stain his shirt.

69

1947

> 'The game so far has been well played ... The Indian problem has been thrust into its appropriate plane of communalism ... a natural, if ghastly, process tending in its own way to the solution of the Indian problem. Grave communal disorder must not disturb us into action which would reintroduce anti-British agitation....'
>
> DIRECTOR OF CENTRAL INTELLIGENCE
> TO THE VICEROY OF INDIA

SIR AKBAR'S mutilated corpse was buried between saplings in the capital's Muslim graveyard, but at Jaya's request, Maharajah Arjun's ashes were not taken to be immersed in the holy river at Benares.

At sunset, the Raj Guru tipped the unadorned clay urn containing the ruler's ashes into the river flowing past the capital and from the crowded riverbanks silent subjects floated thousands of clay lamps on the Brahmaputra River to light their maharajah's soul through the night. When Jaya saw the tiny flames flickering on the black water, she finally gave way to her grief.

Like a child seeking consolation in an unchanging world, she retreated to the Purdah Palace. The cloistered women protected her solitude. Each time the high voices of the Abyssinians announced a visitor, the purdah ladies sent the eunuchs back with a message that the Regent Maharani was unwell.

Jaya tried to make sense of the reports that were sent to her every day, but they had become as meaningless as the snatches of conversation from the women carving vegetable animals below her windows.

As if the placid pattern of their lives would heal the grieving mother, the purdah ladies observed each ritual of the day with minute concern, hoping that Jaya, recovered from her sorrow, might unexpectedly join them at their activities.

At dusk, the melancholic melodies of the river flutes, carried on the river breeze through her open windows, almost eroded the bleak desolation that held Jaya in its iron grip, and when the purdah ladies performed the evening puja with clay lamps and incense, and she heard chanted prayers for her recovery, she sometimes even believed it possible.

In spite of the ministrations of the harem ladies, a full year passed before Jaya could enter the Dowager Maharani's audience chamber to receive the kingdom's ministers.

'You have not named a successor, hukam.'

'There is no heir to the Sirpur throne.'

Jaya's eyes wandered in confusion over the Chinese ladies climbing the blue silk screen. 'The Resident will need to be consulted on the matter.'

'But the Resident is in Delhi, hukam. India and Pakistan have become independent nations. Today the British Empire's partition awards are being announced.'

Jaya wiped her hands on her sari, remembering that it was again August. Only a year ago, communal frenzy had taken her son's and Sir Akbar's lives. What would happen when the British Empire's boundary lines for the two new nations became public knowledge?

THE BRITISH EMPIRE'S partition awards were published, and within hours Jaya's fears turned into sickening reality as the Indians and Pakistanis who had so deliriously hoisted their own flags on the Empire's flagstaffs became intoxicated again, not by freedom but by uncontrollable savagery.

Forcibly dispossessed overnight from lands they had farmed for

448

centuries and which they could no longer defend, Hindus, Muslims, Sikhs fled with their children and the few possessions they could carry to sanctuary in strange countries as fear of homelessness swept the subcontinent.

Millions were crossing borders wherever they could. Refugee trains arrived in stations to be met by anxious relatives who went mad, unable to believe that it was blood they saw seeping through locked doors or that those were the severed heads of children falling against the iron bars of the windows, or that every person in the crowded compartments had been butchered in the name of God.

The new slaughters rendered the murder and arson of Calcutta insignificant, until rape, pillage, burning became such ordinary occurrences the newspapers ceased to record them.

The kingdoms of royal India offered a haven from the communal killings that were ravaging the new nations carved out of British India. Half-mad women came in droves to the Purdah Palace, bringing an endless catalogue of horror. Their litanies went on and on, late into every night, until Jaya sometimes thought she would go mad herself listening to the toneless voices telling of young girls raped so often they had been left to die of their wounds, of mothers forced to watch their babies flung in the air to be skewered on swords while the killers laughed at their sport.

The Sirpur Lancers were placed on constant patrol to prevent Sirpur's citizens from avenging upon each other the tales of horror they heard too often every day from the refugees flooding into Sirpur.

With increasing frequency, when it seemed possible that trouble might erupt, the Lancers asked Jaya to tour the streets herself, a physical reminder of the circumstances of Maharajah Arjun's and Sir Akbar's deaths.

As blood soaked into the pink that had once marked the Empire's Indian possessions, James Osborne returned from Delhi, where Gandhi had undertaken a fast to death, hoping to stop the carnage.

'Your empire created this madness,' Jaya accused the Englishman. 'Why doesn't your army ensure safe passage for the refugees?'

'What army, Bai-sa? There is only a Boundary Force now. The Navy, the Army, the Air Force have all been carved up. Their officers are sitting in Delhi haggling like housewives over how many guns, ships, aircraft and tanks belong to Pakistan and how many to India.'

'Then can't the Boundary Force do something?'

'Nobody wants to use it. It would be an admission of defeat for all three countries – Britain, Pakistan and India. Nobody but Gandhi is behaving honourably, Bai-sa. Do you know what I was doing in Delhi while Hindus and Muslims were murdering each other? The Viceroy, Mountbatten, wants to give the secret files we have kept on the weaknesses and vices of the Indian rulers to Nehru, so India can blackmail them into joining the Indian Union. For weeks I have been with the head of our Political Office, Sir Conrad Corfield, burning those secret reports without Mountbatten's knowledge. Four tons of paper burnt, Bai-sa, and no one even noticed our little bonfire among all the other fires.'

'Why does India want to blackmail us?' Jaya asked wearily.

'Fear. Almost a million people have been killed, another seven million made homeless. The rulers could start hundreds of new civil wars. They have their own armies. They could cut India's railway network, its telegraph and communications system. That is why the rulers are being asked to sign an Instrument of Accession and merge with India.'

Through the open window Jaya could see the Kamini Temple reflected in the river, shining silver in the morning light. 'Merge? Sign away their kingdoms?'

'The rulers are defenceless, Bai-sa. Most kingdoms are landlocked, and the Reformists will now be assisted by the sympathetic Indians around them.' Osborne looked away from the desolation in her eyes. 'It is a highly dangerous time. Sign the Instrument of Accession before your subjects start fighting each other and the butchery begins in Sirpur.'

The iron trident of the Kamini Temple rose like an accusing finger against the cloudless sky, and Jaya thought of the dusty volumes that lay unopened in the stone vaults of the temple, recording three thousand years of existence. The weight of those volumes pressed down on her, reminding her she was the sole guardian of Sirpur's ancient line.

The eunuchs pounded their lances on the marble floor outside the chamber.

'Gandhi has just been killed, hukam! A Hindu fanatic assassinated him on his way to a prayer meeting.'

Jaya stared at Osborne, realizing his predictions could too easily become reality in the madness that was drowning the subcontinent in blood.

The purdah ladies, refugees, maidservants spilled into the corridors, hiding behind the doors as they shouted the details.

'The Mahatma fell to the ground, taking the name of God with his last breath.'

'Each time a bullet entered his body, he said, "Ram. Ram. Ram." '

Jaya remembered her mother's low voice reciting those words as the Raj Guru slashed the taut skins of the Balmer nagaras. Gandhi had used the same mantra as the Maharani: Ram Nam Sat Hai. The Name of God is Truth.

She turned on the radio, unable to believe that the old man who had walked with such determination through the Indian countryside to break the Empire's Salt Laws should already have been killed by his own people before his new nation was even a year old.

Jaya could hear the hidden women sobbing as they listened to the radio's disembodied voice inform India that its Mahatma, its Great Soul, was dead, and she felt unable any longer to carry the burden of their fears.

Perhaps the Sati Mata, with her knowledge of the future, was still sitting in the broken cenotaph on Balmer's border. Or the old Raj Guru, with his knowledge of government, was still writing his treatise on Rajniti in the Fort Temple. She would return to Balmer. She would ask them what to do.

70

1949

> 'The real task has just begun ... We have to
> weave new fabrics into old materials; we have to
> make sure that simultaneously the old and the new
> are integrated into a pleasing whole – a design that
> would fit well into the pattern of India.'
>
> SARDAR PATEL, DEPUTY PRIME MINISTER OF INDIA

DUST STORMS blew sand through the iron bars as the train rolled
through the kingdoms of Rajputana towards the great desert, the
Abode of Death.

The Balmer maidservants stood at the windows, their mouths
covered with their veils, staring at the temples and forts that
quartered the metallic horizon with a monolithic stillness.

Broken battlements crawled down black hills towards empty
reservoirs where crocodiles wallowed in shallow mud, and saffron
flags from distant temples disappeared like sparks thrown backwards
from the engine. To the watching women those brief flashes of brilliant orange evoked whole armies dressed in the colour of sacrifice,
riding from their fortifications to defend their gods from the sword
of the invader.

A car was waiting to drive Jaya into the hills that formed
Balmer's natural barrier against invasion from the desert. Jaya
dismounted near a clump of black rocks. Eagles circled above her

head in a sky almost white with summer heat, and her veil caught on thornbushes as she climbed towards the broken marble cenotaph shimmering in the sun.

Monkeys scampered over the small palms carved into the marble walls, their angry chatter frightening waves of green pigeons from their roosts. Jaya entered the cenotaph and disturbed bats wheeled blindly around her as she moved towards the tattered remnants of an antelope skin still hanging across the doorway.

Jaya swung it aside, hoping to see a laughing woman sitting on a tiger skin while a cobra lapped milk from a coconut at her side. But there was only a fallen trident rusting in the mud, and Jaya turned away, knowing the place held no answer.

Dusk obscured the battlements of Balmer Fort as the car drove up the stone ramparts, and in the darkness Jaya could barely distinguish the Round Tower, or the stone stables carved with the names of the steeds that had carried Balmer kings into battle.

In the glare of the car's headlamps, Jaya saw the Raj Guru and Major Vir Singh waiting at the Fort Temple.

The Raj Guru's white clothes were as unruffled as they had always been, his harsh whisper as he blessed her unchanged from the days when she had sat opposite him in the Balmer Library.

Beside him, Major Vir Singh held himself as proudly as when he had been a young cavalry officer, leading the Balmer Lancers into three wars.

But the painful pace at which they preceded her into the temple reminded Jaya that her teachers were now old men, crippled by time.

They lowered themselves slowly onto the cushions circling a table covered with manuscripts.

'Why have you come here, Bai-sa?' The Raj Guru leaned forward.

Jaya lowered her head and said nothing, feeling again the awe the Raj Guru had inspired in her as a child. The harsh whisper repeated the question.

'Why have you come here, Bai-sa? How will you use the knowledge we have invested in you?'

Jaya looked up. Shadow deepened the colour of the old priest's eyes, and Jaya felt her heart break. Her son's eyes had changed from green to black in lamplight.

'What is the opening lesson of Rajniti, Bai-sa?'

'First there is the praja, the people,' she whispered.

The Raj Guru nodded in satisfaction. 'I once told your father, as I am telling you now, this ancient land is old in the ways of government. It has witnessed the councils of nobles, the fiats of emperors, the whims of kings, the reigns of priests, the tolerance of great republics. Things go wrong only when men forget the first principle of government. The people. What are you planning to do in this changed world?'

Jaya averted her face in shame. 'My father, my brother, my husband, my son are dead. I am told that unless I merge the oldest kingdom in India with a nation that was born only two years ago, there will be more bloodshed. You are my teachers. Tell me what I must do.'

He rose and led her outside. A red cushion rested on the flagstones where the Balmer Lancers had once sat behind their weapons. On it lay an unsheathed sword. They faced each other in the night, dim forms in the white garments of the widow and the priest.

'Your dharma is protection, Bai-sa. You cannot escape your destiny.' In the darkness the disembodied whisper carried the weight of a timeless command, as if spoken by the sages who had sat in the jungles and wrestled with the meaning of India.

The Raj Guru lifted the sword and sliced his thumb. Blood dripped onto his white clothes as he marked Jaya's forehead.

The fanned plume of Major Vir Singh's turban brushed against Jaya's hair. 'I see that the man who anointed your father a ruling king has now anointed you a democrat, Bai-sa.'

A glow of lanterns broke the darkness. Flying foxes swept over the stone ramparts of the fortress, their black wings seeming to burst through the bright stars as men carrying bamboo poles appeared in the temple forecourt. Drums echoed in the forecourt as the bards unrolled a twenty-foot-long mural of a burning city.

A tall man appeared in front of the painted cloth, and the drums fell silent.

'I was a boy of four when I first came to the kingdom. There was famine throughout Rajputana, but my father had news the Maharani of Balmer was with child.

'I had never before entered a great fort. I had never seen the outer walls of a royal zenana. And when the cannon fired from these mighty battlements, I cried out with fear in my mother's lap.

'I am nearing my sixth decade and can no longer count the

royal births I have attended or the times I have recited the history of Rajputana's kings.

'Now we have heard that we are all kings. We have been told our voices will carry the same weight as the voice of an anointed ruler.

'Such news has made us happy. But know this.

'No ruler's voice has ever carried the same weight as ours. Our voices tell of generations that have risen and fallen like the shifting sand dunes of this harsh land.

'Without us, deeds and lives would have long since been blown away, like dust in a desert storm, and proud men would not have been humbled by the greatness that has preceded them.'

He moved away to make room for a relay of singers, and in her head Jaya began composing a letter acceding the kingdom of Sirpur to the Union of India.

The painted flames of the mural flickered in the light spurting from kerosene lanterns. An elephant trumpeted from the distant corral as the declaiming voices of the bards sucked the night into their recitation.

'Two thousand years ago the great Queen Pushpavati was all that remained of the sons of the Sun.

'Her father, her brothers, her husband, all her great line lay slaughtered in the City of the Hundred Temples.

'Queen Pushpavati

'The greatest queen in India

'Famed for her prowess with a sword

'Who could draw a bow almost as well as a man

'Who rode at the side of her husband in pursuit of the cheetah

'This warrior queen was now a widow ...'

455

71

1950

The capacity for mischief and trouble on the part of the rulers . . . is far greater than could be imagined. Let us place ourselves in their position and then assess the value of their sacrifice.'

SARDAR PATEL, THE IRON MAN OF INDIA

OSBORNE WAS waiting at Delhi railway station, hardly visible among the refugees living on the platforms. He steered Jaya through the crowds. 'Jinnah died of cancer yesterday, Bai-sa. At his death he weighed only seventy pounds.'

Jaya nodded, sickened by the misery visible on the streets. Delhi was a city of refugees, its broad avenues and pavements clogged with the nearly three million homeless who had survived the communal slaughters of the North to seek refuge in the capital of their new country.

James Osborne looked at his watch. 'Not bad, Bai-sa. We are only running half an hour late for Mr Menon.'

'What a pity Mountbatten's transfer of power did not run a year late, Major Osborne. If Jinnah was dying, perhaps Pakistan need never have happened. In an ancient land like India, would a year or two have mattered so much?'

Osborne gave her a quizzical look. 'Have you changed your mind about merging Sirpur with India, Bai-sa?'

Jaya looked at the flags flying from the town houses of the Indian rulers, indicating how many princes had arrived to merge their kingdoms with the new nation. 'No, James-sahib. I am saying Gandhi and Jinnah are both dead. And two million other people whom no one will remember until they need an excuse to kill again. Only Mountbatten and Nehru remain. Impatient men now own India's history. Who will argue with their recollections?'

The Secretary of India, V. P. Menon, was waiting outside the high-domed office which only months ago had stored the secret records of the British Raj. He congratulated Jaya on maintaining calm in Sirpur. 'Preventing Hindu–Muslim riots inside Sirpur when the communal madness on your borders was so savage must have been a superhuman task. I remember going to Bikaner during the exodus of many thousands of refugees. In a single day the Maharajah made all the necessary arrangements, including the requisitioning of buildings, the provision of food and the allotment of money for other expenses.'

Jaya turned away from his surprise. 'In our kingdoms we have to consider the needs of all our subjects, Mr Menon. Not merely those who represent the majority.'

He smiled and led her inside. 'Sardar Patel has prepared the Sirpur Instrument of Accession for signature, Your Highness. Please follow me.'

Jaya had seen the leader they called the Iron Man of India only once before, when she had accompanied her husband to a meeting in the old part of the city. But she immediately recognized the man who had stated with precise finality, 'Make no mistake, gentlemen. The royal States will be eliminated if you delay self-rule in India.'

Now he was the Deputy Prime Minister of an independent India, his harshness burned away in the inferno of hatred which was already destroying his nation.

He even smiled when he handed Jaya the papers that would end the existence of a three-thousand-old kingdom.

'This is a historic moment, Your Highness.'

'Sirpur believes it was born before history,' Jaya replied evenly as she sat down at the desk. 'To the subjects of Sirpur, such documents will indicate only that India has merged with us.'

Sardar Patel flung his head back in laughter, and light shone off the dark brown scalp. 'Can Sirpur's citizens be so vain? Will they really believe that India has integrated with them?'

'Their family names are mentioned in the Mahabharata Wars. India's present leaders are mentioned in newspapers used by housewives to wrap yesterday's vegetables.'

Sardar Patel stopped laughing abruptly. 'What would convince Sirpur that history exists?'

She handed him the signed document. 'Exile.'

He gazed at Jaya speculatively for a long moment before turning to James Osborne. 'What do you think, Major?'

Jaya could see the homesickness already tunnelling deep in the Englishman's blue eyes. 'Four generations of my family have lived and worked in this country, sir. Exile may prove a most effective sentence.'

ON HER return to Sirpur, Jaya held audience in the painted Durbar Hall for the citizens who had travelled from all over the kingdom to inquire about the merger. Traders, the scions of Sirpur's noble families, peasants from the fertile Sirpur plains, fishermen and barge owners, sat in rows under the chandeliers arguing about the decision. Only the tribal chiefs were indifferent, and Jaya saw in their indifference the ancient strength of Sirpur.

Week after week, Jaya explained, 'The last Viceroy, Lord Mountbatten, said Sirpur could make its own terms with the new nations of Pakistan and India. He betrayed us. The Indian leaders said we could remain free if we agreed to common policies. They betrayed us. If I had not signed the Instrument of Accession, there would have been more bloodshed.'

When the priests of the Kamini Temple challenged her actions, for the first time Jaya was able to return the challenge without fear of compromising the throne.

'You say you speak for the people. Stand as candidates in the coming elections. If you win, you can change everything I have done.'

In the evenings, Jaya worked late with James Osborne, reorganizing the royal estates. The main chambers of the City Palace were to be converted into a library to house the manuscripts that were slowly rotting in the deserted stone cells in the Kamini Temple. The smaller palaces inside the sprawling palace grounds would become educational institutions. The Purdah Palace would remain a hospice for the harem ladies and refugee women. The boatyards were to be turned over to the fishermen, so that nets could now be mended in the capital instead of having to be dragged back to villages far from the fish markets.

Jaya decided to purchase the British Residency on the prominence of the hill that overlooked the river. The irony that she would soon be living in the house from which the British Empire had controlled Sirpur's rulers for a century did not escape Jaya; and yet she needed to see the water turning crimson at sunset and grey-green with dawn. The river had become part of her, with its seething monsoon torrents and its white sandbanks of summer. She could not have endured living in Sirpur if she could not watch the sails of narrow-bottomed boats billowing with the spring wind as fishing nets were flung across the water where her son's ashes had been scattered, or hear the flutes of the river pilots guiding their lanterned barges downriver to Calcutta, or see clouds of birds spiralling above the river's eddies as the bells from the Kamini Temple rang for the evening pujas.

James Osborne announced his intention to leave India. 'Everything I could do here is finished, Bai-sa. It is time for me to go home.' It had been a long time since Jaya had seen the Englishman's mouth turn in that shy half-smile. 'But I'll wait to make my farewells until your return from your tour.'

For a month Jaya travelled the kingdom explaining that the merger with India had been a voluntary decision, to ensure that no outbreaks of violence would provoke the Government of India into equally violent response. Wherever she stopped, her presence became the occasion for emotional farewells, as if the absence of a symbol had shaken the people's faith in their own identity.

On her return, Chandni ran down the steps as Jaya's car drove into the City Palace. Chandni thrust the morning edition of *The Sirpur Herald* angrily through the car window. 'That jackal of a lawyer has arrived in Sirpur, hukam, wanting to be our next maharajah. Yesterday he gave a big speech in Lady Reading Park.'

Jaya looked at the photograph of Arun Roy smiling from the front page. The headlines urged people to watch him sign his election petition today. She sank back against the leather upholstery, remembering Arun Roy's last speech in Lady Reading Park, and how he had stated with absolute conviction that true justice was proved by the views of a majority. But in the communal killings of the last two years, once ordinary human beings had gloried in the slaughter of their outnumbered victims.

If Arun Roy was elected from Sirpur, what would happen to the kingdom's different tribes and religions? Would he speak for them? Would he give a sympathetic ear to their concerns against the greed of the majority?

James Osborne opened the door and held out a hand to assist her from the car.

Jaya thought of the old Raj Guru's words in the darkness of the Fort Temple: 'Your dharma is protection, Bai-sa. You cannot escape your destiny.' His implacable insistence crushed her with the weight of duties she was no longer strong enough to carry.

'Do you know where the election petitions are being signed, Major Osborne?'

'At the Sirpur Law Courts, Bai-sa.'

'I would be grateful if you could accompany me there.'

Osborne looked surprised, but said nothing.

Jaya motioned the Englishman to wait at the high doorway of the Law Courts as a group of clerks moved aside to allow Jaya to enter the office where the petitions were being prepared.

She closed the door behind her, aware of the faces pressed against the windows watching her approach the man in a threadbare brown suit and spectacles who was sitting behind the desk.

The man looked up from the forms covering his table. 'What can I do for you, madam?'

The man was from Calcutta. His ignorance of Sirpur gave Jaya the confidence to ignore the faces at the windows.

'I want to be a candidate in the elections.'

He motioned her to the chair opposite him. 'Your party?'

'I have no party.'

'Independent.' In spidery copperplate he wrote the word down on a form. 'Your good name, madam?'

'Jaya Devi.'

A sudden smile illuminated the serious face. 'The name means victory, madam. May I wish you good luck in your endeavours?'

Again he bent over his form. Blotting the paper carefully, he offered it to Jaya for her signature.

The door was flung open and the man looked up, frowning at the noise as Arun Roy entered the office, surrounded by supporters.

Osborne pushed his way through the crowd towards Jaya. But Arun Roy was already at the desk.

Osborne took Jaya's arm. Roy laid a hand on her other arm.

'Bai-sa, wait. What are you doing here?'

'Applying to be a candidate in the elections.'

Seeing the shock on the two faces, Jaya felt laughter bubbling up inside her.

Osborne recovered first. 'Congratulations, Bai-sa. It was the dream of the British Empire to teach the princes of India about democracy.'

'What did the British Empire know about democracy?' Arun Roy demanded. 'We taught the Indian rulers that lesson.'

As the two men argued above her head, Jaya remembered the Raj Guru's harsh whisper under the painted frescoes of the Fort Library, demanding, 'What is the first principle of Rajniti, Bai-sa?' and her stuttering reply, 'The people.' The laughter she could no longer control burst through their anger. The election officer behind the desk looked shocked, but she could not silence the laughter welling in waves from somewhere deep inside her, could not halt it from rolling across the Sirpur Law Courts and the narrow lanes of the bazaars until it merged with the silver waters of the river.

Afterword

In 1947, the British Empire's partition awards lost India an area of 364,737 square miles and a population of nearly 82 million.

Disbanding their armed forces, the Indian rulers merged voluntarily with a nation that did not even have a constitution. In return, the Union of India agreed to pay the rulers privy purses to assist in the discharge of their financial obligations.

After the integration of the Indian kingdoms, India acquired 500,000 square miles of territory and 87 million new citizens.

The Constitution of India came into force on January 26, 1950. Reaffirming the agreements made between the Indian Union and the individual Indian kingdoms, Sardar Patel, the Deputy Prime Minister of India, declared to the Indian Parliament:

'The privy-purse settlements are in the nature of consideration for the surrender by the rulers of all their ruling powers and also for the dissolution of the States. Need we cavil at the small – and I purposely use the word small – price we have paid for the bloodless revolution which has affected the lives of millions of our people? The capacity for mischief and trouble on the part of the rulers ... is far greater than could be imagined.

'Our obligation is to ensure that the guarantees given by us are fully implemented. Our failure to do so would be a breach of faith.'

462

In 1970, the Prime Minister of India, Mrs Indira Gandhi, intro
duced a bill in the Indian Parliament stating:
'*The intention of Government is to discontinue the privy purse
and abolish the concept of rulership.*'

In 1971, the Constitution of India was amended to enable th
passing of this bill.